Heart of the Wolf

Black River Moon, Book 1

A. Mariposa

Black Butterfly

Author's Note

The BLACK RIVER MOON trilogy takes place is the beautiful Adirondack wilderness in a fictional town called Black River, NY. Although names and locations might appear to represent places in real life, they are, indeed, fictional. The setting is not meant to represent Black River Village or its population as it exists in the real world.

Please note this book contains adult themes and explicit material. Reader discretion is advised.

Contents

Prologue

She struggled up the hill, her breath laboring in her lungs, rocks biting into her feet. She fled the house without shoes. Her heart pounded, threatening to escape her chest. Her legs shook so badly, she could barely keep herself upright.

The night was perfectly black, darker than her bedroom closet. She didn't have a destination. She fled to escape the trailer and the monster inside of it.

She was only fourteen, but her home had been hell for a long time.

The rain poured down as she fought her way through blackberry bushes and tangled undergrowth. She fell, twisting her ankle on a slick rock, but she pushed on. She ran from a danger as silent and unseen as the night itself. No one followed her, but panic lent wings to her feet.

Finally she could go no farther. She collapsed at the base of a pine tree, her breath heaving, so tired she wanted to puke. She pressed herself against the rough, wet bark. Rain dripped onto her cheeks from the pine branches. She closed her eyes, struggling to breathe.

A bruise like a thundercloud spread across her cheek. She pressed her hand against it.

Since her mother's death, her stepdad's drinking had worsened. Now Maddy knew her father for the monster he was. At least her mother had been generous with her love. Now, she had no buffer between herself and her stepfather's alcoholism.

She curled up into a tight ball at the base of the tree, an attempt to protect herself. She wanted to run away from home, but where could she go? The foster system was a bleak option. She didn't want to live with strangers, or get shuttled around between group homes. No one wanted a fourteen year old.

Tears ran down her cheeks, fueled by helplessness and rage.

Snap! Twitch.

She flinched at the sudden sound. She looked around, near blind in the dark. Mountain lions and wolves lived this high up . . . Still, her stepdad scared her worse than a wild animal.

There—a crunch and rustle—something moving through the underbrush.

Then the blue screen of a cell phone lit up the night. A human shape emerged from between the pine trees. She cringed, a muffled scream in her throat. In the silver-blue light, she saw a man's wide shoulders. His long black hair was slick with rain and fell wildly around his face. His jaw was covered by several weeks of unshaven scruff. His shirt had the grungy look of a hitchhiker. He smelled of wet earth and the forest.

His hazel eyes looked gold in the dark. He gazed down at her curiously. She felt the tension in her stomach ease away. Somehow, though she wasn't sure why, she felt calm. Like she *knew* him.

"You're just a kid," he said, his voice a deep baritone. "What are you doing way out here?"

She opened her mouth to speak, but no words came. She had been struggling with math homework when her stepdad stumbled home from the casino. He reeked of whiskey. He must have lost a lot, because he started cursing and kicking over furniture.

He shoved her into the wall when he passed her in the hallway. He went to the bathroom, and she ran out the back door before he targeted her again.

She touched the bruise on her cheek where he cracked her head against the wall. By now, he was probably watching TV and opening up a new bottle.

How could she tell this stranger all that? She didn't want to go home. But she still had school in the morning.

"I got lost," she whispered, her throat closing.

The man didn't question her. He gazed at her for some time in quiet thought. Then he took her hand and pulled her to her feet. She wobbled and gasped; her ankle was sprained. She staggered, but his arms went around her knees and he scooped her high into the air. He settled her against his strong chest. She disliked being touched or carried, but she could tolerate this. She felt safe.

"Let's get you home."

The man's voice was deep and soothing. He started walking down the forested hill. Exhaustion made her head swoon against his shoulder. She glimpsed the man's feet on the ground below. He wasn't wearing any shoes.

She was half asleep when they reached her backyard. A wobbly, half-assed fence encircled their property. A grown man could step over it—and he did. But he paused beyond the light of her kitchen window. He kept to the edge of the forest, hidden by shadows. There, he set her down on her feet.

"Do you want to come in?" she asked, half-delirious from exhaustion.

"No. You live here?"

"With my stepdad. My mom died a while ago."

"I'm sorry to hear that. Did he leave that bruise on your cheek?"

She didn't make eye contact. Silence stretched between them.

"Go inside, then," he said.

Please, I don't care who you are, stay with me, she wanted to beg. But she knew how adults were. If she told him what was really going on, he would report her to social services, and then she would be ripped away from everything she had ever known.

She didn't remember going inside that night. She just remembered his wild face, half-illuminated by the light from the kitchen window, and that he wore no shoes.

Chapter 1

School sucked, but work sucked worse.

Maddy hated school. Who wanted to study with a drunk stepfather in the next room, roaring at the TV? Between dodging flying bottles and picking up the mess, she didn't have time for homework. And then her job . . . putting up with bitchy customers all afternoon at the local hardware store was not her idea of a fun time. Her father took her paychecks. No money for a car or even to take the bus.

So she walked home. Her feet hurt from standing at a cash register, but it was a familiar ache. At least standing at a register was better than being around the house. Her father was home again after a six week bender, his longest to date. Her life, which had been steadily improving, had spiraled into chaos. She hadn't looked for him even once while he was missing. She had kinda hoped he was dead.

Now he brought friends over at all hours of the night, or drunk women from the bar. They partied it up during those small hours of the morning. The mess quickly compiled until Maddy was an anxious wreck. The house, which had been clean and organized during her father's absence, now looked like a hoarder's home. Food wrappers, pizza boxes, plastic bags and cigarettes covered every surface. The dishes were piled in the sink, which stank of moldy water. Boxes of unpacked online orders filled the living room. Every morning, she made her cup of instant coffee, grabbed her backpack and tiptoed out the front door, as her stepdad snored facedown on the couch. Sometimes, he was pantless.

Her grades were dropping again, dramatically. She hadn't turned in her homework in the last week, because she had nowhere to study and no energy to focus. She didn't know where her father went on his benders, but she wished he would just stay there.

The streets of Black River were narrow and paved with dark asphalt. No sidewalks. Broken down RV's blocked most driveways. Black River was a small town. She passed by yards filled with old lawn chairs, wood pallets, stacked tires, rusty axles and fenders. On her headphones, she listened to *Almost Had Me* by Lights. She had the full album downloaded to her Amazon music app on her shitty old Android phone.

In one yard, a pitbull sat on the front porch close to his water bowl, bored. The dog noticed her, but didn't bark. His tail flapped on the concrete steps. His name was Barney. She brought him treats sometimes, if she had leftovers from lunch. Sometimes, when Barney was off leash, he would follow her down the block for a bit, like a childhood friend wanting to play.

Technically, this was the scenic route home. She could have crossed Main St. from the hardware store and cut off twenty minutes from her walk. But she always took this detour . . . because this was *his* street, and walking down it made each day a little bit less sucky.

There was his house now. As though cued, her playlist skipped to *Star Crossed Lovers* by My Indigo. She still didn't have the guts to ring his doorbell. Other than the few times he found her out on the mountain—cold and wet from rain or fog—she didn't share many words with him. Sometimes he came by the hardware store, and then he would smile at her, with his gold-green eyes and long black hair, and her toes would curl a little. She never knew what to say to him.

Yes, there was an age gap. She was nineteen and just beginning her senior year of high school. She got held back in eighth grade, the same year her mom died. She knew she shouldn't be crushing on grown-ass men. She should be dating boys her own age.

But, she couldn't control the way she felt. Her crush on him was overpowering, making her dumb and speechless whenever she caught sight of him around town. He was over six feet tall, ripped with muscle, built like a wall, his arms covered in tattoos, no hint of boyishness to his face. He was the embodiment of her fantasies. If only she could approach him as a woman now, and not as he must think of her—the scared little girl who kept running up mountains at night.

Maddy sighed. His car, a beat up old Camaro, wasn't in his driveway. No chance of a casual sighting today. Whatever.

She scuffed her dirty Converse on the cracked asphalt and kept walking. She glanced up at the intersection ahead. Then a groan escaped her lips.

There, standing on the corner outside Andy's Market, was a group of kids in varsity jackets. They stood in a loose circle, checking their cell phones and gossiping. She cringed.

Don't they have anywhere else to be? Maddy thought in quiet agony.

She glanced around, looking for a detour, but of course there was none, unless she wanted to cut across someone's yard. Instead, she shoved her hands in her black hoodie and walked a little faster. The quicker she crossed the intersection, she could get past them . . .

It was too much to hope for. A blond beauty with her hair tied back in a cascade of curls—Kaylee Mackovich—saw her coming. A wide smile split her foxy little face. There wasn't an ounce of friendliness in it.

"There she is. Oh my god. She's the girl I was telling you about," she said to one of the guys in their little group. "Go on. Go ask her! Go!"

Maddy felt her feet hesitating as one of the boys split off from the group. The rest watched after him and snickered. *Run. Just run,* she thought. But like an idiot, she slowed down and waited as he jogged up to her.

He held out a $20 bill. She stared at it.

"Hey," he said, a stupid grin on his Peter Pan face. "Kaylee said you'll flash your tits for $20. So like, is this enough?"

Maddy flushed red. "What the fuck?"

"She says you work at The Sapphire Club." He leaned forward. "So like, come on, let's see those porno titties . . . ."

Maddy drew back her fist and punched him square in the mouth, so hard she felt her knuckles pop.

"Oh fuck!" Kaylee yelled. "Adam, are you alright?"

"Oh hell no. Nobody hits my cornerback. Get that bitch!" A football player in a varsity jacket shouted.

The other kids started running toward her. Maddy took off, her feet pounding the pavement. Porno titties or not, she was a fast runner. The group of shitheads fell back after two blocks and gave up, going back to check on their friend. She heard them screaming profanities and cursing after her.

Maddy jumped into a ditch that ran between Black River's old streets and an open, undeveloped field. She followed the ditch for a ways, getting her shoes and pants muddy. When she felt safer, she climbed out. She recognized the old neighborhood on the fringe of town. She knew exactly where she was. She slowed to a stop, her breath heaving in her lungs, her red hair falling wildly down her shoulders. Then she shook out her wrist. Her hand ached.

Kaylee Mackovich was a cunt. She had no reason to be a cunt. She was rich, beautiful, popular, and smart. She had been Maddy's BFF in Middle School before her mom died. Back then, Kaylee was charismatic and already beautiful. The two girls hit it off over music tastes. Soon they were inseparable. For a blip in time, Maddy found herself on a pedestal as Kaylee's best friend, center stage at every school dance and party, and invited to all the most popular sleepovers.

Maddy had followed Kaylee around like a puppy. She even let Kaylee pick out her clothes, her makeup, her backpack. Life was good.

Then Maddy's mom died and their friendship went sideways, like everything else in her life. Maddy got held back a year, which put her in Kaylee's classes. But that only seemed to make matters worse. One day, without explanation, Kaylee suddenly iced her out. Maddy was no longer allowed to sit at their lunch table. Her texts and calls went unanswered. If she tried to speak to Kaylee, her ex-friend would literally turn away and pretend like no one was there.

Maddy confronted Kaylee in Freshman year of High School, only to be told the story backwards. *She* was the bad friend. She gave off *bad vibes*. It was embarrassing that she got held back a year, and Kaylee's mom thought she was a "bad influence."

To make matters worse, Maddy wasn't supportive at all during Kaylee's epic breakup with Trace. Who was Kaylee supposed to turn to? Maddy had *changed* after her mom died and Kaylee needed to cut out the toxic people from her life.

So Maddy punched her in the face.

That was the first time Maddy got suspended.

Unfortunately, that was just the beginning. The bullying escalated. Kaylee spread all sorts of rumors about why Maddy was *held back* in 8th grade. She couldn't read. She had ADHD. She smoked pot. Then in Sophomore year, when Maddy's tits suddenly exploded, Kaylee told everyone she had an STD. Junior year, the confrontations started in the bathroom. Kaylee's group of friends kept cornering her and trying to steal her phone or her wallet. She finally jumped on Kaylee and started to beat her up, but a student ran to get a teacher. Maddy was suspended for three weeks. That solidified her reputation as an outcast and a crazy motherfucker. *Crazy porno titties.*

Senior year, it looked like Kaylee was back at it. Maddy didn't know why that bitch kept targeting her.

"Fucking *Sapphire*?" Maddy muttered. Now at least she knew where the rumors started. The Sapphire Club was a new strip club that just opened on Highway 20. Since the beginning of the school year, random kids she didn't even know kept approaching her to ask, "Are you a stripper? Hey, what about blowjobs?"

Part of the problem was her admittedly massive rack. She was cursed with her mom's excessive curves. It was all people seemed to see.

Maddy sighed. Whatever. She would get through this school year and graduate no matter how many land mines she had to step on. She swept her hair back, pulled up her hoodie and started walking.

She walked fast and listened for any sirens behind her. Hopefully Kaylee and her friends wouldn't call the cops. Maddy was walking so hard and so fast that she didn't hear the voice calling her name at first.

"Maddy! Hey! Maddy!"

She finally stopped and turned around. Sitting on the stoop of a partly-rebuilt porch, smoking a cigarette, was a girl with coal-black hair and thick eyeliner. She had a piercing like a bull's ring through her nose, and a spike in her left eyebrow. The house was old and sagging, with several broken windows taped over with cardboard.

Maddy recognized her.

"Hi Bea," she said.

"Where you running to?"

"Ah, just avoiding Kaylee Mackovich and her flying monkeys."

"Forget those fucktards. Everybody hates them, anyway." Beatrice stood up and brushed off her pants. "You want to come in?"

Maddy thought about it. She wasn't in a big rush to get home, except to avoid walking in the dark. Her house was about a mile outside of town, if she cut straight through the woods. Not too bad a walk, but daunting at night.

"Sure, for a little bit."

"Cool."

Maddy knew Beatrice a bit from school. Bea had gone through similar drama in fifth grade at Pine Hollow Elementary. Her father was arrested for murder. Apparently he was part of a gang dealing meth on the Res, and he executed a rival gang's member. The cops kept the story off the news, but older siblings told younger siblings, and word got around.

She recalled in 9th grade walking in on Beatrice fucking someone in the PE locker room. They were fifteen. It was after school. The person did not look like a student.

Bea's family was like her own—perhaps even more messed up. Her father was serving time in County. She lived with her mother who was also a bartender, like Maddy's own mom. In fact, they had worked together at The B Joint, a roadside bar and truck stop a few miles past Maddy's house.

Maddy had never told anyone about seeing Bea having sex in the PE locker room. She had never spoken to Bea about it, either. They didn't know each other very well.

She followed Beatrice inside.

***

"Really? So you're still a virgin?"

Maddy put out the half-finished cigarette in the wet earth outside Beatrice's back door.

"I don't know why it's such a big deal."

"Because it's sex, and sex is a big deal. Don't you watch TV?"

"No."

Her stepdad hogged the TV when he was home. When he wasn't, Maddy shut off the cable because she couldn't afford the bill. She had a super cheap phone plan, but her data sucked in the mountains. Sometimes she used the wifi at school and the library to browse the internet.

"You sure you don't want a beer?" Beatrice asked again.

"I don't drink."

"Fuck, Maddy. You really are a virgin."

Bea turned up the music on her phone. The speakers' tin-cup ambience seemed appropriate for the gray, cold evening. They looked out at acres of pine trees and a cloudy, troubled sky. It would rain tonight.

Maddy sighed. Most girls had been kissed before the age of nineteen. In this small town, perhaps the coolest thing to do was get drunk down by the river and fuck around. That's where pretty much everyone "lost it." But Maddy didn't drink. She didn't think she would *ever* drink. And so she guessed she would never "lose it" either.

Beatrice cleared her throat and spit a wad of clear mucus onto the ground. Very ladylike. She and Maddy lay, stretched out, on her half-built back patio. The corners of her yard were cluttered with trash bins, old couches and junk, but Bea's house was still nicer than Maddy's doublewide, which had no heat in the winter, no AC in the summer, and held only the vaguest memory of wallpaper.

They lay on their backs as the sky turned dark, watching the mountainside loom above them in a garb of foreboding mist. Her trailer was located in the foothills of that mountain, at the fringe of the forest. From this distance, she couldn't tell which patch of trees hid her long gravel driveway. Maddy liked it that way. Something about the forest and the mountain made her feel safe, like she had a place to hide.

"My grandma used to tell me stories about the mountain," Bea said, following Maddy's gaze. "She said the mountain draws lost souls to it. Helps them find their way."

"Was your grandma Native, Bea?"

"Yeah. Seneca. She used to tell me all sorts of stories. Lots of legends about shapeshifters and trickster spirits. She died when I was nine. I don't really remember them now." Bea blew out a puff of smoke. She looked thoughtful. Then she glanced at Maddy.

"So?" she asked. "Is it true? Do you work at *Sapphire*?"

Maddy grimaced. "No, I don't strip."

"Too bad. My mom used to strip and she made a ton of money, all those tips . . . ."

Maddy grimaced. "Well, I don't. It's not my *thing*."

Maddy fumbled with the zipper on her hoodie.

Bea took another pull from her cigarette and blew smoke up into the air.

"So . . . is there anyone you like?" she asked, changing the subject.

Maddy felt herself blushing. Sometimes she hated her own innocence.

"Not really," she admitted, even as her mind filled with visions of *him*, memories of *him*.

"Come on, there must be someone."

"No one at school."

"Ooh. So he's older? Out of high school?" Beatrice raised an eyebrow. "Who? Does he work at the hardware store?"

Maddy fumbled some more. She didn't want to share her secret. Sharing it meant someone could take it away, take *him* away, and if she lost him . . . .

Beatrice sensed her withdraw, and flicked her cigarette.

"You don't have to talk. I don't care about your sugardaddy. Here, listen to this song. It's my favorite. It's a new album by Halsey." Beatrice turned up the volume on her phone.

Maddy sighed. She wished she could talk freely about him, but she guarded that part of her life even more closely than her dysfunctional home.

Her thoughts drifted with the music. It really was a good song. It seemed to fit with the stormy autumn sky. Her thoughts wandered with the lyrics. She remembered the first time she had seen him around town, and not up in the woods at night . . . when he first became *real* . . .

On her sixteenth birthday, Maddy woke up with the power shut off. That was the day she decided to get a job. Her father, who lived his life dodging responsibility, applauded her work ethic and praised himself for being a good role model.

Maddy didn't know the first thing about finding a job. But she knew she wouldn't have any water or power until she brought home a paycheck, so by some miracle, she managed to get a part-time shift at the hardware store, 4:00-9:00pm M-Th. They started her stocking shelves and scrubbing toilets. It was okay.

Then Arianna, one of the cashier girls, got sick. Really sick. She was out for a whole week, and the General Manager asked if Maddy would cover her register. *"Just for a little while. I can't afford all this overtime."*

Math was not one of Maddy's strong suits — in fact, she really didn't have a strong suit — and the register was ancient. She had to memorize all the item codes and count change manually. Her first day at the register was brutal. She felt completely underwater as she stuttered and fumbled over each new item. She knew she was in trouble when a blond woman, maybe late forties, pulled up to her register with a cart full of house plants. The woman pulled out a wad of dollar bills and loose change.

Maddy rang up the plants, carefully picking them out of the cart and scanning them. Once this ritual was finished, the woman handed her the messy stack of bills.

"I know you, don't I?" the woman said. "Maddy Donovan, isn't it? I remember your mother. You go to school with my daughter Kaylee. Why, you're a bit young to be working here, aren't you? Sixteen? That's impressive. Good on you. So responsible."

"Oh. Hi." Maddy immediately felt uncomfortable. Now she recognized Mrs. Mackovich from the sleepovers at Kaylee's house way back in 7th grade. But that was ancient history.

"Uh, here's your change." Maddy handed over a handful of quarters and dimes.

"You're ten cents short," Mrs. Mackovich muttered as she counted. "And you didn't include my coupon."

"It's expired, sorry. You gave me fifty two dollars, and the total was . . . ."

As they picked apart the transaction, Maddy hoped Mrs. Mackovich would take pity on her, and let her extra $2.74 go, but she didn't. The woman fought for her stupid coupon, and Maddy finally gave up, red in the face and sweaty. She pulled out a calculator and ended up having to cancel and redo the entire transaction. She didn't like confrontation, particularly in public, particularly at work, particularly on her first day at the register. Her fingers trembled as she counted out Mrs. Mackovich's extra change.

Maddy released a pent-up sigh after the woman left. *Why am I shaking?* Mrs. Mackovich might be a bad customer, but she wasn't dangerous. Maddy kept expecting a bottle to fly at her head. *I'm so useless,* she thought. *I can't even count change. I feel like an idiot.*

"You alright?"

She looked up.

He was standing *right there*.

It was her first time seeing him off the mountain. For a moment, they stared at each other so intently that her cheeks turned pink.

To be honest, she hadn't truly believed he was real. Somehow seeing him *here*, in the most mundane place, was impossible. Like a figure from her dreams. It seemed . . . against the rules.

He was buying a set of drill bits and she swished them over the red scanner without thinking. *Beep-beep.* She emptied the rest of his basket without paying much attention to its contents. She couldn't look away from him. *There's no way,* she thought. But she knew the outline of his door-frame shoulders and the loose wave of his long black hair. And she knew his voice, deep enough to make her chest hurt.

Then she realized he had asked her a question.

"Uh, it's nothing. I'm fine." She quickly thrust her hands in her apron pockets, then changed her mind, realizing she had yet to take his payment. "Cash or credit?"

"Credit."

With a sigh of relief, she ran his card and got his signature. He watched her the whole time. She had this crazy flash of an idea that he would write down his number, just like something out of a movie, and slide it to her with a wink. Except he didn't. She was only sixteen. He was much older, she thought. Maybe mid twenties? She should have checked his age on his ID. Instead, she had been so nervous, she had barely matched his name to his credit card before handing it back. She couldn't even remember it.

He lingered for a moment after pocketing his wallet.

"You work here?"

"Uh, yeah."

"Alright." He shifted, leaning his weight on one leg. "You need anything?"

She stuttered. "Oh, um, no . . . I-I'm good."

"Okay. Goodnight," he said.

She watched him leave, every inch of her body vibrating, her eyes devouring him from behind. He obviously lifted weights. She could see the muscles of his broad back through his t-shirt. His skin was deep tan, possibly Native. He made her feel things. Breathless, heart-pounding things.

"Anyway, he pulled out and jizzed on my leg, and that's how I lost my virginity in twenty seconds."

Maddy snorted with laughter, caught off guard.

"What?" Bea asked. "I told you, sex is way overhyped."

"Here, pass me that," Maddy said, and took a puff off of Beatrice's cigarette. It tasted horrible.

There was snow at the very top of the mountain, though it hadn't made its way down to Black River yet. They still had a few months left before winter. Then the snow would creep down to the hills, and the town of Black River would be all but isolated from the world. It was a time of year she both enjoyed and dreaded. Enjoyed for the isolation. Dreaded, because her midnight escapes would be all but impossible.

"I gotta go," she said, climbing to her feet.

"Already? Bummer. I was gonna ask if you wanted to stay for dinner?"

"Maybe next time. I don't want to walk in the rain."

"Alright. See you at school tomorrow."

Maddy said her goodbyes and left down Beatrice's side yard. Then she turned onto the street and walked toward the mountain. Storm clouds swirled overhead, angry and dark blue.

Chapter 2

Maddy walked up the long gravel driveway, surveying the doublewide mobile she called home. They had two acres, the second acre slanting almost vertically up into the forest and mountains. Light blue paint once covered the mobile, but the dirt and cobwebs made it look a mottled sort of gray. The front steps were in disrepair. She went around the back through the sliding screen door into the kitchen.

She heard the TV on. She took a breath, trying to suppress a wave of anxiety.

Her stepdad was sitting on the couch in their tired little living room, rolling a joint on the coffee table. He didn't look up when she entered, not that she wanted to see his red face. A 32″ TV blasted some racy thriller show. Lots of explosions and fast cars zooming across the screen. She crossed the room quietly to the kitchen and reached for a cup of instant noodles from the cupboard.

"Hey, you got money for pizza?" her dad called.

"No. I don't get paid until next Friday."

"Not even $20?"

Maddy sighed inwardly. She wanted to refuse, or say something snarky, but she bit back her retort. She really couldn't say no. If she turned him down, Dean would ask to see her bank account on her phone app. Last time she refused, he threw her phone across the room and broke the screen. Then he would make her go down to the gas station to get money out of the ATM. It wouldn't stop until she handed over every last penny.

She rummaged in her backpack for her wallet. She pulled out $20 and left it on the kitchen counter.

"That's my girl," her dad muttered as he lit up. The smell of old skunk wafted through the living room.

Maddy opened the microwave. It was covered in stains. Before Dean had come home from his last bender, the kitchen was spotless. She bought a bunch of degreaser from the hardware store and scrubbed the walls until the paint started to peel, scraping off layers of oil and sticky cigarette smoke. Then she deep cleaned the oven, the microwave, the fridge—everything. For a few blessed weeks, she had felt good about the space she lived in.

Only to have him wreck it within a few days of his return. What a waste of time.

She impatiently waited 2 minutes for the popcorn to finish, hoping her dad didn't talk to her again. Then she padded quietly up the hall. Maddy closed her bedroom door behind her, wishing she could lock it. She threw her backpack down on the bed with a sigh, then sat down and munched on her popcorn, thinking about Kaylee Mackovich and the varsity crew. She wondered if they would file a police report. Her knuckles on her right hand were bruised; she wouldn't be able to deny it. Too many witnesses. What if she broke the kid's nose? Maddy grimaced. Senior year was not starting off well.

After a while, she heard the TV shut off in the living room and the front door slam.

Her ears perked. Maddy stood up and peeked into the hallway. The living room was quiet and empty. She padded down the hall and crossed to the front windows, where she parted the blinds to investigate. She watched her father stumble down the gravel driveway. An old Silverado was parked in front of a copse of alder trees, idling. She couldn't see the driver except for a red hat. Her father climbed in. Looked like he was heading downriver to the casino with someone. Damn. There went her $20.

Maddy sighed and closed the blinds. She took a moment to pick up her dad's scattered food trash and beer bottles from around the living room. She couldn't get rid of the B. O. stench, but she could at least tidy up. She paused by the coffee table in front of the TV, where a pile of unsorted mail had accumulated over the past few weeks. She started rifling through it. She found a pink overdue bill for utilities, which wasn't unusual. She set that aside. Then she picked up a letter from Gelson's & Associates. She frowned. She didn't recognize the company name. The return address was written in fancy green ink with a little winged logo at the end. It looked pretty official.

She started to open it, then stopped. The mail was addressed to Dean Harvey, her stepdad. He really didn't like her going through his personal business. She knew better than to snoop through his things. Still, she had a bad feeling. It looked like a letter from a lawyer, or a really fancy bill.

Maddy forced herself to drop the letter from Gelson's & Associates back on the coffee table, leaving it unopened. Then she took the small stack of bills back to her room. As she walked back down the hallway, she sorted through them, tearing open each envelope.

Maddy hated going through the mail. It was not a pleasant process. She had no sense for when bills were due, even though she'd been paying them since she was sixteen. The chaos of the house made it difficult to keep track. Bills went missing, or Dean threw them out by accident. She always seemed to be behind on something. It made her feel like she was drowning. Like she was completely inadequate at life, and she would never get the hang of it all.

She imagined someone in their twenties or thirties going through their mail with a sense of ease. They probably had it all organized and a big enough salary to put it all on automatic withdrawal. But she couldn't do that. Last time she tried, the overdraft fees almost killed her.

As she tore open the envelopes, a familiar wave of overwhelming stress began to rise within her.

Her cell phone plan with Mint Mobile was only $15/month and the least of her worries. Utilities were a big one, almost $150. She took a deep breath. That was to be expected. It was never under $120, no matter how many lights or appliances she turned off.

The property tax bill was biannual, she had learned. She needed to save up money to pay it, but she was behind on her savings. Emergencies kept coming up.

She got the WaveTV bill and groaned. It was a nice shade of pink. Her dad was supposed to pay for the TV since that was *his thing*, but it was 65 days past due. Her eyes widened when she opened it. $286.72? *How?*

She scanned over the list of services, trying to make sense of it. Why did he have all these add-ons? She couldn't afford this. It wiped out her paycheck. She wouldn't have any budget for groceries. She was down to a carton of eggs in the fridge, and her last few bags of top ramen. Maybe she could stretch her food another 2 weeks? She'd done it before. Nothing wrong with skipping a meal here and there.

Maddy flopped down on her bed, feeling defeated. She closed her eyes for a moment. *It's fine. Everything is fine. This is just another Wednesday.*

At that moment, her bedroom felt claustrophobically small. It was hardly bigger than a closet. The carpet was a downtrodden greige. The walls were pink from her childhood, when this room had been her nursery. Her eyes searched the glow-in-the-dark stars on the ceiling, looking for a solution. Maybe she would abandon the TV bill to collections. But the last time she did that, WaveTV refused to reconnect their service unless her dad paid the outstanding balance, and all the late charges came to over $700. So Dean opened a new account in *her* name. Or at least, that was his excuse for why her name showed up on the new TV bills.

So if she didn't pay it, she was screwed.

Maddy threw the bills onto the floor with a groan.

Maybe she really should consider becoming a stripper.

How would that look?

She tried to imagine what it must be like to dance on a pole with a crowd of men stuffing bills in her underwear. Maybe it could be fun? She wasn't very confident in her body.

Maddy stood up and shrugged off her hoodie, then slid off her jeans. She stood in front of the mirror in her underwear, trying to imagine herself in sexy lingerie with stylish hair and makeup. Her reflection—frowning, uncertain—stared back at her.

Her face was pretty enough, in a big-eyed, cutesy way. Her hair, a reddish brown color, wasn't very long or very thick. She didn't like her body. She was all curves. Her breasts were two overstuffed pillows that would make Jessica Rabbit blush. Her stomach was flat, bless, but her hips were full. Finding a decent bra within her budget was an ongoing ordeal. She wore three sports bras to PE class and an oversized XL t-shirt to stop the boys from ogling. As someone who didn't like a lot of attention, Maddy felt cursed.

No, she didn't think she could work at a place like The Sapphire Club. She wasn't cut out to be one of those girls on stage.

Maybe if she wasn't a virgin, she wouldn't be so scared of adult stuff like stripping and sex and . . . *well, sex.*

But she wasn't like Bea.

She kept her body to herself, too self-conscious to let anyone see her naked, especially the bare skin on her back. A huge white scar, bigger than her fist, spread across the bottom of her ribcage. When she was fifteen, she had slipped and fallen on broken glass. She had spent two hours in the emergency room getting stitched up. Someday she'd get a tattoo to hide it, but tattoos were expensive.

And if she turned slightly to the side . . . .

She had a bruise where her stepfather had shoved her into the dining table last week. It was still sore. He apologized later, after four beers. Then he forgot about it altogether.

That's what confused her the most—how he always forgot.

She couldn't stand him sober, and she couldn't stand him blackout drunk, but there was an in-between where he was tolerable, almost fun, especially on rare occasions when he had money.

But his denial. His complete fabrication of events . . . .

"I hate you," she whispered in the mirror, looking at the bruise. It was dark and ugly.

Maddy threw herself down on her bed again, kicking the stack of bills on the floor. She pulled out her phone and messed with it for a while. But she was bored and there was nothing on social media to hold her attention.

She rolled over on her side and curled up, trying not to think of Kaylee and that stupid kid. *Fuck I'm dumb.* Why did she have to go and punch him? She knew better. It wasn't like her to pop off that way. Would he tell the school? What would his parents do? She tried to stave off an intense, terrible feeling of trepidation.

She constantly felt like she had her back up against the wall. She couldn't do anything right. If the school administration got involved, she would get raked over the coals for this. Sometimes she felt like the entire world was against her.

Except . . . for *him*. And she didn't even know him.

Her eyes traveled to her window where a full moon was shining through the trees. She wondered if she should take a walk through the woods. She went out there at night more than she liked to admit. The mysteries of the dark forest beckoned to her. But she had a math test the next day, and it was already late.

Maddy fell asleep with her phone on the bed next to her, its cracked screen displaying 11:34pm.

***

Maddy didn't know why she woke up. She lay in the dark with a strange, ominous feeling in her gut. She picked up her phone and checked the time–2:58am.

Something had woken her up, but she didn't know what. She listened and pushed a hand against the knot in her stomach. *Jeezus, calm down.* She thought she heard someone rustling around the kitchen. It was probably her stepdad back from the casino. Still, he usually didn't get back this late. Usually by this time, he was sleeping on someone's couch. She didn't ask what he did all those nights he didn't come home. But she knew some of the girls at The Sapphire Club did a lot more than dance.

She sat up, a bit more alarmed. She could feel her pulse pounding against her jaw. It wouldn't be the first time a meth head had wandered through her back door, though it happened more in the summer, and usually during the daytime. Even crackheads were smart enough to stay off the mountain when the nights got cold around Black River.

She kept a baseball bat next to her bed and grabbed it. The handle was wrapped with duct tape. She had never used it before, but she kept it on hand. Partly because her doublewide mobile was in the middle of the woods. Partly because of Dean's drunken tantrums. The baseball bat made her feel safer when her belligerent stepdad screamed like an asshole outside her bedroom.

She cracked open the door and peered down the hallway. Someone was definitely in the kitchen. The lights were off. The person was opening all the cabinets, dragging out their contents and basically making a mess of the place for no apparent reason.

Maddy gripped her bat and hovered in the hallway. But she must have made a noise, because the man looked up. He flipped on the light. It was not her father.

"Who are you?" Maddy called, trying to keep her voice steady.

The man pulled a gun from behind his back. Maddy stopped, her eyes wide, her stomach falling into her shoes.

"Drop the bat, bitch," the man said. He looked emaciated, like he did a lot of hard drugs.

She dropped the bat and started backing down the hallway. *Shit. This is how people end up on True Crime podcasts.*

"Don't move or I'll fuck you up," the man said, waving the gun.

Maddy froze again as the man pulled a cell phone out of his pocket. He cussed as he unlocked the screen with one hand and tried to find his contacts. Then he gave up on the gun and tapped through his phone. Like, he actually set the gun down on the kitchen counter to scroll through his contacts.

Yeah, he was definitely high.

Maddy glanced down the hallway. Maybe now was a good time to run?

Their eyes locked again as he lifted the phone to his ear.

"Hey bro . . . yeah the house isn't empty, there's a girl here. No, the little shit isn't home. Must've gotten a tip off. What about the girl? Yeah she saw me, she's right here . . . . It's a *girl*, like a teenager, are you deaf? Not an old lady. Fucking stupid . . . ."

He listened for a moment, nodding, then his eyes narrowed on Maddy. She shivered under his calculating stare. *It might not be meth, but he's on something.* He looked pale and sweaty under the fluorescent kitchen light.

She started edging back down the hallway. Maybe she could slip inside her bedroom and grab her phone. She had enough reception to call the cops . . . .

"Hey you, sit down!" he yelled at her suddenly. "Just sit down right there in the hall. My buddy wants to talk to you. He's coming now."

Nope nope nope.

Maddy's survival instincts kicked into overdrive. She ran back down the hallway, overcome by fight-or-flight.

Instantly, a gun went off. *Bam!* It sounded like a thunder strike. A bullet blew a hole through the thin drywall near Maddy's head. She screamed. Her legs almost locked up in shock.

For real? He fired on me? What the hell?

She threw herself behind the first door she came to—the bathroom. She slammed the door shut and locked it. Her legs trembled uncontrollably.

Fuck fuck fuck. What now?

She heard someone slam through the front door.

"Hey dumbass!" a second man's voice roared. "What the hell are you doing? Neighbor's gonna call the cops if they hear a gun!"

"It just went off on its own–"

"That's what the safety's for! Did you kill the bitch?"

"No! She's in one of the rooms."

"You lucky cunt. Good thing you didn't fuck this up any worse, you dumbfuck. Ugh! This is *bullshit!*" Then, to her, the new person yelled, "Hey girl! Come on out. Don't be scared. We're not going to hurt you. We just wanna talk. Where's your old man? We're lookin' for him. Why don't you tell us where he is, and we'll get outta your hair?"

Fuck that! Like she was going to have a conversation with someone who pointed a gun at her. Maddy lunged across the small bathroom and struggled to open the window. The wood frame was swollen shut by moisture. She jammed her shoulder under it and lifted with all her might. Adrenaline made her do superhuman things. Wood splintered. Metal shrieked. She got the window open. She jumped through feet first, no shoes, swinging into the darkness. She landed on the soft earth. *Crunch.* The ground was covered in a layer of frost. Her breath made small puffy clouds on the wind. It was very cold, close to freezing.

She ran north, away from her driveway and deeper into the forest and the cold.

She heard sounds of pursuit—more people were sprinting around the side of her house. She could see their bobbing phone lights when she checked over her shoulder. The ground slanted upward, leading her into the mountain. She dodged through trees and branches, stumbling over hidden rocks and sticks.

Then someone lunged at her from behind, tackling her to the ground. The wind was crushed out of her by a heavy body. She couldn't even drag in enough air to scream. Something cold and metallic struck the side of her head. Her vision flashed white. She tried to curl into a defensive position. Her face was wet—blood.

"Cunt bitch," a heavy voice muttered above her. "Don't move or I'll kill you."

Maddy sobbed. She didn't dare move with a gun pointed at her. She could taste dirt in her mouth.

More men approached through the trees. A bright phone light shined directly in her eyes.

"So what, is this Dean's wife? Fuck, she's young," the man with the gun said.

"It's the guy's daughter."

"Didn't know he had a daughter."

"She's kinda hot."

The men paused. Maddy could almost hear their thoughts. She felt a chill run down her spine as the air filled with tension. They were alone deep in the woods. No one was around. She was alone. Defenseless. No one would hear her if she screamed.

Then the man above her began undoing his belt.

"Keep a gun on her," he said.

"Wait, Pete, this wasn't part of the plan. Marquis said to rough up the guy. Toss his place up, you know. Leave a message—"

"Yeah? Well the fuckers not here, is he? So we leave him a message another way." The big mean one turned back to her. "Ain't that right, sweetheart? Don't worry, we won't make you rat out your dad. But you're gonna give him a message from Marquis—he's gotta pay up."

"O-okay," Maddy gasped, shaking.

"Now be a good girl and spread those legs."

Maddy went numb. She stared up into the blinding phone lights, hardly able to breathe. What did he say?

"I dunno, Pete, this really ain't my thing–" one of the men started.

"Then hold the fucking gun steady and watch the show. I didn't spend five years in County to pass up fresh pussy."

Maddy was too terrified to move. She lay in a freezing ball on the ground, blood running down her face from her head wound. Then a heavy body was on top of her, grabbing her wrists and forcing her legs open.

That's when Maddy finally began screaming.

"Go ahead and scream, hun. Ain't nobody gonna hear you out here," the man laughed.

He smacked her again with the butt of his gun. Maddy lay back, stunned. He ripped her shirt open, tearing through her T-shirt like tissue paper. Her breasts sprung free, totally bare, no bra. Her nipples stung in the chill wind. Meaty paws grabbed her tits. Then someone took hold of her legs and started pulling off her cotton pajama bottoms. She whimpered, tears streaming down her face, too shocked to react.

"Please stop!" she begged. "Please let me go!"

"Shut the fuck up!" the man on top of her yelled.

Suddenly, a low sound rumbled through the woods. It wasn't human.

Maddy felt a primal, instinctual terror at that sound.

The men fell silent. The one on top of her scrambled to his feet, dragging up his pants. The low growl issued again, so deep Maddy could feel it in her own chest. She reached down and tried to straighten her clothing. She pulled up her pants. *Damn.* Her pajama bottoms were damp and warm. She was so scared, she pissed herself.

The men pointed their phones at the darkness, cursing as they stumbled into each other.

"What the fuck?"

"Shut up!" their leader hissed, his gun raised. "I think it's a wolf."

"Is it one of ours?"

Maddy didn't understand the second man's comment. *One of ours? Huh?*

A growl grew in volume, then suddenly went silent.

Someone screamed to her left. The gun went off. The blast lit up the forest for a split second, dazzling Maddy's eyes.

When the darkness returned, it was far deeper, and so was her fear. She heard scuffling, growling, and a juicy, gut-churning sound like ripping flesh. Then the loose *thud* of a body falling to the earth.

If she was smart, she would have run back to her house. She would have gotten inside before the wolf came after her. But she could barely climb to her feet. She was dizzy and she couldn't quite get her limbs in order. Her head throbbed. She fought to stay upright.

Don't be dog food, she thought.

Which direction was her house?

She started back downhill. She kept her hands in front of her, feeling her way through the dark forest. Clumsy. Loud. But her noises were drowned out by the screams of the men behind her. Wild gunshots punctuated the night. Then they stopped altogether.

The night seemed very surreal. Maddy kept placing one foot in front of the other. She told herself to keep pushing through the darkness and the frozen air. Her head hurt. She felt dizzy. It was very cold.

The forest seemed like an endless maze of darkness. Her body grew weaker. Despite her willpower, she eventually collapsed. Her legs simply gave out. She tried to climb back to her feet, but her body refused.

"It's too cold," she whispered, shivering so hard her teeth rattled. "*Too cold too cold too cold.*" She blew into her hands, curled up at the base of a tree. She was lost. She wasn't going to make it home tonight. She closed her eyes and tried to hold onto consciousness.

"Please don't pass out and die," she whispered to herself. She would just take a short break. A little rest, and then she would continue. . . .

Minutes stretched. It was impossible to tell time in the darkness. She might have dozed, she wasn't sure. Then, quietly, she heard a soft voice, barely a whisper: "*Fuck*."

She didn't know if she was dreaming.

Someone knelt nearby. A hand traveled to her face, pushing her hair out of the way, touching the bloody wound on her head. She heard another soft curse.

Strong arms slid around her shoulders and under her knees, and lifted her up. *Warmth*. Suddenly she was fourteen years old again, terrified of the dark and even more terrified of going home. She turned instinctively and buried her face against his muscular shoulder. Where had he come from? How had he found her?

She let out a soft breath and went limp in his arms.

Chapter 3

Maddy cracked open her eyes with a groan. Her first thought was, *I didn't finish my homework last night.* She had a test today. She groaned. Why was her head so sore?

She turned into the pillow and took a deep breath, rubbing her nose against the fabric. It smelled good, but . . . *different.* She breathed again, enjoying the spicy odor of cologne. Aftershave? Tea Tree Shampoo?

Then her heart slammed against her chest. Not her pillow. Not her bed.

The night before came back to her with a jarring burst of pain. Her head pulsed with her heartbeat. Her hand flew up to feel the thick wad of sterile bandages and medical tape covering her forehead. The left side of her head was so tender, even her hand hovering over it made it ache.

What happened? Was she in the hospital? She cracked open her eyes again, cringing at the midmorning light. She was on a king-sized bed covered by a gray comforter. To her left was a window with wooden blinds. The floor was covered in light gray, vinyl-wood panels. The walls were bare of any artwork or decor. The closet's sliding door was open, revealing a secondhand dresser and a laundry basket full of *someone's* clothes. A man's clothes.

A violent reaction overcame her body. She remembered the man who had ripped open her shirt last night. She convulsed and almost threw up.

I was raped? she thought. She reached up to grab her breasts through a loose cotton shirt. No, she wasn't raped. She was *almost* raped. Then . . . . *I was saved. By a wolf?* What kind of stupid luck was that? Some paranormal podcast shit.

Okay. If she wasn't dead, and she wasn't in the woods, *then where the hell. . . ?*

She sat up, slow and silent. Her whole body ached. She was covered in bruises—she didn't remember most of them. Careful not to move her head too much, she slid to the edge of the bed. Standing up was more difficult than she anticipated. The room kept swaying left and right. She placed her feet on the wood-vinyl flooring. She twitched her toes. Nothing seemed broken.

She carefully stood up. She looked around again. The room was smaller from this angle. Then she looked down at herself, staring mutely. It took a moment to register that she was naked except for her panties and a very unfamiliar T-shirt, the color of dried mustard, that fell to her knees.

Her breath caught. Her knees wobbled, threatening to give out. The gun. The men. *I'm okay,* she thought, putting a hand against the wall. *I'm alive.*

Now what? She couldn't go and explore the house in this state, but staying put was out of the question. Did the bastards kidnap her? Then why wasn't she tied up in a closet? She tried the bedroom door. It wasn't locked. She opened it slowly. The hallway was just as ugly as the bedroom. Shag-brown carpet and in-need-of-paint walls. Still a good sight better than her trailer.

She walked down the hall slowly. The old flooring creaked beneath her feet. She passed by a bathroom on her left, then a second bedroom on her right, with a smaller bed and a bare mattress, no sheets or quilts. It looked unused.

Then she heard the suspicious sound of clinking plates and running water. The voice of a News announcer spoke from the TV. She crept toward the sound. The hallway opened up into a large living room. To her left, a deep couch faced a set of massive speakers and a TV hung above the fireplace. The new tech clashed with the 70's style carpet and red brick.

Above the fireplace, a 60" TV was mounted on the wall. It showed the local News station, WWNY. Remembering the commotion from last night, she wondered if anyone had reported her missing.

Probably not, she thought self-deprecatingly.

The unmistakable smell of bacon reached her nose. Instantly, Maddy's mouth watered. Her stomach let out a low rumble.

The sink turned off.

Someone was in the kitchen.

She hesitated at the edge of the living room. She felt frozen in indecision. Did she approach the unseen person, or did she retreat? What if, around the corner, she ran straight into one of the scumbags from last night? She couldn't fathom who else might be in the house. If she was smart, she would sneak out before they realized she was awake. She didn't recognize the interior of the house at all. She didn't even know if she was still in Black River. She glanced down at the mustard yellow T-shirt. Whoever it belonged to, they were way bigger than her.

I should go back, she thought, turning around. Maybe she could climb out the bedroom window and get the hell gone. . . .

"Hey."

She stiffened. Her heart gave a little flutter. She *knew* that voice. His deep, husky baritone was unmistakable.

Maddy looked back over her shoulder.

It was *him*.

Oh good lord.

He stood at the entrance to the kitchen, a towel over one shoulder.

Their eyes met.

She felt a little zap of lightning.

She swallowed. Hard.

Maddy turned around slowly to face him. She was shocked. He was her secret. Secrets were supposed to remain hidden. Not standing before her, face-to-face.

This was her first time standing so close to him outside of work, in broad daylight, without a dark moonlit forest obscuring his physique. His honey-hazel eyes glimmered beneath stern brows. His black hair, a warm tone like rich earthen humus, fell freely past his shoulders. His massive chest made two little mountains under his white T-shirt. He was very tall and packed with muscle; she guessed him to be three or four inches over six feet.

A full sleeve of tattoos covered each arm. She had never really looked at them before. Up near his left shoulder, partly hidden by his shirt, she saw a vibrant, grinning skull in the sinister style of Dios de Los Muertos. The word LOBO in rustic Southwest font ran down his right forearm, while LOCO ran down the left. If his arms were both down, it read *lobo loco*. His right arm also carried the astrological symbol of a Scorpio, or maybe it was just a big fucking scorpion. The rest of the sleeve was too intricate for her to really appreciate at a glance.

His skin was deep tan. He wore blue jeans and steel-toed work boots. Something like car grease stained his shirt. She wondered, not for the first time, if he worked at a garage.

Maddy realized she was staring with her mouth slightly open. She shut it. She met his eyes again. She really didn't know what to say.

"You hungry?" he asked.

Then he walked back into the kitchen.

Maddy followed him with some hesitation. She felt like a stray cat who had wandered into someone's house. He set a plate of bacon down on the kitchen table, and she pulled out a chair and sat down. Next to the bacon was a plate of scrambled eggs and two big waffles with maple syrup.

"I didn't know what you liked," he said, like he needed to explain why he'd served her an entire breakfast buffet. "Eat up. I'll finish the rest."

"Uh . . . thank you," she mumbled.

She picked up her fork and speared one of the waffles onto her plate. The sight of so much food made her suddenly ravenous. She felt like she had burned ten-thousand calories the night before. She started shoving warm, syrup-covered waffles straight into her mouth.

He continued washing the dishes. The voice on the TV droned on. Maddy's ears suddenly perked when she heard her name. *"Now on local news, five bodies were found in the woods just outside Black River, NY . . . Police are saying animal attack . . . nearby mobilehome abandoned . . . currently searching for Madeline Donovan, a student at Black River High School. If you have any information about her whereabouts, please call . . . ."*

So the police were looking for her. Wow. Color her impressed. Someone must have reported her missing. Maybe because of the gunshots. Certainly not her father. Sounded like Dean still hadn't come home.

Another voice interrupted Maddy's thoughts, a memory from the night before: *"Rough up the guy. . . Toss his place . . . Leave a message."*

Maddy's hands started to shake.

Her fork slipped through her clumsy fingers. It clattered to her plate. Then to the floor. It made a lot of noise.

The man turned to look at her.

"Sorry, uh . . . sorry," she muttered.

Her hands clutched the bottom of her shirt as she tried to stop trembling.

He was still watching her. That made it worse. *This isn't normal. Nothing about this is normal.* She was in his house. Her head was bandaged, and she was sitting in his boxers and a T-shirt. She felt a weird sense of vertigo. Everything was surreal.

She stared at her plate. Her cheeks were burning. She tried not to think of the unnegotiable *fact* that she was wearing his clothes, which meant *someone* must have undressed her the night before, which meant he absolutely saw her naked.

"You okay?" he asked.

"Yeah."

He shut off the sink. Then he passed through the kitchen and into the living room, where he picked up the remote. He turned off the TV.

"Sorry if that bothered you," he said.

"It's alright," she said.

She turned in the chair. He was only about ten feet away. She could see him clearly, and she studied his face again. The light from the window cast shadows beneath his high cheekbones. Devilish. He had a masculine neck, a cleft chin, a straight nose and a slightly prominent brow that gave his face a stern appearance. His lips were firm and sensual. His lashes were long and dark. His eyes were a bright, unusual hazel color. Sometimes they were green, and sometimes they were gold. She couldn't tell if he was Native American, Mexican, Brazilian or a little bit of everything. To her, he looked like an exotic model from somewhere warm and tropical.

She felt a flutter in her stomach. It was not a shy tickle, but a steroid-enhanced butterfly striking her ribcage. She liked him *so much*. But . . . he was an *adult*, and she was still in high school. So, like, probably too young for him. God, she could not stop blushing.

"So what happened last night?" he asked.

His deep baritone sent shivers down her spine. She had to force her brain to think. It was their first conversation, beyond a few words at the hardware store. Jeez, she was *so* nervous. It took a moment for her to organize her thoughts.

"Some people broke into my house," she said. It felt weird to hear herself talk. Her brain seemed to lag behind her mouth. *Do I have a concussion?* "I think my dad owed them money. They said something about . . . 'toss the place and rough him up.' Um. But my dad wasn't home. So. Pretty sure they meant to make *me* their message."

"Got it." He crossed his big arms across his chest and glanced over her. Then he asked, "They didn't . . . *hurt* you, did they?"

Maddy grimaced. "You mean, besides this?" she pointed to the wad of sterile bandages taped to the side of her head. "No, they didn't rape me, if that's what you mean. I got away. Some animal distracted them. Like the News said. I guess it was a wolf. I can't really remember." She frowned. "Did you . . . did you find me in the woods?"

"Yeah."

Maddy processed that for a moment. So he was out on the mountain last night. Which made her very lucky. They had never spoken about their little ritual in the woods before. How she kept running away at night, and how he kept finding her up in those mountains, guiding her back home when she got lost in the woods. The first time, she was fourteen.

"What about my clothes?" she asked, her hands beginning to shake again.

"They were torn up pretty bad."

"Oh. But where are they?"

"I tossed the shirt. Your pants are drying."

"Shit," Maddy muttered. Now her cheeks were heating for a different reason. "You threw away my shirt? So you saw . . . ."

Maddy paused. She was pretty sure her shirt had been ripped in half. So, if he found her like that on the mountainside, that meant he got a big eyeful of her breasts. Her head spun for a moment. No guy had *ever* seen her tits! She was mortified. He must have picked her up and carried her back to his car, then driven here, to his house. She was unconscious the whole time. He could have done anything to her.

Her heart jolted in a bad way. He could *still* do anything to her.

It was a terrifying, nauseating thought, how vulnerable she was in his presence. Especially considering the way those thugs had treated her like raw meat.

She met his eyes. He must have seen the fear in her expression, because he uncrossed his big tattooed arms and took a few steps toward her. He paused when he saw her flinch.

"Hey," he said, softening his voice. "I know you don't really know me. But I'd never hurt you. You're safe here."

She glanced away. She knew she was safe. She *knew* that. But . . . .

"Your head okay?" he asked.

"Yeah, it's fine," she said. "How did you find me?"

"I heard the gunshots," he said. "You were easy to find. You weren't far from the mobile."

She reached a hand up to touch her bandages. "Did you do this?"

He nodded.

"So. I guess you saved my life." She bit her lip. "I guess I got lucky. Most people would have run away."

"Fuck that," he said. "I'm not scared of a few punks."

"And a wolf?"

"Yeah. Well. I didn't see one, so . . . ."

A burst of laughter escaped her lips.

"Yeah right. A wolf saved me from getting raped. This is so crazy," she repeated, barely able to believe all the events of the night before, and now she was on the News. Five bodies were found dead outside of her trailer. She could barely wrap her head around it.

"I really shouldn't stay here," she mumbled as she stood up from the kitchen table. "Like, I should probably call my dad or something, make sure he's okay."

She started across the kitchen, but the floor unexpectedly dipped to one side. She lost her balance and tried to catch herself on the countertop. Ugh, she stood up too fast.

He leaned forward and caught her by the arm. She stumbled into him, grabbing his other arm for balance. He steadied her, their forearms locked together, his hands gripping her by the elbows.

She stared at him in shock, his face suddenly very close. She could feel the warmth of his skin beneath her hands and the roughness of his tattoos.

His brows were lowered in concern, but she didn't miss the slightly bemused smile that played across his mouth.

"You dizzy?" he asked.

"Not really, I'm fine now."

"Just slow?"

"Yeah. Stood up too fast."

"Right. Okay. So, you might have a concussion. I should probably take you to the hospital."

"No!" The outburst surprised her. "No, really. I don't have insurance. And like. I'm just waking up."

"I think we should probably go. They knocked you pretty good."

"Please? I can't afford it. Really. I promise I feel fine. I'm just . . . adjusting."

"Guess it's a bit of a shock waking up here."

"Yeah."

She dropped her eyes again. The smell of him was distracting. It was all over his T-shirt.

"Um, I think I should get dressed," she mumbled.

"Your pants are drying. Not much I could do for the shirt. But you can borrow that one." A hint of humor crept into his eyes. "It's a bit big on you."

She smiled shyly. Wow, awkward.

He motioned for her to follow him and walked from the kitchen into the hallway. He opened a third door and stepped into a narrow laundry room where the dryer was running. He selected a pair of gray sweatpants and a hoodie from a clean pile of folded laundry. He handed them to her.

"Bathroom's on the left," he said.

She clutched the sweatpants to her chest and slipped past him into the hallway, trying not to touch him. Then she headed for the bathroom she saw earlier.

His eyes followed her, a pressure on her back.

She closed the bathroom door and set her back against it with a sigh of relief. *Jeeeezus,* she thought, trying to calm the insane butterflies in her ribs. Why did he look like he wanted to eat her?

Chapter 4

Maddy sat her bare ass on the toilet. She didn't have her cell phone. Ugh. She had left it in the trailer. The thought of returning for it filled her with dread. Her whole body tensed.

The bathroom was tiled in 90's linoleum: little off-white squares in a white and green checkered pattern. The cabinets were basic and wooden. The shower was clean, but she saw a little mold on the curtain. Still way better than her bathroom at home, where half the time vomit or piss caked the back of the toilet.

She couldn't poop, her body was all uptight. So she gave up and started going through his bathroom cabinet.

You can learn a lot about people by what they keep in their bathroom, she thought. *Is he safe? Or a creep?*

Deodorant, tissue boxes, band-aids, a million hair ties, razors, toothpaste, mouthwash. There *had* to be something suspicious. He couldn't just be a normal guy. But Maddy was having a hard time finding any dirt on him. She had never seen a bathroom cabinet without pill bottles. *There, some Nyquil.* It was half full. Did he drink it? She pulled open a drawer and found a box of Magnum XL condoms. She slammed the drawer shut with a freaked-out little gasp.

Calm the fuck down. You're acting crazy, she thought.

She rummaged through the remaining cabinets and then under the sink. All she found were normal, everyday, *boring* things. How could he be a regular guy, working at a car garage, and living in a two-bedroom house built in 1973?

Could she trust him? Was he safe? He was her obsession, her daydream, her only comfort on those dark nights when she ran blindly through the forest. So who the hell was he? He hadn't even introduced himself, yet she was wearing his clothes. Somehow, that seemed . . . *naughty*.

"You okay in there?" she heard his low baritone grumble through the door. "I don't hear the shower."

"I'm good. I'm fine!" she called. He probably thought she had passed out on the toilet.

Maddy turned on the hot water. She stood under the shower for thirty seconds, careful not to get her bandage wet. *Axe body wash*, she noted. Then she toweled off. She put on his sweatpants, pulling the drawstring extra tight. When she pulled on the bulky sweater, his scent enveloped her again, and she felt like she had donned a coat of armor. Maybe he intended that?

She stood for a guilty moment, smelling the intensely masculine scent of his hoodie. *Wow,* she thought. So this is what he smelled like. It almost made her dizzy. She wanted to lick it. *Keep it together, Maddy.*

She lifted a hand to the bandage that covered her right temple. She felt a bit of warm fuzziness. No one had ever bandaged her up before.

Then she took a breath and forced herself back into the hallway. Her anxiety tightened in her stomach. She found him in the living room, slouched in front of the TV, the screen on but the sound muted. Again, watching the News. She wondered if he was waiting for something.

She hovered at the entrance to the living room, still uncertain. Now what?

"I'll take you to school," he said, nodding to the TV. "Your picture is all over the local news. You should let them know you're okay."

Maddy blanched. She would rather pass herself off as dead.

"What should I tell the school?" she asked.

"Tell them the truth," he said.

"Um . . . ."

"Some bad guys broke into your house. You ran. You got lost."

"Right. And I went straight to school the next day? I'm not that kind of student."

He gave her a sharp look. She almost felt ashamed. What, was he mad at her for hating school?

"Should I say I spent the night at a friend's house?" she asked.

"Am I your friend?"

"Yeah." She fidgeted. "I can leave you out of it, if you don't want to be involved . . . ."

"It's fine." He stood up and turned off the TV. "Let's go. You're already late."

He's taking me to school. A storm of butterflies kicked up again. She knew this was a serious situation, but . . . how many times had she imagined him driving her around? On particularly bad days, she would fantasize about him picking her up from school, or walking her home, or doing any of the romantic things that boyfriends did. Not that he was anything like her boyfriend. Or could be. How old was he again?

Then he stood up and beckoned her into the kitchen. She followed him like a lost dog.

"Stand under the light," he said, directing her to the lamp over the stove. She did so, a little confused. They stood in the kitchen only a few inches apart. She tried not to stare at the planes of his face or the width of his shoulders.

How can he not feel this? she thought. The magnetism between them was palpable. She felt jittery, like she'd had five cups of coffee. She couldn't think straight.

He reached for her head.

She wasn't prepared, so she flinched back. Her reaction must have been extreme, because he paused.

"Sorry," she muttered.

"Don't be." He watched her closely. When next he spoke, his voice was calm and level. "I need to check your bandages. Is that okay? Do I have your permission to touch you?"

"Yeah. Sorry."

"You're fine, babygirl. You don't have to keep apologizing."

Babygirl.

It slid off his tongue so smoothly.

She felt warm.

When he reached for her again, she suppressed the urge to pull away. His large hands were shockingly gentle as he touched her head. She barely felt the tug of medical tape as he lifted the bandage away from her wound.

"Is it bad?" she dared to ask. She didn't like blood. It made her queasy.

He hissed between his teeth. "That's a big ass bruise, but it's not bleeding anymore. The laceration is shallow. Does it hurt?"

"Yeah," she mumbled. "But it's not bad. I'm fine."

"Mm." He grunted deep in his throat. She didn't think he was aware of the sound. "Take it easy today. No PE."

"Who are you?" she asked abruptly. It was stupid, but since they were standing so close together, it seemed the time to ask. "I mean, what's your name?"

"Gareth Delarosa."

He said it with a sexy sort of accent. He looked so damn hot, she almost forgot to respond.

"Right. Sorry. I'm Maddy, by the way."

"I know."

Her anxiety doubled. She felt a terrible urge to laugh. "What, are you stalking me?"

He grinned at her, like she had said something cute.

"Your name is all over the news, remember?"

"Oh. Right."

"The bandage should be fine for now. But I'm going to change it for you after school."

"Okay."

After school. Did that mean she was coming back here? She swallowed past a hard lump in her throat. Where else did she have to go? She couldn't go back to the mobile.

He turned away, nonchalant, and picked up his keys from the counter.

"We should go," he said. "It's already past 10."

Maddy followed him, a bit embarrassed. Maybe she had misread the situation. Maybe he wasn't that into her. And maybe she was acting *like she had a crush* on him. Like a Freshman flirting with a Senior, but worse. So much worse.

Be more adulty, she told herself. She didn't know how.

His car was sitting in the driveway. He owned a classic '69 Camaro in need of serious rehabilitation. The paint was partially stripped down to the metal. The leather seats were cracking. It was missing a window.

He opened the car door for her. A small gesture, but she noticed. She slid across the cracked leather as he climbed into the driver's side. He slammed the door twice before it clicked shut, then he revved up the engine. The old muscle car choked to life with a roar that felt like an earthquake, and she saw him grimace—half smile, half baring of teeth.

He likes the sound, she thought.

Then Gareth put on his sunglasses and pulled out onto the street.

She watched him from the corner of her eye. He slouched back in the driver's seat and steered with one hand, completely relaxed. With his sunglasses on, she couldn't see his eyes. She glanced at his full sleeves of tattoos. He looked cool and mysterious.

"Do you know how to drive?" he suddenly asked out of nowhere.

"Not yet." Maddy felt young. *No license. He definitely thinks I'm a kid.* She tried to explain, "I got my permit. Like, I'm not lazy or scared of it or anything. Just, my dad doesn't own a car–"

"Got it. You wanna learn?"

"Uh, yeah."

"I'll teach you."

Oh. More silence.

"I, uh. . . I'd like that," she said quietly.

"Yeah. Me too," he said.

Maddy's mind started looking ahead. Driving lessons? With him? She didn't know whether to squirm in excitement or die of embarrassment. It seemed like he wanted to see her again. *This is really happening.*

She thought ahead to after school and frowned.

"So after school, you said . . . " she started, then stopped. "Like, after school, are we . . . ?"

"I'll pick you up," he said.

"Right. Um. I need to go home for a bit. I need to get some things."

She didn't want to go back to that trailer alone. The violence of last night remained with her. Five men had chased her into the woods, tried to rape her, and then got attacked by a wild animal. The memories made her sick and numb at the same time. She gripped her hands when they started to shake again. She didn't think she would ever feel safe in that trailer again.

She waited for him to jump in and offer to take her back to her trailer, but he didn't say anything. Maddy crossed her arms. She couldn't get a read on him.

"Nevermind. I'll figure it out. Anyways. Do you work at a garage around here? I always wondered, but didn't get a chance to ask you . . . . Like, I think there's a garage downtown . . . ." She waited again for him to answer, but got nervous. "I just mean, cuz the stains on your shirt look like oil, I thought cars might be your thing. And the Camaro. It's cool. Are you working on it . . . ?"

They stopped at a red light. He leaned across the car. Maddy went stiff with shock.

He pressed his mouth to hers. His hand cupped her face. Maddy's heart pounded. She felt his warm lips against her own. A brush of stubble. Then his tongue slid into her mouth. Oh wow. It could have been quick, but he lingered. His tongue caressed hers, over and over. Hot and wet and bold.

Maddy had never been kissed before. She didn't know what to do. His breath smelled like fresh mint and burnt coffee. A pleasant tingle shot down to her toes. Her cheeks heated. She felt shy.

Then he released her. He restarted the engine, because the car had stalled, and drove through the green light.

Maddy sat back, her lips stinging. She didn't know what to think.

"Why did you do that?" she asked, curling her knees up to her chest in her seat.

"You seemed insecure."

His answer embarrassed her, because he was right.

"Yeah, well, I'm *not* insecure. My life's a mess. If you were smart, you'd stay far away."

"I don't want to stay far away."

Maddy glanced at him. She couldn't read his expression with his sunglasses on.

"So . . . so what? You want to be my friend or something?"

"Or something."

"Like what? Like . . . my boyfriend?"

He grunted. "Do you have one?"

"No."

"Then yeah. I'm your boyfriend."

Maddy didn't know what he meant. Was he serious? He made it sound like she didn't have a choice. Which was absurd. Of course she did. Did she?

"I'll take you to your place after school," he said. "We'll get your things. Then you're staying with me for a while."

Silence descended on the Camaro, which wasn't very silent at all, but more like sitting inside a thundercloud. Maddy stared resolutely out the window, playing with a lock of auburn hair, pulling and tugging at her uneven bangs. *Boyfriend?* He couldn't be serious. But then, why did he kiss her? *What is happening right now?*

She tried to remain calm as the gray buildings of her high school came into view. Her stomach churned. Just another day at school. Just another day . . . even if the whole town thought she was dead.

He pulled up alongside the curb. Then his car sat there, idling.

The metal gates to the quad were locked at all times, except for before and after school hours. She would have to pass through the Admissions Office to get to class. The moment she stepped through those glass doors, she would be under a spotlight. Her clothes were obviously meant for someone twice her size. She had a bandage on her head. She didn't have her backpack or any form of identification. She realized her hands were shaking *again*. She clenched them tight. Dammit. *Why am I so freaked out?*

Without warning, Gareth reached over and pulled up her hood. He tugged it carefully over the bandage.

"Better?" he asked.

She nodded. Having her hood up made her feel safer.

"If they tell you to take it off, just say you're cold."

She nodded again.

"Hey," he said softly, his big hand landing on her shoulder. "You alright?"

He took his sunglasses off so she could see his hazel eyes. His gaze was steady. Strong.

"I'm okay," she mumbled.

"Pick you up at three o'clock?"

She blinked. "Okay."

He held up a yellow sticky note. It was folded in half. "This is my name and my cell phone. Give it to the police if they need it. You stayed at my place last night."

She laughed weakly. "It's the truth."

"Exactly." He paused, watching her face. "You've done nothing wrong, Maddy."

She looked down. She had the sudden, terrible urge to cry. "Then why does it feel like this is all my fault?"

"It's not."

Maddy drew a firm breath. She forced her hands to unbuckle her seatbelt. Forced herself to open the car door. She gave him a little wave and stepped out of the car, closing the door behind her. Then she walked up to the glass doors of the Administration Office.

***

The Admin Building was a bustle of activity. The morning was in full swing. The doors opened into a white linoleum lobby with leather waiting chairs. Behind a tall wooden counter, five women shuffled back and forth, some carrying manila folders, others filling their cups with coffee.

One woman sat at the counter behind a computer. Her name tag read *Julia Miller*.

"If you're late, put your name on the list," she said automatically, indicating a clipboard. Then she glanced up at Maddy. She looked again.

"Madeline!" she gasped.

The rest of the women turned to stare at her. One had a donut in her mouth. Maddy wanted to dash out of the building and run across the quad. But she headed for the front counter and wrote her name down.

"Hi," she said.

Julia came around the counter to stand in front of Maddy. She had short brown hair, styled in a practical bob, and she wore a red turtleneck sweater.

"Are you okay?" she said as she approached.

"I'm here, aren't I?"

"Your name is all over the News. The police are talking to the principal right now. They will want to see you." Then, after a pause, she added, "We are all so relieved you're okay!"

"Thank you," Maddy said automatically. Her head was reeling. She didn't expect to see the police immediately. She thought it would take some time for a squad car to drive out.

She swallowed nervously. "I have to get to class . . . ."

Julia looked at her kindly. "This is a bit more important, dear."

"Of course. Yeah. I can wait."

"Good. Please. We're all so relieved. Take a seat and I'll be right back."

Maddy sat down in one of the waiting chairs. She tried to ignore the stares from the rest of the women behind the counter. One of them brought her a cup of coffee, which she clutched in her hands, trying not to be nervous. She was shaking again.

She didn't have to wait long. Julia came back after a few minutes.

"Come with me, dear," she said.

Julia led her around the wide counter and through a door, then down a hallway with white laminate tile. Then they entered a break room with the same off-white, linoleum tile floor and yellow walls. She saw a fridge, a microwave, and a yellow countertop. Two police officers stood by the counter. The school's principal, a plump and balding man in a gray suit, spoke with them. They each held a cup of coffee in hand.

Julia led her to them. "Here we are! Madeline Donovan, safe and sound."

"Madeline," Principal Rodriguez said when he saw her. "We've been very worried about you. We are so relieved that you are safe."

Principal Rodriguez greeted her when he saw her. He was a short man with a thinning combover and thick, horn-rimmed glasses. He wore his usual gray suit over a red shirt, and his signature pair of cowboy boots. Principal Rodriguez always wore the same pair of leather cowboy boots, rain or shine, summer or winter. Maddy had never seen him without them. She knew firsthand that his office was full of cowboy memorabilia. Sometimes she wondered if he fancied himself something like a small town sheriff. He definitely played that role at school. All he was missing was the star-shaped badge.

She and Principal Rodriguez had a tumultuous relationship. Last year, she had visited his office almost once a week for all sorts of infractions. Talking back to teachers. Ditching class. He suspended her three times. The third time, he lost his shit and threw her file across his small office. He yelled words like "criminal" and "correctional facility." She hadn't trusted him since.

To be fair, she was doing much better this year. Probably because her dad was gone more often.

Julia gave Maddy an upbeat smile. "Come see me if you need anything, alright? I'll be right up front." With a perky wave, she left the break room, her heels click-clicking on the linoleum.

"Please, Madeline, have a seat," Rodriguez said.

She did so. She felt even more nervous now—trapped, sitting, staring up at the police officers and the principal.

The first officer, short with a blond buzz-cut, started. "We've been trying to get a hold of your father. Do you know where he is? It's concerning that we haven't been able to contact him."

Maddy raised an eyebrow. Principal Rodriguez knew very well that her father was an alcoholic and hardly ever around. Rodriguez had been trying to get hold of him for years. The one time her father had returned his call, at Maddy's begging no less, it ended in quite a few obscenities, on her father's part, screamed into the phone.

When she didn't respond, Principal Rodriguez asked, "Were you aware that your house was broken into last night?"

Maddy tried to arrange her thoughts. Was there any point in lying? Gareth was right. She hadn't done anything wrong.

"Yeah, I was aware," Maddy admitted.

"Why didn't you call the police?" the officer asked. His nametag read Marcus Malone. His partner took out a notebook and a pencil.

"Am I being arrested?" Maddy blurted out.

Marcus spoke in a calm voice, very cop-like. "No, ma'am. We're not arresting you. But we have to take down a report. Do you know who broke in?"

"No. I didn't know them."

"Were you at the house?"

Maddy bit her lip. "I was home. I woke up around 2am . . . ." she began her story. She explained how she had fled the house through the bathroom window into the woods.

Malone spoke again. "A woman driving past heard gunshots. Did you see a gun?"

"Uh, yeah."

"Was it yours?"

"Oh, no."

"And did you go back to the house after the intruders left?"

Maddy hesitated.

"No, I . . . . I called a family friend to pick me up. I didn't go back to the trailer."

Malone's partner jotted that down.

"And who is this family friend?" Malone asked.

She handed over the yellow square of paper in her pocket. "That's his name and number. He said you can call him with any questions."

More notetaking.

"I'm not sure if you're aware," Malone said, "but there was an animal attack in the woods last night in the vicinity of your house. Did you see any animals out there?"

"No but . . . I think I heard a wolf growling. I didn't see one, though."

"I see. That fits with the bite marks on the victims. Our working theory is that the men breaking into your house ran into a wolf or wolf pack. Unfortunately, they didn't survive the attack."

Maddy swallowed uncomfortably. She glanced down at her feet. *So I didn't imagine the wolf after all,* she thought.

"If we find anyone else connected to the crime, do you want to press charges?"

"Huh?"

"If we find the people responsible, do you want to press charges?"

"Well, yeah. I mean, they stole stuff. I think."

"Sorry this happened to you," Marcus said. "You were very brave. We'll write up the report. Here is my card." He handed a slip of paper to her. "Once you have an inventory of stolen goods, please send it to me. We will try to recover what we can. If your insurance has any questions, they can contact me."

"Insurance?"

"House insurance. For the damage."

"Oh."

Maddy had never dealt with house insurance before. She didn't even know if she had it.

Marcus's partner flipped the notebook closed and pocketed it. Both officers looked ready to leave.

"Is that it?" she asked.

"Yup. Unless there's anything you would like to add?"

"No. There isn't." She left out the drugs and the near rape. "Wait. What should I do now? I mean, what if they come back?"

"If you don't feel safe, I suggest staying with friends or family for a few days. Try installing a home security system."

Maddy felt confused. In the past, she had been terrified of cops. Her mother and father had both warned her about social services. She didn't want to end up in foster care. But she was nineteen now. *Duh.* She had forgotten that part. She was an adult and she was on her own.

"What about . . . witness protection, or something . . . ?"

Marcus looked amused, like she had said something cute.

"That's for more serious stuff, like murder. But hey, if anything comes up, call me. We are here to help you." He shook her hand professionally. "Have a nice day, miss."

Maddy watched the two police officers leave. Then she looked at Principal Rodriguez. He was checking his smartphone.

"Would you like to speak to a counselor?" he asked as he checked his email.

"No. It's fine."

"Then you should go to class. Julia will write up a note for you. No more tardies, Madeline. Only two semesters to go. We want to graduate you."

"I know. Thanks."

"Thank you," Rodriguez said automatically. Then he turned and left the break room.

Maddy followed him back down the hallway into the main office. Julia wasn't at the front counter, so Maddy walked through the lobby and out onto the quad. She felt numb. If anything, her day was now even more surreal. The cops had taken their report, she wasn't in trouble, and now she was going to class. Last night's events had been earth-shattering, yet for the rest of the world, life moved on. She was at school without a backpack. The strangeness left her reeling.

Black River High School had been remodeled four years ago. The central quad was brand new, with metal benches, sapling oak trees and fresh green grass. The buildings stood in a ring around the courtyard. To her left was the new science hall. To her right, the auditorium and band room.

She went to her Earth Science class in the new science hall, where everything was metal beams and glass windows. She slipped through the door at the back of the lab, halfway through the period. She took a seat at one of the lab stations and didn't do much, since she had missed the handout and the team assignments. The teacher dropped in briefly to check on her, and directed her to the assigned reading.

"The best you can do with your time right now is study for the test," Mrs. Fleury advised. Her cherry red lipstick clashed with her complexion. "Makeup labs are this Friday at lunch."

Then Mrs. Fleury went to help the kids who were actually doing their work.

Maddy pretended to read in the textbook, but it was hard to focus. Her head was sore, and she felt guilty. Why was she always missing school work? She knew her teachers cared, but they simply didn't have the energy to keep her out of trouble.

That was her life—constantly digging herself out of trouble. Constantly solving the problems her father dumped on her. She couldn't wait to graduate with a "C" average. She wasn't dumb. She just wasn't great at juggling everything.

She didn't want to think about her homework. Her mind turned to Gareth instead, and she touched her lips subconsciously. He had kissed her in the car. It had come out of nowhere. She didn't know what they were doing. She had met him five years ago. He had remained a mysterious figure, more of a fantasy she escaped into when she couldn't handle real life. But he lived at 1110 S. Bickford Ave and drove a Camaro. She barely knew him. He hadn't mentioned their history at all, and yet he had kissed her. Passionately. As though it was his right.

Boyfriend, he said. Was he serious? She knew people had flings. Was this a fling? Was he *flinging* her?

The bell rang, interrupting her thoughts. With a sigh, Maddy closed the Earth Science textbook and funneled into the hallway with the rest of the sheep. She stopped by her locker to get her math book. It was lunch time, but maybe if she went to the library, she could cram a few things into her head before her test . . . .

Chapter 5

It was just past eleven by the time Gareth pulled into his garage—Jack's Auto Repair—off Highway 20 just outside of Black River. Unincorporated Jefferson County, a real backwoods kind of place, which he liked. His garage was not, as Maddy guessed, the Easy Oil on Main St and Herst in town. It was a little shack next to a gas station that catered mostly to truckers and stressed-out moms with flat tires.

"Jack," the initial owner, had left the property long before Gareth ever got there. Gareth took out a loan to buy the place, and he kept the name because it seemed fine.

He shoved open the door and walked into the small lobby, just as a blond woman exploded at the counter.

"You said it would be ready an hour ago!"

His boy Vin stood behind the counter in a mechanic's suit covered in grease. He was a little punk kid around Maddy's age. Vin wasn't so fast with words.

Gareth interrupted them.

"I'm sorry, Mrs . . . ?"

"Mackovich," the blonde woman snapped. She paused at the sight of him and very intentionally lowered her sunglasses. Her eyes raked over him.

Looks like she's in heat, he thought.

The blond woman's tone changed. "Ms. Banner, actually. Recently divorced."

She took his hand. He was hit with a potent whiff of peachy skin lotion and body spray. She looked good for her age, he had to admit, but fuck, he hated perfumes.

"Right. Ms. Banner," Gareth grunted. "Sorry for the delay. An emergency came up and I'm just getting into the shop now. We can have your car ready by 3pm."

"It was supposed to be ready at 10. I have kids to pick up from school and errands to run."

Gareth rubbed his neck, trying to remain calm. He was not in the mood to deal with another entitled rich woman. But his hands were tied. Since the invention of Yelp, small businesses like his garage relied on customer reviews. Soon-to-be Ms. Banner seemed the kind to leave a complaint and not take it down.

"We'll give you ten percent off for your trouble," he offered.

"Twenty percent."

"Ten percent and a free oil change."

"I'd appreciate that." She pursed her lips and stared at him as though he were on the cover of *Men's Magazine*. "You can change the oil today. I will see you at three." Then she turned and walked out the door, hips swaying, her pumps clicking on the cement.

Gareth watched her go.

"Bitch," Vin muttered once she was gone.

"Better not let her hear that," Gareth growled. "Customer first, right?"

"Come on, boss. You really gonna put up with that shit?"

"If she's paying me, yes."

Gareth went through the back door behind the lobby and into their small break room. A row of gray metal lockers lined the wall. He pulled on his gray mechanic's overalls, grabbed a towel from the rack and swung it over his shoulder.

"She's the Passat with the seal leak?" he asked Vin. "I'll start on that first."

"We have the Jeep getting picked up at noon."

"Right. With the new transmission?"

Gareth threw himself into his work. He started with the Jeep, and with Vin's help, they finished the transmission in an hour. Then he started on the Passat. He worked through lunch. He fixed the leaking seals, replaced the rear brake pads and rotated the tires. Then he started on the oil change. He had done so many oil changes in his lifetime, it was almost therapeutic.

As he worked, his mind inevitably turned to Maddy. That girl. In his house. Sleeping in his bed. He liked seeing her in his clothes that morning. His sweater dwarfed her like a dress.

Finding her collapsed in the woods last night had made his heart stop. Her shirt was ripped almost in half down the front, and her sweatpants stank of piss. Maybe he should have taken her to the hospital, but that would have complicated things, because he was covered in blood, too.

So he took her back to his place and held her under the shower to clean off the grit from the mountainside. Then he dressed her head wound. Gently laid her in bed.

What happened to you on the mountain last night, wolfgirl?

Leaving her at school that morning was difficult. She was safe there, he reasoned, but he didn't want to leave her side when she looked so . . . scared.

She had that gray-washed, passed over look that came from poverty. He knew girls her age whose mommies dropped $100 on nails for them at the salon. Those girls went thrifting for *the novelty*. But Maddy didn't have a choice. He had never seen her in new clothes. It bothered him. No one was looking out for her. That much was obvious. Kids in her situation started using drugs or running with gangs. But she didn't. She got a job at the hardware store. That was hard, paying bills at sixteen. Their lives weren't so different; he was just a little farther down the road. So yeah. The hardware store. He checked in on her now and then. She probably didn't even know.

He remembered their first encounter on the mountain at night. Five years ago, now. He wasn't some creep into kids. But he recognized her scent. Something in the blood that called to him. He was a wolf. And she was his lifemate. She couldn't know that yet. She wouldn't accept it. But he smelled it that first night in the woods. She was a wolf, too. *A wolfgirl hidden away in Black River.* That's what brought him down the mountain to her side. A lost, little wolf. He had followed her scent in the dark.

In those days, he was a loner, wandering without his pack. He was just passing through. But then, her scent caught his nose through the stormy woods . . . . It imprinted on some deep part of his soul.

Her bio parents were a mystery to him. Did she inherit the wolfblood from both her mother and father? Or just one? Might explain why she hadn't Changed yet. Female wolves were not common. One born to every ten males, though he suspected the ratio might be greater, with the lack of females he had seen. Maddy was an anomaly. Where was her pack? What was she doing out here, all alone? He recognized her scent the moment he met her. *His lifemate.*

A wolf finding a lifemate was rare these days, but all the signs were there. The instant familiarity. The magnetic pull. The fierce protectiveness. And that addictive, wonderful scent that filled his lungs whenever she was nearby. She smelled like *home*.

They rarely spoke during those rare midnight meetings. It only happened a handful of times. He didn't have much to say. Sometimes she was crying over a fight with her dad. Sometimes, she was just taking a walk. He would walk with her for a while. They would gaze at the moon.

As for what happened last night, luckily he was in the area. Full moon. He heard the gunshots from a quarter mile away. He had arrived just in time. He wanted to go back and sniff around her trailer. Maybe it was a random break in. Maybe not. Some of the men in that group had wolfblood. There must be a pack moving into this territory, likely connected to a drug ring. He wanted to know what kind of shit her father had stepped in.

A new pack in the area would be a pain in the ass for him. He wasn't just a lone wolf. He was an Alpha. Which meant he was a threat, no matter how he laid low.

"Hey boss?" Vin's voice broke through his thoughts.

"What?"

"Phone for you."

Gareth set down the pint of oil and wiped off his hands. Then he crossed to the office. It was located on the other side of the breakroom, little more than a closet with a desk and a filing cabinet. Stacks of billing papers and receipts cluttered the desk. His filing system could use some work. He had a computer, but hadn't had time to set up that Quickbooks shit yet.

"This is Gareth," he said, putting the phone to his ear.

"Hello sir, this is Officer Marcus Malone with the Black River Police Department. I wanted to ask you a few questions about an incident last night involving Madeline Donovan."

"Shoot," he growled.

"Do you know Madeline?"

"I do."

"And what is the nature of your relationship?"

He paused. "I'm her boyfriend."

The cop seemed a little taken aback. "Ah. I see. Alright then. Are you aware that her house was broken into last night?

"I think half the town is aware by now."

"Did you witness the break in?"

"No. I found her after. She was pretty shaken up."

"Did she stay with you last night?"

"Yes, she did."

"About what time did you see her?"

Gareth stuck to the facts—the very watered down facts.

"After 2am, it was late."

The officer paused. "She received a head wound on her left temple. Did you take her to a hospital?"

"No."

"Why not?"

Gareth frowned into the phone. "She didn't want to go." *None of your business, prick.*

"Anything else you can remember from last night?"

"No."

"Thank you for your time, Mr. Delarosa."

"Sure."

Gareth hung up the phone. He didn't think he would hear from them again. The cops in Black River were useless. He was more concerned about the men who had attacked Maddy. He knew the underbelly of Black River pretty well. He knew the kind of petty thieves, drug fiends and dealers that frequented the dive bars down on Broadway and 9th. But these men were from out of town. And they were wolves.

He wasn't sure what to do about that yet. Maybe nothing. They were dead now. Hopefully, their pack's Alpha would get the message and not send more.

He walked through the break room and back into the garage. Then he got back under the hood of the Passat, his mind still working away on this new problem.

If this new pack discovered Maddy, she would be targeted. It worried him. Many female wolves were being targeted, kidnapped and sold for breeding these days. And she was the perfect age.

He needed to keep her safe.

He thought of her sitting in the car next to him. Her bright blue eyes flickering over him when she thought he wasn't looking.

Fuck.

She was so pretty.

Fuck, Maddy.

Why did she have to be exactly his type? Busty frame, not too short, with hair the color of redwood trees and eyes like the summer sky. Smart. She had a bite to her, a bit of fight-back. That came from growing up too fast. She was angry beneath it all. He saw that clearly. She pretended like she was in control, but she was a hurricane. She couldn't see it, but he did.

She hadn't undergone the Change yet. He didn't even know if she felt the same way about him. But after seeing her shy little glances in the hardware store and around his house, he was pretty confident she had a crush.

The impulse to touch her, to pull her against him, was overpowering. That morning, as he stared at the curve of her breasts under his T-shirt, he imagined how they would fit in his hands. Round and plump and biteable . . . *fuck.* He had staked his claim in the car when he kissed her. He had waited for five years. He wasn't going to wait anymore.

That kiss . . . her clumsy, innocent, soft mouth . . . .

You're with an Alpha now, babygirl. Just sit back and enjoy the ride.

"Hey boss," Vinnie called from the doorway. "Mrs. Mackovich is here."

"Shit. What time is it?" He was already unzipping his work coveralls and reaching for his jacket.

"3 o'clock. Is the car ready?"

"Yup. Just gotta close the hood." He slapped the bill on Vinnie's chest. "Ring her up, will you? I'll be back in the morning."

"Eh, morning?"

"You're closing, Vin. You're making overtime. Celebrate."

Gareth swung out the door and walked toward his car with long strides. Damn. His first day as Maddy's boyfriend, and he was going to be late.

***

Maddy failed her math test miserably. Her final period, computer lab, she spent in a daze. Then the bell rang, and it was officially 3 o'clock. Students flooded the hallways, their voices and squeaky shoes echoing off the linoleum floors.

Maddy took a minute to call work from the classroom phone. Her manager was very understanding. She had been "a missing person" on the news, after all. Then she entered the hallway and pushed through the crowd like a ghost. She felt tired and drained. It had been a very weird day.

She dropped off her books at her locker, then left through the metal gate next to the Admin Office. The sky was a crisp, chill blue on this late September afternoon. Perfect white clouds wafted high above the mountain. To the North, a stormhead loomed on the horizon, but she didn't think it would reach them until later that night.

The sky might be blue, but the wind was bitterly cold. Maddy shoved her hands into the pockets of the oversized hoodie. She paused for a moment just to sniff. She had been smelling the sweater all day like a freak. In 6th period, she had pulled it up over her nose and just inhaled. His smell . . . God, why was it so good? It was like . . . spicy woodsy peppery . . . It made her tits tingle. She actually felt her nipples swell beneath the sweater's heavy gray fabric. That was new.

She started down the sidewalk. The basketball team ran past her on their mandatory 5 mile route. Some kids flew by on skateboards. A big crowd was accumulating at the crosswalk. She spotted Kaylee and the varsity jackets waiting to cross the street. She slowed down a little.

She assumed Gareth was going to pick her up where he had dropped her off. As she neared the curb, her heart sank. He wasn't there. She hesitated, figuring she would wait. But as the minutes dragged by, she started to feel stupid. *I'm such an idiot.* He wasn't coming. Or he forgot.

Boyfriend my ass. He was playing her. People always did shit like that. *You need help? I'll fix it. I'll give you a raise. I got a used car you can borrow.* It never panned out. That, and she knew the scales were tipped. She could never pay back their charity, no matter how well-intentioned, and people were entitled, especially adults. How many times had someone's mom dropped off groceries or used clothes, just to spurn her when she couldn't *be* what they wanted? She had learned not to ask for favors.

She turned and started walking in the opposite direction toward the mountains. She would walk her ass home and go back to where she belonged. With each step, she felt her heart sink a little more. That was the problem with fantasies. They were too good to be true. Her life wasn't like that. He was just a flake like everyone else who talked big and then didn't show. She should've known better.

She would change her clothes when she got home, fold up his stuff and drop it on his porch tomorrow. Hopefully he wouldn't be there.

Maddy got four blocks before she heard an engine rev behind her. She would recognize the sound anywhere. Her heart skipped a beat, then she turned.

He pulled up next to her, facing the opposite of traffic, his sunglasses on and driver's side window down, big tattooed arm hanging out.

"Hey," he said. "You need a ride?"

She stared at him. She felt a lump in her throat.

"Get in," he said.

He opened the passenger side door. Maddy walked around the front of the car and slid into the low, leather seat. Then he pulled out from the curb, spewing a cloud of exhaust, and started down the street.

She saw two energy drinks in the center saddle console.

"That's yours," he said, indicating the one that wasn't open. "You walk fast. I'm only 20 minutes late."

Maddy didn't know what to say. She stared at the profile of his masculine face. She felt dumb for getting so upset. He probably got held up at work.

"So," he said, in his deep baritone, "how was your day?"

"Good. Uh. Kinda weird."

"Weird, huh?"

"Yeah. No backpack so ... couldn't turn in anything." She fell silent. He probably didn't want to hear about her school life. He was out of high school by a bit of a stretch.

It was still kinda hard for her to believe that he was here, next to her. She was in his car. They were talking, like two normal people.

"I took work off," she added.

"Smart. Customer service and concussions don't mix."

"How about your day?"

"Busy. Glad it's over."

"So . . . you were at the garage?"

"Yeah."

"What do you do there?"

"I own it." He flashed her a rueful grin. "So a bit of everything."

Maddy's eyes widened. She hadn't realized he owned his own business. So he was like, a real adult.

"You're a mechanic?"

"Yup. Was an Army mechanic. But that was ages ago."

"How long were you in the Army?"

"Active duty for four years. First got stationed in Alaska working on diesel trucks, then sent to Iraq. Came back and was in the Reserve for two more years. Worked for my family a bit. Wandered around. Moved out here."

"So you're still in the Reserves?"

"Nah. I'm just a vet now."

Maddy frowned. She didn't know much about the Army. She didn't know any soldiers.

"So wait. How does that work? They just let you go?"

Gareth shrugged. "Got to the end of my contract and decided not to reenlist. Honorable discharge. It's all good. Helped me get a small business loan. VA rates ain't no joke."

Maddy nodded, absorbing all this. So he wasn't local. She wondered what had brought him to Black River. There wasn't a lot out here except woods.

"I've never left Black River," she said.

"Where would you go if you could leave?"

She gazed out the window. "Anywhere," she murmured.

She caught a whiff of his sweater again when she turned her head. That tingle touched her bellybutton. *I'm wearing his clothes,* she thought. That sense of unreality descended. She wondered if he would try to kiss her again. She kinda wanted him to. But she was also kinda shy. So he picked her up from school, but . . . . Was he serious about being her boyfriend? Or was he teasing her?

He might just want to fuck.

No, that was too creepy and weird. She pushed the thought away. If he was just some perv, he could have tried something in the woods, back on the mountainside, when they were alone. But she had never felt threatened in his presence. He had never leered at her like the gross old men in the hardware store. He had never made any sort of inappropriate move on her. Until the kiss in the car. Which . . . she hadn't been expecting. But she kinda liked it.

She just couldn't figure him out. She knew what she needed from him—protection. But what did he need from her?

She remembered a time, when she was seventeen . . . it was *wrong*, but . . . she was crouched down, restocking the garden supplies, when she felt someone watching her. She stood up and turned. At the end of the aisle, she saw him gazing at her. She stared back. The perfect planes of his face were striking. He looked like an exotic model from Brazil or Greece. Not someone you would find in Black River. Even then, their mutual attraction had been like a gravitational force, drawing them together.

The Camaro came to a stop at a red light. Gareth turned to her. She jumped, thinking he might try to kiss her again.

He grinned. Or . . . *smirked*. Whatever it was, he looked like the devil.

"Easy," he said. His big hand landed on her leg. "Relax."

"I'm sorry—"

"You don't need to apologize."

Maddy dropped her eyes. She didn't know how many times she said sorry in a day. It had become a compulsion.

He watched her face, considering her.

"Are you sure you want to go back to the trailer?" Gareth said. "It might be a bit much for you."

"I need to get my cell phone . . . and like, other things."

"I got a spare toothbrush. Just saying. We can do this another time."

Maddy was silent. Gareth's question stayed with her. Why did she need to go back? She should just leave home altogether. Hitchhike to the next town over. But in truth, she was a coward. She had never traveled outside of Black River before. She had no money saved, no degree, no one to stay with.

"So . . . you really want me to stay with you?" she asked, uncertain. What if he changed his mind in a few hours and kicked her out? "I won't be bothering you?"

"Fuck no, you don't bother me. I wouldn't offer if I didn't want you around. I wanna keep my eye on you."

The way he said it made her shiver in a good way.

"But we just met and . . . ." *I never imagined actually staying at your house.*

"I wouldn't say we *just met*," he grunted.

She stared at him. It was the first time he had eluded to their history.

"Look, you don't have to," Gareth said. "But I think it would be safer for you not to be in that trailer alone."

"You think they might come back?"

He shrugged his massive shoulders. His eyes scanned over the intersection. "Better safe than sorry."

Maddy sighed. She didn't know why she was hesitating. She wanted to stay at his house. It just seemed so sudden. Everything in the past 24 hours had been *so sudden.*

"Let's just get it over with, then," she decided. "I need my backpack and school stuff, too."

"As you wish."

The light turned green and Gareth stepped on the gas. They left Black River behind and sped into the surrounding hills. Soon they were surrounded by thick forest. Then the ground began to slope upward.

"My driveway is up here," she said, unsure if he knew that or not. Maybe not. She pointed to a narrow dirt track that led off the road. There was a very large red mailbox and a street number at the end of her driveway, distinguishing it from the thick ferns. A barrier of wilderness blocked her view of the mobile home, which was placed far back on the property. The foothills sloped upward beyond it, leading into the mountains.

Gareth turned and started down the drive, his engine shattering the silence. Maddy became more nervous as her house came into view. The front door was cracked open. Sometimes her father left it like that when he returned from a wild night. Was he home now?

She checked the driveway. She saw fresh tire tracks and a broken whiskey bottle. Someone might have dropped him off.

"Oh no," she muttered.

"What is it?"

"My dad might be home."

Gareth parked in the driveway and turned off his car. The engine rumbled to a halt.

"Good," he said. "I'd like to meet him."

"No, wait," Maddy's voice hitched. "Don't come inside. I'll be back in five minutes. I'm just going to grab some clothes."

"And if it's *not* your dad in the house?"

They stared at one another.

"Okay," Maddy said, realizing the possible danger. "But . . . ." Her stomach twisted. She knew what the trailer looked like. There was a reason she never invited people over.

Gareth leaned down and pulled a gun out from behind her car seat. Maddy's jaw dropped.

"That's a gun," she said stupidly.

"Safety first."

Gareth got out of the car. With his sunglasses on, he looked like a cop from some sexy, late-night HBO special.

Maddy unbuckled her seatbelt and scurried after him. Together, they walked down the driveway to the trailer's front door. *I'm insane to be here,* she thought. She wondered if she would find her father roaring drunk in front of the TV.

Gareth entered first, his gun held at ready. He used the front door. Maddy followed him over a line of yellow CAUTION tape that was half-trailing on the ground.

"Well, shit," she heard Gareth say ahead of her. He lowered his weapon.

Maddy peeked around his broad frame and sucked in a breath.

Her house was trashed. Obviously someone—maybe those same thugs, or maybe scavengers—had gone through her house. Her furniture was tipped over, picture frames and DVD's strewn about the room. The refrigerator door was open. The food was gone. Her house had been all over the news. Obviously someone had looted it.

Maddy didn't see any sign of her father. She listened. She didn't hear any sounds from deeper in the house. Her trailer was pretty small, and it appeared empty.

Gareth stepped inside and started looking around. Maddy cringed. His sunglasses hid the revulsion she knew must be on his face.

Embarrassment couldn't begin to describe how she felt. She was . . . gutted. In her secret fantasies, she always imagined inviting him over to her house with a clean kitchen and a nicely decorated space. This was . . . the stark opposite. She couldn't hide the fast food trash, the alcohol stains soaked into the carpet, the mounds of unopened mail, boxes of magazines, porno DVD's, scattered beer bottles, and random junk her father dragged home to "fix." Yellow and brown stains covered the couch, where her stepdad got so blind drunk and jacked up on pills, he literally lost his shit.

Her gut sinking, she watched Gareth turn to survey her nasty wreck of a kitchen. It stank.

She hovered back near the door. So now he knew. This was how she lived. In a house that should be condemned.

On pins and needles, Maddy began picking up the living room. Her hands were shaking again. She was so ashamed. She couldn't just leave the place a wreck. She started to straighten the coffee table.

"Maddy," he said softly. He came to her side, taking her wrist in hand. "It's okay. Leave it."

She was trembling. She pulled her wrist free and stepped away from him. She wanted to hide, but she couldn't hide from him anymore. *Do you see me now?*

She went to check under the center cushion of the couch. Her wad of cash was still there. She pocketed it.

"I'm going to get my stuff," she said. She heard the quiver in her voice. She couldn't look at him, so she ducked down the hallway and ran into her bedroom. She shut the door for a moment. She leaned back against the wall. *Okay, so that was humiliating.* She needed a moment to pull it together.

Her backpack was on the bed. It was mostly empty. She rolled up a few shirts, panties, jeans and socks. She threw in her cell phone and a charger. Then she crossed to the bathroom, where she packed her toothbrush, hairbrush, deodorant, pads, and shampoo. What else did she need? It was getting harder to think. Her headache was returning from the night before. Being in this house made her feel claustrophobic.

Oh no, am I going to have an anxiety attack?

"Maddy?" she heard Gareth's voice. It brought her back to herself. "You good?"

"I'm alright," she said, walking unsteadily back down the hall. She met him in the living room. He was standing where the bullet had ripped through the drywall the night before. He studied the size of the hole. Then he returned to her side.

"They fired on you?"

"Yeah," she muttered.

"Fucking pricks."

He took her backpack from her hands. "Is this everything?" he asked.

She nodded. She felt a little queasy.

"You okay? You don't look so good."

"I'm fine," she mumbled. "But. Where are we going now?"

"Back to my place."

She bit her lip.

"You want to stay here?" he asked. He sounded incredulous.

She gazed at him, uncertain. Then some deep, primeval force moved in her belly. No, she didn't want to stay the night in this trailer. She might not know him well, and she might find him somewhat intimidating, but she could trust him. He would protect her—he had proven that much.

She stepped toward him, and he put his arm around her shoulders. He brushed his lips across the top of her head.

"Let's go through Arguello's," he said, a popular taco stand with a drive-thru. "I'm starving."

They left the house and walked down the driveway in silence. He walked closer to her than before, like a bodyguard, his eyes scanning the trees and the shadows. When she glanced at the ground, she noticed animal prints in the mud near the edge of the trees. She pointed.

"Look," she said. "I think those are wolf tracks."

Gareth crossed over to them. He knelt to study them for a moment.

"They look pretty fresh," he agreed. "You always get wolves coming around your house?"

"No. Not that I've noticed." She shrugged. "Weird."

Gareth stood up and brushed off his pants. Then he crossed to his car, circled around to the passenger side, unlocked the door and opened it for her. She climbed into the Camaro and threw her backpack behind her seat. He got in next to her, tucked the gun away behind the seat, and started the engine. The car roared to life like a dragon on steroids.

"So . . . so my house . . . " Maddy tried to find the words. "I'm sorry . . . "

"You got nothing to apologize for." His tone was soft.

She looked away, staring resolutely out the window. She felt vulnerable in the worst way. Living in her stepdad's filth was so immensely, crushingly terrible. It gave her panic attacks. Sometimes she dreamed that she was drowning.

She was too ashamed to invite friends over to her house. And now Gareth had seen the way she lived in raw daylight. She just wanted to be normal. Why did her stepdad have to ruin everything?

She glanced at Gareth out of the corner of her eye. Why was he helping her? She tried to understand him, drawn even deeper toward his mystery. *Who are you?*

As they drove down the mountain, the night flowed past the windshield in a river of darkness.

Chapter 6

True to his word, he picked up a box of tacos from Arguello's on the ride home. They ate at the kitchen table when they got back to his house. Maddy watched Gareth wolf down his tacos with extra hot sauce. She ate two and wrapped up the rest for later.

Then she sat at the kitchen table while Gareth inspected her bandage again. He used a cotton ball dipped in hydrogen peroxide to clean the wound, then wrapped her head with sterile bandages. Maddy wasn't used to being fussed over, and she squirmed uncomfortably.

"Ouch that hurts," she grimaced.

"Hold still and it won't."

She waited obediently, despite her urge to fidget. She sucked in a nervous breath.

"Relax," he muttered in his deep baritone. "Don't you trust me?"

"I don't even know you."

"Huh. But I've been looking out for you for a long time."

His voice was low and rocky. She shivered. The way he said it . . . .

"About that," she hesitated, "why were you out on those mountains last night?"

"I like the fresh air."

He's lying. What kind of psychopath strolled through the mountains at 2am for a little fresh air? Then she caught herself. Actually, she did that, too. Something about the forest and the moon called to her. A certain . . . wanderlust.

"So that's it?" she asked. "Really?"

"Yep. Got lucky. It was a full moon."

"Why does that matter?"

"I'm always out on a full moon."

Maddy had never thought about it before, but now she wondered how often their random, covert meetups coincided with the moon's cycle.

Gareth wrapped a strip of gauze around the side of her head, a duplicate of her old bandage, though not quite as padded. When he finished, he tossed the remnants of her old bandage in the kitchen trash.

"Get up," he said. "Shower time."

"I took a shower this morning."

"Take another one. You'll feel better. Don't get your head wet."

Maddy opened her mouth to protest, but she was too exhausted to argue with him. Going to the trailer seemed to have put him on edge–he was still in protector mode. He walked with her down the hallway. After she entered the bathroom, he stood outside the closed door. Under normal circumstances, it would have been creepy, but tonight, it made her feel safe. She didn't want to be alone. Even closing the bathroom door between them stressed her out. *I feel so clingy.*

Maddy undressed, folding his clothes and placing them carefully to one side. Then she stepped under the hot stream of water. It helped—she began to feel a bit more human. Afterwards, she pulled on her pajamas from home: flannel pants and a black t-shirt. She brushed her teeth. *Normal,* she thought. *Just doing normal things.*

After she finished, she went back into the hallway, where he was leaned up against the wall with his arms crossed.

"You can throw your stuff in the laundry," he said, pointing to the laundry room she had seen earlier.

"Alright."

They exchanged places. He entered the bathroom and shut the door behind him. She felt that bit of anxiety again when he disappeared from sight. *God, I'm like a needy child.* She heard the shower turn on.

Maddy didn't know why, but a sudden wave of numbness washed over her. Her arms and legs started shaking uncontrollably. Now that she had a quiet moment alone, she felt the full effects of the last 24 hours. The gun shots. The brutal attack in the woods. Waking up in a strange place. School. *Him.*

Going to the trailer might not have been the best idea. Whatever cocoon she was hiding in began to unravel. Her knees became wobbly, and her strength slowly drained from her body. She sank to the floor. She found herself wrapping her towel around her shoulders like a blanket. Her life rose up like a big, black ocean inside of her. She was this little boat spinning around.

Her breath came in low, soft pants. She pressed her forehead to her knees. *A panic attack. This is a panic attack.* She couldn't summon a single thought, and yet, it seemed like some distant part of her brain was processing, processing, processing . . . .

She sat on the shag carpet, her arms folded tight around herself, and stared at the wall, her eyes glassy and vacant.

He found her like that in the hallway. His shower finished, he stood over her, looking down at her. Then he lifted her to her feet.

"You're out of it," he murmured.

He led her into the living room, holding her hand, and sat her down on the couch. She felt fragile and empty. If left to her own devices, she probably would have stayed in that hallway for the next ten hours.

He put on a movie: an old Western with John Wayne. The TV flashed pictures of the wild wild West, and John Wayne looked ten feet tall on horseback. She stared at the screen blindly.

He sat down and pulled her against his wide chest, his arms around her, one leg up on the couch, their bodies partway overlapping. He was careful with her head as he settled her against him. She relaxed in the warm circle of his big arms. She could hear his heartbeat, strong and steady, beneath the cushion of his pectoral muscles. She stared at the TV screen, her mind blank, her gaze faraway.

Maddy floated like that for a while. She wasn't sure when she came back to herself. It seemed like hours had passed. She was lying across him on the couch, his big tattooed arms around her waist. The movie was finished, and he held the TV remote in one hand, flipping channels. He absently brushed his lips against the top of her head when she stirred.

"You back yet?" he asked.

"Mm-hm," Maddy murmured. She kept expecting something crazy to happen, like a car to drive through the wall, or a bullet to shatter a window. But he was calm. They sat undisturbed, surfing channels, finishing out a wild day in front of his 60" TV.

Gareth settled for the National Geographic channel—some documentary about Aztec tombs. He watched the screen. The tension in her stomach started to fade. She inhaled. Exhaled. She focused on his scent. Old Spice? Axe? It was very manly.

Finally, she mumbled, "What are you doing?"

"What boyfriends do."

She heard his voice rumble up through his chest beneath her ear. That word, *boyfriend,* brought a warm feeling to her stomach.

"No," she mumbled again. "Like . . . what are *we* doing?"

"Watching TV. Why? You want to watch something else?"

"No, this is fine . . . ."

She gave up. She wanted to know more about him. Why he seemed so chill, so unconcerned, about their strange relationship. Her mind traveled back to the hardware store. After she started working there, he would come in every couple of weeks. In the beginning, she wasn't always at the register. The manager had her stocking shelves and doing inventory. *Clean up on Aisle 3.* Basic stuff. Usually, she caught sight of him when he was already leaving. But she remembered, once, she was covering the paint counter, and two men approached her. She was sixteen. They hovered around the desk, asking questions about outdoor paints that she couldn't answer.

Then one guy leaned over and said, "Hey, my friend thinks he knows you."

She remembered the uncomfortable drop in her stomach.

"No, I don't think so," she said, wishing she had a hoodie on, so she could pull up her hood and slouch away.

"Naw, he knows you from somewhere. You ever go to Davenport? You go to the clubs there?"

"No."

It was a stupid question. She was obviously young. They were way older. The guy leered at her over the counter. His 'friend' stood nearby, his hands shoved in his pockets, staring at her with gross intensity.

"Hey, when do you get off work?" the guy asked.

Maddy cringed. She didn't want to answer that question. But everyone knew the hardware store closed at 9pm.

"Tell me when you're off. We can grab some beers. Come on. You drive here? Or you having a friend pick you up?"

She looked around, wishing for someone to swoop in and interrupt their conversation. Then, suddenly, her eyes landed on *him*. He walked into the paint section silently. His presence sent a little shock through her system. She hadn't run up the mountain for a while—she was older now, and she knew better how to avoid her stepdad when he was drinking. These days when he was belligerent, she walked into town and sat at a diner until it closed, messing on her phone.

Although she still thought of Gareth often, they hadn't encountered each other on the mountainside in a while.

He came up to stand behind the two men. She met his gaze. He must have seen her desperate look.

"Hey," he said over their heads. "You got deck sealant?"

She nodded, her palms sweaty.

"Where? Show me."

The sleazy customer at the counter turned around, his face scowling, then stopped when he saw Gareth's towering frame.

Gareth glared down at the two men.

"You gonna buy something? Or you just pissing around?" he growled.

The two guys stepped back quick.

"Naw, we're good man," the first guy said. He and his friend slunk off through the store. Gareth watched them go.

Maddy walked out from behind the counter. She led him over to the deck sealant, barely able to look at him. She could *feel* him standing next to her.

"Here's what we got," she said, motioning to the shelf. Then, awkwardly, she muttered, "Uh, thanks. Those guys . . . ."

"Yeah. You should tell your manager."

She glanced up at him, feeling her face flush. She nodded silently.

"Men are shit," he added. "Don't be nice. Tell them to fuck off. You got mace?"

"Uh . . . no."

"You sell it here?"

The hardware store had a self-defense cabinet in the back, next to the outdoor furniture section. She nodded and pointed. "It's, uh, at the end of Aisle 15 . . . ."

He grabbed a can of sealant and walked away. She stared after him, confused. Maybe twenty minutes later, he returned to the paint section and handed her a little keychain mace. It was still in the plastic wrapper. The price tag read $30.00. He bought her a nice one.

"Keep it on you," he said. "Ask someone to drive you home tonight."

She took it. She watched him go. She remembered feeling a warm sense of relief. A sad, pouty part of her wished that *he* could drive her home. She should ask him. She hesitated as he walked away.

Don't be weird, she told herself. She was the obsessive stalker in this situation. He was just some guy she met in the mountains. She didn't really know him.

"Where'd you go?" Gareth's voice grumbled deep in his chest, bringing her back to the couch, his arms, the TV. His hand lifted up her hair, then gently cradled her head against him. "You tired? You can fall asleep."

The thought of falling asleep on him sounded divine. She listened to his breathing, lulled by the gentle rhythm of his chest rising and falling. His spicy scent filled her nose. *Is this real? Am I dreaming?*

She might have slept for a minute before the sound of the heater kicking on startled her awake

He resettled his arms around her. His thumb gently stroked over her cheek.

"Just relax, Maddy," he murmured.

He kept saying that word–*relax*. Was she really that tense? She had carried tension her whole life. Maybe she didn't know how to relax.

His hand started kneading the top of her shoulder. It felt nice. Her breathing deepened automatically as he worked on a knot near her neck. Usually she didn't like being touched, but she could lean into this. *Just breathe.*

He shifted, pulling his other leg up on the couch so she was lying completely on top of him. Then he started massaging her back. A tiny moan escaped her lips before she caught herself. His thumbs went to the base of her neck, into the fleshy parts of her shoulder blades, then down her spine. It felt heavenly.

She didn't know when it happened, but suddenly she was kissing him. Her face lifted and his mouth met hers, his lips soft and sensual. He took his time, his mouth lazy and gentle, his fingers mindlessly rubbing small circles on her back. Then heat flared. She squirmed on top of him, as a warm ember began to grow into a flame. His tongue slid between her lips. Then he shamelessly thrust inside to taste her, his tongue exploring the soft walls of her cheeks. Her jaw went slack. He held her hostage, kissing her like he would devour her face.

At first she tried to mimic what he was doing–she didn't know how to kiss–but then she couldn't think.

Countless minutes passed. Gareth paused only to let her breathe for a second before thrusting his tongue inside her again. Strange and wonderful sensations moved through her body. She thought she might drown, but she didn't want to stop. She felt like he had no intention of ever stopping–like he had waited a long time for this moment, too.

It's happening, she thought. *This is really happening.*

She felt a hard bulge against her belly through his sweatpants. He didn't try to hide it. She was lying on top of him, partly cradled between his legs. His bulge dug into her waist. It was . . . a *lot* larger than she expected.

His hand slid up under her shirt to rest on the bare skin of her back. It traveled from the band of her sweatpants up the flare of her hips, exploring the dimples in her lower back. Then his rough, warm palm traveled up to her ribs. His hand brushed the scar on her left side–a big spiderweb of raised, white skin, where she had landed on a broken bottle.

She flinched at the touch. Her anxiety spiked.

"Wait!" she said, and sat up with a start. "Wait, stop."

He stopped. He gazed up at her in surprise. She sat up on top of him, her legs to either side of his hips, one hand braced against his chest. She winced when she moved her head too fast. Then she grabbed her shirt and tried to pull it down. She pushed his hand away.

"What?" he said. His lusty eyes, full of simmering heat, widened. "Did I hurt you?"

"I-I don't like being touched! Just stop!"

She wanted to throw her hands over her face in embarrassment. *Fuck me*, she thought. *I'm such a fucking loser.* She finally had him all to herself and she went and fucked it up.

He removed his hands from her back and raised them slightly so she could see them. He watched her face.

"Sorry," he said. "I got carried away."

They stared at one another. She was breathing heavily. Her lips were buzzing, her chin wet with his saliva, the taste of him all over her mouth. Her entire body was humming. She knew he felt it too. The bulge between her legs was rock hard and . . . *so* thick . . . . Was that really supposed to fit inside of her?

"Maybe this was a bad idea," he murmured, his voice low and guttural. "You've been through a lot."

His words crushed her. A bad idea? Like *she* was a bad idea?

"No, no, it's not a bad idea," she rushed to say. "I like kissing you."

He relaxed a bit. He looked relieved. He reached for her waist again, then stopped.

"If you liked it," he said slowly, "why did you want to stop?"

"I don't," she said.

He frowned, puzzling through her words. He looked so fucking manly, she thought she would melt. *Dammit. I ruined the mood,* she thought, forlorn. What if he never touched her again? *I suck.*

"We can stop, you don't have to do this for me," he said.

"I don't want to stop. I . . . I'm just not used to people touching me."

"Okay. I get that." He paused, considering her. Then he asked, "Can I touch you, Maddy?"

She nodded, breathless. Then he moved to sit up. She grabbed his shirt.

"Wait, what are you doing? I said it's okay . . . ."

"You have a concussion. Let's keep it chill."

"Alright. Yeah. So . . . ."

"Lay down on the couch. I'm going to give you a massage. A real one."

Maddy stiffened. "Can I keep my shirt on?"

"Yeah, if you want."

With a bit of hesitation, she climbed off of him. She'd never had a man give her a massage. Or anyone, really. It was way outside her comfort zone–but not a bad idea.

He disappeared into his bedroom and returned with a bottle of warming lotion. She tried not to make a nervous joke about it. He probably used that lotion to jerk off. *Shut up shut up shut up,* she told her brain.

Maddy found herself lying on her stomach on the couch. The warm leather was beneath her cheek. His lips brushed against her neck. A satisfying tingle ran down her spine.

He settled between her legs. He applied the lotion to his hands, then placed them spanning her lower back, his thumbs feathering the little dimples above her hips. True to her request, he left her shirt untouched. He ran his hands up her spine under the cotton fabric. She gasped.

"Do you like it?" he asked.

"Yeah . . . ."

"Good."

He kept rubbing his hands over her back until her body felt warm and loose. She thought she would melt into the couch.

"Why do you always help me?" she asked in barely a whisper.

His silence lasted so long, she thought he didn't hear her.

"Because you're alone," he finally said.

Maddy felt a lump form in her throat. Yeah, she was alone, even with her stepdad coming and going like a hurricane. Sometimes she felt totally invisible.

Gareth's hand traveled up to her shoulders beneath her shirt. His palm left a path of fire across her skin.

"Let's say I'm a wolf," he murmured.

She closed her eyes, listening to his deep voice, imagining it.

"I've been wandering for months, lost, no pack, no territory. I'm running through the forest. It's night. Suddenly I smell something *different.*"

His hands traveled over her shoulder blades, warm and steady. She could feel the hard calluses on his fingers.

"I come across a girl, all alone. I take her back home, where she's safe. But she keeps running away. It seems that half the time I'm on that mountain, she's out there too. I can't help but wonder why."

His hands roved across her back, slick with massage oil. His fingertips found the scars left by her father's drunk rages.

Across her left side was the biggest one, from a broken handle of rum that shattered on the wall next to her head during one of Dean's worst tantrums. She was fifteen. She took money from his wallet to pay for groceries.

"I ain't raising no thief!"

He threw a handle of rum at her head. It shattered on the kitchen cabinet. Then she slipped in the rum and fell on the glass. He got pissed at her for falling.

A neighbor two lots down drove her to the hospital. Thirty stitches in the ER with a doctor asking her a hundred questions. *I fell. I don't know. I just fell.* So much blood, it made her sick to look at it. It took the nurses two hours to remove all the shards of glass from her skin.

Remembering that day almost ruined her mood.

She focused on Gareth's palms sliding down her ribcage. His thumb ran over the edges of her scars. He stroked them over and over again, as though memorizing them.

Then his hands grew still. He lifted up her shirt, exposing the length of her back.

She stiffened in surprise, ready to spring from the couch, but he pinned her down with one hand.

"Shit," he said softly.

Maddy's good mood dissipated.

"Get off," she said, trying to sit up.

"No."

He held her down easily and lifted her shirt higher. She could feel the weight of his body behind her on the couch. She stopped struggling and submitted to his gaze.

"*Fuck*," he muttered, touching the big white web of scar tissue on her left side, just beneath her ribs, where the glass had gouged her.

"How did this happen?" he asked.

"I fell off my bike as a kid," she lied.

"Bullshit."

His hand brushed over the bruise on her left hip, where she had slammed into the table just last week. It was almost healed. A pleasant green color.

"And this bruise here? Who did this?"

She opened her mouth. Her jaw worked for a moment. Then a terrible, overwhelming sense of shame filled her.

"Fuck off," she snapped. "It's none of your business!"

She tried to slide away from him, off the couch, but he grabbed her hips. He dragged her back under him. They wrestled for a moment. But she wasn't very strong, and he wouldn't let her slip away. She ended up in the corner of the couch, his arms locked on either side of her, his face hovering over hers. She cast her eyes down, staring at his wide chest, unable to look him in the eye.

"Alright," he said in his gravelly voice, "let's talk. Since I'm your *boyfriend* now, I've got some questions. First, how long have you lived like that?"

Her lip quivered. "Like what?"

"The house, Maddy."

"Yeah . . . um, I'm sorry, I know it's bad . . . ."

"You don't gotta apologize. But I want to know how long?"

"Since my mother died." Maddy began to tremble. "I was thirteen."

"Right. Sorry. That's hard. So your stepdad. I get the mess. But why are you afraid of him?"

She clamped shut her mouth. How was she supposed to tell him? She had never told anyone before. She kept her eyes fixed resolutely on his strong chest.

His hand brushed a lock of red hair back from her face. He leaned in close.

"Why you keep running up mountains at night, little girl? You gonna tell me the truth? Or you gonna keep lying?"

She stared at the ink on his arms, at his long black hair spilling over his shoulders. Anywhere but his eyes.

After a long, silent pause, he smirked.

"Right. So you wanna wait this out? I'll wait."

The minute stretched, his big body imprisoning her in the corner of the couch, his arms like a cage. His scent made her skin tingle with electricity. Shame and desire warred within her. She wanted to run. He wouldn't let her off the couch. She glanced down at the floor, then over at the kitchen, looking for an escape route. He casually reached down, clasped both her wrists, and pinned her.

Finally, she broke.

"My stepfather hits me, okay? When he gets drunk. Sometimes he's completely incoherent. He gets angry . . . and you know, I'm the only one around." Tears sprang to her eyes, and she let out a choked laugh. "He threw a bottle at me. It broke and I slipped on the glass. I had to go to the ER. That's why I have that scar."

His shoulders grew rigid. The energy shifted between them. Gareth's face looked dangerous–almost feral. She could almost believe he was a wolf.

"I'll fucking kill him," he growled, his voice so guttural she could barely understand him.

"What? No. You can't." She thought of his gun. Her dad was a complete waste of life, but she didn't want him dead.

"Why do you care?" Gareth spat. "He treats you like shit."

"I don't care. I'm over it, Gareth. Please listen to me. My life isn't normal. Other kids wonder if their parents love them. I wonder if I'll have running water next week. But that's how it is. Hating my dad doesn't change my life. So whatever. I'm over it."

"You're not over it."

"I am. I'm doing just fine on my own."

"No." His face hovered close to hers. "No .... You're hanging on by a thread. But don't worry. I've got you. You don't need that piece of shit. I'll daddy you all you want."

Her mouth opened in shock.

He kissed her, his tongue sliding between her lips. His hand went to her jaw, holding her face as he tasted her. When she tried to kiss him back, he groaned and sucked her tongue into his mouth. His teeth bumped against hers.

A heady rush of fire moved through her body. Everywhere he touched began to burn – her arms, her neck, her stomach. His head dipped down. He didn't hesitate – his mouth fastened on her nipple through her shirt, hot and wet through the thin cotton. He ran his teeth gently over the hard peak. Then he drew it deep into his mouth, sucking on her flesh. Shivers of pleasure racked her body.

"Oh my god," she groaned.

He lifted up her shirt and she didn't stop him. He gazed at her naked breasts for a long moment, his eyes devouring her. Then he fell upon them, squeezing the soft flesh with his palms, rubbing her nipples between his fingers. He pushed one breast into his mouth and took a big bite, stuffing his face like a starving man. He growled. Then he bit down on her nipple, making her gasp. He sucked on her tit, flicking it with his tongue so she moaned.

"Fuck you have nice tits," he groaned. "*Fuck,* Maddy." He switched to the other one, leaving a trail of bites and kisses across her chest.

Maddy found herself mindless and panting, overcome by his assault. She didn't want him to stop. She didn't want to think. She just wanted to feel him. When he slid down her pants, she lifted her hips and helped him get them off, kicking them to the floor. He caught her legs and pulled her closer to him, so he was leaning between them. She lay with her naked back on the leather couch. Her panties were already soaking wet.

"Pink," he said, his voice thick with lust. "That's the girliest shit. I fucking love you."

"What?" Maddy yelped.

"You heard me."

His fingers found her swollen clit, which he rubbed through her panties just enough to make her gasp.

"You like that?" he murmured as she moaned. He did it again, trailing his finger over her clit, making her shiver with pleasure.

"What are you doing?" she gasped. She had never felt anything so divine.

"What boyfriends do," he grinned. "You look surprised. You ever been touched like this before?"

He stroked his thumb over her clit through her panties. She jumped a little, she was so sensitive. She gazed up at him, unable to hide her vulnerable expression. He seemed caught by her look. He leaned down and gave her a deep, wet, devouring kiss.

"Spread your legs for me, babygirl," he said softly as she made room for him.

His head dropped down to take one hard nipple into his mouth. He sucked on it, making her groan. She had never felt pleasure from her breasts before–not this kind of melting weakness. His thumb rubbed little circles over her clit, applying more and more pressure. Maddy ground her hips against his hand, unable to resist.

He played with her clit, trying different things, rubbing and tapping and stroking her. He studied her reactions like he was memorizing a map. She felt a wave of tension growing in her body. She sighed and arched against his hand.

"There it is," he murmured.

He pressed against her again.

"Hah!" she started, her voice catching in her throat. Deep pleasure flared behind her bellybutton. *What is he doing to me?* "Oh!" The pressure kept building. He kept rubbing his thumb in slow, steady circles, his hand braced against her crotch. She threw her arm over her mouth and bit her wrist. He watched her face with the sexiest grin she had ever seen.

"Gareth!" she gasped. "Oh!"

"Come for me, babygirl . . . ."

She cried out when the wave of pleasure crashed over her body. Her legs clenched around his wrist. Her back arched off the couch. She felt herself gush deep inside, her hips convulsing, her whole body squeezing down on him.

He continued to rub her, his touch gentle and persistent, pulling her into a second peak. She didn't know how he did it, but she orgasmed a second time, right on top of the first, her heart hammering in her ribs, her muscles contracting powerfully.

"No! Ah!" she cried, almost falling off the couch.

He laughed and gathered her up in his arms, pulling her into his lap. Her second orgasm made her limbs like jello. She felt loose and uncoordinated, completely in his power. His lips grazed her forehead, then he kissed the wound on her temple, holding her close.

"Was that your first orgasm?" he asked, holding her body against his.

She nodded, unable to speak words. He looked smug as hell. She was naked except for her drenched panties, but she couldn't make herself care. His arms tightened around her, and he kissed her nose.

"That's my job, to make you feel good."

She couldn't respond immediately. She felt like melted butter. She just stared into his eyes, all brown and green and gold flecked.

Then, shyly, "So . . . you're serious. About the boyfriend thing."

"Fuck yes I am."

He kissed her again, wet and sloppy across her mouth, getting his saliva all over her lips, totally shameless. She felt completely dominated by his strength, his heat. She tried to turn her face away to breathe, and his mouth trailed down her neck. His hands easily moved her in his lap, placing her legs on either side of him, their crotches rubbing together. She could feel the hard bulge of his erection. He *wanted* her to feel it.

She moaned. Damn. She wanted more.

Then his arms went under her ass, bracing her against him as he stood up from the couch. He scooped her into the air like she weighed nothing at all. Her legs wrapped around his waist and she grabbed him hard around the neck. She knew he wouldn't drop her, but she wasn't used to being carried.

"Wh-where are we doing?" she asked shakily.

He walked into his bedroom and lay her down on the bed. Then he pulled off his shirt, revealing his chiseled abdomen. She had never seen a six pack up close. Her mouth went dry and her lips parted. His body was *delicious*–toned, hardened, with a wide chest and massive shoulders. Nothing like the boys at school. Every muscle in his abdomen stood out like rock, his skin smooth and tan. His pectoral muscles were like two small mountains across his chest, with a deep indent between them. His shoulders were just as defined.

She stared up at him, wondering if he was going to finish what he started. Would she lose her virginity tonight? Her eyes dropped to his crotch where she could see the outline of his hard cock through his sweatpants. The little cuts in his abdomen trailed down past the rim of his pants. His hard on looked way bigger at this angle. Fuck.

He groaned and layered himself over her on the bed, propping her legs up on his shoulders and spreading her wide open, exposed and vulnerable. She felt submissive beneath him, overcome by his natural dominance. The giant wall of his body pressed her into the mattress. His cock nestled against her crotch in the most intimate way, completely sexual. He nestled the hard length of his erection against her dripping cunt. She caught the whimper in her throat.

When he finally broke their kiss, she was hot and panting. He hovered over her, their faces an inch apart.

"You ever fucked before, little girl?" he murmured against her lips.

Maddy shivered, hard. She couldn't reply at first.

"I . . . I . . . ."

"Hm. Maybe not then . . ." His hand gently went to her head, touching her bandage, then her hair. "I could hurt you."

No no no I want it! Don't stop! She wanted to beg him but she couldn't get her words in order.

He bent down and kissed her again, lazily devouring her mouth. She felt her legs pushed farther back by his shoulders, opening her, trapping her beneath his body. His tongue slid across her bottom lip. *Heat.* She could feel it down to her toes. Her hips flexed instinctively, and he pressed his hard-on firmly against her, riding her gently.

"Hmm. Maybe I will fuck you," he whispered into her ear.

Thoughts of his cock filled her head. What would it feel like, to have him fill her empty, aching core? To fully submit to his body? To give herself over to him completely?

"Y-yes," she murmured, barely able to speak.

His tongue slid in and out of her mouth. She moaned, overcome with desire. He was a lot stronger and heavier than her. He kept grinding against her, and she gasped, her clit sensitive, feeling another wave of pleasure begin to grow. She writhed and groaned. God, was she going to come again? He grinned, watching her face, moving his hips with deliberate slowness.

The thought barely passed through her mind before another climax took her body, wringing her out like a towel. She gasped and cried out. He watched her face as her legs gripped him and her spine bowed off the bed. His hand gripped her neck as she cried and moaned, holding her by the throat possessively.

"Look at you, coming again like a good girl . . . ." He growled low into her mouth. "Mmm Maddy. You smell *good*."

His voice was so deep, she felt it in her belly. She collapsed beneath him, sweating, hardly able to breathe as the wave passed. Her arms and legs were completely useless. She felt like a doll.

"You have the sexiest eyes," he said, his hand still wrapped around her throat. He stroked his thumb over her jaw, then across her bottom lip, then pressed it into her mouth.

"You're a puddle now, huh?" he murmured.

She couldn't answer with his thumb filling her mouth. She looked up at him, helpless. Three times, she had submitted to him, feeling her body weaken and melt into his strength. He enjoyed seeing her meltdown. He was dominating her slowly, imprinting himself on her, bringing her into a state of deep arousal, more than she had ever comprehended or imagined.

She began to understand what he meant when he said *daddy*.

Her mouth opened softly, her lips swollen.

"I want to . . . I want to have sex with you," she said. Perhaps in the most un-sexiest way, ever.

"You do?" he murmured. His thumb dipped into her pink mouth again, brushing her tongue. Then he withdrew it and spread her saliva across her lips. He was teasing her.

He pushed his hips down. "Like this?"

She nodded, speechless.

"Hmmm," he groaned.

His hands went under her ass, cupping her against him. His arms flexed. He moved for real this time, thrusting against her body like he was really fucking her. Maddy gasped at the taste of his power.

"Ah!" Her eyes widened. Oh god. He was really strong. It scared her, and she clung to his neck in shock.

He kept it up for a minute, thrusting against her like he was fucking her, his hips moving so powerful she thought she might break. She clung on tightly to his neck. Oh, wow. Was this what he wanted to do to her?

Then he slowed down, pressing her back into the mattress. He kissed her jaw.

"Horny girl. This cock is too much for you. Maybe I'll just keep giving you orgasms until you faint."

She shuddered. She knew a threat when she heard one. And she knew he would do it, too.

"Please can we . . . *do* it?" she asked. *God, am I whining?* "I mean, I've come this far . . . ."

"Tits out," he agreed.

"Hey, that's a big deal for me."

"It's a big deal for me, too." He bit her left nipple to prove it and gave her breast a little shake, like a dog with a bone, and she yelped.

"Stop it!"

"Okay."

"No, I mean, stop teasing me. You're not taking me seriously."

Gareth paused. He held her pinned against the bed as he considered her.

"You ever fucked before?"

"I . . ." Maddy blushed. "Like, yeah. Totally. Many times."

"Really?"

He watched her face with a discerning look. His eyes narrowed and lost some of their humor.

She cringed. "I mean, no. Not really."

"Oh. Not really? I see. So you were gonna lie to me again."

"I wasn't–"

"Yeah, you just did."

He pushed his cock against her drenched lower lips. His grip tightened on her ankle and he pushed her leg back a little farther. She felt a twinge of fear at how completely he was in control of her body.

His voice dropped, growing serious. "That's twice tonight you lied. I don't like it when you lie to me, little girl."

"You make it sound like a big deal–"

"Because *it is*. If you don't tell me you're a virgin, you're gonna get hurt."

She recovered and scoffed. "Yeah, whatever."

"Have you ever had a finger inside of you?"

She blushed at the intimate question. She opened her mouth to answer, but she was too embarrassed. No, actually. She was totally inexperienced. She had played with herself on occasion, and she had tried exploring a few times, but she didn't know the first thing about her own anatomy, except for what she had seen in porn.

Gareth groaned. "I'm serious, Maddy."

"Look, my head is fine. I'll be careful."

"No, I don't mean that." He paused. "I'm larger than average. Sex hurts the first time. You know that, right? You can get hurt a lot if you're not ready. Or if the guy is a fucking moron."

She shivered at his tone.

"So then what?" she asked. "You're not going to sleep with me because I'm a virgin?"

"I didn't say that."

"Then why not?"

"You're not ready. It's too much for you."

Maddy felt embarrassed. The more the silence stretched, the awkward tension grew, until she didn't know how to dispel it. He released her legs so she could wiggle out from under him, his hand slipping over her body as she moved away.

Maddy felt embarrassed. *He probably doesn't sleep with virgins,* she thought. Or he was having a moment of regret over her age or something. Either way, she didn't buy it. What guy with his level of testosterone wanted to go slow?

"Anyway," he said, pushing himself off of the bed. "You need to sleep. It's late. And you have a concussion. I'm gonna take the couch."

He ripped a t-shirt down from his closet and threw it at her.

Maddy caught the shirt and sat up, feeling a pang of rejection. She gazed up at him with big, confused eyes.

"Aw, don't look at me like that," he said. "I'm trying to be the good guy."

She opened her mouth to respond. He swooped down and kissed her open mouth, sticking his tongue down her throat, then broke away with a devilish grin.

"Goodnight, Maddy."

"Oh!" she started, surprised. "Yeah . . . yeah, goodnight. Gareth."

He left the room and shut the door behind him.

A little put out, but also exhausted, Maddy slid under his sheets and pressed her face into his pillow. She took a deep, steadying breath, waiting for the pent-up, sexual heat to drain from her body. As the darkness settled around her, she tried not to feel rejected. *I'm so stupid.* She had thrown herself at him–practically begged him to have sex–and he turned her down.

A few hot tears slipped down her cheeks. Why did her life have to feel so fucking awkward? It wasn't her fault that she was *behind*. Most girls got a boyfriend in Middle School. She knew one couple who had been together all of high school. It's not like she hadn't tried to date. She had a few crushes. Just . . . no one wanted to date Crazy Porno Titties.

He was probably having second thoughts right now. Maybe he would dump her in the morning. Why would a guy like him want to be her boyfriend?

I have to make myself better somehow, she thought. *So he'll want to stay with me.*

Then she fell asleep to his scent on the pillow.

Chapter 7

G areth stayed awake that night. Sleeping on the couch was not his favorite place. Technically he had a spare bedroom with a mattress leftover from his old room- mate—now that was a shitshow that didn't work out—but he hesitated to use it. He should've thrown it out by now. The guy had terrible hygiene.

He groaned and rubbed the raging hardon throbbing in his pants. No matter how much he longed to hold her, he couldn't sleep next to her yet. He wouldn't be able to control himself. And with her big eyes looking up at him all confused and sexy and heated . . . beckoning him . . . *begging* him . . . .

The Alpha in him wanted to finish what he started. Bend her over doggy style and take her from behind. He groaned. She would be tight at first, but she would adjust with time. Her body was very responsive to his touch. He wanted to tie her up in his bedroom and keep her as a pet, plying her with orgasms until she was incoherent, mating multiple times a day, just to work out this raging frustration he'd carried for years. It was his darkest fantasy. One he had entertained before, seeing her bent over stocking shelves in the hardware store. Carry her off somewhere secret in the woods. Keep her naked for his use. Pleasure her senseless.

He remembered the day his lust hit him in a wave. It was about a year or two ago, now. It was summer. He was building the deck in his backyard. He dropped by the hardware store on a Saturday to pick up another box of deck screws. The store was busy. A voice over the intercom called, *"Cashier number three to the front!"*

He remembered her running down an aisle from the back of the store, looking flustered. She was wearing a white tank top under her shop apron with a black bra underneath it. He didn't expect to see her. She didn't work weekends. He turned and froze. Her tits almost popped out of her shirt—everything jiggled and bounced. The impulse to reach out, grab her, drag her down onto the white linoleum floor and bite into those big breasts was overpowering. He almost lunged. Half of him wanted to ravage her. The other half wanted to throw himself over her body so no one else could look at her.

He knew every man in the store caught an eyeful of those bouncing titties. If they had a dick and balls, they went home and wanked it. He hated that, but the image stayed with him for days. That's when the hunger started to grow. When he stopped seeing her as a little girl needing his protection, and realized he wanted her—no, *craved* her—as a woman.

She was his lifemate, so it was inevitable.

But he still had to control himself. He didn't want to hurt her. Much as he would love to press his thick rod into her tight flesh, she wasn't ready yet. He needed to ease her into it.

Dammit, Maddy. He would wait for a little longer until she fell asleep. Then he'd take out his frustration with the hand lotion in the bathroom. Fuck. He hadn't felt this horny since *he* was a teenager!

He thought back to her trailer. What a sorry wreck of a place. Now that he was alone in the dark quiet of the living room, he had a chance to digest everything he had learned. His feelings swung between disgust and rage at her father. And then, deep sadness for all she had endured. He felt bad, knowing *that* was the home she had fled so many times. If he had known how bad it was . . .

What? What could he have done? Rescued her? How could he make that move? Under 18 it would have been kidnapping. But. He would have done *something*.

She was his lifemate. He didn't know if she felt the same. She hadn't Changed yet. Did she have any wolfsense at all? He caught her sniffing his sweater a few times. Maybe his scent filled her with that same intense, smoldering *craving* he felt whenever she walked close. He could only wonder.

He sighed, rubbing his pants again. It was going to be a long night.

***

Maddy woke up the next morning to someone sitting on the bed. The whole mattress dipped.

She opened her eyes, still exhausted. Her body felt like it was made of sand.

"You awake?" Gareth asked.

"Now I am," she muttered weakly. Ugh. Five more minutes.

"I made coffee. I gotta go to work. You feeling ok?"

She sighed and tried to sit up, then slouched back against the pillows. She blinked up at him, stunned by his handsome face in the morning light. His black hair was swept back in a ponytail, accentuating his firm jawline. He looked fresh out of the shower and smelled like . . . like . . . .

Memories of the night before flooded her, and she felt her nipples harden beneath the cotton shirt.

She tried to sit up again, but she couldn't quite fight her way free from the pillows.

"I feel like I'm eighty years old," she muttered. "I'm so tired."

His gaze grew firm, like he had made a decision.

"I'm calling the school. Stay home. It's Friday."

"But . . ."

"Sleep in. You'll feel better."

He took out his cell phone and called the school in front of her. Maddy watched, her lips parted in surprise.

"Yeah. I'm calling in for Maddy Donovan. She's gonna be out sick today."

A woman's voice babbled into the phone.

"I don't give a shit about her attendance. She's got a concussion."

Another pause.

"Okay. Yeah. Have a good one."

He hung up. "See? Easy. Anyway. Let me give you my number. Text me if you need anything."

Maddy's mouth was slightly agape. She shut it. *He called the school for me?*

"Oh, um, right. I have it."

"You have my number?"

"Um."

She paused awkwardly. Technically it was against company policy to steal a customer's information. But. She remembered a year ago at the hardware store, her manager slapping a yellow order receipt in front of her for a stack of 2x6's for a deck.

"Call the guy and tell him his lumber is ready for pickup."

She didn't know it was him until she heard his voice over the phone. No one had a voice that deep or gravelly. It made her all nervous. She stuttered when she told him his order was ready. Then she hung up.

She held the receipt for a couple of minutes, battling with her conscience. She told herself she was *just crushing* and not illegally stealing someone's personal information. Then she put his number into her phone.

She never used it. But she took it out at night sometimes when she was alone in her room, the TV blasting away down the hall, and wondered what she would text him. How he would respond. Maybe something like:

Sooo lame. She remembered cringing in the dark, squirming with anxiety, too scared to take that first step. She took selfies in her dark bedroom, wondering if she should send one. The angle was bad and her hoodie hid everything but her face and her luminous eyes in the screen light. She liked the ones with a little pout, her cheekbones accentuated, some hair framing her face. Then she would delete them, embarrassed.

If she sent him a selfie, maybe their conversation would go like . . . .

Then her imagination fizzled. She'd have to admit to stealing his number from the store, which made her look crazy.

For that reason, she never texted him.

"I got your number, uh . . . like a year ago . . . ." Maddy trailed off.

"Breaking company policy?" Gareth guessed at her prolonged silence.

Then he threw back his head and laughed. The deep, rugged sound shocked Maddy. He almost sounded like his Camaro.

"Damn," he said. "Stealing my number. You're a rebel. So, were you ever going to use it?"

"I don't know, maybe?"

"*Maybe.* Glad I made the first move, then." He stood up from the bed. "Anyway, give me *your* number."

"Okay, it's . . . " she rattled it off. He saved it to his phone. Then he sent her a text. She heard her phone ping somewhere in her backpack.

"Alright. I'm going. Get some sleep. I'll be home tonight."

"Have a nice day at work," she squeaked.

He leaned down and claimed her lips, his tongue entering her mouth and stroking lovingly against hers.

"Now I will," he growled.

Then he turned and left the room. She listened to the front door open and close. He locked it.

Maddy lay back and closed her eyes. Why? Why was he so hot? And why was she so so *lame*. Ugh!

She thought of getting up, but the bed was too inviting. She sighed and let herself drift back to sleep.

***

When Maddy next opened her eyes, afternoon light filled the bedroom. *Whoa, did I sleep all day?* She didn't remember the last time she had slept for so long.

She got up and used the bathroom, then she walked through the quiet house. She stood in the living room for a minute and breathed deeply. Now that she could recognize it, she noticed his scent filled the house in a warm, pleasant way. She looked at the couch where he had pinned her down the night before. Where she had lost herself in his arms. Her first orgasm. Two orgasms. No, actually. *Three.*

He was intense. And masculine. And dominating. And totally unfamiliar in so many ways. But somehow, she felt like she had known him forever. Even in the woods on those dark rainy nights, his presence comforted her. He was rough around the edges, a molten volcano of testosterone, but he seemed genuine. And the way he said *boyfriend* made her toes curl.

Finally. She was 19 and she had her first boyfriend. She had made it to the 2nd day of their relationship. She hadn't fucked up yet.

She entered the kitchen and looked in the fridge. Half a gallon of milk. Some oranges. A few eggs. An ancient container of pasta. No beer or alcohol. His freezer was also sparse. She rummaged through his cupboards. She found a bunch of random cans of beans and peas and stuff. But no hidden handle of vodka shoved above the fridge. No little sacks of weed or anything that looked like drugs. Where her paranoia came from, she didn't know. Was he sober? He seemed so . . . wild.

She made herself an omelet. Then she washed her plate. Then she checked her phone. With a little *ba-dump*, she saw a text message from him.

> Hey.

> It's Gareth.

> You up yet?

> Text me when u get this

So serious. No smiley faces or anything. Her hands trembled as she stared at his texts. Her stomach squirmed. How many times had she taken out her phone and stared at his number, wondering what to say?

Clumsy, she wrote back: *Hey yeah it's Maddy. I'm awake. I can't believe it's already afternoon. How was your day?*

No no no. Too much. She had to play it cool. She deleted it, then wrote:

> Yeah I'm awake now. Wat's up?

She sent the text and cringed. Since they were dating, shouldn't she send him a little heart emoji or something? Was it too soon? What about a kissy face? Any of that made her want to die with embarrassment. She started to pace around the living room, throwing her arm over her face, feeling totally silly. How long until he texted back?

Her phone buzzed.

Hey good morning, sleepyhead.

Was getting worried u ghosted me.

How ru feeling?

Maddy typed back:

A lot better

Send. She waited. Then:

You got homework?

Maddy blinked at the phone. Actually, yeah, she had a ton of makeup assignments for her math class from this past week. And nothing else to do around the house. She really should get out her assignments and get to work.

She sighed. She hated school so damn much.

Is he really going to tell me to do my homework? she thought with a bit of annoyance. He was treating her like a child. She remembered, with sudden stark clarity, her embarrassment the night before. She groaned. *Damn.* She had actually pouted! After *begging* him for sex. But he turned her down because she was a virgin. It was *humiliating.* He thought of her as *a kid.*

The boyfriend thing is bullshit, she told herself, trying to calm the butterflies in her stomach. He couldn't possibly see her that way. They barely knew each other. All of their interactions up until now had been distant and covert. So what if he kissed her and touched her and said all those sweet words last night? She couldn't believe it was real. Fantasies didn't cross over into reality. He was acting more like an older brother or . . . .

"I'll daddy you all you want."

She turned bright pink. After what she had felt last night, the way he overpowered her body, making her melt into the bed . . . .

She squirmed. She felt . . . naughty.

So maybe she was into it?

She couldn't leave him on "read." She texted back:

Yeah I'll work on that now.

Then, after a long moment, feeling bold and a little sassy, she wrote:

Thanks dad.

She was surprised when her phone pinged back:

Good girl.

Ugh! Why? Maddy threw herself down on the couch with a dramatic flop and threw her arm over her eyes, writhing in embarrassment. Why was he like that? Teasing her about their age difference. And why did she like it? Why?! *What's wrong with me?* She must be a lot more messed up than she thought.

It's harmless, she told herself. She didn't actually want to fuck her father. Now that was *gross*.

She struggled for a moment with her awkward, confusing feelings. Then she went to get her backpack and returned to the couch. She put her phone on the charger. She took out her math assignments. Maybe now, with some peace and quiet, she could get some work done.

The silence of the house soothed her nerves. Maddy preferred the quiet. She had spent plenty of time hiding in the school library during her lunches. She finished two assignments before her head started to hurt. She was focusing for too long. Time for a break.

She got up to get a glass of water. She stared at the magnets on his fridge. She saw a big fiesta-style one that read *Phoenix, AZ*. Was he from Phoenix? She really didn't know much about him.

She was crossing back to the couch when a loud car drove by on the street. It backfired just outside the house. It sounded like a gunshot.

Maddy jumped. Physically, her feet left the floor. Then she froze. Thick, clammy fear lodged in her throat. Her heart jarred painfully in her chest, and her hands started shaking. She stared at the front door of the house, frozen for a moment, half-expecting to hear someone rattle the knob. She waited, every muscle tense.

Then, like something out of a nightmare, she heard a loud *clunk* from the back of the house.

Maddy spun around. Her eyes dilated. Sickening dread washed over her for a second time. *Someone is in the house.*

Her body flew into overdrive, hijacked by a sense of unknown danger. She stood, frozen, listening. The hair on her arms and neck prickled. What should she do? She tried to think rationally. The likelihood of anyone coming in through the back of the house was slim. They would have to slip through a window, and Gareth's property was slightly slanted, so the back windows were much higher off the ground than they seemed.

Maybe I imagined it? She was doubtful. But. She should check.

Maddy looked around for a weapon and grabbed the poker next to the fireplace. *Don't be crazy,* she thought. *I'll just take a look and....* Heart pounding, she tiptoed down the hallway. She checked the unused bedroom and the closet. Nothing but stacked storage boxes and a bare mattress. Then she peeked into the bathroom. Looked behind the shower curtain. Then she finally crept into Gareth's bedroom. His window was securely closed with a stick to keep it from sliding open. She even checked nervously behind the bed.

Which left the laundry room.

She snuck down the hallway to the closed door, telling herself to calm down. Her ears strained for any hint of sound. She cracked the door open.

Nope. Just a pile of laundry waiting to be folded on top of the drier.

Maddy breathed out slowly. *See? It was your imagination.* She should have felt better, but she found herself walking through the house again on high alert, her gaze combing every corner, even the utility closet where the water heater was kept. She was convinced she had heard someone rustling around. But no one was there.

Then she sat down uneasily on the couch. She kept the fire poker next to her, her homework spread out and forgotten on the coffee table. Her neck prickled uncomfortably. She couldn't relax. Adrenaline circulated in her veins. She couldn't make herself calm down.

Okay, I've lost it, she thought. *I'm going to have another panic attack if I don't get my shit together.*

Her phone pinged, making her jump again. Then she released a breathy laugh. *It's fine. I'm fine.*

She checked it.

Gareth.

How's homework going?

It was a little after 4pm. She imagined he would be heading home soon. She didn't know how late he usually worked.

Her hands shaky from the adrenaline, she texted back:

> It's good

Normally she would have played it cool. But her fear got the better of her. She still was not entirely convinced someone wasn't in the house. Her rational mind said it was fine, nobody home, but her body told her differently. She didn't know which one to believe. For the moment, she was locked to the couch, overwhelmed and fearful.

She texted him:

> so I'm kinda freaking out

> What's wrong?

Her phone started ringing. He was calling her. Oh god. She picked it up.

"Hey," he said, his voice very deep.

She realized they had never spoken like this on the phone before, except for that one time she stole his number.

"Hi."

"What's up?" He must have heard something in her tone, because his voice had an edge. "You okay?"

"I-I'm fine," she said.

"What's wrong?"

"I'm, uh . . . Well, this car went by. It backfired and . . . then I thought I heard something in the bedroom and . . . ." She sounded crazy. "I don't know. I don't know if there's someone in the house. I think maybe there is. But I can't tell."

He listened. Then calmly, he said, "Go outside and wait for me on the porch."

"O-okay. Should I call the police or . . . ?"

"No, I'll be there in a few minutes." Then she heard him say off the phone, "Hey Vin, I gotta go. Close up when you're done? . . . Yeah I know it's Friday. Then tell him Monday. Ok."

Then to Maddy he said, "Are you outside yet?"

She climbed to her feet, her legs wobbly. She crossed the living room, unlocked the front door, and walked out onto the porch in her bare feet with no bra. She felt dumb.

But once outside, she didn't want to go back in. She sat down on the cement front steps, tears stinging her eyes. She felt trapped by her own body. *What is wrong with me?*

"Yeah, I'm outside," she said.

"Okay. I'm leaving now."

"Do you think there's someone in the house?"

"Babygirl, I trust your judgment, but . . . you might be having some PTSD."

"I don't know what that is."

"You don't . . . ah okay. Look, I gotta drive so I'm gonna hang up, but I'll be there in fifteen minutes. Just chill on the porch for me."

"Okay. Bye."

"Bye."

He hung up and she put her phone down, defeated. PTSD? Was that like some sort of mental disorder? She sat her ass down on the cement step with a sigh, propping her face in her hands. So he really thought she was crazy. Maybe she was. Maybe she had been crazy for a long time.

She waited anxiously until she heard the roar of the Camaro down the street. Gareth pulled into the driveway, his sunglasses on. When he got out of the car, he was carrying a paper bag.

Maddy stood up when she saw him. He came up the steps, reached out and dragged her into a full body hug, wrapping his arms around her. His heat and smell enveloped her. She felt the tension drain out of her instantly.

His big hands cupped her face and he looked into her eyes. "You okay?"

"I'm better now."

"Good."

Then he opened the front door. She followed him hesitantly inside. Somehow, with his presence there, the house didn't seem nearly as big or foreboding. He noted the fire poker still leaning on the couch. Then he stalked down the hall, checking each room.

When he got back to her side, he looked satisfied.

"Right," he said, finally closing the door behind them. "Checked everything. No creeps hiding out anywhere. You got spooked. I mean, who wouldn't? You've had a hell of a few days."

"I-I'm sorry."

"You're good, babygirl. Look. It's probably not the last time. So. Here." He handed her the paper bag.

Maddy opened it. Inside was a soft, fuzzy white bear and a CBD pen.

"Hold the bear, it helps," he said. "And the guy at the weed shop guarantees this is the best pen for anxiety."

Maddy was in disbelief. She looked down at the bear in her hands and squeezed it. A basic bear with two little black eyes. She almost cried. Then she started unwrapping the CBD pen. Her fingers felt cold and clumsy. He took it from her and finished opening it.

"Just hit the button like this. It heats up. Inhale. Not too long. Like this." Gareth showed her and let out a little poof of vapor. "Now you try."

Maddy hesitated. She had never messed with weed before.

"Will I get high?" she asked, a bit suspicious.

"No, it's just CBD. You'll feel better. Takes the edge off."

Maddy hesitated, then took a little puff. She coughed. It tasted *grassy*.

"So . . . " she said, still choking a bit. "So I imagined it? It felt so real."

"Yeah. It feels like that. You had a flashback."

"I almost called the cops."

"I'm glad you texted me." He wrapped her in a second hug, longer than the first, and kissed her forehead right next to her bandage. "Don't worry. Nobody's gonna get you here. You're safe. You got me protecting you, now. You trust me, right?"

She nodded into his chest.

"Good."

Maddy felt tears well in her eyes. She couldn't hold them back. She gripped him hard and started to cry. He held her, pushing her deep into his chest, like he would absorb her into his body. She cried big, sloppy tears into his shirt. She didn't hold back. She didn't think she could. Snot dripping, breath heaving, she sobbed and sobbed.

"Hey hey," he murmured, stroking her hair. "Yeah, let it out. I got you. You're safe."

Finally the tears started to slow down. As she choked and hiccuped, he pulled back to wipe the hair from her face. He kissed her forehead.

"Hey, you know what?"

"What?" she hiccuped.

"I haven't taken you on a date yet."

She started laughing through her tears. "What? *Really?*"

"Yeah. It's Friday night. You hungry? You like pizza?"

She nodded.

"Okay. How about you wash your face and let's get pizza."

He released her, his hand clasping hers until she could stand up straight. Then she pulled her hand away and wiped it over her snotty face.

"Sorry about your shirt . . . " she mumbled.

"I was gonna change anyway."

Gareth walked behind her down the hall. She turned into the bathroom and washed her face. It was all puffy and gross. She grimaced at her reflection in the mirror. Why did she cry like that over a stuffed bear? She totally lost it. She never cried. Why did she always come undone around him? No matter how hard she tried to be strong, she kept falling apart. *God. He must think I'm a mess. I have so many problems. Why isn't he running away yet?*

But he had never run away before. Instead, he seemed intent on drawing her closer to him.

Maddy cleaned up and crossed to his bedroom to change out of her pajamas.

Gareth took over the bathroom and showered.

She met him a half-hour later in the living room. She felt her heart do a little flip-flop. He wore a black crew neck sweater with a subtle knit weave. The sleeves were pushed up to his elbows, revealing the tattoos on his forearms. His jeans looked nice, no stains or holes, like the kind he set aside for special occasions. She noticed a big silver watch on his left wrist. Shiny.

She had changed her outfit twice. She hadn't brought a lot of clothes. She wore her ripped jeans and a black t-shirt that said "NOPE" across it, and her favorite black hoodie. She applied a little eyeliner and mascara and brushed out her hair, but that was it.

"You ready?" he asked.

"Yeah. Where are we going?"

"You know Zippy's?"

She should have guessed–but it didn't stop her from grinning. Zippy's was the only pizza joint upriver. It wasn't a fancy place by a longshot, but it was a local hotspot. Maddy could never afford to eat there. An X-Large meatlover's cost almost $40. But sometimes she ducked in after school and wasted $5 on videogames.

Gareth must have seen her perk up, because he grinned and reached for her hand.

"Come on. Let's go."

Chapter 8

Zippy's was a weird hodgepodge pizza joint over the bridge on the South side of Black River. It used to be a house that got converted into a pizza parlor. Then the owners built an arcade off the front, and turned the rear parking lot into a beer garden. Now it was part "family" pizza place, part arcade, part late night hangout. Behind the gravel parking lot was a few acres of empty grass leading into the forest.

Zippy's attracted pretty much every crowd in the upriver community. On a Friday night, it was noisy and chaotic. It was pretty much the only thing to do in Black River besides the mini golf course down Highway 20 and the new climbing wall that closed at 7pm.

The gravel parking lot was packed. Gareth found a spot at the far end next to the woods. Night had fallen, and the parking lot was lit by a lonely street lamp half buried by foliage.

Gareth held her hand as they walked inside, but Maddy found herself hunching her shoulders as they neared the crowded restaurant, worried she might run into someone from school, or worse, her dad's friends.

Out back, a big group of college kids were playing competitive cornhole on a mowed area of the yard. Behind that was a bonfire surrounded by outdoor furniture. The 21+ crowd filled every seat. Indoors, families packed into the front restaurant where a big TV blasted a football game, and little kids crawled under tables. It was the second week of October. The windows and ceiling were hung with little paper bats, ghosts and jack-o-lanterns. Maddy saw fliers taped up for "Fright Farm Haunted Manor" out at Beaumont Farms. It was a historical site that put on a haunted house every year. It was pretty famous to the upriver area, but she had never been.

Gareth pulled Maddy through the chaos to a small booth at the side of the dining room, far away from the counter and the long line of people waiting to order.

Gareth emptied his pockets on the table and threw down his heavy plaid jacket in the booth. Maddy remembered the thick flannel from about a million times he had worn it in the hardware store. That surreal feeling descended again. It felt strange to be sitting here at Zippy's, sharing a table with him in public. No longer just a fantasy.

"Large pepperoni okay?"

"Sounds good," Maddy agreed.

"You want a beer?"

Maddy looked up at him, surprised, then saw a glint in his hazel eye. He was teasing her.

"Right," he said gruffly, reading her face, "a Coke?"

"Um . . . iced tea?" she said.

"Got it. See you in a minute."

Gareth left her alone at the table and went to stand in line. Maddy sighed and looked around. She shifted uncomfortably. Her eyes immediately spotted a group of kids staring at her from one of the booths nearby. She thought they might be Juniors. They were pointing and whispering, then giggling and texting on their phones.

"Is that the missing girl who was on the news?" she thought she overheard.

"Yeah didn't you hear? She just turned up at school randomly like nothing happened."

Then, *"Lame. I thought she got eaten by a wolf!"*

Maddy slouched down a bit in her seat. Black River High School had less than 400 students. Of course she would be recognized.

She messed around with her phone for a moment. Then suddenly she heard a buzzing sound. With a frown, she picked up Gareth's jacket. His scent assailed her like heady perfume, and for a moment, she couldn't think straight. That annoying, potent, *masculine* scent made her tits swell pleasantly beneath her sweater. *Damn.* Why did his smell have such a strong effect on her?

Then she reached into his pocket where his phone was buzzing.

The screen was locked, but she still saw a missed call from "Roxie."

Roxie?

It sounded like a stripper's name.

Maddy bit the inside of her cheek. Her stomach dropped. *Holy shit.* She knew, deep down inside, that another woman must exist in Gareth's life–like an ex living on another planet somewhere–but she didn't expect to see a missed call on his phone. Was Roxie his ex? Why would an ex call him on a Friday night?

His phone started buzzing again in her hand. Maddy jumped and almost dropped it. Roxie's name appeared again on the cracked screen. *Oh no.* Two calls back to back? She must be more than just an acquaintance.

Then a text popped up: *"Hey wat r u . . . ."*

Maddy couldn't read all of it because his screen was locked, so she just glimpsed the preview. Her face turned bright red. She didn't know whether or not to feel pissed, guilty or embarrassed. She shoved his phone back into his jacket and tossed it down on the booth, like she was trying to cover a fire. Damn. Why did she have to be such a snoop? She had no right to be going through his phone. Even if it was his own fault for not updating his privacy settings.

Just forget it, she thought. It was none of her business. They had only just started . . . um, *dating.* But the name ate away at her. She found herself picking at her nails, filled with a sudden, terrible anxiety.

Maybe it was his sister?

A customer at the garage?

An employee?

Maybe an employee. How did she feel about a female employee named Roxie calling him twice on a Friday night? Girls crushed on their bosses all the time.

Please dear God be a sister, she thought.

"Here we go. One large pepperoni. And breadsticks. Here's your drink. I guess it's a fountain."

Gareth slid the pizza onto the table and flopped down across from her. Without hesitation, he put two slices on her plate and set it in front of her. Then he took three pieces for himself. He began tearing into the pizza like he hadn't eaten in a year.

Maddy reached for a breadstick, her appetite somewhat curbed. Her mind worked over the missed phone calls as she watched him eat. She should just ask him about Roxie. But she couldn't say she was snooping on his phone. That was like . . . a huge breach of . . . something.

"So like, how many years have you lived in Black River?" she asked innocently.

He raised an eyebrow. "Five or so. Why?"

"Just curious. Um. Do a lot of people work for you at the garage?"

He swallowed his first slice almost whole and started on the second one.

"Just Vin. Probably gonna have to hire more. Business is picking up this year. It's a good thing. Almost closed up the place a few times."

"Right. So, um . . . any girls work for you?"

He gave her a side glance. "No."

"Do you have any sisters?"

"No. Two brothers. Why the interrogation?"

Maddy shrugged, still feeling nervous. "I don't know. I'm an only child."

"Yeah. I figured."

Maddy sighed, frustrated. How was she supposed to ask him about Roxie? She sounded like an ex. It was getting difficult to look at him. *Why am I so sensitive? It's not like we've been dating for years.*

She stood up with her cup.

"I'm going to get a drink. I'll be right back."

Then she turned and walked across the crowded dining room to the drink fountain near the counter. Kitschy decor hung from the walls: old-school pizza ads, posters, license plates, strings of lights, stuffed animal heads, and a vintage bike frame. Twice she almost got toppled by a child running back and forth from the arcade at the back of the dining room. She saw some familiar faces from school, but no one she really knew.

She stepped up to the fountain and got ice, then started filling her glass with iced tea. She tried to clear her head. *Just forget about Roxie.* She glanced at the booth over her shoulder and saw Gareth checking his phone. She tried to get a look at his expression. Did he seem happy? Was he reading Roxie's text messages right now? A terrible knot of jealousy and insecurity formed in her stomach. She honestly couldn't tell what he was doing.

"Oh look. This bitch!" said a nasty voice from behind her.

A bit of electricity ran up Maddy's spine. She turned to see Kaylee and two of her cheer squad friends standing in their cheerleading outfits behind her.

She blinked in shock. Then she looked around the pizza parlor. Why were they here of all places? Guessing by their outfits, a high school football game must have just ended. As the thought went through her head, she noticed the inrush of jocks in their varsity jackets streaming through the door. Luckily, they were all sitting on the other side of the restaurant.

"Are you going to move so we can get our drinks?" Kaylee sneered.

"Fuck off," Maddy said.

Kaylee's blond ringlets were pulled back in a high ponytail. Her pointy face turned into a scowl.

"You better watch your back, *Muddy*. After what you did to Adam? You're lucky his parents didn't press charges. You should be in jail where your redneck ass belongs!"

"What the fuck are you talking about?" Maddy said, rage boiling beneath her skin. She turned to face Kaylee, her iced tea forgotten. "You're the one who provoked me!"

"You psycho bitch broke his nose!"

The girls on either side of Kaylee crossed their arms. They might be cheerleaders, but they looked athletic. Maddy didn't fancy fighting all three. Not without a baseball bat.

The one on the left, a gorgeous Black Barbie, took a threatening step forward.

"You got some real issues. You know that? Like you're crazy toxic *for real*. You think you can just fuck up someone's face and walk away? You mess with one of us, you get the whole pack!"

"You're basically dead!" the other girl glared.

Maddy took a deep breath. *So I'm the toxic one?* She wanted to scream, but she couldn't lose it here in front of a hundred people. *Just let it go. Disengage. Violence is not the answer.*

She picked up her drink and turned to walk away. Then one of the girls—she didn't see who—shoved her. Hard. Maddy rammed her ribcage into the edge of the countertop. She spilled her drink all over a basket of hot pepper packets. Her cup went tumbling across the countertop onto the floor. The rest of her drink went on her hoodie.

"Fuck you!" she screamed, and whirled on Kaylee, ready to rake her nails across the bitch's face.

Then someone grabbed her from behind. Giant arms went under her armpits and dragged her backwards, lifting her feet off the ground. She kicked for a moment.

"Put me down!" she exclaimed.

Kaylee and her two cheerleader friends stared past Maddy at the man behind her. Kaylee's eyes were wide. Her cheeks turned bright red.

Gareth set Maddy down but kept a firm grip on her arm.

"What are you doing?" he asked, his usual baritone growl somehow even deeper.

It wasn't clear who Gareth was speaking to, but the three cheerleaders stared at him as though they had seen a god. Black Barbie's mouth gaped open just a bit. Girl Number Three looked winded.

Then Kaylee recovered.

"Oh wow, thank you so much! That crazy cunt was about to attack me!" She looked at her two friends. "Right girls? She's psychotic. You saved us! That was so heroic of you!"

"What?" Maddy exclaimed. "You shoved me and spilled my drink—"

Maddy tried to rush at Kaylee again, but Gareth's grip on her arm was like an iron chain. He dragged her back toward him.

Then he pointed at Kaylee.

"I saw all of it," he said. "Next time I won't be nice."

Then he dragged Maddy with him away through the packed restaurant. Maddy felt hot tears stinging her eyes. God, she felt crazy. Why did Kaylee make her feel so unhinged?

She felt like the whole room was staring at her, though in truth, the place was so packed that maybe only a handful of people had witnessed the exchange. Even then, they'd just seen her spill her drink.

"Let's go," Maddy said, trying to pull her arm away, her cheeks hot with shame, and her ears ringing with adrenaline. "Let's just get out of here and go home."

"No."

"Gareth, please? If we stay, they'll come back around and . . . ."

"Yeah? And what? We're gonna give up good pizza cuz some little cunt wants to fight you?"

He dumped her back into the booth and slid in next to her, his big body trapping her against the window. His scent washed over her again, warm and spicy, and she felt a tingle move through her belly. He was so close. His leg pressed against hers under the table. She found herself glancing away, struggling against a natural urge to submit. Outside was so dark, she couldn't see the parking lot.

"So? You gonna explain that to me?" he asked, holding her barred with his shoulder.

"How much did you see?"

"All of it. Don't try to lie to me again." His voice was soft with warning. "They said you were lucky some kid didn't press charges. What did you do?"

She stared up at him, gaping. His face was stern. This close, she could feel the heat of his body through his sweater. He had rolled up his sleeves to his elbows, revealing the tattoos that covered his muscular forearms. His black hair fell across his shoulders. He looked five-star hot and intimidating as hell.

His words rang in her head. *"What did you do?"* Why was he looking at her like that? Did he really believe Kaylee's story? He was no better than the teachers and the school principal.

Maddy spat angrily, "You too? Yeah. Fine. So I'm the bad kid. I always fuck up somehow. So now you're on my case?"

"Just tell me what happened."

Maddy sighed. It was embarrassing to talk about. She couldn't go into every detail—it would take a freaking hour to explain Kaylee's superbitch psychosis. Some of the stuff was so passive and insidious, it didn't even sound like bullying to a third-party. The belittling. The subtle negs. Spreading rumors. It didn't sound real.

But physical fighting? Oh right. That was real.

"Look, that's Kaylee Mackovich. She's like . . . my enemy. I dunno. It's dumb. She told this boy Adam to give me $20 to flash my tits–"

"What?"

His anger shocked Maddy into momentary silence.

Then she quickly continued, "She's been spreading rumors that I'm a stripper and I work at *Sapphire*. So like, kids have been coming up to me since the beginning of the school year, asking for blowjobs and shit."

"Okay."

"So this guy Adam offers me $20 to flash my tits and I decked him. Like I think I broke his nose. I don't know, I just ran. It was the same day that . . . . The same day that . . . that night, my trailer got broken in . . . ."

Her words were unraveling. Her hands started to shake again, remembering the night of the break-in and the gunshot near her head. Maddy felt dangerously close to crying, and she had promised herself not to cry in front of Gareth again. At least not so soon. She was supposed to be mature and responsible. *Like an adult*. But almost getting into a fight at Zippy's on their first date really wasn't making her look good.

What if he broke up with her?

"I'm sorry," she said, suddenly scared. "I'm really sorry, okay? Like, I wasn't thinking. I know I shouldn't have hit him. I'm lucky his parents didn't report it. I've been suspended for fighting before and I didn't want it to happen again–"

"You're a hot fucking mess," Gareth said.

Maddy opened her mouth, shocked by his bluntness, and hurt that he would use those words.

"I'm not. I'm really not. I'm responsible. I've been working since I was sixteen. I'm not fighting at school. I only hit Adam because . . . . Ugh, look, I'm going to graduate this year no matter what!"

"Yeah? You sure about that?"

"I . . ."

He shocked her by turning his head and catching her lips in a sudden, deep kiss. It could have been short, but he drew it out, his tongue pushing between her lips, his mouth slanting over hers. Over and over.

"Fuck," he said softly into her mouth between kisses. "You're a . . ." He slid his tongue across her lower lip. "Hot. *Fucking*. Mess."

Maddy's face was bright red. He held her trapped between his body and the wall, shielding her from the restaurant with his big shoulders as he massaged her mouth with his tongue. He was going to turn her into a *hot mess* if he kept kissing her like this! A wave of passion began rising between them. Her heart was racing. He turned his upper body toward her. His hand found her jaw, cupping her face in his big palm, gentle yet firm as he controlled her mouth. She gripped his thick wrist, her hand trembling against his onslaught. His kiss deepened, sucking her tongue into his mouth, where he trapped it with his teeth. She felt a hot wave of testosterone rising off of him like smoke from a fire. She was going to suffocate.

"*Jeezus*," he muttered when he finally released her lips. "Come on. Come with me."

"W-what?" Maddy stuttered.

He slid out from the booth, dragging her behind him.

"Come on. Let's play some games. Make the most of it. I want to beat my crazyass girlfriend at air hockey."

"What! I'm not crazy!"

Gareth laughed from deep in his chest. "What do you want to play?"

It took Maddy a moment to process that she wasn't in trouble, and that he seemed to be enjoying himself. If he meant to take her mind off the confrontation with Kaylee, then he had succeeded. Despite it all, she felt herself begin to smile. Then she pointed to a game where two people sat in a fake Jeep and shot dinosaurs with toy guns.

"Let's start with that one."

Gareth got ten dollars worth of quarters and climbed into the seat next to her.

"Ready to get your ass kicked?" he said with a grin.

Maddy grinned back. "You're going to regret this."

"I hope so."

Then she lost track of time shooting T-Rex's. Maddy couldn't remember the last time she had gone to the arcade. Never on a date. And it *felt* like one. Gareth paid for their games and collected the tickets for Zippy's little prize counter. He kept finding small ways to touch her: his hand on her lower back as they left the dinosaur game; brushing her hair back from her face; sliding his hand up her wrist as he showed her how to play ski ball. He kissed the top of her head when she beat him at *Street Fighter II*. He pulled her into his shoulder as they waited in line at the ticket counter. He got her a little plastic ring with a spider on it, and a handful of Halloween candy.

Maddy forgot to look around for Kaylee and the Varsity jackets. She forgot to feel claustrophobic in the crowd of screaming children. All that mattered in the warm, sweaty chaos of the pizza parlor was his big body next to her, his hands drawing her attention back to him, and the way her stomach fluttered every time their eyes met.

***

"The thing is, Maddy, with bullies, you gotta just leave 'em be."

They sat in his car. It was about eleven o'clock in the evening. Behind them, the pizza parlor had slowly transformed from an after-school fun zone into a late night pub. Maddy was sweaty from a few hours playing videogames in the humid arcade. She couldn't remember the last time she had laughed so hard. Her fingers were sore from button mashing. They must have played *Street Fighter II* for an hour. Then other classics: pinball, air hockey and ski ball. The list went on and on.

She leaned back in the bucket seat of the passenger side with her sneakers kicked up on the dash and her hoodie pulled up. Gareth sat next to her with his elbow on the door and his head propped on his hand, watching her. She sighed, messing with the string of her hoodie.

"Kaylee and I used to be friends back before my mom died. I don't understand why things changed," Maddy said sadly. "She told me it was my fault for being a bad friend. I guess I wasn't there for her when she needed me. She said I was toxic."

Gareth snorted. "When your mom died, you mean? She can fuck right off then. Don't take that shit to heart, Maddy."

"I mean . . . I *wasn't* there for her at all that year . . . ."

"So what? So you deserve to become a target? Bullies don't think like you or me. They don't need a reason. Seeing you weak and vulnerable is reason enough. They just like the rush of pinning someone down." He hesitated. "You said her name was Mackovich?"

"Yeah, why?"

"Her mom was a customer at the garage."

Maddy groaned. Just thinking of Mrs. Mackovich gave her anxiety.

"Yeah. She's the worst. Her mom comes through the hardware store like she owns the place. Nobody wants to deal with her." Maddy rolled her eyes. "I guess maybe she *does* own this town in a way. Their family is super rich. I think she's on the town council, or the school board, or something like that."

"Ain't nobody that rich if they're living in Black River," Gareth grunted.

"There's million-dollar houses out in Elk Haven," Maddy pointed out. She rarely went out that way. Elk Haven was a gated community down Highway 20 for fancy folk who wanted to pretend they lived in a wilderness resort. They even had a little community gym and campground with showers and RV hookups. Maddy remembered going to Kaylee's house a few times in Middle School. She'd never seen so many bedrooms and staircases, and the kitchen island was a solid sheet of quartz.

"Kaylee acts like it's the Hamptons," Maddy said. "Her house is like an apartment complex, it could fit so many people. She's so lucky. She lives like a princess."

Gareth was quiet, then he shrugged. "Yeah, well, that might change. I heard they're getting a divorce. Mrs. Mackovich will be Ms. Banner soon."

Maddy narrowed her eyes. "How do you know that?"

"She told me."

"At the garage?"

"Yeah."

"Why would she tell you that?"

Gareth raised an eyebrow. "Why else? She wanted to see if I'd bite."

It took Maddy a moment to figure out what he meant. Then, in horror, she exclaimed, "You mean, *Kaylee's mom* wanted to date you?"

Gareth laughed. "*Date?* No, I don't think she wanted that."

"Then . . . ." Maddy's eyes widened. "She wanted to *hook up*? Like, *fuck you?*"

Gareth shrugged.

Maddy looked him over, reminded of their age gap. With all the fun they were having at Zippy's, she had almost forgotten about it.

"That's weird."

"Is it?"

"Yeah, a bit."

He leaned toward her. "How weird? Too much?"

"I don't know . . . ." Maddy started to feel self-conscious. She had all but forgotten about Roxie's calls and texts, but now her mind jumped to them. She knew Gareth had a lot more experience under his belt than her. She could easily imagine him being happy with someone his own age.

"How old are you, anyway?" she asked.

"Twenty-eight."

Oh.

Suddenly Maddy felt shy.

"I'll be twenty-nine next month. What about you?"

"Nineteen. Uh. My birthday was in August."

Maddy cringed. A solid ten years. Of course, she had always known about their age difference, but hearing him say it out loud put their years in stark contrast. She had no idea what it meant to be twenty-eight. Or even twenty-five. And here she was, whining about being bullied in school. He really must see her like a kid.

What was she doing with a guy like him? Maybe she had daddy issues, after all.

He should be with someone his own age, she thought.

The imaginary vision of Roxie rose up in her mind. She imagined some badass chick with tattoos and black pinup hair working second shift as a bartender. Someone wild and fun in cherry red lipstick. Not some sad teenager like herself in a secondhand sweater—a tomboy getting picked on in school. He could do a lot better.

"I mean, isn't it weird for you? Dating someone in high school?" The question dropped from her mouth. "Like, dealing with bullying and homework and stuff. Probably not what you signed up for."

He studied her in the dark, quiet cab of the car. His eyes glinted gold in the night. The roof of the car cast his face in deep shadow, shielding him from the harsh white light of a lone streetlamp. He looked a lot like a wolf, she had to admit. She was reminded, suddenly, of the times he would find her on the mountain, a silent presence with his secretive, gold-glinting eyes. She was much younger then. Fourteen. Fifteen. Her secret crush had grown slowly over time as she noticed more and more how good-looking he was. But in the beginning, he had been a ghost. A mysterious god of the forest. Someone who made her feel safe and less alone, despite the strangeness of their connection. He was . . . her secret.

What we are doing is forbidden, she thought. If she told anyone their story, they would think he was some predator. But she was the stalker in this situation. Normal people would never understand how he had saved her, just by showing up in the darkness.

"Do I find it weird?" he mused. "No. Why? Do you?"

"I mean, a little. You're almost thirty. You're older than some of my teachers. Maybe I have, like, *issues*. You know. It's kinda wrong, isn't it, for us to be together?"

"Do you feel like it's wrong? Like you'd rather be with someone your own age?"

His question made her tremble, though she wasn't sure why. She thought of the white bear he had given her to hold. How he always came to her rescue. The thought of losing him, even going back to the way things were before, left her gasping for air.

"No," she said quickly. "No, I like this."

"You like this?"

"Yeah. I mean. I like you." She hesitated. "It feels right. But what if I have 'daddy issues' and there's something super wrong about me?" She cringed saying it out loud.

"Alright. So let's talk about that. Daddy issues. Do you know what those are?"

"I think it's when you're into older guys?"

"Sure. So do you get a lot of crushes on old dudes?"

"Um, no. Not really."

"Just me?"

"Yeah."

Gareth grinned wolfishly. "Then maybe you're just into me. *Anyways*. So what if you want a daddy, Mads? You don't have one at home. Well you do, but he's a piece of shit."

Maddy blushed. She glanced away, a little embarrassed. He was so direct. It made her feel like she was under a spotlight.

"To be honest, Mads, I think I met you for a reason. You need someone to protect you. I think that's what you want. Call it 'daddy issues.' But you just want *protection*. Nothing wrong with that."

Maddy was silent for a minute, digesting his words. She huddled into her hoodie self-consciously. He obviously didn't care about their age gap, or any other issues she might have. It's like he knew her. *Really* knew her. In a way she didn't even know herself.

She looked up at him, searching her eyes, feeling something deep inside of herself relax. She had never talked like this with anyone before.

She finally asked, her voice soft, "But shouldn't you want to be with someone more independent? Someone you don't have to protect, or take care of?"

Gareth grunted like he found her question funny. "That's just what boyfriends do, babygirl."

She stared at him.

"Let me put it this way. A man protects the people who need him. That's what I believe. And you need me. So here I am."

"I mean, what if you get tired of protecting me?"

"Hasn't happened yet. We've known each other a while now, Mads. You think I haven't thought this through?"

"Uh . . . no, not that . . . ."

"You don't think I'm genuine?"

"No?"

"You think I'll abandon you eventually, right? So you're testing me?"

Maddy stared at him. It was like he could read her mind.

"How did you . . . ?"

"We're not that different, Mads. My old man had a substance abuse problem, too. Worse than drinking. So I get it."

Maddy blinked. "I didn't know that."

"Well, how would you?" Gareth sighed and sat back against the door, his eyes turning to the night outside the window. "You know how much crazy shit I've seen, Mads? I've seen women in Iraq who hide their faces their whole lives from everyone but their families. Nude spas. Orgies. I know married couples in Black River right now who are poly, with three, even four or five partners, and twice as many kids. There's swingers who swap spouses at parties. Transgender couples, asexual, pansexual, heteroflexible, you name it. Just last year I read an article in the Davenport newspaper about a Middle School history teacher caught with an 8th grade boy. Now *that's* nasty shit."

Maddy grimaced. "Yeah, I remember. It went viral on Picplace. They held an assembly about it and everything. She was tutoring him over summer vacation right?"

"I just read the headlines. But *this,* what we're doing, is not *that,* Mads. This is between two consenting adults."

"Right. So you're happy dating some kid like me."

"And what's so wrong about you?" Gareth asked with an arched eyebrow. "You're a good person. You work hard. You're fun. You got a job and pay bills. You got the shit end of the stick with your stepdad. I get that. But hey. You're still cute."

Maddy laughed.

"You said you were eighteen? Nineteen?"

"Yeah. Nineteen."

"So what?

Maddy felt better. Maybe the age gap wasn't that weird after all. It worked for them.

She gazed at the angular planes of his face and his masculine neck. They had known each other for so long, but this felt like their first real conversation. Her mind went back to the hardware store and all those years they spent dancing around each other.

"Do you remember when you bought me that mace?"

"When those two creeps were bothering you?"

"Yeah."

"Yup. That was a few years ago. Why?"

"I wanted . . . ." She took a breath and looked out the window. God, why did they have to be sitting so close? Admitting all this made her stomach squirm in a delicious way. "I really wanted you back then. Like. *For real.* I had such a crush on you."

He grinned. "Yeah? So you had a little crush back then?"

"It was a big crush."

He laughed. "I figured."

"What? No!"

"I knew it. I could tell." He reached over and pinched her chin suddenly. "You turned all cute and pink any time I came over."

Maddy thought she was going to die.

Gareth leaned in and caught her lips. In the privacy of the Camaro, Maddy felt like they were on the dark side of the moon. He kissed her slow and gentle, his lips brushing over hers, his mouth soft.

"So," he murmured deep in his throat, speaking against her mouth. "You still got a crush on me, Mads?"

She shivered, hard.

"*Hmm.* Now that you told me, maybe I should've teased you more in the hardware store."

Maddy closed her eyes. His words sent a jolt of electricity through her body.

His kiss deepened, his tongue entering her mouth, tasting her. She tried to kiss him back, and he playfully sucked her tongue into his mouth. His hand reached up to cradle the back of her head. He kissed her like that for several minutes, wet and bold and hungry. Maddy couldn't think. Couldn't breathe. All she could feel was the heat pooling in her belly.

Then he broke away, his lips hovering over hers, a trail of saliva dripping down her chin.

"I should've called you back to the scrap lumber section. Yeah. That aisle is always empty. Could've been fun."

"Gareth!" she gasped.

His hand went up under her sweater, unhooking her bra with ease. With a hungry growl, he pulled her shirt up and took her breast into his mouth, sucking on her swollen nipple. She gasped at the intense sensation. He squeezed her breast with his hand, pushing it deeper into his mouth. He sucked on her tit, his tongue flicking across her sensitive peak.

Maddy heard herself moan. She didn't know she could make sounds like that.

In her mind, she imagined the hardware store. She would take him to the very back of the warehouse, between the long stacks of baseboard and timber framing. There, he'd catch her wrist. Push her up against the wall between the piles of wood . . . .

It was *so wrong*, why did it make her so wet?

"Ah," he groaned. "Look at what you do to me."

He picked up her hand and pushed it against the crotch of his jeans. Maddy gasped as she felt his erection. He was *so large*. He held her hand against him. He wrapped her fingers around his length through the fabric, making sure she felt his size.

"Fuck, Maddy," he murmured.

"I-It's really big," she gasped.

She met his intense gaze, his eyes like dark whiskey, hooded and heavy with desire, his hair a wild mess around his shoulders. He searched her face. Then he leaned forward and took her lips again. His kiss was hot and forceful, full of fiery, pent up desire.

"You really want me inside you?" he murmured.

She felt like she was drowning. She nodded.

Suddenly her phone started to vibrate.

Maddy groaned. It took her a moment to switch gears. Her body felt hot and heavy, her thoughts sluggish and heated.

She pulled her phone out of her hoodie. She didn't recognize the number on the cracked screen. But it was close to midnight. Seemed like it might be an emergency.

She glanced at Gareth. He looked about as frustrated as she felt, his face drawn and intense, his eyes burning with lust. He took a deep breath and cracked the window to cool off.

Then she picked up the phone.

"Hello?"

"Hello. This is Officer Langirik with the Davenport Police Department. Is this Madeline Donovan?"

"Yes?" Maddy's heart stopped. Was she in trouble?

"Your father is here. We need someone to pick him up. He says you can give him a lift home. He was arrested for public drunkenness and threatening an officer."

"Oh. Um, it's pretty late. . . ."

"If you don't get him now, then we will have to surrender your dog to the animal shelter."

"My dog? What? My dad has a dog with him?"

"Yes. He says it's his dog."

She shared a look with Gareth, who could overhear the conversation easily in the quiet car, even if the phone wasn't on speaker. He shrugged.

"Well, if it's a dog that needs rescuing. . ." he said.

Maddy almost laughed.

"Right. Sure. Um. We're driving from Black River, so we will be there in forty five minutes," she said into the phone.

"See you then, Ms. Donovan."

Click.

Gareth straightened up and put his keys in the ignition.

"Not how I planned to spend the evening," he said, "but I think it's worth saving a life."

"How the hell did my dad get a dog?" Maddy muttered.

"I guess we will find out."

Maddy buckled in as Gareth's Camaro roared to life like a jet engine, utterly destroying the silence of the night.

He turned out onto the street and started toward the interstate.

Chapter 9

They spent most of the drive in silence. It was cold in the car, even with the heat on, and Maddy snuggled into her hoodie to keep warm. Now that the rush of the arcade was fading, she was growing tired.

"So he's your stepdad?" Gareth asked after a while.

"Yeah. Dean Harvey. I have my mom's last name."

"You know him a long time?"

"Most my life," Maddy explained. "Only dad I ever knew, really. My mom met him when I was five."

"Right. A real part of the family." Gareth sounded nonplussed.

Maddy stared out the window as the Camaro passed through a low fog bank. The highway to Davenport was black and empty. They had passed one car in the last fifteen minutes. In these parts, they were more likely to hit a deer this late at night.

Her mom met Dean down at The B Joint when Maddy was five. He was a lot different back then. He worked laying brick for the union. Drove a new truck and owned a little fishing boat. He was a fun guy back then. Maddy recalled him taking their family on camping trips. That was a long time ago. Before his back injury, then the spiral of drinking and painkillers.

Maddy didn't know if Dean and her mom ever got married officially. She knew her mom wore a ring, but she didn't remember the wedding.

"What about your bio dad? You ever hear from him?" Gareth asked.

"No. Mom called him my sperm donor. I think he was a trucker just driving through. Or something like that."

Maddy shrugged. The mention of her bio dad pissed off Dean, so she rarely brought it up. She didn't have a name or nothing to go off, anyway.

Gareth stopped asking questions after that. She didn't blame him. It was late and he was probably exhausted. She couldn't banish her creeping sense of guilt. She felt bad, like she had messed up. Driving out to Davenport to rescue her dad from jail wasn't the ideal ending to a first date.

"I had a lot of fun at Zippy's," she said as they pulled off the freeway and started down Davenport's main strip. "I'd love to do it again sometime."

Gareth looked over at her like she'd said something cute. He reached over and squeezed her leg.

"Same, baby," he grunted.

Gareth parked on the empty street outside the Davenport police station. They went in together. Maddy walked up to a cop sitting at a bulletproof glass counter. She introduced herself and handed over an ID. Soon after, another officer brought out her stepdad from the back hallway.

Dean Harvey was a short, stocky man with a beer belly and a face like a wrung out Leonardo DiCaprio. He was probably handsome in his youth, though Maddy couldn't really see it. He now resembled any other bar rat. He was squat and barrel-chested, with thick arms from laying brick most of his life. He had wispy blond hair that he usually wore under a baseball cap when he was working the odd job. A week's worth of gray scruff covered his neck and jaw.

On this particular evening, vomit stained the front of his denim jacket. His face was red and puffy from drinking for several days straight. His blond hair was greasy and mussed. He reeked of liquor.

"Maddy! My girl! You're a good, good kid, you know that?"

"Hey Dad," Maddy said.

Dean stumbled a few steps forward like he meant to wrap her in a hug. Then he caught himself on the wall. His bloodshot eyes traveled to Gareth. He seemed to sense intuitively that Gareth was not just a friend.

"Who's this?" he barked.

"Dad, this is Gareth. He's my . . . um . . . my *boyfriend*."

It was her first time using that word to introduce anyone in her life. It should have been a special occasion, like a homecoming game or prom night, or maybe a dinner with her folks. That's how normal kids broke the news to their normal parents. But here she was at a police station at 1am, talking to her old man with vomit on his jacket.

"You have a boyfriend? How'd that happen? You owe him money or something? Hah! Kidding. Look here, *dude*. You hurt my daughter and I'll shove my shotgun up your ass!"

The cops exchanged a glance.

To his credit, Gareth stayed silent with his hands shoved in his pockets. He was a good half-foot taller than her dad. He didn't seem put off by the threat. But he also didn't act friendly at all.

Another cop emerged from a hallway to their left with a young pitbull mix on a leash. It had a faun colored coat with big white paws. It looked maybe part lab.

The dog ran up to them, tail wagging enthusiastically. It walked like a puppy who hadn't grown into its legs.

"And who's this?" Maddy asked, relieved to have a distraction. She let the dog sniff her hand. Then it began licking her fingers.

"This is Joker," her dad said. "Picked him up last night from a buddy. What do you think, Maddy? You always wanted a dog. Remember?"

"I think I was like ten years old when I said that. I don't know, Dad. I didn't realize it was a puppy. She's going to need training . . . ."

"Pssh, you're always so serious! You worry too much for a kid your age. Just look at his lil face. Let's keep him. We're keeping him. What's a home without a dog?"

Maddy sighed. Despite the added responsibility, the dog was adorable. Little Joker—who was a girl, actually—was just too cute. She sat down and scratched, losing balance and half falling, then wiggling in a happy circle.

"Yeah," Maddy said, "I guess it's alright. What's a home without a dog?"

The cop handed Joker's leash to her. The puppy immediately went up to Gareth and rolled onto her back with an eager whine.

Gareth reached down and scratched the pup's soft pink tummy. Joker promptly started to pee.

"Shit," Gareth muttered, stepping back to avoid the stream. "You got paper towels?"

"The janitor will get it," one of the cops said. "We got some paperwork for Madeline to sign before we release Mr. Harvey. His license is out of date, so we'll need a current address for the ticket and the fines."

"Fines?" Maddy asked, feeling a little sick.

"Drunk and disorderly conduct, and destruction of private property," the female police officer rattled off. "He broke the window on a man's car. We will forward the fines and any subsequent rulings by the court. His case will need to be reviewed, but I don't think the damage will exceed $250. So. That's good news. No criminal charges."

Maddy glanced up at Gareth, unable to read his expression. He was frowning at her stepdad again, who was clinging to the wall for balance.

"How much do you think all that will cost?" she asked.

"We will send the damage assessment and any follow up tickets via mail. Make sure to update that home address. Failure to pay the fines within the allotted time will only add more fees."

Maddy sighed. She crossed to the counter and started filling out the paperwork, then signed the release. Already her mind was running its old program. The last 48 hours spent with Gareth disappeared as though they had never happened. This was just another typical Friday night, getting a call from somewhere to rescue her stepdad. She would take Dean back to the trailer, but then what?

She chewed on her bottom lip. Gareth wanted her to stay at his place. But, would her stepdad mind? Or would he throw a tantrum? This was brand new territory. She might be over 18, but she had never tried to spend several days away from home before. Dean could get needy and controlling. Honestly, he was unpredictable. And someone needed to take care of the dog.

Maddy felt the weight of her life start to suffocate her again.

"Come on. Let's go, Dad," she said, trying not to sound sullen.

She left the station with Joker's leash in one hand, and Gareth walking silently beside her. She couldn't get a read on him. She knew he was unimpressed with her father–who wouldn't be–but his face was stoic, his lips firm.

He unlocked the car and her dad slid into the back seat, where he sprawled out. Joker jumped in after him. Then Maddy and Gareth got in the front.

The drive back to Black River was excruciating. At first her dad rambled on and on about a big win at the Casino and a subsequent party spree around Davenport. His story wandered in and out of bars, clubs and hotel rooms. He talked about a fight with a stripper that got him and his buddy tossed out of a club. Throwing his beer bottle at a parked car that cracked a window, which ended in his arrest. Some cursing and ranting about the oppressive sociopolitical system in America. He offered Gareth a bunch of money, like $200, to drive an extra 30 minutes to South Davenport to pick up cocaine from a buddy. Gareth declined with a few words.

Then Dean's muttering faded into snores as he toppled over and crashed. Joker wiggled around the back seat, whining.

Maddy was overwhelmed.

"Sorry about that," she said nervously to Gareth. "Really, I'm so sorry, he's just drunk. I don't think he can really afford cocaine."

"It's fine, Mads. Don't worry about it."

She couldn't tell if Gareth was pissed or just tired. She sighed. She always felt shaky and fragile when her stepdad got like this, maybe because he was unpredictable. She picked at her fingernails as the Camaro shot down the highway like a bullet.

Gareth's big, warm hand suddenly landed on hers, covering both of her hands with his own, interrupting her anxious fidgeting.

Maddy glanced up at him. His eyes were focused on the road. He still hadn't said anything. But he kept his hand over hers. She wondered what he was thinking.

***

They got back to her trailer well past midnight. Gareth carried her dad into the house without needing to be asked. He dumped Dean on the couch with a grimace.

Maddy took Joker out to pee, then let the dog back in the house. The big pup immediately jumped onto the couch next to her dad and curled up to sleep.

Maddy wondered how she was going to afford dog food.

Then she started picking up the living room. Gareth hesitated before helping her. For a half hour or so, they picked up trash and moved furniture around. Then, finally, he came to stand by her side.

"Let's go," he said.

Maddy hesitated. She dropped her eyes and shoved her hands in the pockets of her hoodie. She still hadn't figured out where she was going to stay the night.

"Maddy," he said. "You're coming home with me."

Maddy felt her shoulders grow tense. She swayed on her feet. She wanted to go with him. God, she would like nothing more. But some terrible chain held her bound to the trailer and the absurd man sleeping on the couch. She might hate her stepdad, but she also cared about him, in that foolish, stubborn, childlike way. As Dean reminded her often, how many step-parents would have abandoned her to the foster system? He wasn't a perfect person by any means. But he looked out for her, for her mom's sake. He called her his daughter. She couldn't just abandon the old fool.

Her hands curled into fists.

"Let's talk outside," she said. It was better if her stepdad stayed asleep.

They walked out the back door into the yard, just beyond the light from the kitchen window. How many times had Gareth led her back to this spot from the mountainside? Now they stood face to face. He crossed his arms, the treeline at his back, his eyes solemn.

"Don't tell me you're staying here with that sorry sack of shit," Gareth said.

There it was. Anger. Maddy flinched at his words.

"Look," she said levelly, "I don't like him either. But he's my dad. I can't just leave him. You see how he is. He could hurt himself. And . . . this is my home."

Gareth was silent.

Maddy bit her lip again. She hated feeling like she was disappointing him.

"I know you want me to come with you," she continued, "but I don't think it's a good idea. Not yet, anyway. I need to keep an eye on Dean."

"Alright. So let me ask. How bad does it have to get before you leave?"

Maddy's eyes widened. She sucked in a breath.

"What do you mean?"

"Just how long do I have to wait before I drag you out? Until he beats you again? Or burns down the trailer with you in it?"

He looked pissed. Maddy's thoughts flashed to the gun in his car.

"Gareth, that's my business, not yours."

"I'm your boyfriend now. Those scars on your back? Those are *my* business. Someone's gotta take care of you."

"That happened a long time ago. You don't have any say over what I do."

"I think I have some say, especially over your safety."

"No, you fucking don't! I'm an adult and I can make my own decisions."

Gareth half-smiled, but it was not a nice look. More of a grimace.

"So now you're an adult and you're gonna make all the big decisions. Alright."

Maddy was furious.

"Don't mock me."

"Then stop acting like a child."

"Fuck you!"

"You're protecting him."

"I'm not—"

"You're *enabling* him."

"What?" Maddy glared. "So this is my fault? I can't help who my dad is."

Gareth spoke in a low growl.

"But you help him every day. You pay the bills. You clean up his shit. You buy groceries. When are you calling it quits? You're not his daughter, Mads. You're his housekeeper and his caretaker. That's it. That man doesn't give a shit about being your father. He's using you."

His words pierced her. She bit her cheek in sudden pain. The brutal honesty was more than she could take. What did Gareth know about her family? Dean was the only father she had ever known. She felt herself shutting down.

"Thank you for reminding me that my stepfather doesn't give a shit about me," she said coldly.

Gareth's expression changed, his anger fading from his face.

"Maddy, I didn't mean–"

"You did. And you're an asshole for saying it."

Gareth hung his head.

Maddy continued, her words direct and practical, "You're right. I don't really have a dad. Or a mom. No one really cares about me. But that doesn't change anything. I've been on my own for a long time. I don't need you looking down on me. Or pointing out everything that's wrong with my life."

Gareth stared at her. He looked at a complete loss for words.

Maddy folded her arms around herself.

"I think you should go," she said. "I need some time to think about all this."

"Right."

"Really, Gareth. Just leave."

"Okay." He reached into his pocket and pulled out his keys. Then he paused. He looked back at the house. "Do me a favor?"

"Yeah?"

"Call me if you need anything. I mean it."

She wondered if he would try to touch her or kiss her before he left, but he didn't. She watched him walk away. Every muscle in her body yearned to spring after him. To run and wrap her arms around his back and beg him not to go. But she couldn't move. Her feet remained glued to the ground. *How did this happen?* She felt torn in half. Strange, how just a few hours ago they'd been laughing together in the arcade. And now the night ended with this sour pit in her stomach.

Maddy heard the Camaro roar to life. She ached as she listened to his car run down the gravel driveway, growing more and more distant. Then she turned back to the house. She felt like she had made a mistake. With a surge of anxiety, she reached for her phone, intending to call him. But she stopped herself.

He called her a child. It was a slap in the face. He couldn't use her age against her like that. Just because he was older than her didn't make him her keeper.

He didn't have to speak such ugly truths out loud, to her face, like he did. Her stepdad might be a pain in the ass, and a belligerent drunk, but he was her only family. Was she supposed to abandon Dean to move in with some guy she had known for two days? Putting it like that, it seemed insane. How could Gareth ask her to make such an impossible choice?

She was used to taking shit from people. But his words shot straight through her defenses and struck a nerve. He was the first person to get a front row seat of her messed up life. And instead of helping her, she felt judged.

Alright. So that's it. Maybe it really was over.

Maddy sighed. She felt sick to her stomach. Was she really ready for a relationship? For two days, she had lost herself in the rush of being with *him*. Her fantasy come to life. But now her stepdad was home and reality was knocking. Dean Harvey was a hurricane. Her stepdad's chaos took up so much of her energy, now she wondered if she had room for Gareth or anyone else. Maybe it would be better for her to call things off.

Fuck. She felt like she wanted to cry and scream at the same time.

Maddy went back into the house. Dean snored and grumbled on the couch. It was a familiar scene. Everything back to the way it should be, as though the terrifying night of the break-in had never happened.

Whatever stash of drugs those thugs had been after would remain a mystery. She doubted Dean would remember. Or tell her.

She wanted to cry, but instead she sucked in a deep breath. If she gave herself time to wallow in her feelings, they would swallow her alive. She'd figure out her problems on her own, like she always did.

Joker jumped off the couch and followed her down the hallway, her skinny tail wagging. Maddy let the big puppy into her room. Together, they climbed into bed. Joker stretched out instantly against her back, as though she had always slept there. Maddy felt a little better. She turned and pushed her face into Joker's sleek tan fur.

"I'm sorry you're part of this mess," she whispered to the dog. "But you don't gotta take care of me, okay? I'll take care of you. I'll figure it out."

Maddy wondered if she should text Gareth, but she didn't know what to say. She was too exhausted, physically and emotionally, to hold a conversation. She hadn't planned to be back in her trailer so soon. In truth, she was surprised she was falling asleep.

She closed her eyes, trying to ignore the deep, painful throb in her heart.

Chapter 10

Dean sprawled on the couch and moaned the following day. Maddy brought him water and ibuprofen. Then she tip-toed around the trailer, picking up and straightening what she could. She tried not to bother him. He was always in a sour mood the day after a long bender. Sometimes he was in a bad mood the whole week. With any luck, he'd sleep it off.

She was a nervous wreck. Memories of the break-in haunted her as she cleaned up the trailer. She tried not to look at the bullet hole in the wall. She kept glancing out the front windows, thinking she saw someone in the driveway, but of course no one was there.

Congratulations, Maddy, she told herself. *You've reached a new level of 'paranoid.'*

It was afternoon by the time Dean got his ass up off the couch. Maddy was in the kitchen trying to clean the massive stack of dirty dishes in the sink. She wasn't making much progress. The sink kept clogging, and they were on a septic, so she couldn't use a garbage disposal. She kept emptying the little strainer into the garbage. The stench of mold made her eyes water.

Then her dad groaned, sat up and climbed unsteadily to his feet. His face was red and swollen. He wandered through the living room and turned down the hallway, trudging to the bathroom. Maddy heard the fan turn on.

When Dean finally came back out, he was still zipping up his trousers and buckling his belt. He paused at the entrance to the living room. That's when he noticed the crumbling drywall and the bullet hole.

"Something happen to the wall?" he asked. He poked at the hole with his finger. "*Wowzers.* That's a bullet. And what's with all the caution tape on the front porch?"

"There was a break in," Maddy said.

"No shit?"

"Yeah."

Dean looked around the living room again.

"Did they take anything?"

Maddy cleared her throat. She had been dreading this moment all day—her inevitable confrontation with her father.

"No. But they were looking for you. They wanted me to give you a message. They said you owed them money. I think . . . I think they might come back if you don't pay them."

"Pay *them?* Pay who?" Dean asked with a bewildered look.

Maddy blinked. Denial. Alright. His act was pretty convincing, but she had learned not to take him seriously. Ever.

"So . . . you don't know anything about that?" she probed.

"I don't owe anyone a damn thing," he said with a scowl.

Maddy found that hard to believe. She felt a little nauseated. It might not mean anything to her father, but she remembered the giant man's body on top of her from that night, his weight suffocating her, holding her down, ripping her shirt. "*Now spread your legs like a good girl.*"

She was pretty sure these guys meant business. Something was up. She couldn't let her dad sweep it under the rug.

She gripped the side of the countertop where her dad couldn't see her hands.

"What about those letters from Gelson's & Associates?" she asked.

"What the fuck? You reading my mail?"

"No, I just noticed—"

"Mind your own fucking business."

She pushed on, for her own self preservation.

"I didn't read any letters," she explained. "I just saw them on the table. I didn't recognize the company. Are they bills or something?"

"Nope. Probably advertisements. Just ignore them."

Bad news. Now she was doubly worried. She didn't know what her stepfather had gotten himself involved in, but it seemed pretty dangerous, and he was hellbent on hiding it from her.

"These guys were pretty serious," she insisted. "They're going to come back if you don't pay them. I'm worried about you, dad. Are you in trouble?"

"No. What trouble? I'm the life of the party! Anyway, I got money. So I'll handle it."

Handle it. Sure. Like he handled everything else?

"Dad, if you just tell me—"

"So these guys who broke in, did the cops get them?" Dean cut her off.

Maddy blinked. She scratched the back of her head and glanced outside, remembering the story on the News.

"No, actually. It's a little weird. I guess they were attacked by a wolf. They didn't survive."

"A wolf? What the hell?"

"I know. Um. It was kinda wild. That's what the cop said when I made a report. A wolf attacked them."

"In our own backyard?" Dean repeated, softer. "Well, dang. So they're dead?"

"Yeah. They found five bodies in the woods."

"What are you all worked up about, then? Look at you, making a mountain out of a molehill. If these fuckers are dead, then no one's gonna come hassle us again."

Maddy looked down at the sink, feeling frustrated and a little embarrassed. How did he always make her feel stupid?

"Fucking ridiculous. Thinking I'm in some trouble. Psh. You're just a kid. Don't forget that. You might pay a few bills, but you don't know *jack* about jack shit."

Dean slumped back onto the couch with a deep sigh.

Maddy bit her lip, a mixture of troubling emotions warring inside of her. She felt angry, ashamed, and invisible. Dean didn't seem to care that she was home when the break-in happened, or that her head was bandaged. He didn't ask if she was alright. She was a missing person on the news. The whole town knew, but he didn't.

It never bothered her before how Dean never asked about her. But now it did.

It disturbed her. The more she thought about it, the less safe she felt in the trailer. She doubted Dean would lift a finger to protect her if more thugs showed up.

"I gotta call my buddies," Dean said, rummaging for his phone between the couch cushions. "They're not going to believe this. A fucking wolf? Dang."

"Yeah. Do that," Maddy mumbled.

Dean pulled his phone out and fumbled around with it.

Maddy went outside. She took Joker with her. Having the puppy around the house was a nice distraction. But it came with its own challenges. She didn't have any dog food, so she fed the dog scrambled eggs and a can of tuna fish that morning. She didn't have a leash either, so she used a length of nylon paracord she found in one of Dean's boxes of random junk. She tied it in a loop around Joker's neck. Then she took her on a little walk through the woods.

As she walked, Maddy checked her phone to see if Gareth had texted her. It was almost noon. She hadn't heard anything yet from him, not even a platonic "good morning." She refused to text first. She didn't want to chase after him and look clingy, especially after telling him to go last night. But damn. Didn't he care?

You said you needed time to think about things, she reminded herself. But she still hadn't arrived at any answers. She felt angry and sullen. His words from last night still stung.

You're not his daughter.

You're enabling him.

That man doesn't give a shit about being your father.

Stop acting like a child.

Tears welled in her eyes. She knew Dean took advantage of her in many small ways. But she was orphaned after her mom died. She could have been homeless. Or put in foster care. Dean stepped up in his own way. He was her only family. What did Gareth know? Despite her stepdad's nastiness, she was relieved to see him safe at home. Sometimes she wished he was dead, but she didn't really want to see him hurt. Deep down, she hoped someday he would kick his drinking habit and straighten out. She believed it was possible.

Joker pulled at her leash suddenly. She whined at something in the woods. Then, without warning, she lunged.

Maddy didn't have time to react. Her grip slipped on the leash and the dog took off through the forest.

"Joker, no!" Maddy yelled.

Joker bounded off through the underbrush, her tail wagging furiously. Without thinking, Maddy took off after the dog. She plunged into the woods, following Joker's yellow body through the ferns and blackberry vines.

Luckily, Maddy was a fast runner. She caught up with Joker about ten minutes later. The pitbull mix was barking excitedly at a tree where a fat raccoon sat on one of the lower branches. The awkward little rascal looked disgruntled. She guessed that Joker had startled it and then chased it up into the tree.

"Joker, no, bad dog!" Maddy grumbled.

Joker ignored her and kept bouncing around at the foot of the tree.

She wasn't any good at scolding animals. She sighed and looped the paracord leash around Joker's neck again. She would have to get a sturdier collar or maybe a harness. Joker was surprisingly strong for her size.

She dragged the dog away from the tree. Then she paused. She turned and looked around. They were deeper in the forest now. All she saw were trees in every direction and the deep emerald canopy of pine needles. She couldn't see any mountain peaks or familiar landmarks through the dense branches. The sky was overcast, so even the direction of the sun seemed debatable. It was uncanny how every direction looked identical to the next. She had no idea where she was.

She turned in a slow circle, trying to remember which way she had come from. She couldn't see the mobilehome or her yard. *Oh no.* A cold, clammy knot formed in her gut. Usually she didn't go running haphazardly through the woods. She stuck to the trails and familiar spots near her house.

Now that she was paying attention, the forest was awfully quiet. She usually heard the trill of bird song and the rustle of squirrels. But everything seemed very still.

A branch snapped behind her. Maddy whirled around. Some desperate part of her hoped to see Gareth standing between the trees.

She froze.

It was a wolf.

Her heart raced. She felt her knees begin to quake. She couldn't believe it. A black wolf stood between the trees. It was almost the size of a horse. *This must be the monster who killed those men.*

After telling Dean all about the wolf attack, she didn't expect to encounter the creature in the woods. *I'm an idiot,* she thought. Of course the predator would still be wandering around the mountainside. Where else would it be?

Joker whined and hid behind her legs with her tail tucked and her ears down.

Maddy felt like she would pass out. Her hands went numb and her heart pounded painfully in her chest. She had never been more terrified in her life.

The wolf gazed at her with golden eyes. It was completely silent.

Maddy stepped back and almost tripped over Joker. Her instincts told her to run. But her knees were shaking so bad, She found herself sinking to the ground, unable to remain upright. *Fuck fuck fuck. This is it. I'm going to be eaten alive.*

But the monster didn't lunge at her, as she expected. Instead, it seemed to copy her. As she sank to the ground, the beast sat on its haunches. It crouched between the bushes, its ears perked forward, watching her.

Maddy felt confused. It wasn't acting wild or aggressive. Was it someone's pet? No way. She didn't see any collar. But it wasn't acting like how she would expect a man-eating predator to act.

It's fucking huge. That monster could eat a whole cow, she thought.

She didn't know what to do. She could pull out her phone, but who was she going to call? She wasn't even sure she had reception.

Unexpectedly, the wolf stood up. It walked toward her, completely silent. Maddy sat on the ground, shaking, ready to meet her fate. She was going to become dog food. A fitting end to her pathetic life.

Then Joker ran out from behind her, her belly close to the ground.

"Joker, no!" Maddy cried, terrified. She didn't want to watch her new dog get eaten. That seemed a lot worse than forfeiting her own life.

Joker ignored her and approached the wolf with a sad whine. She flipped onto her back in the pine needles and showed her pink belly. Maddy felt like doing the same thing—she almost considered it. She held her breath, unable to predict what would happen next.

The big black wolf looked down at Joker, almost as though it was amused. Then it walked around the dog and approached Maddy. It leaned in and sniffed her face. Maddy held her breath, waiting for its massive jaws to chomp down on her head. The wolf sniffed her chin, then her forehead, then her hair. She was shocked when she felt a cold nose press against her ear.

Then the beast licked her cheek.

Maddy stiffened at the roughness of its tongue.

Maybe she didn't taste very good, because after that, the wolf turned away and started walking back through the woods. Maddy watched it go, still holding her breath. After about ten feet, the beast paused to look back at her. It waved its tail twice in a lazy sweep.

Maddy stared after it with wide eyes. It beckoned to her again with its bushy black tail.

It's taking me home, she thought.

No, no, this is real life, wolves don't do that.

Except, it was totally waiting for her.

Feeling surreal, Maddy stood up. Joker got up too and ran after the wolf, keeping a careful distance from the creature, her ears back and tail tucked submissively.

Maddy started walking behind the wolf. Once it saw that she was following, the beast continued on through the woods.

Maddy wondered why the wolf was alone on the mountain. Usually lone wolves were solitary males looking for a female to start a new pack. She checked the beast's anatomy tucked up under its long, bushy tail. It was definitely a male. Maddy wondered about that. Maybe it was looking for a mate.

"Sorry I'm not a female wolf," she said to the beast as she walked.

The black wolf's ears perked at her voice.

Maddy felt a little crazy.

"You should find yourself a nice lady and settle down," she said. "Somewhere far away from here."

The black wolf turned its gold eyes back on her. Then it kept walking.

It was the most bizarre thirty minutes of her life, as Maddy followed the wolf through the forest. They didn't take any discernible path that she could recognize. But sure enough, after a bit of time, she noticed some familiar pine trees, a few rock formations and fallen logs. She passed by an old, empty box of Bud Light that must have blown out of the trash can weeks ago. Definitely a Dean.

The beast was leading her back home. *This can't be happening.*

The wolf paused when her trailer came into view through the trees. Heavy clouds were gathering in the sky. It looked like it would rain soon.

Joker started wagging her tail when they reached the edge of the back yard. She made an unexpected play bow and barked at the wolf.

"Quiet, Joker!" Maddy hushed. She hoped her dad didn't come outside. It would ruin the moment. Then she turned to face the beast.

"Thank you," she said to the monster.

The black wolf regarded her with its intelligent yellow eyes. Then it turned and slunk off through the trees. It moved in complete silence, like a ghost.

Maddy shivered. She felt like she was coming out from under a spell. *Did that really just happen?* Damn, she hadn't gotten a single pic on her phone. No one was going to believe this. Well, maybe Bea would believe her.

Was it really the same beast who had saved her from those men in the woods? She couldn't think of any other explanation. Ironic, that she was just talking about the wolf with Dean. Maybe it had a den close to the trailer?

She stood out on her deck for a moment, surveying the forest. Oddly enough, knowing the beast was out there didn't scare her. If it had saved her from those dangerous men, and led her back home, then maybe, despite all odds, it was a friend. Maybe some sort of magic existed in the world, after all. Or maybe she was just a very lucky girl.

Then the sliding back door opened and Dean stuck his head out.

"There you are! Soup's on," he said.

"What?" Maddy asked, confused.

"I made soup. You know. That ramen stuff you like. Even put a fried egg on top. Come on, slowpoke. Let's eat!"

***

Maddy ate her ramen as Dean talked on and on about his big win at the Casino.

"I'm gonna get you a new phone. I mean it! Or maybe a computer."

"Sure, dad."

Yeah right. Maddy listened with half an ear, blindly staring at the weather report on the TV. Dean always talked big when he won a little extra money. She remembered when she used to believe in him and his absurd promises. She used to hang on his every word.

Now she wondered when that had changed. Maybe around seventeen? Yeah, probably about that age, she began to realize her stepdad was just . . . useless.

She had gone out of her way to get him a job at the hardware store as a maintenance tech. She hassled her manager for months to get him the position. It would cover all their bills. She thought Dean just needed help getting a job. Maybe once he had a job, he wouldn't lie around on his ass all day. She blamed her mom's death for the alcohol problems. She told herself he was just broken up and grieving and needed help. She took it on herself to dig him out of the hole. That's what family did, right? Help each other?

Dean acted like he wanted the job. He even went to the interview sober. He started talking about the new Honda truck he was going to buy. How he'd repair the deck. Maybe install AC on the mobile. All that.

Then, on his first day of work, she found him face down on the couch, an empty handle of vodka next to him, too drunk to even sit up, his pants soiled with shit. She tried to get him up, but he wouldn't budge. Then he disappeared for a week. She went to work ashamed and told her manager her dad was sick. They gave the job to someone else.

Yeah. About then, she had realized he was just a flake. Totally useless. She shouldn't have expectations for him. Or really, for anyone.

"How bad does it have to get?" Gareth's words echoed in her thoughts.

She didn't really have an answer. The break-in two nights ago was pretty bad.

Her mind returned to Gareth. Why hadn't he texted yet? She checked her cell phone. No new messages. Maybe he was done with her mess. Despite his big words at the arcade, she had scared him off after all.

"You think I'll abandon you eventually, right? So you're testing me?"

She wasn't testing him. She didn't even know what that meant. She just wanted to see if he would text her first. And so far, he wasn't.

Maybe he's just not that serious about you. Maybe he's not even thinking about you.

Yeah, that was probably true. She needed to protect herself. She didn't think she could survive a real breakup with him, if she actually let her guard down and opened her heart. She closed her eyes for a moment, took a deep breath, and pushed the thought of him far away. She didn't need him. She had learned long ago to rely on herself.

Then her stepdad's words caught her attention.

"So lemme get this straight. That guy last night was your boyfriend, no joke? Or was I so shitfaced, I hallucinated all that?"

Maddy glanced at Dean.

"Um, yeah, sorta," she muttered.

"Sorta? What does that mean? You fucking him?"

Maddy flinched. "No."

"Right. Alright. So what's he want with you, then?"

"We're just . . . hanging out."

Her stepdad laughed. "Classic line. Coming at you like he don't want teen pussy. He's just waiting for you to put out." Her dad swallowed a mouthful of ramen. "He's a little old for you. Guys his age only want one thing. Trust me. It's not your brain. Hah! Take it from your old man."

Maddy pushed the noodles around her bowl. She deflated a little. She knew she wasn't that smart. Truth was, she had no idea why Gareth wanted to "be" with her.

"He's actually a really good guy. He gave you a ride back from the police department."

"Out of the goodness of his heart. Right." Her step-dad rolled his eyes. "He's got you fooled. He'd better drive me home from Alaska if he wants to fuck my daughter. He's just playing nice, Maddy, waiting for you to put out. You guys really not fucking?"

"No, we're not. We just started dating."

"Sure." Dean scoffed. "Some advice? Don't nail yourself down. You're young and tight, and you got great tits. Get yourself three boyfriends. Then all our problems will be solved. You'll have them paying all our bills." He let out a loud laugh.

Maddy set down her bowl of ramen. She didn't think she could eat anymore.

"You know what? We gotta get you set up at *Sapphire*," her dad rambled. "I'm telling you, I know the owner. He'll get you a nice job there. Those girls make bank off tips. You don't even need to graduate. You'll make more than all those college kids. And it's close to home. Hell, you could walk there. *Anyway.*" Dean's tone suddenly turned serious.

Maddy felt herself shrink down. She knew that tone.

Dean pointed a swollen finger at her.

"Stay the fuck away from that guy, Maddy," he said with a glare. "He's too old for you, and he looks like a pain in the ass. Last thing I need is some dickhead thinking he's gonna fuck my daughter. What next? Coming 'round like he owns the place? If I find out you're hanging around him, I'll knock you into next week. You understand?"

Maddy dropped her eyes. She nodded. She knew she should feel something—hurt, fear or disappointment—but she just felt numb. Her hands were suddenly shaking. She was thirteen again with a grown man raging at her. She wanted to run and hide.

"You understand, *chickadee?*" he repeated. He made the cutesy name sound threatening.

Maddy nodded again. "Yeah. I understand."

"You wanna date some old guy, I got buddies at the bar who'll treat you right. You can have your pick."

"That's funny, dad. It wasn't really a thing anyway. We just hung out a few times. It's not serious."

"Damn right."

Maddy felt a little sick. Everything Dean said about men and sex made her feel gross. She stood up. She went into the kitchen and dumped out the rest of her dinner in Joker's bowl, who was more than happy to finish her noodles.

Maddy felt hollow inside. She grabbed her phone and walked down the hallway to her cramped bedroom. She shut the door behind her and flopped onto the bed. Murky twilight filtered between the trees outside her window. She popped in her earbuds and turned on her favorite playlist. A mix by Phantogram. Then she checked her text messages again. Still nothing from Gareth.

She remembered, suddenly, the missed calls from Roxie on his phone. The thought struck her numb. Maybe that's why she hadn't heard from him. Maybe he was tired of her teenage drama and spending time with Roxie right now.

It was too painful to think about.

Hot tears stung her eyes. She let the tears begin to spill down her face. *I'm a fucking worthless idiot,* she thought, sniffling like a baby. Why couldn't she just handle her life?

Outside her window, the sky deepened into late evening. It started to rain.

Chapter 11

G areth got into the garage early on Sunday morning. He was in a low mood, and he wanted to do something productive.

He parked his Camaro in front of Jack's Auto Repair in the chill, foggy morning. The sun was still climbing over the mountains and the air was frosty. His breath rose in little puffs of vapor. He wore a heavy, quilted flannel jacket and work jeans. It was fucking cold. Black River was nothing like Arizona where he grew up.

He glanced at the clock on the dash and gauged the time difference. It would be early morning over there, but his mom should be awake. She was a gym rat and preferred to work out before the sun came up.

He took out his phone. He scrolled through his contacts. He hit the dial button.

The phone rang a few times before a woman picked up.

"Am I imagining this, or is my boy calling me?"

Gareth grinned. "Hey, momma."

"*Mijo*. I guess I haven't lost my mind."

"Yeah, not yet. You still got time."

His mom laughed.

"So why are you calling me? You doing well? I've got your cousins here visiting this weekend. They're asking about your new address. No one knows where you moved to. Are you going to tell us or just stay mysterious?"

"Eh," Gareth dodged, thinking of his old man and his brothers. His family was pretty nuts. He didn't want unexpected visitors.

"Nah. Not yet. Say hi for me," he said.

"Alright, *chico loco.*"

"Hey though. I got a question for you."

"What is it?"

"It's about wolves."

His mom went quiet on the phone. He heard a slight scuffling as she moved through the room, and a soft click as a door closed. He guessed she had stepped outside on the porch.

"What about wolves?" his mother asked, her tone laced with curiosity.

"I think I met one. A girl."

"*Verdad?* That's very rare these days."

"Yeah. But she hasn't gone through the Change yet. When does that happen? Is it the same as males?"

"*Ay, mas o menos,* it can vary," his mom said, pursing her lips over the phone.

Gareth could almost see her standing in the silver early-morning light, a light shawl wrapped around her shoulders, overlooking a pristine swimming pool in the backyard of a Spanish-style mansion. His family had struggled for years when he was a teen, but these past few years, the Sonoran pack was thriving. Gareth didn't know what kind of business his father was involved in. He'd rather not ask. But at least his mother and his brothers were doing well. He couldn't say he didn't benefit, either. His mother fronted the money for the downpayment on his place. He could afford the house now, but those first few years running the garage had been a bit dicey.

She continued, "The Change can happen suddenly. I know with you boys, it was like *una granada* blowing up as soon as you turned fourteen. *Pero los mujeres son delicadas.* Your aunt Juana and Roselia all entered the Change at different ages. *Para chicas,* the age she becomes a woman will make a difference. How old is she?"

"Definitely past puberty," Gareth said. "She's turning twenty."

"*Ai ya,* that is late. Ok. Sometimes being all alone can stop it."

"Alone?" Gareth echoed. "Like separated from her pack? Does that happen a lot?"

"*A veces,* it's more common now because of the foster system. Wolf pups need other wolves to stimulate them. *Les dan vitalidad*–they pass along their vitality. If they're isolated, then pups never really get a chance to *come out.*"

"I didn't realize that was a thing," Gareth said.

"Yeah. Well. Your *tio* and your cousins took you boys on *a lot* of fishing trips. And you had me and *papi* at home. It's why we stick to the pack," his mom explained.

"Right."

Gareth didn't miss the subtle nag about *sticking to the pack*. He knew she didn't approve of him leaving their family behind in AZ. But he couldn't live around his dad anymore. He and his old man never got along. Their last altercation got bloody. He ran a hand down the tattoos on his forearm. It was better for the family if he ducked out.

"Any other reason?" Gareth asked.

"Well, there's one more. If a wolfchild is malnourished, or living under a lot of stress, that can also stop the Change. Natural self-preservation, I think. Or just the physical toll of the stress."

"That's . . . something to think about," Gareth murmured.

"You sure this *chica* is a wolf?"

"Oh yeah," he said "*Absolutamente*. But she hasn't Changed yet. So she doesn't know."

"Was she adopted?"

"Kind of," he said shortly.

"Careful *mijo*," his mom cautioned him. "Remember your father is an Alpha. Your wolfblood is potent. If you're spending a lot of time together, you might trigger the Change without meaning to."

"Oh, I mean to," he muttered.

"Tsk! *Mijo, escuchame,* she's going to need support if she starts to Change and no one tells her what's going on. It can be very dangerous. You know what happened to Roselia. And we only just got her back."

Gareth's brow darkened. Yes, he knew Roselia's story very well. His mom's youngest sister was abducted by slave traders and sold as breeding stock on the black market when she was fifteen. Unfortunately, it was a common story in Lycan families. Females were rare, and they could be auctioned for as much as a quarter-million dollars.

Her mother's family had searched for Roselia for twenty-five years before they were finally reunited. His aunt lived in Phoenix now with the rest of the Sonoran pack, but she was a very private person. He didn't know much about Roselia's life. His aunt didn't share her story with many people. His mom and cousins knew more about it than he did.

"I hear you," Gareth said. "I know the danger. Don't worry, *mama*. I can handle it. I'll keep an eye on her."

"I worry for this girl. You watch over her, Gareth. Remember Roselia. Bad men are everywhere."

Gareth was distracted by Vin's truck pulling up in front of the garage. He'd forgotten that Vin was coming in for overtime today. He was hoping to get some space to think. He suspected Vin had a girl now and needed the extra cash. But he didn't know for sure. If it didn't relate to work, they didn't talk much.

"Gotta go, mama," he said. "Gotta work."

"*Ai, mijo*, I hope it works out."

Gareth grinned. "Sure, mom. Say hi to my cousins. Love you."

"Love you, too. Call more often, okay?"

"I will. I promise. *Adios.*"

He hung up the phone with a sigh. He felt a little better having this information in his back pocket. He had been thinking about Maddy's wolfblood since last night. If she Changed, then he could explain the lifemate thing to her, and all this wouldn't seem so strange. She'd get it. She would have to.

But she was very delayed.

Now he knew what was delaying her. Of course it was Dean.

The stress of living in that house, her isolation and the whole fucking situation had compounded into this mess. His instincts were right. Living in that mobile home wasn't healthy for her. He had to get her out.

"Remember your father is an Alpha. Your wolfblood is potent. If you're spending a lot of time together, you might trigger the Change without meaning to."

So his Alpha blood might trigger her Change. Alphas were not like regular Lycan. They were a cut above the rest. Stronger. Fiercer. A little crazier. His father was a prime example of that. Gareth had spent the last several years trying to get away from the devil blood that defined him. Now it was finally coming in handy.

Supposedly only Alphas had lifemates, though he wasn't sure of that, so little was known anymore about the bond. He could have asked his mom, but he didn't want to get her excited. A lifemate was a very big deal. She would want to fly out to meet Maddy, and that wasn't a good idea right now.

He got out of the car and slammed the door behind him. Then he went to unlock the garage. His jaw was clenched.

"Hey boss," Vin said, climbing out of his black truck. "Thought you were taking Sundays off."

"Plans changed," Gareth growled as he unlocked the two big garage doors and slid them up overhead.

He had hired Vin over the summer to help him handle the rush. The kid wasn't much good with customers, but he was a whiz at fixing cars, and he learned the new diagnostic equipment in a day. He liked to tinker and figure stuff out. He was awkward, but useful, and he wanted to work. Gareth wanted to keep him around for as long as Vin wanted to stay.

Luckily, the busy summer season was slowing down. Over the summer, they were both working seven days a week and raking in the cash. Now in October the mountain passes were closed due to heavy storms. Less traffic coming through from the other side of the mountain. So the garage got a break.

Still, there was always something to do.

Gareth stood face to face with a big diesel F250 that needed a new head gasket. Easy enough to swap out, and the part just came in. He rounded the truck and went to change into his work overalls.

"You hittin' the Mercedes?" he called to Vin.

"Yup, just finishing the tires."

The kid turned on his Bluetooth speakers and started blasting music. He hit the button and boosted up the Mercedes on the other lift.

Gareth thought of Maddy as he put on his work uniform. He had been pissed since Friday night. It all went South like a landslide after Dean showed up. Maddy was a different person around her stepdad. He regretted taking her to get the dog. But he supposed her stepdad's return to her life was inevitable. He just wished it wasn't so soon, right when he was gaining her trust.

For a moment in the arcade, she had let down her walls and acted her age. He loved it. She was laidback and hyper all at once, curious and ready to play. He was high energy and she kept up easily. She laughed at his dumb humor. He saw her genuinely smile at him, and she had *dimples*. Fucking adorable.

But then he'd gone and fucked it all up. He called her out on her caretaking. She reminded him of his mom that way. He saw the pattern so he said something. But she was young. And he was too honest. Too blunt. He let his anger get the best of him. He wasn't a perfect man by any means, and he had been too harsh.

He knew she had some figuring out to do.

He couldn't make her leave her stepdad behind, though after seeing the ragged scars on her back and the trash throughout the trailer, it seemed like a no brainer.

But good people were loyal. Sometimes loyal to the wrong people. And, in her twisted world, that was the only father she knew.

Gareth knew how addiction worked. He had dealt with it in his own family. His dad, Alpha of the Phoenix pack, was straightened out now after suffering a major heart attack and losing half his kidney function. But he was still a cold and violent man. How the rest of the pack put up with such an Alpha, Gareth was done wondering. He wouldn't go back. Not until his old man was dead.

He was worried about what would happen to Maddy if he left her alone in that house. Dean Donovan was a fool, not a manic tyrant like his own pops, but he was still dangerous. Would she turn up with more bruises? Gareth pulled in a deep breath. He might have to murder Dean if he saw one more scratch on that girl.

Gareth grabbed the box with the new head gasket and walked back into the shop. Sunlight spilled into the garage through the two open doors. Looked like the heavy, overcast sky was breaking up a bit. Nice to have a break in the rain.

He got Vin lined out on the Mercedes. Then he opened the hood on the F250. Time to get his hands busy. His cell phone buzzed from the shelf behind him. He paused to check his phone.

Damn. Another text from Roxie.

> *Hey big guy. You busy tonight? You should come over. <3*

Roxie was alright. They had messed around for a bit, off and on. Usually late night stuff. He never invested or talked about his life. She never met the family. When she started trying to get closer to him, he took a big step back. That was the last they spoke. He was surprised she still had his number. They hadn't spoken in a few months.

He felt a bit guilty. Maddy was his lifemate, but for the past five years, she had been way too young for him to approach her, and wolfblood ran hot. So Roxie became a hookup for those nights when he thought he would break his wrist from beating off. He never meant to use her; he thought their arrangement was mutual. They had both agreed to keep things casual. But last July, Roxie confessed her feelings to him.

He simply didn't feel the same way. So he'd been forced to break things off.

He hovered for a moment, wondering what to say. Then he texted:

> *Hey, sorry I can't. I'm seeing someone.*

> *for real?*

> *Yeah. I got a girlfriend now*

> *Since when? U told me u didn't get serious*

> *well I'm serious now*

> *So when you said you didn't get serious, you just meant with me?*

She sent a much longer text. He glanced over it, but all he saw were a bunch of expletives. He didn't read it.

He selected her name in his app and blocked her number.

Then he went back to work.

***

Sunday morning, Maddy woke up late. She was exhausted, but the dog was whining to go out. Right. New responsibility. She got up and used the bathroom. Her head wound looked healed enough to take the bandage off. She felt wistful throwing it in the trash.

She pulled on her hoodie and a pair of black leggings, tied on Joker's paracord leash, then opened the back door to take Joker on a walk.

She almost tripped over a giant bag of dog food and several grocery bags laid out on the covered porch. Next to the groceries was her backpack.

She stared at the collection, stunned. Then she dropped the leash and almost collapsed. She had cried most of the previous night and slept terribly. If her backpack was there, that meant Gareth had delivered these groceries for her. But he hadn't said a word. Hadn't asked to see her or talk. No texts or missed calls.

Maddy shuffled nervously through the groceries. He even bought her toilet paper. Damn. He must have dropped almost $200 on all this. Her kitchen would be stocked for weeks.

Alright. The groceries were probably to relieve his conscience. But . . . he returned all her personal stuff, too.

She brought everything inside. Then she went through her backpack. She found her homework and her change of clothes, phone charger, CBD pen, the white stuffed bear, and other items. She even found the little spider ring he had won for her at Zippy's. But still no text.

Maybe it really was a breakup.

Tears stung her eyes again.

This wasn't how it was supposed to work. She was supposed to give him a silent treatment while she "thought things through." Then he was supposed to cave in. He would send her a text message admitting he was mean and wrong for all the stuff he said on Friday night. He was wrong about her stepdad. Wrong about her enabling. Wrong about her life. He was just *wrong*. Then he would beg her to forgive him.

But now the tables were turned.

Was he done with her?

Had she pushed him too far?

Her stepdad was still asleep on the couch. Maddy retreated to her bedroom with her stuff and shut the door behind her. Then she held the bear for a moment, feeling anxious and sad. She didn't know what to think. Was this his way of saying goodbye?

Summoning her courage, she took out her phone.

> *Thanks for the groceries.*

She typed out the message and hit send. Then she waited. It became apparent that Gareth wasn't going to respond quickly. So she shoved her phone in her pocket, flipped up her hood, and went to take Joker on a stroll through the woods. As she walked, she remembered her surreal encounter with the wolf the day before. She looked around the woods a lot more than usual, jumping at every rustle in the bushes or snap of a twig, but she didn't see any big black beasts roaming about. She sighed. Wolves hunted over a wide range of territory. Maybe the beast was on some other part of the mountain, and maybe that was a good thing.

On the way back, her phone pinged.

> *Sure thing*

> *Make sure you eat*

She didn't know what it meant. Why did he care if she ate, if he was breaking up with her? A bit timid, she texted:

> *U busy?*

> *just working. Wat's up?*

> *didn't hear from u yesterday*

> *u said u needed space*

Maddy chewed her lip. She had never been in a relationship before. She didn't know what to do. She typed out:

> *are we broken up?*

Then she hesitated, scared to hit send, knowing it could unleash a domino effect and completely break whatever threads still bound them together.

But she couldn't stay in limbo. It was driving her crazy.

She hit send.

She waited.

She finished walking Joker and went back inside. Then her phone pinged:

> *do u rlly think i'd buy groceries for u if we were broken up?*

Maddy blinked at the text.

> *i don't know*

> *i thought maybe u felt guilty*

> *nope*

> *but we need to talk*

> *come over*

Fuck. Maddy felt sick to her stomach. He sounded so serious. Maybe he wanted to break up with her officially in person? Why couldn't he just do it over text? She felt like the ground was falling out from under her.

With shaky hands, she texted:

> *ya ok*

> *your place?*

> *I'm at the garage*

> *It's on highway 20*

> *Here's the address*

Maddy felt a spike of anxiety. Shit. She hadn't planned on going to his workplace. It was kind of intimidating, the thought of seeing him out in the adult world, doing adult things. She knew he worked at a car garage, but she didn't know where. *I guess I'm about to find out.*

She entered the address for Jack's Auto Repair into her phone's GPS. It was only a two mile walk down the highway from her house. Not far at all, actually. She was surprised.

Three miles was about her daily commute to school. She could walk there in less than an hour.

One thing was for sure. Gareth did not text like the kids at school, who spent all their time on the phone. His messages were brief and to the point. She felt like she was talking to an authority figure. And now she felt like she was in trouble.

> yeah omw

Maddy dropped into the trailer briefly to tell her dad she was taking Joker on a walk, and wouldn't be back for a while. Dean waved her off. He looked groggy from just waking up, and he was lighting up a joint.

"Hey, pick up laundry detergent while you're out," he grumbled as she shut the door behind her.

Maddy rolled her eyes. She was going the opposite direction from town. So that wasn't happening. He could buy his own damn detergent. Though she would probably pick some up from the store tomorrow on her walk home.

Then she started walking toward the highway, Joker following happily along on her paracord leash.

Chapter 12

Maddy walked down the long black ribbon of highway through the mountains. The rain had stopped for a bit, though the sky was still overcast. She had no idea Gareth worked this close to her house. Jeez, no wonder she saw him so often in the woods. If she or her dad owned a car, maybe she would have encountered him a lot more often.

Highway 20 was the only route from Black River over the mountain into upstate New York. The highway cut through an old growth pine forest before it climbed upward and turned east into the Adirondacks. The woods were filled with black bears, moose, white-tailed deer, bobcats and coyotes. It was unusual to encounter a predator like a wolf. Maddy wondered if she would ever see the beast again.

Maddy loved watching the wildlife on the mountain. It was better than a movie in her opinion. Nature always seemed busy, if she took the time to slow down and watch. Overhead, a flock of honking geese flew by in V formation, their necks stretched out and white wings flapping. Over the summer, it wasn't unusual to see clouds of monarch butterflies making their way through the meadowed woodland. October was a bit late in the year, but she kept an eye out. Butterfly watching was one of Maddy's secret, hidden pleasures. She had a whole sketchbook full of drawings. She wasn't very good. But she tried to capture all the different patterns on their wings.

Through the forest to her left, if she went far enough, she would encounter the banks of the Black River, which flowed into Lake Ontario a hundred miles away. To her right, the mountain reared its mystical, white-crowned head.

At this time of year, the passes were closed higher up the mountain, which meant less traffic on the highway. It took about forty-five minutes to walk to Jack's Auto Repair. Joker made the walk a bit more challenging, because she kept trying to chase after squirrels, or follow weird smells off into the brush. Maddy kept the leash tightly wrapped around her wrist. Joker might be a puppy, but she was strong.

As she walked, Maddy thought over her argument with Gareth on Friday night. She was still hurt by everything he had said.

"You're not his daughter, Mads. You're his housekeeper and his caretaker. That's it. That man doesn't give a shit about being your father."

Dean was the only father she had ever known. She knew he wasn't her real dad, and she wasn't his real daughter. But the reminder of it stung. This was her life. She couldn't change it. Gareth owed her an apology.

Maddy saw the sign for the gas station first—a small convenience store with four pumps out front. Jack's Auto Repair was across the parking lot. A slight incline separated the two properties, covered in gravel and tall grass. Only a few cars were at the pumps. Maddy walked past the gas station to the garage.

Jack's Auto Repair was painted light gray with a new red sign. It had two big garage doors open, revealing the service ramps inside. Two cars were boosted up on metal lifts: a big F250 and a little red Mercedes.

A steel gate enclosed a car lot at the back of the garage where it looked like a few trucks were being kept overnight. Maddy assumed they were waiting on parts.

A small office with a blue door hung off the side of the building. Maddy didn't know if she should go into the garage directly or through the office. She didn't see Gareth anywhere.

Then she caught sight of someone. A skinny kid close to her own age was working underneath the Mercedes. He might have been twenty-two or twenty-three. He noticed her approaching and stepped away from the car. He wiped his hands on a rag that he thrust into his back pocket.

Maddy's eyes swept over him curiously. He wore gray overalls with the words "Jack's Auto Repair" embroidered over the left breast pocket. Besides that, he had an edgy look about him. His face was thin with hollow cheeks, and Maddy thought he sorta resembled a goat. He had a little triangular soul patch on his chin, black plugs in his ears, and an eyebrow piercing. Maddy imagined him and Bea making a cute couple. They definitely had the same aesthetic. He wore a black beanie, and she would bet money that under the beanie, his head was shaved.

"Cute dog. Can I help you?" he asked.

"Yeah. Um. I'm here to see Gareth."

He looked her up and down. Maddy couldn't tell what he was thinking. She was a little sweaty from the walk, but she didn't think she looked that bad.

"He's busy right now. Can I help you? We got a tow truck if you're broken down. I can haul you back here for a fee."

"Oh, no, it's not that. Um. He told me to come by. I think he's expecting me."

"Oh-kay? What's your name? He didn't say anything to me."

Maddy frowned. Was she supposed to make an appointment? Who was this guy?

"Look, it was kind of last minute. I just walked here—"

"Maddy?"

She heard Gareth's loud, deep, booming voice echo from the other side of the garage. They both jumped.

"Yeah, it's me," she called, her own voice high and timid in comparison.

"Bring her back, Vin!"

The punkish guy gave her a bashful smile. "Sorry. I'll take you back now. My bad."

As he led her into the garage, he explained, "Boss says not to bother him when he's working. But then he goes n' changes his mind all the time. He wants me to get better at handling customers."

"It's okay," Maddy said.

They found Gareth at the back of the second garage, where another car was parked with its hood up. He was bent under the hood with a pair of pliers in hand. His black hair was tied back in a messy, partial bun at the base of his neck. His jaw and cheek bones looked sharp enough to cut a finger. His eyes glimmered bright hazel gold in the soft autumn daylight.

"Here she is, boss."

"Thanks Vin. You almost finished with the Mercedes?"

"Just aligning the tires."

"Right. Keep an eye on the front."

Vin nodded. He gave Maddy a little wave, then walked back through the garage.

Maddy didn't know what to do. She hovered nervously, watching Gareth's broad back as he finished working on the transmission. She glanced around the interior of the garage. She hadn't spent much time around cars. She saw metal shelves lined with oil canisters and transmission fluid, different sizes of wheels and hubcaps, some larger tools and machinery. But the shop was clean and well organized. No garbage or clutter lying around.

So this is where he works, she thought. He owned this place. It was his garage. He was running his own small business. He even had an employee. Someone called him boss.

I'm dating a boss, she thought.

Or at least, she had been dating a boss for all of three days. Their talk would probably put an end to that. Now she felt like a kid who had been called to the principal's office. Especially in a place like this. All heavy metal and cement. No softness. Their meeting felt like all business.

Finally Gareth finished and straightened. He sighed, stretching out his back.

"You walk here ok?" he asked, turning to look at her.

She could tell just by his tone that he had something on his mind. He reached up and undid his hair, shaking it out, pulling it back, then tying it again at the base of his neck.

"Yeah. It wasn't bad. I brought Joker with me."

Then he noticed the dog. Joker was lying on the cool cement floor. He stooped down to scratch her ears and she thumped her tail. She was much more calm after the long walk.

"Come with me," he said.

She and Joker followed him through the garage into a small break room. The walls were unapologetically gray, the cement floor covered with black rubber mats. Harsh fluorescent lights hung from the ceiling. One of them was out. She saw four lockers, a card table, a mini fridge, and a microwave.

Gareth unzipped his work overalls and stepped out of them, then tossed them in one of the lockers. Underneath his gray jumpsuit, he was wearing a white T-shirt and jeans. She stared again at his muscular, tattooed arms. *Lobo Loco.* She knew loco meant crazy, but she didn't know the other word.

He took a minute to get a plastic bowl down from a cabinet in the break room and fill it with water from the sink, which he gave to Joker. Meanwhile, Maddy looped the end of Joker's leash to one of the cabinet doors.

"Stay," she said.

Joker wagged her tail. She wasn't trained, but she seemed happy enough to sit on the floor next to the water bowl and pant.

"This way," Gareth said.

He led her through the break room into an even smaller office, with barely enough room for a filing cabinet and a desk with a new computer on it. The computer was turned off and looked like it hadn't been used in a while. The desk was covered in paperwork. It was a bit chaotic, and Maddy felt slightly better about the state of her house.

He shut the door firmly behind them.

"Alright," he said. He pulled up a metal stool and pointed to the computer chair behind the desk. "Have a seat. Let's talk."

Maddy took the computer chair while he sat on the metal stool. The chair was very low to the ground, and he was higher up than her. She gazed up at him nervously.

"You don't gotta look so scared," he said with a bit of humor in his deep voice. "I'm not gonna punish you."

"What do you mean?"

"You look like you think you're in trouble."

"Oh. Yeah. Hah." Maddy gave an awkward laugh. "So, um. I texted you a question."

Gareth released a slow breath. "Right. You wanna know if we're broken up."

Maddy fidgeted with her fingers. She stared down at her hands in her lap.

Gareth leaned forward slightly, trying to catch her gaze. "Why'd you ask me that? You freakin' out?"

Maddy released a breath she didn't know she was holding.

"Well," she began, "Yeah, I guess so. You didn't text me yesterday, and you brought my stuff back to the trailer. I thought maybe it was a sign. Like maybe you're over it." She glanced up and searched his eyes. "Are we breaking up?"

"I don't plan on it," he said, his voice level. "But Mads, I'm not gonna lie. We gotta talk about Friday night. Cuz I'm pissed."

"What? Why?"

"You agreed to stay at my place. But the moment Dean appears, that changes."

"Well, I had to take care of him."

"You don't owe him that. He's a grown man. And I don't want you staying in the trailer after what you showed me."

"What did I show you?" Maddy felt herself growing petulant.

"On your back. Those scars."

"Oh."

"That's right. 'Oh.' After seeing those, I don't want you anywhere near that guy. I want you far away from him."

Maddy glowered. "So what? You want me to move out?"

"Something like that."

Maddy bit back a laugh. Her voice had a hysterical edge. "That's wild. Where would I go? You want me to move in with you?"

Gareth raised an eyebrow. He didn't need to respond. Maddy glanced away from his steady gaze and swallowed past a hard lump in her throat. Yeah, that's what he wanted. She knew that. And she liked his house. It was quiet. Peaceful. She could see him every day, which was kind of mind-blowing. But the thought of moving out was overwhelming. There was too much uncertainty.

She wrapped her arms around herself.

"That's a lot to ask of me right now," she said.

"Why?"

"Because . . . because someone has to take care of the dog."

"That's not a real reason, Mads."

Maddy knew it wasn't. She could always bring Joker along, or find the pup a new home. She couldn't really vocalize her reasons. It was all instinctive. Reality was, she didn't know Gareth that well. She was drawn to him, but they had barely spoken over the last five years. She felt that cosmic force pulling them together, but he was intimidating as hell. There was plenty about him she didn't know.

On top of that, she was afraid of leaving the trailer. She had lived there her whole life. It would be a lot easier if Dean liked Gareth, but he didn't. Maddy would get her ass kicked if Dean found out they were dating. What would happen if she left the trailer to live with Gareth?

"You're not gonna tell me why?" Gareth prompted her.

Maddy realized she had been quiet for a long time.

"I can't stay with you," she repeated. "It's . . . too much, too soon. We've been dating for four days. I can't just move in with you."

"Sure, Mads," Gareth said. "I get that it's fast. But you're a special case. We didn't *just meet,* and I've got a problem with someone leaving bruises on you."

She dropped her eyes, ashamed.

"He beats on you, Mads," Gareth repeated in a low voice.

"He hasn't hit me in over a year."

"Then what's that bruise on your back?"

"That's different. It was an accident. He pushed me because I was in the way."

Gareth was quiet. His shoulders stiffened. Maddy fought the urge to over-explain. Her excuse sounded weak, even to her own ears. But it was the truth. Dean had apologized for shoving her. He was drunk.

"Just give me some time to figure some stuff out," she said.

"Alright. How long?"

"Really? We're going to put a deadline on it?"

"Yeah. We are. So how much time do you need? A week? Two weeks?"

Maddy stared at Gareth with wide eyes. He looked dead serious.

"Try, like, a year!" she exclaimed. "You can't force me to do something I don't want to do."

"You're right, I can't. But I'm warning you now, little girl, if I see one more bruise on you, I will drag you out of that trailer by the scruff of your neck."

"Like hell you will!" Maddy exclaimed.

"You wanna try me?" he growled.

Maddy stared at him, biting back her retort. She could have been snarky, but something about his voice—so low and gruff—made her throat close up. Actually, no, she really didn't want to try him. He looked like he was about to drag her back to his house right now.

"I'm not moving out in two weeks," she repeated. "I told you my life's a mess. I warned you to stay far away from me. So this is it. Take it or leave it."

"You really want me to stay away from you?"

Maddy dropped her eyes. She shoved her hands into the pockets of her hoodie. "No."

Gareth released a deep, put-upon sigh. Then he reached out. He caught the front of her sweater and pulled her over to him. Maddy stumbled forward, out of the chair, as he dragged her into his arms. Her eyes widened as his warmth enveloped her. She found herself standing between his legs, leaned up against his inner thigh. He held her loosely in the circle of his big arms.

"Alright," he said in a husky voice, "Let's try this again. So. We left things kinda open-ended on Friday night. You wanna talk about that?"

"Um, yeah," Maddy said.

She swallowed. Standing this close to him made her heart race erratically in her chest. She was really bad at talking about her feelings, especially face-to-face like this. Throwing a tantrum or yelling seemed so much easier. She felt her anxiety spike. She clutched her hands together, embarrassed that her fingers were beginning to tremble. Jeez. Why did he have this effect on her?

"So Friday night," she said. "You really hurt my feelings. You said some harsh stuff."

"Yup, I did. So what hurt you?"

"You said Dean's not my real dad."

"Well, he's not."

Maddy flinched. She felt her temper flare again.

"That's a fucked up thing to say," she protested. "You basically said my stepdad doesn't give a shit about me."

Gareth brushed a strand of red hair back behind her ear. He studied her face as though considering his next words. Still, she thought he could have considered them longer, since when he spoke, it wasn't exactly sweet.

"Mads, sorry to be blunt, but he *doesn't* give a shit about you. I know it's not black and white. He's probably an 'alright' guy sometimes. But trust me. He doesn't care about anyone but himself."

Maddy felt tears stinging her eyes. Damn.

Gareth's voice gentled.

"I'm sorry I hurt your feelings," he admitted. "But I'm not sorry for what I said. I meant every word. It's tough love, babygirl. I gotta stand my ground on this. You need to move out and leave Dean and his problems behind."

"You can't just demand that of me. You have *no idea*," Maddy shot back. "You have *no idea* what it's like to grow up without parents. You're wrong about me. I'm not a caretaker. I can't help my stepdad's issues. He's the closest thing I've got to family."

"No excuse," Gareth said. "He's abusing you. *Using you.* And he's got you pinned down."

"I can't just abandon him."

"There it is," Gareth said.

Maddy flushed. She hated how he looked at her, his gold eyes piercing her like they could see into her soul. She felt like he had the upper hand, and she hated it.

"You gotta stop lying to yourself, babygirl," Gareth said, his gaze steady. "You're in denial. I saw the bruises. How do I know he hasn't done anything since Friday? Would you tell me?"

Maddy hesitated, shocked by his question. She didn't have time to react. Gareth turned her suddenly in his arms and yanked up her sweater, his eyes running over the skin of her back. She gasped. His warm, calloused hand brushed the spiderweb of raised scar tissue. He rested his palm there for a moment. Her heart quickened. She felt the possessiveness in his touch. He didn't hide it. A shiver of anticipation went down her spine, and warmth settled in her belly. He owned her. She knew it. But she couldn't give in yet. She couldn't just "belly up" like a lost puppy. Trusting people came at a price.

He dropped her sweater back down and turned her around to face him. He pushed up her sleeves to check her arms.

"Good. No new bruises. So I don't have to kill a motherfucker today," he growled. Then he held her wrists and looked into her eyes. "Mads, you deserve better. You don't owe that piece of shit anything. Give me one reason why you should stay loyal to him."

Hot tears stung her eyes. She felt her face grow pale. Her heart was racing in her chest. She wasn't sure why, but she felt like she might have a panic attack.

"He didn't . . . he didn't throw me out when my mom died."

"What? Is that it?"

"Yeah." Saying it out loud sounded pathetic somehow, but Dean had thrown it in her face a hundred times. "I was an orphan. He could've sent me to social services, but he didn't. He gave me a place to live."

"In your mom's trailer."

"Yes."

"Does he own it?"

Maddy hesitated. She actually didn't know anything about that.

"I don't know."

"So the generous and benevolent Dean Harvey let you stay in your mom's trailer after she died. Maybe the trailer belongs to you. Have you thought about that? Maybe he couldn't send you to social services because he would lose *his* home."

Maddy blinked at him. In truth, she hadn't considered that. She had no idea whose name was on the title of the property. It hadn't occurred to her to check. She had always thought of it as "mom's place." Maybe he had a point.

"I don't know. That's a lot to think about. But Gareth, you and me, we only just started dating. I *really* can't move this fast. I've never had a boyfriend before. I've never been kissed before . . . until you . . . in the car, when you . . . ."

Gareth squeezed her wrists gently. "Mads," he murmured, "I know. . . ."

"Dad says you got me fooled. He thinks you're just after 'teen pussy.'"

Gareth grimaced. He glanced down briefly. A look of disgust flickered across his face, probably at Dean's raunchy language.

"Well, some guys would be," he said.

"I think it's better if we're just friends right now," she blurted out. "Like, slow down a bit. Let me take this one step at a time. I can't move out of my house to live with you. That's *psycho*. No one would make that demand of someone they just met. I just . . . I need to breathe. I need to slow down."

Gareth looked thoughtful. He searched her eyes. His thumb stroked the inside of her wrist in a slow circle. The small touch made her relax; she felt some of the tension leave her shoulders as she waited for his response. He brushed another stray lock of long auburn hair behind her ear. Each small caress of his calloused fingers made her heart flutter.

His eyes flickered over her face. He sighed.

"Alright. Maybe I jumped in too fast and you weren't ready. You've been through a lot this past weekend. You're overwhelmed. I get it."

"Thank you . . ."

"I'm not finished."

Maddy bit her lip.

"We can slow down if that's what you need. But I see what's going on, Mads, maybe better than you do. You're a caretaker. You think it's normal, but it's unhealthy. You might put up with Dean's bullshit, but I won't. He's got addiction issues and it's running you into the ground."

Maddy frowned. "He's not just some addict. He's my dad."

"Yeah. Well. That's hard."

"You really think I'm unhealthy?" she asked. "Like I'm toxic?"

"I think you're in a toxic situation," Gareth pointed out.

So, yes, he thought she was toxic. She almost heard Kaylee's voice in her head, taunting her. Maddy struggled with that for a moment. She knew her homelife was unhealthy, how could it *not* be? But it was the only home she had ever known. *This is all my fault. Why am I so fucked up?*

"You know what I saw on Friday?" Gareth asked.

"What?"

"Dean comes first. Before yourself. Before me. Before anything else. You might say you hate that guy, but he calls you at midnight from an hour away, and you go running. Your world revolves around that wasted son of a bitch. So, sure, let's go slow. Let's be friends. Because if I'm your boyfriend, I'm not sharing you with Dean. And I won't watch you caretake his sorry ass. I gotta nip this threesome in the bud."

Maddy felt frustrated and confused. He was turning the tables on her. Like being friends was *his* idea. She crossed her arms angrily in front of her chest and glared at him.

Gareth sat casually on the stool as he considered her. Why did he have to look so calm?

"Alright. Then we're just friends," she said.

"Yup."

"You act like it's no big deal."

"I want you to sort out your situation with your dad, before I sort it out for you."

Maddy scoffed. "You don't have to sort out anything for me. I already think Dean's an asshole."

"So you gonna move out?"

Maddy was silent.

"Alright. You gonna tell him you saw me today?"

Maddy bit her lip. She glanced up and met Gareth's eyes. She couldn't answer him.

His face darkened the longer she hesitated.

"I don't like you sneaking around. I get you learned to lie to protect yourself. I know you're scared of him. But it's a bad habit, Mads."

She felt ashamed. Why did he have to make her feel like a kid?

"You don't have to worry about me lying anymore," she pointed out. "We're not together. We're just friends. So you can ghost me whenever you want."

Maddy tried to sound tough, but she saw Gareth's face soften.

"I'm not abandoning you, Mads."

"Sure." She hesitated. "Fine. Right."

They stared at each other for a long moment. Maddy couldn't handle the tension in the room between them. She felt angry and sick and hurt. The office was so small and cramped, she thought she would suffocate. She needed fresh air and space to think.

She stood up in the small office and turned to the door.

"I'll just go now," she said.

She started to push by him, but his arm snaked out. He caught her easily by the waist and dragged her back into his body, between his legs. His strong arms trapped her against him.

"What–?" she gasped.

One hand went to the back of her neck. He angled her head as his mouth boldly slanted over hers.

Maddy froze. Her lips parted instinctively as his tongue dipped into her mouth. He tasted delicious. His breath mingled with her own, his kiss deep and sensual. She felt a slight brush of stubble from his jaw.

His kiss deepened, his tongue thoroughly exploring her mouth. A little whimper of pleasure fought up from her throat as her knees grew weak. Her nipples began to tingle and swell beneath her sweater. His fingers wove into her hair, gripping her head firmly, holding her captive. She could feel the heat of his body through his white T-shirt. He was so big. Spirals of pleasure moved through her at his touch. His arms held her bound.

Her fingers started to travel on their own, inching up his back to his muscular shoulders, then up his neck into his thick hair. The messy bun at the base of his neck came loose in her hands. His black hair fell soft and silken across his shoulders. She ran her hands through it in a daze.

He shifted against her, pulling her more firmly against his body. He wasn't shy in the least as his arms slipped down and his hands gripped her ass. He manhandled her through her black leggings. His long fingers pressed into her intimate folds through the thin spandex material.

Maddy gasped in shock, squirming away with a little mewl of protest, but he held her ass firmly in his big, strong hands. His fingers probed along her slit through her leggings. She thought he might tear her pants off, he was so aggressive.

She felt herself grow wet and creamy down below.

"*Friends*," he repeated into her mouth, his voice thick with passion. "Let's be friends, Mads."

She moaned. She felt like melted butter. Her eyes slitted open. His face was dark with passion as he kissed her. She knew her own gaze must be sultry and vulnerable. He pulled her flush against him, letting her feel the size of his erection through his jeans against her crotch. Then he leaned in close to her ear.

"Why are you pushing me away, Mads?"

"I'm not . . . ."

"Don't lie to me."

He pinched her ass, hard. She squealed, squirming against him, arching in his arms like a cat. He caught her lips in a deep kiss, taking her noises into himself.

"You know what I think?" he said into her mouth. "I think you're afraid."

She murmured something incoherent. Maddy tried to respond, but her words were muffled. He kept drowning her in kisses, passionate and slow, then soft and playful, then deep and lusty. She groaned. His lips traveled back to her ear, where he nibbled at her earlobe, catching it between his teeth, then down her neck, leaving a trail of pleasure. His hand went between her legs and he pressed against her clit. Maddy gasped and weakened, gazing up at him with a helpless expression. He gazed into her eyes, his own dark with lust.

"Your fucking beautiful," he murmured.

She blushed. For a wild moment, she thought he would take her right there in his office. Drag off her panties and claim her virginity, make love to her like a scene from some steamy, late night HBO special.

She never got the chance to find out. One of the metal lockers in the break room slammed shut, and she heard Joker whine in excitement. Sounded like Vin was making lunch.

Gareth released her with much reluctance. Maddy sucked in a deep breath. Her lips were swollen and soft, her cheeks flushed, her head spinning. She tried to stand up, but she overbalanced and fell against his chest. Why did she feel drunk?

"You okay?" he asked with a rueful grin.

She met his eyes. His look pierced her. She couldn't deny the hunger in his gaze. She felt it to her core.

"Gareth . . . I'm sorry . . . I can't . . . ."

"Why're you apologizing?" he asked softly, drawing her close again.

She shivered as his big, tatted arms looped around her. His lips brushed her forehead. The gentle caress brought tears to her eyes.

"I meant it, when I said we should be friends." She felt terrible saying it again, but she knew it was the right thing to do. "I can't . . . I can't handle this right now. I don't know how to be in a relationship. I just . . . I can't."

He hushed her gently. "It's alright. I know you're overwhelmed."

"I'm sorry."

"You don't gotta apologize, babygirl."

"I'm *really* sorry," she repeated. Damn. Why did he always make her cry?

She tried to push away from him and stand up straight, but she overbalanced again, feeling dizzy. The room dipped slightly to the left.

Gareth grabbed her by the forearms. He steadied her. He looked concerned.

"You doin' alright?" he asked.

"Yeah, I'm okay. I think. The lights are kinda bright."

He raised an eyebrow. "Bright, huh? You look pale. You gonna faint on me?"

"I . . . no, I don't think so . . . ."

The room kept spinning. She clung to his arms as her heart raced. She felt like she couldn't catch her breath. Why was she so dizzy?

"Mads?" Gareth asked. His voice seemed far away.

"Something's wrong . . . ." she mumbled.

Her vision narrowed. His arms went around her. He drew her against his chest as her legs lost strength. She felt like her limbs had turned to water and she was melting into the floor. The last thing she saw was his concerned face as she fell forward.

Chapter 13

Gareth paced up and down the driveway outside, his cell phone raised to his ear, listening to it *ring, ring, ring.*

Inside, on a wooden bench in the break room, her head propped up on his jacket, Maddy lay unconscious. It wasn't the most comfortable place to 'take a nap,' but he didn't have a couch she could lay on. Her cheeks were pale, but her pulse was steady.

He suspected what the problem might be. But he didn't want to assume anything before he talked to his mom again.

If Gareth craned his neck, he could see through the break room door. He glimpsed Vin sitting next to Maddy on a foldable plastic chair, scrolling through his phone. A bemused half-smile crossed Gareth's face. The kid was probably looking up "home remedies for fainting spells" online. Luckily, Gareth was well-versed in First Aid, CPR and other survival skills from his time in the Army. He wanted to laugh. Fuck the internet—*he* was the damned home remedy.

He remembered Vin's look of shock when he carried Maddy from his office into the break room. Vin had just sat down at a small card table with a meatball sandwich for lunch. He looked like he was about to watch an episode of something on his phone. Joker was eagerly sitting by his feet, her puppy eyes trained on the meatballs, a bit of drool puddling on the floor between her paws.

"Whoa. What happened? She okay?" Vin asked, dropping his sandwich.

"She got dizzy. Gonna lay her down here for a minute."

"Is she alright? Did she hit her head?"

"No. I'm gonna make a phone call. Watch her for me?"

"Sure thing, boss." Vin nodded, his face a little pale.

"Don't you go passin' out on me too," Gareth growled as he grabbed his phone from his jacket pocket. Then he folded up the flannel jacket and tucked it under Maddy's head. "I'll be right back. Come get me if she wakes up."

"Right. Yeah. No problem." Vin looked nervous but determined to help.

Gareth left the break room, his cell phone in hand. He walked through the garage to the driveway before dialing. He had his suspicions about what might have caused Maddy to faint, but that was wolf business, stuff that Vin wouldn't understand.

As the phone rang and rang, Gareth paced up and down in front of the shop, trying to stay calm. If everything his mom said was true, then maybe all this fucking around had triggered Maddy's Change. It might be happening a lot faster than he originally assumed. When he tried to remember his first werewolf Change, all he remembered was being ravenously hungry and horny all the time. But maybe that was just called "being a teenage boy."

Finally, the phone picked up.

"Mijo? What's wrong? Two calls in one day. Now I know somet'ing happened."

"Hola mama, quick question for you. It's about that girl. The one I told you about before."

"Yes. The wolf girl. She must be *una persona muy preciosa para ti*."

Gareth paused. He spoke alright Spanglish, but it had been a second. *She must be a very precious person to you.* His mom's voice was laced with heavy implication.

He couldn't deny it, but he didn't want to say too much more. His mother was an intelligent woman. She would put it all together if he gave up too much. He hadn't called her since her birthday, and here he was, calling twice in the same morning about a girl. Yeah. She knew something was up.

He asked quickly, "So what are the signs of the Change?"

"I already told you a few. Can you be more specific?"

"This girl. She's having dizzy spells. Like she will faint suddenly."

His mother made a clucking sound with her tongue as she thought. He could almost imagine her pursing her lips with one hand propped up on her hip.

"I am no doctor, mijo, but wolves need to eat. Use your head. The Change takes a lot of energy. You know this is true. You don't need me to tell you. So she might be burning a lot of calories in preparation for The Change. If she's not eating enough, because she doesn't know her own body, she might pass out from hunger. So make sure she eats." Her mom hesitated. "And if she keeps fainting, for God's sake, take her to a hospital."

"Yeah, yeah, trying to avoid that unless I have to."

"Don't be stubborn. Use your head and be safe, mijo."

"What else?" Gareth asked. "What happens when a wolf starts to Change for the first time?"

"*Ai,* let me think. Increased energy. Or she might sleep a lot. Vivid dreams. She might find smells and sounds to be very strong. Sometimes it starts off slow with little changes like that. Then suddenly, boom! Her full transformation. Not necessarily at the full moon. You said she was very delayed, so hard to say. It might be especially hard on her. So what do you t'ink? Is she starting?"

"I don't know. Maybe."

"I will send you a care package. What's your address?"

Gareth hesitated. "It's alright, *mama.* Just text me a list of things. I'll buy them."

His mother sighed. "My mysterious son. You got Wholefoods out there, mijo?"

"Naw, just basic groceries. But I can make a trip into the city."

"Basic groceries? So you're in the country somewhere?"

"Mom, I can't. . . ."

His mom chuckled. "Okay, okay. I'll let it go. But I'm so curious where you live now! Someday, I'm going to visit you and meet this girl who's got you so worried."

"Sure, mom. Whatever you say. I gotta go. Text me the list."

"Alright. Take care."

He hung up the phone and started through the garage, his muscles strung tight as a bow, unable to hide the tension running through his body. He didn't know much about Maddy's food habits. She wasn't skinny or emaciated like some girls. Actually, her body was all soft feminine curves, with a delicious jiggle that made him want to sink his teeth into her thighs. But she probably didn't eat a lot of nutritious food, considering her low income. That's why he bought her groceries that morning. He remembered her fridge was empty. But maybe she hadn't eaten yet today?

He entered the break room at a fast pace. Vin looked up, startled, from his phone. He was watching a Youtube video on how to resuscitate a drowning victim. Joker, the dog, was sitting under the kitchen table staring intently at Vin's meatball sandwich.

"Better keep an eye on your lunch," Gareth said. "Dog's lookin' pretty keen."

"Yeah I know, I see her," Vin said. "She's a super chill puppy. We could use a shop dog."

Gareth shrugged and didn't reply.

"So what did you find out?" Vin asked. "Who'd you call?"

"Not a doctor, but someone just as good," Gareth grinned, thinking of his mom's words. "It's probably low blood sugar."

"So what can we do?"

"We just gotta wait, I guess. Then make sure she eats something when she wakes up."

Gareth opened up his iron gray, gunmetal locker, where he kept his work overalls, some deodorant and a change of clothes. On the shelf above his clothes was a little box where he dumped his wallet and keys. He grabbed a $20 bill out of his wallet. Then he shut the metal door with a slam.

"I'm going to the gas station. I'll be right back. If she wakes up, make sure she doesn't move around too much. She could fall again."

"Where are you going?"

"Getting some sugar."

He left the break room and jogged through the garage, dodging around the side of the Mercedes, then out into the brisk mountain air. It was just past noon. White nimbus clouds filled the crisp blue sky. Across the highway from the garage stood a wall of solid forest, where frost still covered the grass in the shade. Still, it was a pleasant day in the mountains.

It took Gareth five minutes to cross the parking lot to the gas station, walk into the tiny convenience store and grab a bag of M&M's off the shelf. An old asian man named Johnny was sitting at the register, smoking a cigarette and reading a newspaper. He was covered head to toe in tattoos. The ink had bled together on his wrinkled skin to resemble wavelike patterns or big blotches. He and his wife owned the gas station and a small convenience store in a strip mall downtown. It was called "Sunshine Grocery" but the locals referred to it as "Tiny Costco." Mr. and Mrs. Sato bought Costco bulk goods and resold them at a higher price, so folks didn't have to drive downriver. Gareth had shopped there plenty of times. It was a great service.

"Hey Johnny," he said as he threw down the pack of M&M's and the $20. "How's your weekend going?"

"Slow as shit," Johnny said, slurring his "L's." "You read the paper? Murder down the road. Five men killed by wolf." Johnny's eyes narrowed on Gareth. "I wonder, why would a lone wolf kill five men?"

"What's that, like a riddle?" Gareth grunted.

Johnny blew out a ring of smoke. He tapped his cigarette in the ashtray by his elbow. Gareth waited. Some people knew about werewolves, but it wasn't an everyday topic of conversation. He wondered if Johnny was an avid reader of the werewolf subreddits online.

"No riddle," Johnny said. "Me? I think it was a 'gang execution.' Back when I was 'yakuza,' that's how we did it. Bad employees everywhere. Bad for the whole organization. Take 'em out in one hit. If you join up but you waste time and money, you don't live long."

"Why not just fire them?" Gareth asked with a side-grin.

Johnny laughed. "Yakuza don't get fired. Yakuza get dead."

"Right. Something to think about. I don't think there's a mafia this far out, though. We're pretty far in the sticks."

Johnny shrugged. "Plenty of drugs coming off the Res. That's my opinion."

Gareth took his change and waved goodbye, then headed back to the car garage, his mind returning to Maddy.

When he reached the break room, Vin was still sitting next to her in his fold-out chair. Maddy was still on the bench, small and pale. He knelt next to her, his face drawn into a thoughtful frown. His hand rested against her forehead, his thumb feathering against her temple. Her pulse was steady. Her breathing deep and even. She didn't have a fever. She didn't smell sick to his wolf senses. And yet, something about her scent was subtly different. It made his blood stir. He told himself it was his imagination, and yet . . . could it be . . . the Change was already happening? So soon? His brow knitted with worry.

Vin scooted his plastic chair a little closer to Gareth next to the bench. His eyes flickered over Maddy's generous chest area, which was distracting even through her oversized sweatshirt. Then he looked studiously at the ground.

Gareth noticed the look, but didn't say anything. He didn't like it, but he couldn't really expect anything from the kid. Only a goddamn saint would fail to notice her . . . proportions.

"She your girl, boss? Are you guys dating?" Vin asked after an uncomfortable silence.

"Yeah. Something like that."

"Didn't know you were seeing anyone," he said. "So how did you two meet?"

"Eat your sandwich, Vin."

"Right. Okay. Just sayin', you never talk about yourself. I didn't know you had a girl. Thought you were more of a . . . ."

Gareth raised an eyebrow, turning to look at his employee. "You thought I was what?"

"I dunno. Figured you were just a Netflix and chill type of guy."

Gareth honestly did not know what to say about that.

"Oh, look. She moved." Vin pointed. He looked more than a little relieved to change the subject. "I think she's waking up."

Gareth looked down at the bench. He gazed intently at Maddy's face as she stirred. Her eyelids fluttered.

Then he half-turned to Vin and reached out his arm. "Hand me a water bottle."

***

Maddy opened her eyes. She blinked woozily as she gazed up at the ceiling. A hand swam into her line of vision, offering her a bottle of Arrowhead water.

"Easy," Gareth said as she grasped it. Her hand was shaking. He helped her to wrap her fingers around the bottle.

"You're okay. Just go slow," he encouraged her.

"What's wrong with me?" Maddy groaned. Her head was throbbing.

"Hypoglycemia."

"Hypo-what?"

"That's low blood sugar. But you're doing fine. You just gotta eat something."

He helped her into a sitting position. Maddy's grip was pathetically weak on the water bottle. She tried to undo the cap, but her fingers weren't working quite right. Gareth took the bottle back and opened it for her, then passed it to her lips. Maddy took a few deep sips. The water cleared her head a bit.

She met his warm, hazel gaze. Gareth knelt next to the bench where she was sitting. It was a long way for such a tall man to bend down. His shoulders and chest were like a wall blocking out the rest of the room. His big hand rested on her knee. She could feel the gentleness of his touch through her leggings. Just that small gesture sent a spiral of tenderness through her belly. Somehow, it was doubly endearing to see such a rugged man show so much concern. She felt herself melt a little.

Then he tore open a bag of M&M's. He spilled a few into her hand. He waited as she chewed on the candy and swallowed. She felt a little self conscious. By his intent gaze, she was certain he wouldn't let up until she finished the whole bag. She ate a few more.

"She's looking a lot better, boss," Vin said.

Maddy glanced over and recognized the gaunt, herstine face of Gareth's young employee, Vin, standing a few feet away. The young man was obviously gauging their relationship. Maddy wondered if he had ever seen Gareth act this way around anyone before. He almost seemed amused by it. He crossed his arms and put a hand to his chin, hiding a grin.

"What happened?" Maddy said, blinking in the harsh overhead light.

"You passed out," Gareth answered her. "Like I said, it's probably low blood sugar. You eaten yet today?"

"No. Not really," she said with a wince.

"That's probably it, then."

"She can have some of my sandwich," Vin suggested. "Or like, half of it."

Gareth glanced over his shoulder with a raised eyebrow.

Maddy rushed to say, "No, I don't want to take your lunch. The candy is enough. I feel much better already. I should really get home. Thanks, though."

Vin shrugged. "Cool. Well. Glad you're feeling better." Then he went back to the table where his sandwich, and a begging Joker, was waiting.

Gareth turned to Maddy. "You sure you're feeling alright?"

"Yeah. I was just dizzy for a moment."

"You still dizzy?"

"I mean, a little bit."

In truth, the thought of food made her feel nauseous. Chewing and swallowing the M&M's was a bit of a challenge. But she knew Gareth was right. She had likely passed out from low blood sugar. She had skipped breakfast that morning, and she walked two miles up the highway to the car garage on an empty stomach. She was probably hungrier than she thought. She hadn't slept very well last night. Plus all the stress from their fight. So it was probably a little bit of everything.

"You think you can walk to the car?" Gareth asked. "I'll drive you back home."

"Yeah. I can do that."

A furry head bumped her hand. With a grin, Maddy looked down at Joker, who was crowding close to the bench and wagging her tail.

"Aw, I didn't forget about you!" Maddy grinned and scratched the dog's ears. Then she picked up Joker's leash. As she petted Joker, she avoided meeting Gareth's eyes. She felt shy. Kind of embarrassed.

I actually fainted while he was kissing me, she thought, trying not to blush. Like something out of a bad romance novel. How pathetic! She wanted him to take her seriously and respect her as an adult. But now he probably thought she was some weak, frail invalid.

Gareth got his keys and wallet out of his locker. Then he put on his sunglasses. With his eyes hidden behind the dark glasses, he instantly became mysterious and unapproachable. She gazed up at him, watching him get ready. Her eyes traveled over his tatted arms, bulked-out shoulders and loose hair. He tied his hair back at the base of his neck. Then he pulled on his heavy flannel jacket with fleece lining.

He held out his hand. She took it and he pulled her to his feet.

"I'll be back in a few, Vin," he said.

"No worries, boss," Vin said around his sandwich. He was sitting at the little card table watching videos online. He ignored Gareth and Maddy as they left the break room.

Maddy followed Gareth through the garage, blinking in the harsh overhead lights. She felt a little nervous as she followed him to the Camaro out front. She wondered if she was getting a migraine. The big, white fluorescent bulbs that illuminated the garage seemed brighter than she remembered, and the scent of oil and rubber was overpowering. If she didn't know any better, she would think she was pregnant. Except she was a virgin. So that was impossible.

Gareth unlocked the passenger side door and let her into the Camaro. Then he climbed into the other side of the car. The engine choked to life. Maddy cocked her head slightly and listened. The engine sounded better than she remembered. The car didn't shake or shudder quite as much, and the roar was more subdued. She also noticed his door shut and locked smoothly.

"Did you do some work on the car?" she asked.

"A bit, yesterday," he said. "Replaced the engine belt and a few spark plugs. Nothin' too crazy."

"It sounds better. I can tell."

He grinned as he pulled out the driveway. "Thanks, sweetheart."

Maddy blushed. She didn't know what to say to that. She glanced down at her hands as he pulled onto Highway 20 and turned in the direction of her trailer.

"So we . . . we're friends?" she asked, uncertain.

"Yup."

It was not exactly the outcome Maddy had been hoping for. But she knew it was better for her in the long run. She needed to slow down. After the past few days, she needed some time to breathe. She didn't function well when she was overwhelmed—and in her life, that happened often.

Reflecting back on their conversation, she knew Gareth was right. In the long run, she needed to move out and leave Dean behind. But she needed to go at her own pace. Which, considering every other area of her life, was a bit delayed.

She was held back in 8th grade. She didn't have a driver's license. Up until four days ago, she had never been kissed, never had a boyfriend. It was a bit embarrassing. Some girls her age were already sophomores in college. She would be turning twenty next year. She was old enough to move out. She should want to.

But what Gareth suggested felt more like jumping off a cliff.

"We don't have to be friends," she said suddenly. "If you'd rather break things off completely, I understand."

"I'm not doing that," Gareth said.

Maddy wondered if he meant his words.

He glanced over at her. She couldn't read his eyes with his sunglasses on, but he seemed to notice her insecurity, because he reached over and took her hands in his own. His warm, calloused palm stilled her fingers. She hadn't realized she was picking at her nails again.

"When you get home, I want you to eat something," he said. "You gonna do that for me?"

Maddy was a little taken aback. "Yeah. Of course."

"Good. Just reminding you. As friends."

He flashed her a grin. He was so handsome, his jaw square and sharp. The little cleft in his chin was the manliest thing she had ever seen. She stared at him stupidly for a moment. Then she turned and gazed out the window, her cheeks bright pink. *Fuck my life.* Just a two-second smile made her forget what she was thinking.

The rest of the short drive back to her house was laced with tension. With his hand resting in her lap, Maddy couldn't stop thinking about his sensual kiss in his office, his heated gaze, or the feeling of his tongue caressing her mouth. His calloused fingers remained protectively over her own. His scent seemed more potent somehow. It filled her with a terrible sense of yearning. The memory of their little makeout session in his office aroused her, and the heat wasn't going away. He had awakened something powerful in her blood.

She rubbed her thighs together, thinking of his muscular, six-foot-four body pressing into her soft curves. This was hard. How was she supposed to be friends with him, with all this pent up sexual tension between them?

He pulled into her driveway but stayed close to the street, the Camaro hidden from her trailer by a line of pine trees. Maddy was relieved. Dean would freak out if he saw her in his car.

"Well, I guess this is it," Maddy said awkwardly.

She couldn't kiss him goodbye if they were just friends, and a hug over the center console seemed strained. So she opened the passenger side door and swung her feet out onto the gravel.

"I think I owe you a driving lesson," Gareth said, catching her off guard.

"Oh, right." Maddy's heart leapt despite herself. "I didn't think you really wanted to. I mean, we don't have to. I know you're busy."

Gareth raised an eyebrow and regarded her through his dark sunglasses.

"I'm not that busy, little girl. You said you got your permit, right? When are you free this week? Let's hang out soon."

"Yeah, I got it over the summer. I just need to check my schedule at work. I'll let you know on Monday?"

"Alright. Do that."

"Okay. I will."

She tried not to look as pleased and excited as she felt. They were 'taking things slow.' But she couldn't help herself. The thought of Gareth teaching her how to drive kicked up a storm of aggressive butterflies in her stomach. It definitely checked a box on her "Super Secret Fantasy" list.

She glanced at him out of the corner of her eye, trying to gauge if he was excited too, but she couldn't get a read on him with his sunglasses on. How could he act so casual?

He noticed her little side-look and gave her a wolfish grin.

"Come over anytime, Mads. *Mi casa su casa*. Don't be a stranger."

The way he said it, she felt a delicious shiver down to her toes.

"Hah. Alright. Um. Bye, Gareth." She almost said thank you, but she wasn't sure why.

"Call me if you need anything. I mean it."

"Yeah. Okay. I will."

She shut the door and gave him a little wave. Then she walked back down the driveway toward the trailer, Joker following along on the paracord leash.

Maddy chewed her lip as she walked. The words "hang out" bothered her the most. But they shouldn't bother her. This was what she wanted.

Why was she still so aroused?

How was she supposed to be "just friends" with a guy she'd crushed on for five years? Those feelings wouldn't just disappear. Actually, they seemed to have increased tenfold since she exited the Camaro.

Dean barely acknowledged Maddy when she came in through the sliding glass door off the back deck. She started for her bedroom at first, then she remembered her promise to Gareth to eat something. As though waking up from a coma, her stomach let out a loud groan. Oh yes. She could definitely eat.

Her stomach rumbled again as she went into the kitchen. She felt a sudden, strong craving for chicken. *Mmmm.* She rummaged through the fridge. Didn't she remember a pack of chicken breast in the groceries? She checked the freezer.

"Hey kiddo! What are you looking for?" Dean called from the living room.

"Where did the chicken breast go?" she asked.

"I cooked it. There's some left in the pan."

Maddy checked the skillet on the stove top. She wrinkled her nose. The chicken breast looked oily and a little burnt. But her stomach rumbled, and her craving for protein was strong. She picked up one of the greasy, over-seasoned breasts and bit into it. Dry, as she suspected. But her appetite was suddenly overwhelming. When she finished her first piece, she ended up grabbing another. She finished off what was left in the pan.

As she ate, she kept checking her phone for texts from Gareth. She wondered what he was thinking after their conversation in his office. Maybe he wasn't thinking much at all? She imagined him and Vin working together at the garage, blasting music and fixing up cars. She almost felt a little jealous of Vin, getting to see Gareth like that—not being a protective boyfriend or a guardian, but just a busy guy at work.

It made her smile. She wondered what he was like as a boss. She remembered that glimpse of admiration she had caught in Vin's expression. Again, it made her feel a bit more confident about Gareth. He must be a good boss to inspire that kind of loyalty from an employee.

"What're you smiling about?" Dean asked suspiciously as she walked through the living room.

"Nothing. Joker's just super cute," she said.

"Yeah. Dogs are the best," Dean grumbled. He eyed her as she walked past him to the hallway. Maddy avoided his gaze.

"You meet up with anyone on your walk?" Dean called after her. "You were gone a long time."

"Just took the old switchback trail," Maddy said vaguely.

The hair prickled on her neck. Her stepdad glowered at her for a long moment. Maddy knew he wanted to ask her more. She was gone for several hours, and she didn't come back with laundry detergent. She knew as well as he did that she rarely took walks in the forest that long.

She knew what he was really asking. *"You still seeing that guy?"* She could almost hear the question on his lips. *"Tell me the truth, Madeline. You getting fucked in the backseat of some shitty brokedown sports car?"*

She waited for him to probe deeper. But then his phone beeped. Someone was texting him. He picked up his phone off the couch and frowned at the screen.

With a quiet sigh of relief, she started up the hallway to her room. She shut the door firmly behind her. Then Maddy opened her backpack and spread her schoolwork out on the floor. After a few minutes, the TV's volume turned up in the living room. She forced herself to do makeup homework while her father roared at a football game on the tube. Just like old times. Except for Joker, who pawed at her door after a half-hour, and slunk under her bed with a whine. She obviously didn't like the noise.

"You're really not much of a guard dog, are you?" Maddy teased her, and scratched the nervous pup behind the ears.

Around 10 o'clock, she saw the screen on her phone light up. She checked it.

Gareth.

Go to bed

You got school tomorrow

She stared at the text in surprise. Really? How did he know she was awake? Then she glowered at the screen. She started to text him back, angry that he would try to set a bedtime for her. It was a little ridiculous. Then she stopped. She breathed deep. *Yeah, well.* It was getting late. She had to go to bed soon, anyway. It was kind of sweet, maybe, that he was thinking of her.

Ugh. Fuck that.

Her anger came back. She would go to bed because it was *her* choice, and she was going to do it anyway. Maybe she should leave him on "read."

But some part of her caved inside. She didn't want to push him away. She touched her lips, suddenly remembering his kiss, his smell. God. A flood of visceral memories assailed her. She thought of her weak, helpless state in his office, when she collapsed against his chest. His promise of pleasure as he devoured her mouth. She could still taste him.

She wondered what it would be like to feel him inside of her. She couldn't imagine it. A little shiver of anticipation ran down to her toes.

She clutched the white bear to her chest that he gave her. She closed her eyes and sucked in a breath. Then she texted him back.

Yeah ok I'm going to bed now

She typed it out. Sent.

She dragged herself into bed and lay down. Joker jumped up next to her and curled up against her back. Maddy held her phone in hand, waiting for his reply. Eventually, her screen lit up.

Sleep good, little girl

Maddy started typing, unable to control herself.

Why do you care when I go to sleep? I thought we were just friends. You can't set a bedtime for me. Don't treat me like a kid.

She hesitated before hitting send. She read the message over. It sounded pathetic.

She fell asleep with the text unsent on her phone.

Chapter 14

Monday was super fucked. Maddy got to homeroom late because Joker decided to tear apart the trash before she left the house. Her homework was only half finished. She spent so much time on her makeup assignments, she completely forgot US History. Her laundry didn't dry all the way so her pants were still a little damp. But. She was at school and breathing, so that was something.

Around 9am she received a text from Gareth:

You in class?

She texted back:

Yes, I'm here

good

How's the dog?

she's super cute

but stressful

it's kind of a lot

Dad doesn't do anything

sounds about right

put your phone away

pay attention in class

Maddy rolled her eyes and even sent him back a little eye roll emoji. He didn't respond.

Between her second and third period classes, there was a fifteen minute break called Nutrition. Students rushed to use the bathrooms. They crowded around the vending machines. The halls of the school were packed and noisy, as usual.

Maddy went to her locker. She frowned as she walked down the busy hallway. Her locker looked . . . *different*. Her steps slowed down and she paused. Someone had written "Porno Titties" across the gray metal door in big, black permanent marker. Her cheeks began to burn with embarrassment.

Gee, I wonder who did this? she thought with sarcasm.

She recalled her altercation with Kaylee and the cheer squad at Zippy's. Knowing Kaylee, she got one of her flying monkeys to do the work for her.

Maddy felt herself shrink a little, but remained calm as she undid her lock. She would report it to the Admin Office. The janitor would probably scrub it off that evening. It wasn't a big deal. She would be fine for one day.

When she opened her locker, a big waterfall of rainbow wrappers fell out. At first Maddy thought they were Halloween candy, then with growing dread, she realized they were *condoms*.

The kids in the hall began turning and laughing. Phones popped out. They started taking pictures and filming her as she stood amid a pile of condoms.

Maddy clenched her fists. She felt so much rage, she thought her head would explode. She could hear people FaceTiming their friends.

Don't turn around, she thought. *Don't look. Let them laugh. Just get your books and go to class.*

She pulled her book out of her locker. Fuck Kaylee Makovich and her dumbbitch friends. She slammed her locker shut and stalked away. A few kids followed her with their phones out, but she flipped them off until they gave up and fell back.

Even if she tried to report the harassment, she doubted Kaylee would fess up to anything. Kaylee had a ton of people to cover her back. Her mom was on the school board and the PTA. To make matters worse, Principal Rodriguez did not like Maddy. She had a record of fighting and suspensions. So, the administration would never believe her.

With a heavy cloud of shame hanging over her head, Maddy went to third period, and spent the rest of the day in a strange daze. She stared out the window, wishing to leave her body and just float away over the mountains. Maybe tonight would be a good night for a forest walk. Maybe she would live her life in the woods as a hermit and completely recede from society.

The condom video went viral around the school. Maddy spent her lunch hiding in the library between bookcases, trying to avoid every group of laughing students she passed.

By fifth period, she was called to the principal's office and asked if she was soliciting sex from students. When she explained, furiously, that someone had pranked her, Principal Rodriguez sent her across the hall to one of the counselors "to talk." Maddy was fed up. She walked back to class instead.

A slip of paper arrived for her in sixth period, and her teacher gently informed her that she was receiving 3 days of detention for bringing sexual paraphernalia to school.

Maddy left school at 3pm with her hood up and her hands shoved in her pockets. As she walked, she seethed. So, Kaylee Makovich had gotten her revenge. Maddy knew from past experience if she kept her head down, the wave would pass, and a new viral video would take over campus by Friday. But it still wasn't fair. Kaylee pranked her, yet Maddy was the one with detention. In what fucking world did that make sense?

She wanted to find Kaylee and smash her face into a wall. But. Maybe Gareth was right. The only way to handle bullies was to completely disengage. She should ignore Kaylee completely. She already had 3 days of detention. She didn't want to get suspended.

She got out her phone for a moment, wondering if she should forward Gareth the video, since it was all over Picplace. But then she thought better of it. What good would that do? They were supposed to be "just friends," she shouldn't run to him for comfort if they weren't dating. She needed better boundaries.

Besides, she sorely wanted him to see her as an adult and an equal, not a little girl in need of help. Being bullied at school was too humiliating.

Maddy continued down the sidewalk, shoving her phone back into her pocket, feeling completely dejected. The long days of summer were gone, and the sky was gray and blustery. She found herself at the corner of Gareth's street. Her feet automatically turned down the sidewalk to his house. But she stopped. Her day had been fucking awful. She could not handle seeing him right now.

Then her feet turned toward the hardware store. She wanted to skip work, but she couldn't. She knew better than to bail on her shift last minute. With a sigh, she started walking toward Main Street.

She remembered her first year working at the store and how hard it was to juggle school and work together. Archie Hawkins, her boss, had almost fired her several times. But he took pity on her, and the other employees had talked him into keeping her on. She considered herself lucky.

She couldn't really say that working part-time and going to school had gotten any easier over the years. Last summer, she had retaken her math class because she fell behind on studying and failed the final. Summer school wasn't fun, but Maddy had kinda given up on having fun. She didn't really know anything other than work.

It was hard. The impulse to ditch was strong. But she took a big breath and walked to the hardware store. *Just show up,* she told herself. She had learned that trick when she was seventeen. As long as her feet got her to the hardware store, the rest of her shift would take care of herself. *Just show up and be a warm body.*

She reached the store fifteen minutes early for her shift. It was payday. Right, money. She changed course halfway across the parking lot and headed for the building next door.

Next to the hardware store was a thrift shop called *Calico's Vintage Wares* with a studio apartment on the second floor. Archie Hawkins, the owner of the hardware store, rented out the little apartment as his office. Maddy climbed a wooden staircase at the back of the thrift shop to the second story. The blinds were pulled over the windows, but she could see a yellow glow from inside. She knocked.

Archie's secretary slash HR manager slash accountant opened the door.

Sarah was another redhead in Black River. Maddy felt a vague sense of kinship with her, even though Sarah was twice her age and a mom of three young boys. She wore a maroon knit turtleneck sweater and a pair of tight jeans. She looked tired.

Behind her, Maddy saw a big square room with basic tan carpet. It smelled like Clorox wipes. The chemical smell seemed extra strong today and tickled Maddy's nose unpleasantly. Long IKEA desks lined one wall with three different computer monitors. The other wall was filled floor to ceiling with filing cabinets and bins of office supplies. A half-open door led to a small bathroom.

"You back? Feeling better?" Sarah asked.

"Yeah, doing a lot better," Maddy sorta lied.

"I can't believe your house got broken into and it was on the news. So scary, you were a missing person for a bit. We were all pretty worried. It's all the girls downstairs would talk about. So what happened?"

"Um," Maddy paused. Memories of the break-in still left her little shaky, though now she mostly felt numb about it. Almost like remembering an out-of-body experience.

Sarah waited for her to talk with wide, curious eyes.

"It was intense," Maddy finally said. "Some guys broke into my house in the middle of the night. I got out, though. Spent the night at a friend's place after."

"That's good. Like I said, we were so relieved to hear you were safe."

"Thanks. It was a close call."

"So did the thieves really get attacked by a wolf?"

Maddy winced. Everyone she knew at school kept asking her the same question. She tried not to think of the terrifying growl in the dark, and the sound of ripping flesh, screams and gunshots.

"I don't know if it was a wolf, but yeah, the cops told me they found bodies in the woods. They were attacked by an animal."

"That's nuts. And sad. There's an alert out for wolf sightings, so they must be pretty set on it."

"Really?"

"Yeah. I've been listening to the radio nonstop. I'm a bit of a wolf activist, myself. They're still under Federal protection in most areas. I didn't realize they had released them this far east. Or maybe the wolves escaped from a nature reserve? Anyway, it's a little scary. A lot of hiking trails are being closed until they catch the beast, and local animal control is saying we should report anything we see. So be careful walking around, okay?"

"Yeah. Definitely."

Maddy thought of the big black wolf she had encountered last Saturday. How it had appeared out of the forest like a ghost, walking in complete silence. How the predator had come forward and sniffed her face. She should report it to the police, but somehow, she felt a bit reluctant. As frightening as the wolf looked, it was a beautiful creature, and it had led her back to her trailer when she was lost. If it was the same creature who had killed those men, then technically, that meant it had also *saved her life*.

For that reason, she felt a strange sense of loyalty to the animal.

No, she decided, she would keep that encounter to herself.

Sarah pulled Maddy's check out of a small stack next to the door.

"Anyway, here you go. We need to get you set up with Direct Deposit. Printing checks is getting expensive."

"Thanks, Sarah. I'll do that next time."

"Sure thing, hon. That's what they always say. Drop into my office whenever you have the time, and bring your routing and account numbers. Anyway, have a good shift."

Maddy ran back down the wooden stairs, the paper envelope clutched in hand. A chill, moist wind blew past her off the mountain. A shower of red leaves fell on the cement as she crossed the parking lot. Patchy clouds filled the butternut-orange sky. It felt like autumn. She had a sudden craving for a warm cup of cinnamon tea.

She entered through the loading bay of the warehouse at the back of the hardware store. From there, she went into the break room. She checked the schedule and sighed. Ugh. She was covering the "Returns" counter. She groaned. She just wanted to turn off her brain and stock shelves.

Gabby and Marciela, her coworkers, were both on break. They were sorting through two different tubs of Halloween decorations.

"We need new stuff, Gabby," Marciela said in her cute, lilting accent. "Dees pumpkin lights are 20 years old. Everyt'ing in de box stinks funny."

"Yeah, you're right, what is that smell? This fake tombstone is kind of sticky. All right. I'll see what I have in my garage."

"Oh hey Maddy!" Marciela said, noticing her. She rushed forward and wrapped Maddy in a big hug. "Ai chica, you had us worried! I'm so glad to see you safe and sound. Yeah Gabby?"

"That's right, kiddo. That was a lot of drama on the news, wasn't it? You're like a little Black River celebrity this week. 'Kid survives wolf attack and house robbery.' Good to see you all in one piece."

Gabby was a 50-something mom with a blonde perm. She was chewing a stick of gum at manic speed. Her press-on nails were an inch long and Barbie pink. True to her name, she was often the center of gossip at the hardware store. She also liked to give well-intentioned but screwball advice.

Maddy had never met Gabby's daughter, she was off at college in Florida, but Maddy sometimes wondered what it was like having such a high intensity mom.

"Thanks guys," Maddy said with a weary smile.

Marciela released her and stepped back.

"You doing anyt'ing fun for Halloween? We were t'inking of going to the haunted house later dis month. Senior Hawkins said he would buy tickets for everyone. They're good any time."

"Yeah, he slipped them in with the paychecks," Gabby winked at her. "Don't forget it's payday!"

Maddy waved her white envelope around. "I got my check here."

Their manager, Archie Hawkins, was a pretty good guy.

"You get paper checks, Maddy?" Marciela asked, surprised. "You should really get direct deposit. So much safer. You're old school!"

Maddy rolled her eyes. "I just haven't set it up yet. Anyway, yeah, I'll probably go to the haunted house. I don't know."

"Ayiii Maddy! That's great!" Marciela gushed. "Aw, I remember Halloween at your age. It was *so much fun.* All the costumes and *de boys.* You've had a hard month. Time to party, ya?"

Gabby gave Maddy a sympathetic look. "Marci is right. You should go celebrate with your friends this Friday. Do something fun. Watch scary movies and eat candy."

Maddy nodded. Most kids by senior year did a lot more than eat candy. At least in Black River, they did. But she didn't say that out loud.

"Anyway, I gotta get out there. See you guys later." Maddy tied on her red apron and headed out onto the floor.

By the time she clocked in and got to the "Returns" counter, five customers were standing in line. Archie Hawkins, her boss, looked a little flustered. He was a tall, scare-crow-looking man with a thick reddish beard and a terrible comb over. Maddy guessed him to be in his mid-forties. She knew he was married because he wore a ring, but she had never met his wife. The hardware store was a family business, and she guessed they ran a little contracting company on the side, though she didn't know much about it.

Archie glanced up as she approached. He looked relieved.

"Thank God you showed up. I though you might skip your shift," he said. "I need to get a shipment sorted out in the warehouse. Can you finish this?"

Maddy stepped up to the counter as Archie bowed out and ducked away. She finished handing the customer his refund for a box of screws the wrong size.

"Next!" she called.

She tried not to groan when she saw none other than Mrs. Mackovich standing across the counter from her. Kaylee's mom looked like she had just gotten her hair done. It was very blond. Her foundation was dabbed on extra thick, and she was wearing a low cut purple top. She looked good, Maddy hated to admit it, especially for a forty-something mom.

She was suddenly reminded of her conversation with Gareth that night in the Zippy's parking lot. It made her cringe all over again. Had Mrs. Mackovich actually hit on him? Ugh.

Well, at least now she knew one extra piece of small town gossip: Mrs. Mackovitch was getting a divorce. Maddy didn't want to be petty, but after the condom incident with Kaylee, she really couldn't hold back.

"Oh hi, Mrs. Mackovich. How is *your husband* doing?"

Mrs. Mackovich looked startled by the question. "Fine, Madison."

"It's Madeline."

"Oh."

"Really, I hope things are *going great* with you two."

Mrs. Mackovich narrowed her eyes. She clacked her long nails on the countertop, as though debating whether or not to react to Maddy's taunting voice. Then Kaylee's mom said, "I brought these two boxes back for a refund. Terrible product."

Maddy looked at the two opened boxes of plant food.

"What was wrong with them?" she asked.

"Does it matter?" Mrs. Mackovich snapped. "I didn't like the product. It didn't work."

"Well, both boxes are opened, so we can't put them back on the shelf. Do you have a receipt?"

"No. I thought you had a store guarantee on all your products?" Mackovich pointed to the front door. "That's what the sign outside says."

"We do," Maddy assured her. "When did you buy them?"

"Back in August."

When Maddy was younger, she might have let the return slide, since she hated confrontation. But today, she was in a bad mood, and she was especially pissed at Kaylee. This woman had spawned Kaylee from her womb. So she was done being nice to the Mackovich family.

"It's a 30 day guarantee," Maddy said with a China doll grin. "So unless you have a receipt, I really can't process the return. Store policy."

"This is ridiculous! Where is Mr. Hawkins? I've been a regular customer at your store for almost ten years!"

"I'm sorry. But that's our policy."

Maddy saw a few of the people in line beginning to shift back and forth, looking irritated. One old man turned to the fellow behind him and rolled his eyes. Maddy ignored them. Entitled customers could wait their turn.

"Maybe you don't understand," Mrs. Mackovich repeated herself with an arched brow, her nose in the air. "I bought these boxes back in August and only used them once or twice for my hydrangeas. It's the wrong PH. It turned them bright pink."

"Okay, but because it's outside of our 30 day policy, I can't accept a return without a receipt."

Mrs. Mackovich scoffed. "Can't you look up my credit card purchases?"

Maddy glanced at the archaic computer next to her. "Honestly, this thing can barely search addresses and phone numbers. We don't keep a record of credit card purchases. That's what receipts are for."

"So you can't look up my account?"

"We don't have accounts like that."

Mrs. Mackovich was pursing her ruby red lips. She looked pissed. But Maddy didn't really care. It was satisfying to see Kaylee's mom struggle with being told "no." The apple didn't fall far from the tree.

"This is the most unprofessional, disrespectful customer service experience I've ever had," Mrs. Mackovich exclaimed. She picked up her boxes of plant food and shoved them back in her bag. Then she pointed threateningly at Maddy. "You better watch it, girly. Archie and I are good friends. We go way back. I'm going to tell him exactly what happened here."

Maddy raised an eyebrow. "You do that, Mrs. Mackovich."

"So unprofessional!"

The stuffy blond lady picked up her bags and flounced off, storming toward the exit. Maddy imagined her leaving a little trail of fire in her wake. She wondered if Mrs. Mackovich would seek out Archie Hawkins to complain, and if Maddy would hear about it later. She tried to make herself care. But she couldn't. It was store policy. Her hands were tied. She turned to the next customer in line.

"Next?" she said.

Time passed, and before she knew it, it was 8:30pm. A half-hour before closing, Mr. Hawkins came to relieve her and close up the customer service counter, since the store was almost empty. He handed her a mop and bucket, and told her to start at the back of the store and work her way to the front. Maddy took the mop from him and started up Aisle 15. She was eager to finish up and go home.

If Mrs. Mackovich had complained to her boss, Mr. Hawkins didn't mention it. He looked tired from a long day, too. Hopefully the whole thing would blow over and she had nothing to worry about. As much as she hated to admit it, the Mackoviches scared her. It seemed like they wielded some strange power over the town. She didn't know if it was money or something else.

Maddy was starting on the second aisle, sliding her wet mop back and forth across the speckled white linoleum tiles, when she heard someone clear their throat behind her.

She looked up, surprised to see Vin standing in the aisle. She recognized his black beanie and soul patch.

"Oh hey," she said, a little startled.

"Hey. I didn't know you worked here."

"Yeah."

"That's cool. So do you know where the ant spray is?"

"It's down Aisle 7. Here, let me show you."

"It's alright, I can find it."

"Mr. Hawkins wants us to show customers where things are at," Maddy said. "It's this way."

She led him down the first aisle, then cut across the back of the store to where the sprays and outdoor fertilizers were kept.

"Hey," Maddy said on impulse, "thanks for your help the other day."

Vin was walking slightly behind her. He shoved his hands in his pockets. "Sure thing. It's no big deal. So are you feeling better?"

"Yeah. A lot better. Right as rain." Maddy glanced over her shoulder at him. "So how's working at the garage? You like it there?"

Vin was chewing on a toothpick. He shrugged. "Yeah, it's great. Best job I've had in a while. I couldn't do retail anymore. Fucking people are the worst. I'd rather work on cars."

"So you're a mechanic?"

"Mr. Delarosa is training me. He's a good boss."

Mr. Delarosa. It was weird hearing someone call Gareth by that name. Dang. It sounded so official. Maddy felt a little weird thinking about it.

"So like, you've worked for him a long time?" she asked.

"Since over the summer. He hired me at the beginning of June."

"What's he . . . ." Maddy paused. "So . . . what's he like?"

Vin blinked at her. They had reached Aisle 7. She pointed to the ant spray on the shelf, next to a variety of cockroach traps and mosquito repellents. Vin reached up and grabbed a can of "Ant B'Gone." He flipped it around in his hands. She wondered if he did graffiti art. He seemed very comfortable with spray cans.

"Honestly? I don't know the guy well," Vin said. "But he works his ass off. Gives me all the overtime I want. Doesn't yell at me if I fuck shit up. Knows a lot about cars. I think he was in the Army? He has dog tags hanging up in his office. So yeah. I think he's a good guy, if that's what you're asking." He looked her up and down. "How old are you?"

Maddy blushed. "Nineteen."

"Right." He looked her over again. "So like, you guys together?"

"We're . . . friends."

"Oh. Not what he told me."

"It's kinda complicated, I guess." Maddy folded her arms across herself, feeling a little anxious, though she wasn't sure why. Despite his punkish appearance, Vin seemed like a soft-spoken, intelligent and thoughtful young man. She could definitely imagine him and Gareth getting along.

Vin scratched the back of his head. "Well, I gotta get going. For what it's worth, I think he's really into you. He was really worried when you fainted back at the garage."

"Thanks." Maddy felt her cheeks growing hot again.

"No problem. I hope you guys work it out, whatever it is. Anyway, I'll see you around."

Maddy watched Vin walk away down the aisle. Something about him kinda reminded her of Bea, though she wasn't sure why. Maybe their sense of style? She shrugged it off and went back for her mop. It was almost closing time, and she still had half the store to wipe down.

As she cleaned, she thought of what Vin had said about Gareth: *He works his ass off . . . doesn't yell . . . knows a lot about cars.*

It made her feel a little bit better, hearing Vin's perspective. It was reassuring, especially after Dean spouted all that bullshit about "teen pussy." Her stepdad's words still made her cringe: *"Guys his age only want one thing. Trust me. It's not your brain. Hah!"* She knew Gareth wasn't like that, but her stepdad had a way of undermining her self-esteem, and making her question her version of reality. Vin's opinion gave her an outsider's perspective. Her suspicions were confirmed—she could tell Vin really liked his boss.

Mr. Delarosa.

She blushed. Ah. So official.

Did that mean, if they got married, she would become *Mrs. Delarosa?*

It was way too early to be thinking about that.

Still, she felt her toes curl just a little.

Chapter 15

Tuesday morning, Maddy walked onto campus with her hood up and her head down. She cringed when she heard laughter in the hallways. Every time she saw a group of students hovering over a phone, she ducked down and looked away.

Despite her best ninja impression, she knew people recognized her. The condom video was still circulating. Black River High School only had about 400 students in total, so it was pretty excruciating. Younger students who didn't know her before now pointed at her and sniggered. The Freshmen were the absolute worst. Well, they were all the worst.

Maddy knew the video would continue to spread for another few days or so before the wave died down. By next week, a new viral video—probably homecoming or something—would take over. But for now, she was Black River High's #1 entertainment.

Thank you, Kaylee Bitchovich.

Maddy went to her locker, which the janitor had scrubbed clean the day before. Some of the permanent marker was still visible. She sighed. The "p" from "porn" and the "s" from "titties" were still noticeable. Someone had written "Penis" connecting the two letters with a ballpoint pen.

Maddy rolled her eyes. Maybe she should ask for a new locker.

On sudden inspiration, she snapped a pic of the word "Penis" and sent it to Gareth. She hadn't heard from him last night. She guessed that was okay. After getting home from work, she had fed the dog and finished her math worksheet, then collapsed in bed.

Her phone pinged as she walked into homeroom.

> wat's that?

She sent back an eye-roll emoji.

> i don't get it

> my locker

> some kid wrote penis on your locker?

> Fucking punks

Maddy laughed to herself. She could almost hear his voice.

> ya they suck

> So how's your day?

> started good

> got a workout in

> now just bullshit

> i imagine fixing cars is easier than dealing with people

> yup

Maddy thought of her encounter with Vin last night at the hardware store, and the glowing review he had given *Mr. Delarosa*. She sniggered, thinking of Gareth's last name and how formal it sounded. She just couldn't picture him that way.

> i saw Vin last night at the hardware store

> he says he likes working for you

oh man

that's nice, Vin's a good kid

what did u do before opening the garage?

i was an NCO in the Army

what's that?

non-commissioned officer

maybe I'll tell u about it sometime

Maddy blinked.

u in class now?

ya i just sat down

good. put ur phone away

pay attention to your teachers

they don't want to be there either

Maddy rolled her eyes for real this time. Then she stuck her phone in her backpack. The bell rang and all the students sat down. The teacher at the front of the class began to take roll-call. Then he read over a list of announcements.

Maddy barely listened. Her mind wandered to Gareth again and his career in the Army. How long did he serve? Six years? That was a long time from her perspective. Longer than she had been in high school, which felt like forever. He must have learned a lot of cool stuff. She remembered how comfortable he had been with a gun when they checked out her trailer last Thursday. How he knew exactly what to do with her concussion.

As her teacher droned on about upcoming school events, Maddy slipped out her phone again and searched for NCO online. Non-commissioned officer and squad leader. It sounded interesting. She really didn't know anything about the Army.

She found on a website:

An Army squad leader oversees their soldiers on wartime missions. Using their tactical knowledge of the battlefield, they fulfill mission objectives. Successful squad leaders are physically fit, mentally prepared, and can lead their squad under stressful situations. They are cool under pressure, with strong leadership skills, good weapon handling, and great marksmanship.

Maddy scrolled down the page a bit. She chewed on her lip. Wartime missions? So maybe he was a bit more of a badass than she initially realized? She wondered if he saw a lot of action in Iraq. He was so casual about it. But a squad leader sounded pretty intense.

He must be downplaying, she reasoned. She hadn't considered before, with everything else going on, that he might have actually seen some action.

The day passed by in a blur. She didn't have work after school; she was only scheduled on Monday and Thursday that week. It bothered her. She needed to remind her boss, Archie Hawkins, that she needed a full twenty hours. He was always forgetting. Sometimes other employees harassed him for extra shifts, and it was a slow time of year at the hardware store. Summer projects were completed and the weather was turning rainy. Last year, she recalled picking up a canvassing gig on the weekends to make ends meet. Ugh, that had been a lot of walking. She didn't want to do that again.

Without anywhere else to go, Maddy walked home after school. Her steps led her through an old neighborhood, where giant, ancient maple trees spread over the street. The yards were overgrown. Moss grew on the rooftops of peeling houses, and broken down trucks sat in gravel driveways, abandoned.

She recognized a big tan house with brown eaves and a covered front porch. A pile of rubber tires sat to the side of the driveway under a cold autumn sky.

Beatrice sat on her front porch smoking a cigarette, checking her phone.

"Hey Maddy!" Bea called, catching sight of her.

"Oh hey," Maddy waved back. She found herself slowing to a stop in front of Bea's house. The two girls looked at each other across the front yard. Bea flicked her cigarette.

"So? You're having one hell of a week." Bea pointed to her phone. "You're like a celebrity porn star now with all those condoms spilling out of your locker. Do you have any left by the way? I'm running low."

From anyone else, the words would have been offensive, but Maddy felt herself grinning. Bea grinned, too. Maddy flipped her off, and Bea returned the gesture with a pointy black witch's nail. Then she blew out a puff of cigarette smoke like a wizard.

"You want to hang out for a minute?" Bea asked. "Sounds like you had a day. My mom's at work. You can have a beer if you want."

"I don't drink."

"Right. I remember now."

Maddy felt a sense of relief. It was nice to have an ally. Still, she hesitated before walking up the driveway to join Bea on the porch. She had to take care of Joker when she got home. But maybe she could stay for a half hour.

They ended up on a broken down swing set in Beatrice's backyard. The yard was square and narrow. It slanted downwards to a wobbly wooden fence that ringed the back of the property. On the other side of the fence, ancient beech trees plunged down a hill into a deep gully, where a little meandering stream made its way to the Black River.

The ground was red with fallen leaves. Beneath the leaf cover, the grass was nothing but weeds, with a few sad tomato plants struggling in the corner of the yard. They sat side by side on the old swing set. Bea wore a pair of Doc Martens she had had since Middle School. They were banged and scuffed, and held lovingly together with black electrical tape. She kicked her feet back and forth.

"Karma's a bitch. Kaylee and those preppy fucks will get what's coming to them eventually. Hopefully sooner than later."

Maddy tried, but failed to feel better about it all. Kaylee's perfect life seemed untouchable.

"Hey, can I tell you something weird?" she asked Bea.

"Sure. I like weird."

"I was out walking on the mountain last Saturday, and I saw this big black wolf."

"A wolf, huh?" Bea blew out a puff of smoke. "That's pretty cool."

"No, like, it led me home."

"Really?"

"Yeah. It led me through the woods back to my trailer. It even looked at me a few times, like it could understand me when I talked."

"Wow. You even talked to it?"

"A little bit."

Bea was quiet, staring at Maddy with a raised eyebrow.

"You think I'm crazy, don't you?" Maddy asked.

"No crazier than my grandma. And that's a compliment." Bea grinned. "Didn't a wolf attack those guys who broke into your trailer? I think I saw that on the news."

"Yeah. I think it was the same one."

"So maybe this wolf is your guardian spirit. Like an angel watching out for you. You know, the mountain hides a lot of strange things. I believe it. You ever listen to the Upriver Paranormal Podcast? It's local. I'll share their Picplace page with you."

"No, I didn't know that was a thing."

"Oh yeah. They get all sorts of people on there. People who've seen Bigfoot. Ghost hunters. UFO sightings. Anyway, that wolf sounds pretty neat, Maddy. I hope you see it again."

"Yeah. Me too."

Maddy glanced down and smiled at the grass. She liked the idea of having a guardian wolf spirit.

"So what else is new?" Bea asked. "You never really told me about that guy you liked. So does he work at the hardware store? It's not . . . Archie Hawkins, is it?"

"Gross, no!" Maddy gasped.

Bea laughed.

Maddy smiled awkwardly and fidgeted. Right. Last time they talked, Bea asked her about her crush. Maddy hadn't shared any details. But now she felt like she needed someone to talk to. So much had happened over the last five days, it made her head spin. Bea seemed like a sympathetic ear.

"Um. So, we're kind of dating now," Maddy admitted.

"What? You have a boyfriend? That's fast. Wow, a lot's happened to you since last week."

"It's been a little crazy. But I wouldn't call him my boyfriend. Not yet, anyway. We decided to take it slow. But yeah. I think we're dating."

Bea raised an eyebrow. "You *think* you're dating? Okay. Spill the tea. Who is this guy?"

Maddy remembered walking in on Bea in the PE locker room in eighth grade. She remembered a flash of bare ass cheek from the guy who had her pinned up to the wall. The grunts and the groans. Bea had her own crazy secrets, and whatever she said, she didn't think Bea would judge.

Still, she didn't want to reveal her whole history with Gareth. Sharing their secret past together felt like a betrayal of trust. It belonged to them. It really wasn't Bea's business.

She decided to tell Bea a slightly truncated version of the story.

"We met at the hardware store," Maddy admitted. "I've had a crush on him for a while."

"Like how long?"

"A few years."

Bea raised an eyebrow. "Okay. So you really like this guy."

"Yeah. Just. He's kinda older."

"How old?"

Maddy fidgeted. "He's almost 29?"

"Dang. Alright. So definitely a sugardaddy. Do you have a picture? I want to see him."

"No, not really . . . ."

"What about Picplace?"

Maddy blinked. She felt dumb. "I never thought of that."

Bea got out her phone. She was already opening the app. "Are you for real? You never stalked him online? Here, I'll look him up. What's his last name?"

Bea started tapping away with her long nails, her cigarette held in one hand.

"Search for Gareth Delarosa," Maddy said, spelling out the last name.

She looked over Bea's shoulder at the Picplace search results. A bunch of accounts popped up, of course. She expected that.

"Sort by mile radius," Bea muttered, tapping on options.

Then a profile appeared at the top of the list: *Loboloco444*.

"That's him," Maddy said.

"Lobo loco?" Bea asked. "That means 'crazy wolf' in Spanish. Is he Mexican?" Then she waggled her eyebrows. "Hey, Maddy! It's your wolf!"

"Good one, very funny," Maddy said with some sarcasm. "I don't know if he's Mexican or not. I think he's from Arizona? He's got these tattoos . . . ." Maddy described Gareth's sleeves as Bea clicked on the account.

Gareth's profile pic was a photo of a bald eagle taken from his phone somewhere on the mountain. She sucked in a nervous breath, watching over Bea's shoulder as she scrolled through his account. His profile was sparse. The last photo posted was around November last year. So almost a year ago. It was a picture of a new sign being mounted on *Jack's Auto Repair*. It had two likes.

Bea started scrolling farther down. In his earliest pic, he was wearing Army fatigues. It was from eight years ago. Maddy barely recognized him. His head was shaved, he had sunglasses on and his skin was dark tan. He wore a green helmet and carried a big automatic rifle. Behind him was a harsh, flat, arid desert and azure blue sky. Was he in Iraq?

"Is he a soldier? Okay, that's kinda hot. I love guys in uniforms," Bea said. "That's a big gun, too."

"Yeah, he was in the Army," Maddy said. "He said he was a squad leader."

"That's pretty cool. So he can protect you."

"Yeah, I guess . . . ." She shrugged. She kind of liked that idea, too. "I don't see any recent pics of him."

"Let's check his tagged photos. Maybe someone took a pic of him and posted it on their account."

Bea switched to "Tags" and scrolled down. The first picture showed Gareth in a bar next to a beautiful girl with a bleached pixie cut and ruby red lipstick. His big arms were propped up on the counter, his tattoos visible in the dim bar lighting. The girl looked dressed up for a date. Was this Roxie?

"No way," Bea gasped. "That's him? He's super hot, Maddy. And he really doesn't look that old. I'm relieved, to be honest. I thought you were into Mr. Hawkins."

"Hell no," Maddy groaned. "You really thought that?"

"Hey, I've seen your trailer. You gotta get your lunch money somehow."

"Shut up, Bea!"

Bea laughed and stuck out her tongue. "No shame! I got this follower on Picplace from Iceland. He's like 70 or something. He likes Goth girls in Lolita dresses. So I send him a few pics and he sends me funds on PayUp. That's what you need, Mads. A follower from Japan or something who's into redheads with big boobs."

"I dunno, Bea. That's kinda intense."

Maddy was barely listening. She was staring at the picture of Gareth, worry knitting her brow. The description under the pic had a bunch of kissy faces and the words, "*love this animal.*"

Maddy checked the date. "July 4th?"

"Not that long ago," Bea said, following her gaze. "Who's Roxigrl25?"

Roxie.

Maddy's stomach twisted into knots. She thought she would puke right there on the grass. So that was her. The girl who called him at Zippy's.

"Is that his ex?" Bea asked.

"I don't know. But I think I saw a missed call from her on his phone," Maddy admitted. "I'm actually not sure who she is."

"'Love this animal?' Sounds sus," Bea muttered as she read the caption on the pic. She clicked on the girl's profile. "Ugh. Limited access. Damn this bitch. Just let me stalk you!"

"Is that all you can see on her profile?"

"I'm looking now. Hold on. There's a few photos that aren't private. Oh man. This bitch works at Ladybug Coffee?" Bea laughed.

"What's that?"

Maddy saw a tagged photo of Roxie hanging out the drive-thru window of a coffee stand with a big smile.

"It's off exit 206. You know where the Black Bear Diner is? Yeah. Same parking lot. It's a drive-thru coffee stand where the barista girls all wear bikinis. My sister Becca used to work there. I wonder if they know each other? Do you want me to ask her?"

"Um, no, it's fine," Maddy rushed to say. "Just forget about it."

She felt weird prying deeper into Gareth's personal life. She wanted to hear the truth from him directly instead of snooping around behind his back. Still, the urge to play detective and poke around was strong. Roxie looked fun and sexy and outgoing. Everything Maddy wasn't. She thought of Gareth kissing Roxie's big, glossy, bubblegum lips. . . . Thought of him undressing her, feeling up her body, fucking her . . . .

Maddy thought she would be sick. It felt like cheating. Even though she had only dated him for a weekend. Technically, they were "friends" right now, not officially together. She had no real claim to him, but she still felt confused, jealous and hurt. Here she was, scared of going too fast, while Roxie had probably jumped right on board.

Part of her wanted to send Gareth a screenshot and demand an explanation. Another part of her didn't want to look crazy and desperate.

"Bea," she said, her voice catching, "last Friday night, Gareth and I went on a date. And, uh, Roxie called him. I don't think he knows that I know. But I saw her name pop up on his phone. I thought it was weird."

"Dang. So they're still talking?" Bea sounded unimpressed. "Look, you gotta protect yourself, Maddy. These older guys think they're smarter than us. Just remember: boys are dumb. Always. We're the smart ones. Now you know about Roxie. So when do you see him again?"

"Um, probably Wednesday. We're meeting up after school."

"Alright. When you see him again, ask him what's up. Who is this bitch? Are they fucking? Cuz you don't play games. Then you tell me what you find out. I wanna know, too."

Maddy nodded, borrowing some of Bea's sassy determination.

"Yeah. Alright. I will, Bea. Thanks for the advice."

"Anytime, kitten."

They hugged. Bea scratched Maddy's back with her long claws.

Bea handed her a cigarette, and Maddy took a drag. She tried not to imagine Gareth with the Ladybug barista and her spunky pixie haircut. She could never measure up to someone like that. She had way too many hang-ups and problems.

"Don't look so down, Maddy!" Bea exclaimed, noticing her gray mood and dour expression. "Don't let this Roxie chick get under your skin. You're, like, a unicorn."

"A unicorn?"

"Yeah. Like a super-rare wonderbitch. How many girls got that skater vibe, all laid back, with giant porno titties and still a virgin? This guy is lucky you're even looking at his Picplace account right now."

"Please don't call me 'porno titties.'"

"Sorry, but you know what I mean."

Maddy blinked at Bea again. She hadn't ever thought of herself that way. A unicorn? Her life was such a mess, and she had so many problems, she struggled to comprehend why Gareth might be into her. Was it really because she wore Converse sneakers and had giant boobs?

No way. Their connection went much deeper than that.

But maybe not, if he was still talking to Roxie.

"So you guys haven't had sex yet. Have you done anything at all? Like how serious is this?" Bea asked.

Maddy turned pink again. She thought of her evening on Gareth's couch, how he had touched her with such dexterity and skill. How his hands brought her to multiple orgasms. How she had begged him for sex, but he turned her down. She had almost forgotten that exquisite humiliation.

"We got to second base. I wanted to have sex. I kind of threw myself at him," she lamented.

"He turned you down? Is he insane?"

"I'm a virgin, so he didn't want to rush in all fast. He said I could get hurt."

Bea looked skeptical. Maddy felt embarrassed.

"Either he's really into you, or the virgin thing scared him off."

"Why would being a virgin scare him off?"

"You don't know? Jeez, you're innocent. Because virgins are clingy as hell, Maddy! Trust me. Older guys don't want to deal with that. Virgins are crazy emotional. They get super attached."

"Oh. I didn't know."

Maddy bit her lip. Bea was so confident, now Maddy was second-guessing herself. Was she clingy? She didn't know anything about relationships. She didn't have any frame of reference. And she didn't think Gareth would tell her honestly if she was bugging him.

"So guys don't like it when you're clingy?" she asked Bea.

"Fuck no. They hate it."

Maddy fumbled with the string of her sweater. Well, shit. How did she know if she was being clingy or not?

"Hey, I got an idea," Bea suggested, "Becca and I are hitting up Fright Farm this Friday. Are you free? It's at Beaumont Farms on their old plantation. Why don't you invite him along? Becca's really good at reading guys. We'll check him out for you. If he's sleazy and gross, we'll let you know. And hey, if you find out bad news about this Roxie chick, you can come hang out with us and have fun."

Maddy considered it. It sounded like a good idea. She remembered the ticket she got with her paycheck yesterday.

"The timing really works out," Maddy agreed. "I got a free ticket from work. I'd love to go with you, if that's okay."

"Haha! Of course it's okay, silly. Lighten up a bit! You sound *so excited*," Bea teased her. "I'll text you the details on Picplace. This is going to be so much fun. I love Halloween!"

Bea hooked her arm in Maddy's and leaned in close, giving her a little half-hug.

Maddy returned the hug. She had never been to a haunted house before, and Bea's excitement was contagious. "Fright Farm Haunted Manor" was famous in Jefferson County. All the cool kids went there. And now, at the late age of nineteen, she would finally get her chance.

With that thought, Maddy stood up and brushed off her pants. She picked up her backpack and glanced at the overcast sky. It was getting dark.

"It's been fun hanging out, Bea, but I gotta get home," she said.

"Yeah. I should do homework," Bea agreed. "Senior year is taking too long, I'm so done. Hey though, I'll see you this Friday? Don't bail on me."

"Yeah, text me. I'll see you at school."

Bea made a little cat paw with her long nails. Maddy waved back. Then she jumped off the swing and started down the side yard.

Chapter 16

That night around 10pm, Maddy finished brushing her teeth. Then she picked up her phone and stared at Gareth's number. She hadn't heard from him since that morning. She wondered what he was doing. She tried to picture him at his house, maybe sitting on his couch in front of his bigass TV watching an old western movie, fresh out of the shower. Or maybe he was at the gym. Or maybe he was asleep. Ugh. She really shouldn't be thinking about him this much.

Dean and his friends were still out on the deck smoking cigarettes and gabbing, just like she had done with Bea after school. Except Dean's friends would keep it up all night, getting louder and louder as the beer flowed. They wanted to see the bullet hole in the wall. They cracked open beers and listened to Dean's concocted version of the break-in and the wolf attack. He loved telling stories. Nevermind he wasn't home when it happened.

Since getting home, she had been preoccupied with thoughts of Roxie. A jealous, hard knot had formed in her stomach. She even checked Picplace again to stalk Gareth's profile. So eight years ago, he was in Iraq. She stared at that photo a lot. He didn't have his tattoos, but his arms were just as big, and the gun even bigger. There was a lot she didn't know about him yet.

He had a few pics after that, mostly car stuff. The pic with Roxie was one of three tagged photos. The others were random graphics for events in Arizona from years ago.

She felt like an idiot. If she had checked him out on Picplace sooner, she would have known about his *other girl*.

She sighed. It was no use. She couldn't ignore the Roxie situation. She needed to talk to him about it. The hard knot in her stomach wouldn't let her relax. How is she supposed to sleep with all this anxiety? Her head was practically spinning. She needed to get her truth out.

She thought of Bea's advice. With a bit of courage, she started texting. She rewrote the text several times. Reread it. Deleted it.

Finally, after several minutes, she sent the longest text message she had ever written in her life. It filled up her phone screen:

> hey so I'm having second thoughts

> I don't think we should talk to each other anymore

> I know we said we would be friends and go slow

> But I don't think you've been honest with me

> I don't want to be your side piece

She wondered if he would have the balls to reply. Or if he was even awake. She tucked her phone into her pocket. Then she finished in the bathroom and crossed back to her bedroom. Joker was lying on the floor in the hallway and thumped her tail when she saw her. Maddy scratched her ears. Then she went into her small, dark room and laid down in bed. She slipped under her light blue comforter. The bed was chilly from the cold mountain air. It would take a moment to warm up from her body heat. She closed her eyes determinedly. It was time to go to sleep and forcefully empty her mind.

Then her phone buzzed.

> can we talk?

Maddy stared at his text for a long moment. It was not what she expected. She didn't really know what to say. Her heart started to pound in her chest.

> I'm tired and I'm kinda done talking right now

alright

But maybe i can clear some things up

Maddy took a deep breath. She didn't know how to have this conversation. But she didn't think she could sleep without laying the Roxie thing to rest.

okay we can talk

Her phone started to vibrate. He was calling her. Shit. This was hard.

Maddy picked up, unsure of what to expect.

"Hey," she said.

"Hey."

Gareth cleared his throat. It sounded like he was chewing on something and had just swallowed. Was he eating dinner? She heard a paper bag rustle, and the clang of his metal trashcan lid opening and closing. She suddenly imagined him standing over his kitchen sink, munching on a sandwich. Had he just got home from work? Was he working this late?

"Are you eating dinner?" she asked.

"Yeah, just got home. You all tucked in?"

"Yeah."

She still wasn't used to hearing his voice over the phone. It sounded even deeper and more guttural than in person. It made her skin tingle.

"Good," he said. "So why you calling yourself my side piece?"

Maddy struggled to stay composed. She needed to speak coherently, not just garbled up emotional nonsense, no matter how much she wanted to unload.

"My friend Bea and I checked you out on Picplace. I saw the pic from 4th of July."

"What?" Gareth asked. He sounded confused. "I'm never on there. What 4th of July pic?"

"It was at some bar. And . . . I saw the missed calls on your phone at Zippy's. I know about Roxie." A lump formed in her throat. She struggled past it. "She looks like a lot of fun. And like, probably more your age. So. You should date her. Just forget about me. It's not cool you strung me along like you did. Like, thanks for all the help. You really saved my life after the break-in. But you don't have to keep after me like this. I get it."

Gareth was quiet. Maddy had no idea what he was thinking. She wondered if he was going to hang up the phone. She kinda wanted to hang up before he got a chance to respond. This was agonizing.

"Alright," he finally said. "I'm on Picplace but I can't see the picture. I don't know how this app works."

Maddy rolled her eyes. "Like does it really matter?"

"I want to know what pic you're looking at."

"Why, are there more you're trying to hide?"

"No, Mads. I'm not trying to hide anything."

He paused for another long moment.

"Fuck it," he muttered. "Look, forget the app. I haven't seen Roxie since the 4th of July. Yeah, we went to a bar. What do you want to know?"

"Are you still seeing her?"

"No."

"Is she your ex?"

"Not really."

"What does that mean?"

"We never dated. We just . . . kept it casual."

"So she's a fuck buddy?"

Gareth sighed. "Yeah. A fuck buddy, I guess. I don't like calling people that. We just messed around a few times."

Maddy didn't know how she felt about that. She was still a virgin. Sex was still a big deal to her.

"So you were just friends?" Maddy pointed out. "Kind of like us?"

"No, nothing like us, Mads."

"Bea thinks you're still fucking around with her."

"Who's Bea?"

"She's my friend. So like, do you have a lot of different girls you hookup with? Are you a player?"

"No, Mads, that's Hollywood. I'm not like that. Roxie knew it wasn't anything. I told her that upfront."

Maddy bit her lip. She closed her eyes for a moment and took a breath. She could sense Gareth's frustration over the phone. She could almost see him run his hand through his hair. He let out a deep breath.

"What we got is different, Mads. Roxie never came over to my house, or my garage, or met Vin. I offered for you to move into my house to get away from Dean. That's more than I'd ever do for Roxie or anyone else. I get that you need to go slow and just be friends right now. But that doesn't change . . . *anything* . . . between us."

Maddy bit her lip. Damn. He was making sense. But this was hard.

"So you're not seeing her?" She repeated.

"No. I cut things off."

"She called your phone that night at Zippy's," Maddy pointed out. "So I guess you didn't cut her off that well."

Gareth sighed. "Yeah, well. It's been months. I didn't expect her to call. It was bad timing."

"How do I know you're telling me the truth?" she asked.

"I don't know, Mads. You gotta trust me. Why would I lie to you?"

Maddy took a breath. Trust was not her strong suit. She had to take him at his word until she got to know him better. But that was hard for her to do.

Her mind returned to Roxie and she tried to stave off another surge of jealousy. Maddy remembered that 4th of July holiday from earlier in the year. She had worked that day and earned double-time. Then she walked home, watching the fireworks blast off over Black River High's football field. She was exhausted, but grateful for the money.

So that very night, he had fucked some girl? It didn't seem fair.

"How long were you two together?" she asked quietly.

"We weren't 'together' like that. We hooked up a few times—"

"For how long?"

"I don't know. Six months? Off and on? I didn't see her a lot."

Maddy tried to remain calm. "That's a long time. Six months sounds pretty serious to me."

"Well, it wasn't. I cut things off when she tried to get closer."

Maddy gnawed on her lips. "Right. What about now? Is she still calling you?"

"She texted this morning, but I blocked her number."

Maddy sat for a moment and processed everything.

Gareth's voice was calm and patient. "Look, Mads, I know we've had this . . . *thing* between us for goddamn ever, but I couldn't do anything. You were too young. You get that, right?"

Maddy had never heard him speak like that before. *You were too young. You get that, right?* She felt her hands tremble slightly on the phone. Yeah, she was too young, and his explanation made sense, but that didn't make it easier for her to trust him.

"You get that, right, babygirl?" he repeated. "You were too young."

"Yeah," she said softly.

He pressed her, "You probably felt like you had dibs on me this whole time. Right?"

"Yeah," she said. "Yeah, I did. I guess."

She heard the grin in his voice. "Well, I'm all yours now. I don't have time for two women. That garage is my life. I mean it. Roxie and I had nothing serious. You're my first girlfriend in a long time."

Maddy wavered. "Girlfriend? It's too fast, Gareth. We're still figuring that out."

"Sure we are."

"How long since you last dated anyone?" she asked.

"I don't know. Six years?"

So, he hadn't dated anyone since before he moved to Black River. That was a long time. She reminded herself that he was older than her, and sex for him probably wasn't such a big deal. Maybe the Roxie thing really wasn't serious at all. She shouldn't be surprised that he had a casual hookup. She wasn't dating Gareth six months ago. It's not like they had some secret arrangement.

Roxie booty called him last Friday night and he blocked her number. What else did she want?

I'd prefer she didn't exist at all, Maddy thought, feeling petty.

"You doin' alright over there?" Gareth asked.

Maddy realized she had fallen silent again. She wasn't used to expressing herself like this. Communication wasn't her strong suit.

"What's wrong, Mads?" he asked, softer this time.

"I . . . I want to be the only girl you think about," she said lamely.

"You are. I promise." He sounded relieved, like he had finally figured out the problem. "You don't gotta worry about Roxie. I never think about her. She's gone, babygirl. Don't worry about that. You and me, what we got, that's something totally different. It's real. You have no idea."

Maddy clung to the phone, feeling a lump lodge in her throat. Why did he have to go and say stuff like that? He'd done more for her in the last four days than anyone had since her mom died.

"I'm sorry—" she started.

"Don't apologize. You did nothing wrong."

"Yeah but . . . I checked your phone at Zippy's without telling you. That's, like, not cool."

"I don't care about that, Mads. Just so long as you're alright."

Maddy heard her stepfather's heavy footsteps pounding down the hallway as he went to the bathroom. She shrank down beneath her covers. Her pulse quickened. She didn't want Dean to overhear her on the phone. If he caught her talking to Gareth, she was scared of what he might do. Probably break her phone or throw it in the river.

"What is it?" Gareth asked again.

"It's my stepdad. Hold on."

Gareth paused. Then he said, "You sound scared."

"I just don't want him to hear us on the phone."

Maddy turned her volume way down. Her bedroom door was almost directly across from the bathroom. She heard her stepdad pause outside her door for a bit longer than seemed necessary. Was he listening? This was totally new Dean behavior. Since when did he give a damn about anything she did?

"I have to hang up," she whispered softly into the phone. "I'll text you." Then she ended the call before Gareth could answer.

She waited for a breathless moment, hoping her stepdad hadn't overheard her little whisper into the phone. Then she heard the bathroom door open and close. The fan turned on. She sighed.

Her phone pinged. Gareth was texting her.

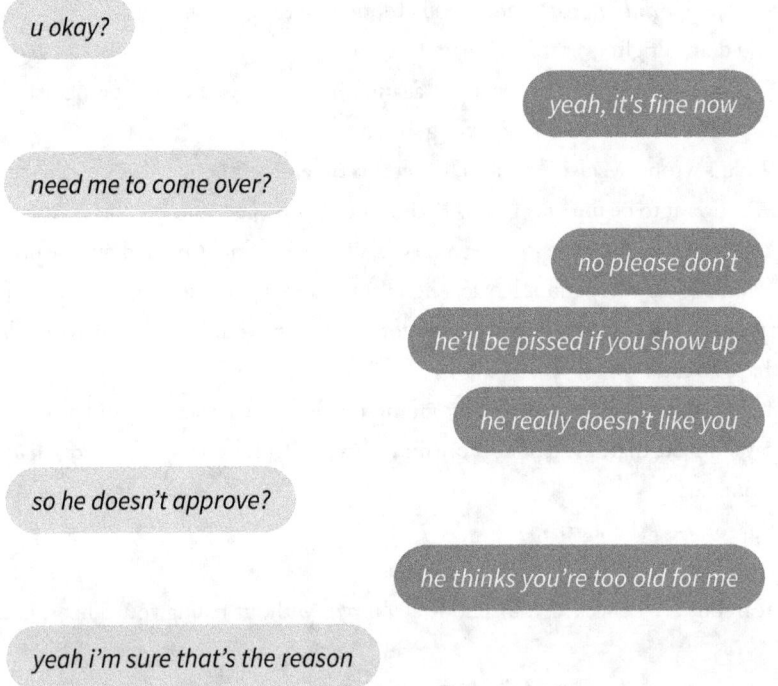

Maddy sighed. If she told Gareth about Dean's threat, "*if I catch you talking to that guy again, I'll knock you into next week,*" he would probably lose his shit. She could see that situation quickly escalating.

Sorry i didn't trust you

stop apologizing, you're fine

It's all good

you still wanna do the driving lesson?

Maddy stared at the text in surprise. She blinked. She hadn't considered canceling the lesson. Though if the Roxie conversation had gone differently, she might have.

yeah for sure

I'll pick you up from school at 3pm tomorrow

usual spot

bring your permit

The usual spot? They had a usual spot? She put the phone down for a moment and tried not to "*squee*" quietly into her blanket.

Then her phone pinged again:

you should go to bed. It's late.

Maddy chewed her lip. Part of her wanted to tell him to fuck off. But it was nice, actually, having someone take the reins and tell her what to do for a change. It gave her a sense of relief. She wasn't doing everything alone. With the whole Roxie thing sorted out, she felt closer to him than before. She hadn't realized how much those phone calls at Zippy's were hanging over her head.

ok I will

good girl

Chapter 17

Gareth didn't exactly love running a car garage. He liked working on cars and fixing things, sure. But *running* a business? He didn't really have the head for it. He wasn't into sales. He didn't network or try to sling his services at everyone he met. He still had the stack of business cards he ordered four years ago in his desk drawer.

His primary means of getting business was the highway right outside the door. You never knew what kind of people were going to blow in day by day. Some neighbors had accounts from way back before he owned Jack's Auto Repair. They even remembered "Jack," who ran the place some ten odd years ago. Gareth didn't know the guy. "Jack" had sold the place to Stewart Markham, who couldn't turn a profit or fix a car. Then Stewart sold the place to Gareth in a desperate bid to get out of debt *and* out of town.

Gareth thought he had turned the place around in the four years or so that he had owned it. When he first decided to stay in Black River, he got a job as a maintenance tech for an HVAC company. He worked that gig until he earned enough to buy a car. Then he got the VA loan for the business and bought the garage. His mom fronted the money for the downpayment on the house. He kept promising to fly her out to visit. But he hadn't shared his new address yet with anyone in his family. He liked to keep his life separate. Mainly because wolves were territorial, and once he opened that floodgate, his brothers would come to Black River and probably try to stake a claim. They wouldn't like seeing him with something nice they couldn't share.

It was Wednesday morning, about 7am. Garage didn't open until 9am, but he was sitting in his cramped office trying to get his accounts all sorted in Quickbooks. He was a few weeks behind tallying up expenses and charges and invoices and billing. He needed an accountant, but he didn't want to hire anyone.

Somewhere out on the garage floor, he heard Vin blasting away some suped up EDM music while he finished the last few vehicles. The kid came in early; he'd been working since 5am, or at least, that was the punch-in on his timecard.

Gareth sat back from the computer with a sigh. He took a moment to sip his coffee and run a hand over his tired eyes. Then he stared at the edge of his desk, where just two days ago, he had wrapped Maddy up in his arms and kissed her senseless. She wanted to *go slow*. How was he supposed to do that, when every muscle in his body wanted to pounce?

It took all of his self control to hold back. He wanted her badly. She was his lifemate; her scent called to him; she lit a fire in his blood. His wild nature yearned to claim her. Honestly, fucking her senseless would solve a lot of problems.

First, she'd get attached. She might be scared of it, but he liked the thought of her being all clingy and needy with him. He wanted that. Then she'd think twice before pulling that "friends" crap again.

Second, it meant he could fuck her twice. And he would. Immediately after he spilled into her the first time, he would make love to her again and again. He could feel his shaft swelling at the thought of it. He couldn't wait to hear her little noises as he emptied into her sweet womb. And he had a feeling she would enjoy it very much. She wanted him, too. He knew that with certainty. She was just scared of getting close.

Third, he would finally make her submit—show her the Alpha wolf. That urge was overpowering, especially after their little fight. He wanted to bend her over his desk and thrust into her from behind, doggy style. Ride her until her mind broke, until she forgot her own name, until she was sloppy and incoherent from pleasure. He would pin her down and take her with long, deep thrusts, marking her body with his own. Then she would know where she belonged: beneath him.

If he had to drag her out of that mobilehome by the nape of her neck, he would.

He wasn't going to let Dean lay another hand on her.

The "friends" thing was total bull.

He stretched out his back in his office chair. He put his arms behind his head. Undid his ponytail. Shook out his hair. Then wrapped it up again in a messy bun at the base of his neck. He glanced at the cell phone on his desk.

He would check in with her again in a few hours. Make sure she got to school okay. Any other girl, he wouldn't be concerned. But Maddy was a special case. She needed the extra.

Gareth turned off his computer. He cracked his neck and stood up. He hated staring at monitors.

"Vin!" he yelled as he came out of his office. He looked around the garage. "Vin! Turn that shit down!"

The pounding EDM music suddenly stopped. "What's up, boss?"

"You done with the Ford truck? It's getting picked up at noon."

"Yeah, it's ready." Vin tossed him the keys.

"I'll move it to the back lot," Gareth said.

Gareth picked up a few empty oil cans on his way out and tossed them in the big trash barrel in front of the garage. The truck Vin finished earlier was temporarily parked in the front driveway while they worked on a different vehicle.

Gareth grabbed the keys to move the truck to the locked car lot behind the garage. He needed to get better security. He had two security cameras on the lot and a floodlight, but anyone could climb over the fence. He was holding off hiring a security guard, but if business picked up again next year, he might have one just for the summer. He wondered how much that would cost in wages. Ugh. It all made his head hurt.

He climbed out of the old Ford and locked the door. Then the wind shifted and he smelled something strange and unfamiliar coming from the forest. The hairs on the back of his neck prickled. He frowned, sniffing again, wondering if he was imagining it. Then he heard the crunch of boots running across the dirty, pebbly asphalt.

He started to turn when something hit him from behind.

Oof!

With a grunt, Gareth was dealt a stinging blow to his back, right between the shoulder blades. He fell forward onto the truck and caught himself against the door. He saw the reflection of his attacker behind him in the truck window. He ducked as a metal pipe came swinging at his head. Crash! The window shattered. Shards of glass went flying. Gareth threw up his arm and spun away, trying to get some space between him and the crazy motherfucker with the pipe.

"What the *fuck?*" Gareth roared.

He turned to face his attackers. Two men were on him at the same time. A few others hung back in a loose circle in the car lot. The first thug with the metal pipe was tall and skinny. The bigger, burlier one had a knife. He saw the man's sharp, jagged blade glint in the floodlight from the back of the building. Shit. It wasn't just a box cutter or a pocket knife. It was a hefty Rambo-looking hunting knife with serrated edges.

The gang of thugs had women's pantyhose covering their faces to hide their identities. They looked like bank robbers. He thought for a moment that they were thieves trying to steal a car from the back lot, but that didn't make sense. Why show up in the morning, when the garage was just opening?

That, and their scent was unmistakable. They were wolves.

"Really? You gonna wear women's underwear to come at me?" he said. "The fuck. Take that shit off. Who are you?"

"You fucked up. Messed with the wrong pack," the biggest one said with the Rambo knife. The guy was built like a big-rig truck with a voice that smoked a pack a day. He must be six and a half feet tall. Every visible inch of skin was covered in tattoos. He looked straight outta prison, if Gareth had to guess. He sniffed the air, catching a whiff of the man's strong wolf-stench. Not an Alpha. So he must be their Beta.

Gareth's eyes narrowed. "So what? This an execution?"

The big one pointed the jagged Rambo knife at him threateningly.

"You killed my brother. So yeah. That's exactly what this is."

Oops.

He wasn't surprised. These goons were from the same pack that had attacked Maddy's trailer. The same pack that had come after Dean. He had gone a little overboard that night in the woods, and killed all of the men who had tried to rape Maddy. They were werewolves, so it didn't seem quite as serious of a crime. The laws of the wild were different for their kind. Anyway, of course their pack would want revenge. It was only a matter of time before they came after him.

Gareth reached into his back pocket where he carried a pair of brass knuckles. He slipped them onto his fist. *No time like go time,* he thought. Then, with a deep growl, he rushed the smaller guy with the pipe. He blocked a swing aimed for his head and struck the little asshole across the face. Something cracked. A spray of blood misted the air. The skinny man fell to the ground with a high-pitched scream.

The group of wolves started to move. Another man rushed at him from across the lot with a wild howl. He was swinging a big rusty hammer. Gareth kicked the hammer out of his hand and caught the man in the throat with another deft punch. His opponent stumbled back with a choking sound, clutching his throat, his eyes bulging. He collapsed next to his friend, wheezing and grappling at his neck.

"Who else wants a taste?" Gareth said angrily.

He turned to face the mob, kicking the pipe away under the truck as he did so. The big one—Rambo—stood at the fore of the group. The lesser wolves hung back, waiting for a signal from their Beta. They looked less certain now. Probably weren't expecting someone who could kick ass.

"Who are you?" Rambo spat.

"Wouldn't you like to know," Gareth growled.

He hoped none of them had brought a gun. He didn't think so, because they would've used it by now. Guns were easy to trace, and a bullet raised more questions than a guy getting beat to death in a car lot.

"Took ya'll long enough to find me," he said when no one moved. "Where ya'll been? That trailer's only two miles from here. Your Alpha must be pretty dumb."

"Big words for a lone wolf. We've been watching you all week. Marquis owns this area. You're out of your league."

"Who the fuck is Marquis?"

Another wolf piped up from the party in the back: "Alpha of the Grayridge Pack. We own every county between here and Canada, and we're gonna take this one too."

"Shut the fuck up, Steve," Rambo growled.

The smaller wolf who'd been talking went quiet.

"Doesn't matter who Marquis is," Rambo said. "You're a dead man."

With a nod of his head, they all rushed him at once.

The first one to reach him, Gareth clocked in the jaw with an uppercut that sent blood spattering across the side of the Ford truck. He went down like a pile of bricks.

Then a second goon jumped on his back. Gareth twisted, using his krav maga training from the Army. He was a little rusty. His muscles bulged in his arms and chest as he grabbed the man in a headlock and threw him over his shoulder, body slamming him against the hood of the truck. The man's head cracked back on the metal hood and he went limp. Fuck. Gareth hoped he wasn't dead—murder was illegal—but these wolves were trying to kill *him*.

Gareth turned fast. Rambo was on him like an avalanche. The knife whizzed past his torso, barely missing him by an inch, to scrape across the hood of the car. Sparks flew. Paint scratched. Dang. That would be expensive to fix.

Gareth grabbed Rambo by the wrist, engaging him head on. He shoved the giant wolf backward against the truck, keeping the knife far away from his face. He delivered two quick punches to the man's gut, driving the brass knuckles deep into his abdomen. Rambo didn't seem phased. He shoved Gareth back and then fell on top of him, trying to stab the knife into his stomach.

Gareth crashed to the ground, dragging the big guy with him. He twisted around, trying to grab him in a headlock.

Rambo put up a good fight. The big bastard was prison strong. If this was some skirmish in the prison yard, he might have had more luck. But Gareth was not just a regular wolf. He was Arizona royalty. Alpha blood. And he was his father's son. That made him stronger, crazier, and meaner than any fucktard with a knife.

With a roar of adrenaline, Gareth pried the man off him, flipped him, and hooked his arm around Rambo's corded neck. He locked him in a stranglehold, squeezing the air out of him.

Rambo dropped the knife and started clawing at Gareth's arms. His nails turned into claws that dug deep and tore up Gareth's skin, ripping into his flesh.

Gareth felt blood trickling down his forearms to his wrists, but he did not let go.

Out of the corner of his eye, he saw the two remaining wolves circling around. One reclaimed the metal pipe from under the truck. They prowled forward, waiting for their chance to bash in his head.

It didn't look good. Damn. Maybe he'd have to kill these fuckers after all.

"AAAGH!"

With a roar, Vin flew onto the scene swinging a crowbar. He came out of nowhere, dropping from the sky like a bat out of hell. He came up behind the two remaining goons, swinging the iron bar with two fists.

Thwack! He hit one of the thugs in the back of the head, and caught the other one across the knees. They both fell down, howling and moaning.

Then Vin turned to Gareth, the crowbar held high. His face was flushed and his eyes were wild. He looked a little crazy. He started wailing on the guy locked in Gareth's grip. He struck him in the gut, then the balls, then the knees.

"Shit!"

Gareth jumped up before Vin hit him, too. He shoved the big bastard away and stood up, backing off from Vin's swinging crowbar.

"Vin, ease up!"

He grabbed Vin's arm before he went too far. He applied pressure to a point on his forearm that forced him to drop the iron bar.

"Ow!" Vin yelped. "Fuck, why'd you do that?"

"To stop you from committing a goddamn felony!"

As they yelled at each other, the pack of wolves scrambled to their feet and ran off. The big one was limping and clutching his nutsack. The scattering of smaller ones chased after him, leaving a trail of blood behind.

Gareth watched them go. They sprinted across the parking lot, setting off motion detector lights as they went.

"Better get the fuck outta here!" Vin yelled after them. "Now what? We can't just let them get away!"

Vin danced on his feet, looking ready for a fight, but also cagey as hell.

"Fuck, boss. You got tore up good."

Gareth glanced down at his bloody forearms. Cuts and gashes left by the Beta's claws ran from his elbows to his wrists. He sighed. More cuts to cover the tattoos that covered his scars.

"Well?" Vin repeated. "What should we do?"

"Forget 'em," Gareth muttered. "Unlock the doors. We're open for business, Vin."

"For real?"

"Yup. For real."

Then he winced. He rolled his shoulders experimentally. His back was sore between his shoulder blades where the metal pipe had hit him.

"You okay boss?" Vin asked.

"Just that fucking metal pipe. Damn."

Gareth half grimaced, half bared his teeth. Now that his adrenaline was wearing off, he was beginning to feel every bump and bruise where those assholes landed a blow. It was not pleasant. He took a moment to breathe and clear his head. Adrenaline coursed through him, making him wild and angry. He could see his breath rising in little clouds of vapor.

"Let's start the day, Vin," he repeated. "We got customers coming to pick up cars at 9am."

"Alright, boss."

Together, they started walking back to the garage. Vin picked up the crowbar and walked next to Gareth closely, his head turning this way and that. He looked jumpy and excited.

"We really showed them, huh? That was crazy. With the crowbar? Like, I saved your life. I want a raise!"

"You're really going to ask me for a raise now?" Gareth growled.

"Well, I mean . . ." Vin looked suddenly nervous. "If not, it's cool. I'm just sayin'."

"I'll think about it," Gareth grunted.

"We need, like, better security or something. Like an alarm system. They broke the window on the Ford. What are we gonna do about that?"

"We're gonna wash that fucking blood off the truck before anyone sees it," Gareth said. "Then you're gonna make a very nice phone call to the owner to explain what happened. Vandalism. Probably a bunch of meth heads looking for parts to sell. Then we're gonna replace the window for free."

"What? Me? Why do I have to make the call?"

"I thought you wanted a raise."

"Man!"

Vin whined the rest of the way through the parking lot. At the entrance, Gareth stopped for a moment to close up the gate. He wrapped the heavy chain around the bars and closed the padlock. Ugh. His arms were throbbing. He was ready to go home, but the hardest thing about owning a business was that he had to be the boss.

He headed to the unisex bathroom next to his office. It was a surprisingly large restroom for the size of the shop. It even had a shower stall and an eyewash station. He kept a hefty first aid kit in one of the metal storage cabinets, thanks to all the nicks and cuts they got on the job. Time to clean up these gashes before they got infected. Human nails and wolf claws were fucking disgusting. Luckily the cuts were shallow.

As he walked through the shop and got the first aid kit out in the bathroom, he thought about the brief skirmish. Attempted execution, rather. It pissed him off. So the Grayridge Pack had finally found him. At least he had a name now for the pack and their Alpha.

He wanted to know their numbers. They might have a broad territory, but most of the counties between Black River and Canada were farmland or forest. They might be backwater strong, but that didn't mean they were a match for the Phoenix Pack.

These goons obviously didn't know who Gareth was. If they did, they probably wouldn't have swung a metal pipe at his head.

Or who knows, maybe they want a war.

He didn't know how much sway his father's name held this far from Arizona. Phoenix was a harsh place, and the Phoenix Pack was the largest in the Southwest since the LA empire fractured and broke apart. His family controlled one of the five largest wolf-kingdoms in the U.S., or at least, they did last he checked the reddit boards. He didn't know where they stood now. It had been a few years. But he doubted a lot had changed.

These fuckers wanted to kill him. That put him in a shit mood. He liked his life in Black River, and he didn't want to leave. That meant he needed to become such a pain in the ass, they left him alone.

Did he tell his family about this? Did he involve them in this conflict? It meant opening a whole new can of worms.

What about Maddy? Did the Grayridge Pack know about her yet? They hadn't mentioned her, so maybe they didn't realize she was a female wolf. If they did, they would snap her up in a heartbeat and use her as mating stock. It was the sad condition of their kind.

He needed to protect her.

He needed to make sure she was okay.

He needed to check on her.

Gareth left the sink in the break room and walked into his office, where his phone was sitting on the desk. He unlocked the screen, ignoring the bit of blood still leaking down his arm from the cuts. He reasoned she was alright. But he had to be sure. It was after 8am. He selected her name from his texting contacts: Mads. Then he typed out his message and hit send.

> *u in class?*

He waited for her to respond. It was agonizing.

> *yes, dad*

He grinned. Or bared his teeth. Something like that.

> *don't be a brat*

> *see u after school*

With sudden inspiration, he opened up her Contact info and changed her name from "Mads" to "Brat." Fuck. Making him feel old. Someday he was going to spank that ass.

He shut off his phone's screen and slipped it in his pocket.

If they came after Maddy, heads were gonna roll.

Chapter 18

That morning, Gareth texted her just after 8am, while she was sitting in homeroom trying to wake up.

you in class?

yes, dad

don't be a brat

see u after school

Maddy paused, reading his text. She sighed. She was nervous about the driving lesson. And even more nervous about seeing him again. But she felt a lot better after sorting out the whole Roxie thing over the phone last night. And his allusion to their past history stayed on her mind.

He still hadn't told her why he started helping her on the mountain. She had asked back at his place, the same night she showed him her scars. He had made up some story about being a wolf without a pack. *Lobo loco.* It wasn't really an answer. But the fact remained, this "thing" between them had been building *for-fucking-ever.*

She remembered the first time she had caught sight of his face. When she had first noticed how handsome he was. It was maybe two months after their first meeting. It was a hot, humid summer night. Crickets chirped under the back porch. Owls hooted in the trees. The forest was full of noise. She wore cotton shorts and a thin, loose nightshirt. She was walking along her favorite trail through the woods.

Dean had taken a swipe at her. He was a lot more violent back then, and she was a lot more vulnerable. She flew out the back door before he could catch her and leave a bruise. In bare feet, she ran down the side of the mountain, skidding through soft dirt and mossy grass. Eventually, she found a familiar trail that ran along the side of a stream, through a thicket of paperbark birch trees.

It was a clear, warm night. The moon was full. She followed the trail to where it ended at the banks of the Black River. She remembered standing next to a dead fir tree, staring at the moon's reflection in the dark, swirling water. For a moment, she considered throwing herself into the river. The current was fast and deadly. She wondered how long it would take for her body to sink to the bottom. How would it feel, to have the icy water embrace her and put an end to this hell? She wondered if her mother was waiting for her on the "other side." Did people who commit suicide go to heaven? Or maybe there was no afterlife, and her body would just return to nature, to the natural cycle of things. Becoming nothing at all seemed better than living through this pain. Every day was agony. She just wanted the pain to stop.

She remembered climbing on top of a big rock next to the river, where she gaged the water's black depths, wondering if she had the balls to do it.

It took her a moment to realize she wasn't alone. Something moved out of the corner of her eye, and she glanced up. She saw him standing across the river from her, watching her silently.

She was scared at first, but then she recognized him. She wiped the tears from her cheeks. She was too scared to talk to him. He seemed to notice her distress and forded the stream, walking along the big fallen fir tree like a bridge. He approached the rock where she was standing.

"You lost?" He asked when he reached her side. Even now, she remembered the manly baritone of his voice.

She shrugged. "Sort of."

She gazed up at him curiously, squinting through the moonlight. She remembered the angular shape of his face. When she first met him, he looked like a homeless hitchhiker, but now he was clean shaven. He wore fresh clothes and his face looked younger than she expected. She noted his gaunt cheeks and strong jawline, the cleft in his chin, his straight nose and arched, black eyebrows. He was . . . *handsome.*

He folded his arms and leaned on one hip. "So what're you doing out here so late? You gonna jump in the river?"

It was like he could read her mind.

"No," she said. "No, that's dumb."

"You're right. It's pretty dumb."

His eyes wandered over her face down to her bare feet, taking in her loose cotton pajamas. He seemed as curious about her as she was about him. But if he had more questions, he didn't ask anything else.

"Follow me. I'll take you home."

That was the second time they met. It was July or August, a few months before she turned fifteen. The vision of his face stayed with her after that night. When she was out on the mountains, she always looked for him. He didn't always show up. But often enough, they would encounter each other on the mountainside under the moonlight. They didn't have long conversations, but he would walk with her for a ways. He would lead her back home.

And now he was her driving instructor.

She felt a little shiver of anticipation. She texted him back.

> yeah I'll see you at 3

The day flew by. She spent her lunch in the Admin Office in a special room for kids serving detention. After school, Maddy stood outside on the sidewalk, her backpack slung casually over one shoulder. It was just past 3pm. The sky might be blue, but the wind was bitterly cold.

Maddy shoved her hands into her pockets. She started down the crowded sidewalk, jostled to and fro by her peers. The basketball team ran past her on their mandatory 5 mile route. She checked her phone but didn't see a text. She assumed Gareth was going to pick her up at the same place he had dropped her off last Thursday, just outside the Admin Office.

As she neared the usual place, she saw two things that made her heart sink. First, Gareth wasn't there, and it crossed her mind that he wasn't coming. She couldn't silence the tiny, evil voice at the back of her mind that taunted her: *"He's going to ghost you."*

Then she saw Kaylee Mackovich and the Bitch Crew sauntering down the sidewalk. She recognized two of the girls from Zippy's. Annoyed, Maddy pulled up her hood and tried to make herself invisible. But it was impossible. They were walking straight toward her.

She braced herself for a confrontation.

The varsity jackets walked past her, then they slowed down a little. One of the girls elbowed another, and they turned to stare at Maddy. They stopped. Kaylee turned with them, but she had her phone out and she was texting someone. She acted like Maddy didn't exist. The other girls noticed her, though. The one that reminded Maddy of a black Barbie doll sneered. Maddy tried to remember her name. Was it Amy? She had blond braids woven into her thick, beautiful black hair. She wore bright blue eyeshadow, and she had full glossy lips. Maddy tried not to feel a little jealous of her perfect complexion.

"I heard you got detention for bringing condoms to school," Barbie sneered.

"You know those condoms weren't mine," Maddy said. "So which one of you stuffed them in my locker?"

Barbie raised an eyebrow. "I don't know what you mean."

"I can't believe you'd accuse us of that!" the short blond girl said from the rear. Then she stuffed a hand over her mouth and laughed.

Maddy rolled her eyes. "You're a terrible liar."

"We didn't do anything!" the little blond exclaimed.

"Nothing you can prove, anyway. You better watch your back. We're not even yet," Barbie snarled. "I still owe you a beat down for what you did to Adam."

"You're seriously going to beat me up? That's rich. I'd like to see you try," Maddy shot back.

Barbie took a threatening step forward. "You think you're tough shit just because you're trailer trash? I'll take you any day, slut."

A loud, rumbling engine interrupted them. Both girls turned as a classic '69 Camaro pulled up across the street. It parked along the curb, across from where they were standing. The car shut off and the door opened, and Gareth stepped out. His hair was tied back. He wore his sunglasses, a faded gray T-shirt, casual athletic-style black pants and Nike running shoes. His muscular, tatted arms were fully visible. He shoved his hands in his pockets as he started across the street.

Barbie's mouth gaped. "Kaylee, it's him! That hot guy from Zippy's!"

Kaylee's head shot up and her cheeks turned instantly pink.

"Oh my god, look at his shoulders," Girl Number Three whispered. "His tattoos are so hot! Is that a scorpion? That means he's a Scorpio, right? According to my zodiac book, they're supposed to be super temperamental and, like, *crazy* in bed.'"

"Fuck, why is he here? Where did he come from?" Black Barbie muttered. "Kaylee, is he here to see you?"

Kaylee was quiet, staring at Gareth with unnerving intensity. Maddy recognized that look. *No,* she thought. *No, no, no!* Maddy felt slightly sick. Kaylee must have a crush on Gareth, too.

Maddy stepped back from the three girls, her mind reeling. She hadn't realized her enemies would remember Gareth from Zippy's. By the expression on the girls' faces, he was definitely "a thing," and they had definitely talked about him.

She shouldn't be surprised. Apparently Kaylee's mom had hit on him, too. Gareth was probably the hottest guy in Black River. Still, it left her with a sour pit in her stomach.

Gareth caught sight of them. He started toward Maddy.

"He's coming over here," Barbie said.

"Is he coming to talk to you, Kaylee?" Girl Number Three said in awe. "Maybe he remembers you from last Friday. I mean, of course he remembers you!"

Kaylee straightened up a little and tossed her hair to one side. For a moment, she had an expectant look on her face, like she fully thought Gareth would breeze by Maddy, swoop up to her and ask for her number. Kaylee was super hot. She was probably used to guys approaching her that way.

But Gareth ignored her, of course. He reached Maddy's side and stood in front of her on the street. Even a step down from the sidewalk, he was a few inches taller than her.

If he saw Kaylee and the Varsity jackets, he didn't acknowledge them.

Maddy met Gareth's hazel eyes. She hadn't seen him in a few days, and for a moment, she had forgotten just how good looking he was. It was strange seeing him here outside the school in broad daylight. Her secret crush, her midnight hero, now just a part of everyday life.

"Hi," Maddy said, for lack of anything better.

"Hey," Gareth said with a grin.

"Yeah, hi," Kaylee added.

His eyes passed back and forth between them. Maddy was standing with a bit of space between her and the other three girls. It was pretty obvious they weren't hanging out as a group.

"Hey, what's your name?" Barbie called to him.

He completely ignored her and turned to Maddy.

"Ready to go?" he asked.

Maddy tried to keep the little smirk from her face, but it was impossible. She glanced at Kaylee, then she joined Gareth in the street. She saw the look of shock on Kaylee's face. For a blissful moment, she basked in the glory of making Kaylee Mackovich jealous. Gareth's hand touched her lower back as they started across the street. She thought he might put his arm around her, then he let his hand drop. Right. They were still just friends for the time being.

"Slut," she heard Girl Number Three hiss at her back.

Surprisingly, Gareth turned.

All three girls jumped.

"What did you say?" he said.

The Varsity Jackets all stared at Gareth with wide eyes. Kaylee looked especially pale.

"Gareth, it's fine, let's go—" Maddy started.

But he raised his big muscular arm and pointed at them. "Drop the bullshit. Dumb kids. See this girl here next to me? She's better than all you all combined. You better leave her alone, or you're gonna be hearing from me."

They blinked at him. Nobody said a word. Then Gareth turned around and put his arm around Maddy's shoulders. He guided her back across the street.

"You eaten? I got you tacos in the car."

"No, not yet." Maddy glanced down at her shoes. She didn't know what to say. "Uh, thanks for standing up for me."

"They giving you a hard time?"

"Yeah, kinda."

He opened the door for her and she got into the passenger side. She found a bag of tacos and an energy drink in the center console. He started up the engine and pulled away from the curb, then headed toward Main Street.

Maddy looked out the window as they drove away from the high school. Kaylee and the Bitch Crew were still watching her. She took a deep breath. The confrontation unnerved her a bit. She suspected the Varsity Jackets weren't done with her. Now they'd seen her twice with Gareth, and Kaylee's narrow, jealous eyes meant something bad. Kaylee wouldn't be second best, especially to Crazy Porno Titties. Despite Gareth's protection, Maddy anticipated more bullshit would be coming down the pipeline.

"You got your permit with you?" he asked.

"Yeah, it's in my backpack."

"Good."

"Where are we going?"

"I know a spot. An old rest stop up on the mountain. It has a nice empty parking lot. Perfect for a new driver."

Maddy grinned. She felt a sense of relief. She wasn't ready to tackle driving down a busy street, even if Black River only had around 1500 residents.

Gareth turned the corner. They headed toward Highway 20. Maddy ate her tacos as they passed through a few intersections in silence, the radio buzzing on Gareth's dashboard. It was tuned to a local news station. Maddy caught a crackly voice saying: *"–largest storm system in recent years predicted to hit Jefferson County as early as next week. Residents advised to stock up on fresh water and other necessities in case of mudslides or road blockages. On other news, wildlife services received the coroner's report for the mysterious deaths of five men found in the forest just outside Black River . . . report confirms a wolf most likely predator . . . so far the hunt for the man-killing wolf continues . . . ."*

Maddy glanced at the radio, then over at Gareth. He was wearing his sunglasses and his lips were set in a firm line.

"I saw a wolf up on the mountain," she said.

"Yeah?"

"Yeah. It was near my trailer. Do you think it's the same predator that killed those men?"

"Probably. Who knows? Anyway, I've been meaning to ask," Gareth said, "did you ever find out why those guys came by your place?"

"No." Maddy sighed. "I confronted Dean about it. I think he owes them money. But he denied it all. I can't force him to tell me anything."

"I see," Gareth grunted. He sounded very capable of making Dean talk. But Maddy didn't want a confrontation between the two men. She knew Gareth was a hair's breadth away from committing a felony where her stepfather was concerned.

"No one's come around the trailer, though?" Gareth asked.

"No, not when I've been home, at least."

Gareth grunted again.

Honestly, Maddy had been trying very hard not to think about it. She didn't feel very safe in the trailer, even with Joker following on her heels wherever she went. The possibility of the criminals showing up again hung over her head like a dark cloud.

Main Street turned into Highway 20, and the windy road took them up into the mountains. The Camaro sped by her driveway and her mailbox, then past the gas station and Jack's Auto Repair. They were going pretty high up.

"What happened to your arms?" Maddy asked, finally noticing the long cuts that covered Gareth's forearms.

"Banged them up on a truck. No big deal," he said.

"They look like claw marks," she pointed out.

He shrugged. "Don't worry about it. They'll heal up just fine."

Maddy stared at the cuts again. Then she glanced up at his face. She sensed there was more to the story, but she couldn't imagine why he'd lie to her about that. She sat back in her seat, chewing on her lip, wondering about the cuts on his arms and the general mystery that was Gareth Delarosa.

Chapter 19

They drove for a little while longer until Gareth pulled off the highway. The exit was obscured by big trees. Maddy saw a brown sign that read "Eagle Outlook Campground and Rest Area." The sign underneath it read "Closed for the Season."

Gareth followed the winding road through the wilderness to a large parking lot. It looked abandoned. Maddy saw a trailhead blocked off by a metal barrier. Another sign read "Campground Closed."

The parking lot was wide and spacious. No signs of people or parked cars. There was plenty of room for a new driver to get comfortable behind the wheel.

"I didn't know this was here," Maddy said, amazed.

"There's all kinds of hidden little places on this mountain," Gareth said.

He parked the car and turned to her. She jumped a little. He was so close. Over the last few days, she had forgotten what it felt like to be in his presence. His heat. His scent. The energy between them. She felt a little jittery, or maybe that was the energy drink kicking in.

"You ever driven a car before?" he asked, giving her a pointed look.

Maddy blushed, embarrassed but eager to impress him. "Yeah. Of course. Duh. Like who hasn't?"

His eyebrow went up, a look she definitely recognized. But he didn't question her. He held out his keys.

"All you," he said.

Maddy took the keys nervously. In truth, she had never sat behind the wheel of a car before, and she didn't know anything at all. This was her first time.

Then Gareth opened the car door. They both got out and traded places, so that she was behind the wheel and he was in the passenger seat. The leather was warm from his back. She felt like a creeper, but she enjoyed the residual heat.

"Pull up the seat so your feet can reach the pedals," he reminded her.

"Right. Sorry. I know that."

"No need to apologize."

She blushed as she pulled up the chair. Her legs were much shorter than his. Then she fastened her seatbelt. He made her adjust the rearview and the side mirrors until she could see her surroundings comfortably. Maddy felt nervous as she stuck the keys in the ignition.

"Alright. Show me what you got," he said.

Maddy turned the key and the engine started. She knew that much. Then she tried to put the car in Drive but nothing happened. The stick wouldn't move.

Gareth pointed down below to her feet.

"I want you to put your foot on the brake. Okay, good. Now you can change gears. Put it in Drive. That's neutral, one more. Okay, good."

He talked her through it slowly and gently. Then he made her take her foot off the brake. The car jumped forward. She braked suddenly and gasped as the seatbelt caught her weight.

"It's a big engine," he said. "It has a kick. You okay?"

"Yeah." Her hands gripped the wheel. She was a little shaken. It took her a moment to relax. He took off his sunglasses and hooked them in the neck of his washed-out gray T-shirt. Then he waited until the tension left her shoulders and she loosened her grip on the wheel. She took a deep breath, forcing herself to relax.

"Alright," he said. "Let's try again."

This time, Maddy drove in a slow circle around the lot like a limping deer. *Go. Stop. Go. Stop.* She was so nervous. Her anxiety was like a high-pitched whine in the back of her head. He encouraged her with soft words as she got used to the feeling of the car and the wheel. Then he started explaining what all the knobs on the dashboard meant: the oil, the speedometer, the engine light, the mileage.

The sound of his voice was soothing. He continued explaining to her how the starter worked, and how to tell if the battery was dead or if the starter was broken, or if the car had an engine problem. He rambled a bit. It took her mind off her anxiety, and she discovered that she liked seeing this side of him. He seemed relaxed and open. As a mechanic, he knew a lot of technical information about cars and engines that she would never remember. Still, she listened to him with her lips slightly parted, nodding at intervals and trying to follow along as the car moved forward.

Over time, she grew more confident. She pushed her foot farther and farther down on the pedal. The car rushed forward.

"Shit!" she braked again. "Sorry!" she gasped when they came to a sudden halt.

"That's okay, babygirl."

"Jeez. Don't coddle me. I can handle this," Maddy said, annoyed. She didn't know why she was irritated. Maybe because she wanted to impress him with how independent, capable and 'adulty' she was. But by now, he probably guessed she had lied about her driving experience. Which was twice as embarrassing.

"I just don't want you to freak out," Gareth said. He seemed amused by her irritation. "This is new for you. And you got that anxiety thing."

"What anxiety thing?"

"The one that gives you panic attacks."

"Yeah, well, I'm not going to have a panic attack right now."

"If you say so. Ready to go again?"

"Of course I'm ready. Don't go easy on me. I can handle it."

"Okay." His eyes flashed. "I won't go easy on you."

Maddy shivered, wondering at the private meaning of his words.

She went in a circle around the parking lot again. This time, he told her to step on the gas. The car leapt forward. He made her bring it up to twenty miles per hour as they cruised down the length of the lot. The Camaro wanted to go faster, she could feel it, but she focused on following Gareth's directions and controlling the vehicle.

Gareth was a good teacher. He was very calm and gave clear directions. After a while, as she got used to the feeling of the car, Maddy forgot to be nervous. She almost started having fun. She liked the feeling of the big car beneath her, and the little kick it gave when she accelerated. She caught herself grinning and glanced over at Gareth.

He was watching her with a half-smile on his lips, which pulled into a full grin when she met his eyes. His white teeth flashed. She felt her heart flutter. Jeez. His smile was so fucking charming.

Suddenly a squirrel shot across the parking lot. Maddy gasped and swerved, dragging the wheel to one side. She tried to hit the brakes, but she hit the accelerator instead. The Camaro shot forward. With a cry, she panicked and shut her eyes.

Gareth's hand grabbed the wheel.

"Hit the brakes!" he said.

Maddy managed to lift her foot off the accelerator and push down on the brake.

The Camaro fishtailed and skidded to a halt, coming to rest a few inches away from the edge of the lot, where a hill sloped down into the tree line. Gareth grabbed the gearshift and put the car in Park. Then he reached over and turned off the engine.

Maddy was breathing hard. She sat back, staring out the windshield at the wall of pine trees. A dim, orange sunset filtered through the thick branches, reflecting off the glass window.

The silence was deafening.

Then Gareth reached over and unfastened her seatbelt.

"You alright?" he asked.

She nodded, her heart racing. She thought she might throw up.

"Let's get out of the car. Take a breather."

"I-I'm sorry."

"For what? Nothing bad happened."

"Is the squirrel okay?"

Gareth laughed—a big, manly guffaw. Then he opened his door and got out. He looked around.

"Yeah, the little fucker is fine," he said.

He walked around to the driver's side and opened the door for her, then helped her climb out of the vehicle. Maddy's legs were shaky and her eyes were watery.

"You alright?" he asked. "You sure you're not having a panic attack? We should've brought your CBD pen."

"No, no, I'm okay," Maddy said weakly.

She felt better standing on her own two feet. Less claustrophobic. Safer. She looked behind her at the car. It sat innocently with a bit of steam rising from the hot engine.

Now she just felt embarrassed.

"I'm sorry—" she started again.

"Stop," Gareth said. "It was my fault. I distracted you. Shoulda reminded you to keep your eyes on the road."

"Shit happens fast when you're driving," Maddy muttered.

"Yup. It does." Gareth pushed his hands in his pockets and glanced up at the sky. "I say we call it quits for today. You did a good job, Mads. We got some daylight left. You wanna take a walk?"

"Yeah, sure," Maddy said. She smiled a little awkwardly. He grinned back. Then he nudged her with his arm.

"Hey, you did good," he repeated.

She let out a breath she didn't realize she was holding. Then she nodded. "Yeah. It was alright."

"Next time will be easier."

"Sure. If you'll trust me with your car again."

He snorted. "This POS? Dent it up as much as you want. I'm rehabbing it anyway."

Maddy grinned. He winked at her.

Then Gareth walked across the parking lot to the grass. The head of a walking trail opened up near the far end of the rest area. It looked like it led to the abandoned campground that Maddy had spotted earlier. Walking down forgotten trails always made her feel like she was on an adventure.

She followed Gareth onto the winding dirt path. They started into the woods. The trail hadn't been cleared in a while. She wondered how long the rest area had been closed. At least a year, she surmised, looking at the amount of ferns, grass and fallen branches obscuring the walking path. A thick layer of pine needles cushioned her feet. Birds chirped merrily in the tree branches. She saw the pesky squirrel again running up a large old pine mother, its bushy tail teasing her.

"Watch out here," Gareth said, stepping over a rather sharp, pointy tree branch.

"I see it," Maddy said.

Being in Gareth's presence, looking at his broad shoulders and muscular back from behind, made her feel safe. She was reminded again of their first meeting in the woods when she was fourteen, when he carried her back to her trailer in the middle of a summer storm. He knew the mountain well; he was an outdoorsman, she could tell. They had that in common. The woods were also her happy place.

As they walked together under the magical emerald canopy, she felt the tension leave her shoulders. She took in a deep breath of pine-scented air. A chill autumn wind brushed her cheeks. Not everyone loved the dense woods, but for her, this place was paradise.

"So how was your week?" Gareth asked as they walked.

She shrugged. "It was kinda rough. I got detention."

He turned to look at her. His gaze was surprisingly stern. Not what she expected at all. "Really? What did you do? You fightin' those girls again?" he asked.

"I didn't get into a fight," Maddy jumped to her own defense, "so you can stop looking at me like that."

"That's good. So what happened?"

She fiddled with the string on her hoodie, trying to gather her thoughts together and evade his intense gaze.

"I got three days," she admitted. "But, like, I already went to one session at lunch. I'll finish the rest this week. So it's no big deal."

Her hands trembled, giving her away. She shoved her hands into her pockets, but not before he saw through her bravado. Maddy tried to look unphased, but it was hard. It was *humiliating*. He made her feel guilty for no reason.

"Three days is a lot, Mads. We talked about this at Zippy's. Tell me honestly. Did you get into a fight?"

"No," she said. "I didn't do anything."

"Then why'd you get detention?"

"I was set up."

"Now you just sound crazy."

Maddy sighed. "The principal would agree with you. He didn't believe me either. Look, Kaylee Mackovich and her freak friends lockerbombed me. They stuffed my locker full of condoms–"

"What?"

He sounded incredulous. It made her pause, her feet coming to a halt on the dirt trail. He stopped next to her. Then she continued in a rush, staring down at the ground.

"Yeah so, they stuffed my locker full of condoms. When I opened it, the condoms all spilled out over the hall. The video went viral and I got detention for having sex stuff in my locker–"

"You got detention for the condoms?"

"Yeah."

"So that's why you said it was a setup."

Gareth ran a hand through his long black hair. He looked away, then back down at her.

"Did you tell the principal what happened?"

"Yeah, but . . . like I said, he didn't believe me. I have a record of different offenses with the school district. Like, an ongoing one."

"For how long?"

"Since Middle School?"

Gareth was quiet.

Maddy felt anxious, trying to discern the expression on his face. He was gazing out at the woods in thought. She felt as vulnerable and exposed as she had that night at Zippy's when Kaylee confronted her by the soda fountain.

"You're a hot mess," he had called her.

Maybe it was a little less cute now.

"The administration doesn't like me. We don't have a great relationship," Maddy added, then her voice trailed off.

"You don't trust authority, huh?" Gareth asked.

She shrugged. She felt awkward answering him. She had never really thought about it before.

"Not really, I guess," she said. "Not like they've ever helped me at school, really. And my dad's worthless. I've always been on my own."

"Do you trust anybody?"

She bit her lip. "Sure."

"Who?" He turned to stare at her with piercing eyes and she avoided his gaze.

"Myself?" she finally said.

He didn't seem pleased by her answer. "But not me?"

"I . . ." Maddy hesitated. She couldn't lie. Honestly, they barely knew one another. "I think you're trustworthy," she hedged. "I just . . . it's a 'me' problem, okay? Not a 'you' problem."

"I get that. But have some faith in me, Mads."

She thought of last year when Principal Rodriguez threw her file across his office. She didn't think she could do anything to restore her reputation with the school, and she was almost beyond trying. It felt pointless. She just wanted to graduate and leave the whole mess behind. Principal Rodriguez definitely felt the same.

Gareth searched her face. She felt like he saw too much. Then his hand cupped her cheek. She hadn't heard him approach her, crossing the short distance between them with a few quiet steps. She flinched at his touch.

His thumb wiped away a stream of tears running down her cheek. Maddy hadn't realized she was crying.

"Mads. I said to *call me*."

"I'm sorry . . . ."

"Don't apologize. I should've checked up on you. It's my fault."

"No. We're just friends now, remember? I didn't want to tell you. It was embarrassing."

Gareth sighed. "You should have told me. I would've . . . ."

"What? Beat up Kaylee Mackovich?"

Gareth grimaced. Maddy felt like he wanted to. Somehow seeing him get all protective made all the bullshit worth it.

He stood next to her, his hand cupping her cheek, gazing down at her. His eyes were deep and sensual, like warm whiskey. He looked like he would lean forward and capture her lips with his own. Was he going to kiss her?

"You're shaking," he murmured.

"S-sorry."

He leaned closer instinctively, sensing her weakness.

"You using your CBD pen?"

"No. I forgot. Why do you even care?"

"I told you I wasn't going to abandon you."

"But I'm a shitshow," Maddy said, ashamed.

"Yeah, well, that's just life."

He rested his forehead against hers, leaning down from his great height. She trembled. Why did he seem so drawn to her when she was like this? When she was on the verge of falling apart, that's when he seemed unable to keep from touching her, from pulling her into his body, his strong and protective arms enveloping her.

He held her like that for a few minutes, until Maddy felt her powerful emotions subside. When she was truly calm, she pushed away, and he released her from his embrace. She wiped her eyes and looked around. The woods were a lively place, full of birdsong and rustling leaves. It was difficult to stay sad when she was surrounded by this much raw beauty. There was still an hour or so of daylight left. Let's make the most of it, she thought.

She grinned up at Gareth mischievously. He caught her look and gazed at her as though entranced.

With a burst of energy, Maddy playfully dashed up the path ahead of him.

"Come on!" she called over her shoulder. "I'll race you!"

"Race me where?" Gareth called after her. He sounded amused. "Guess that means you're feeling better."

"Better get moving, slowpoke!" she teased.

"This time I'm *not* gonna go easy on you."

He lunged after her, and with a yelp, she dashed off down the trail.

Chapter 20

Running through the forest with Gareth behind her was exhilarating. He was tall and athletic, but Maddy was a fast runner despite her curvaceous figure. And she had a lot of energy. She bounded through the woods, the trail at times becoming obscure and difficult to follow, then emerging again between ferns and bushes. She laughed as she made her way down a stair-like series of tree roots. Then turning, she followed the trail along the banks of a little stream.

Gareth followed right behind her. He allowed her to lead for a little while. Then he jumped ahead when the trail widened out. He yanked her hood up over her head as he passed her.

"Hey! Not fair!" she laughed, pulling her hood back down.

She fell into step behind his broad frame. She was impressed by his stamina and easy elegance as he ran through the woods. They ran for about a mile before her breath began to labor in her lungs. But Gareth looked like he could jog up the whole mountain. She started to slow down, a stitch in her side, and he glanced over his shoulder. He shortened his stride so that she didn't fall too far behind.

Damn him, she thought. *He's in way better shape than me.*

Her eyes focused on his long black hair. For a moment, he reminded her of the black wolf that led her and Joker home the other day. As she stared at his back, she felt like she was going into a strange trance. Suddenly, her vision swam. The light beneath the trees seemed to change. She felt like she was moving underwater.

As though a dream had overcome her, Maddy found herself running behind a black wolf. He loped ahead of her through the woods. She knew him. His presence. His strength. She followed him naturally, her paws thrumming on the soft earth, the mysteries of the wet forest apparent to her keen ears and nose. Her hot breath rose in little puffs of mist in the cold air.

She glanced down. She was a wolf, too. It didn't surprise her at all. It felt right.

Maddy came out of her wolf vision as she tripped over a rock. She stumbled forward with a gasp. Her head spun and she lost her balance.

"Gareth!" she shouted, suddenly dizzy and scared.

He turned just in time to catch her. She barreled into his chest as she was falling. He grabbed her in a bear hug and spun her around so they both didn't collapse on the ground. She clung to his powerful embrace, pressed into his chest, her head spinning.

"What happened? You alright?" he asked, alarmed.

"I don't know," she panted, her heart racing. She gripped him tighter for balance. "I need to sit down."

"Alright. Over here."

He helped her to a log, where she half collapsed onto it. Maddy sat down heavily and put her head in her hands. For a brief span of time, she felt like all of her senses had become more vivid. The sound of birdsong was almost painful. The sharp scent of the forest floor was filled with mold, hummus and beetles. She could smell beetles?

"My head is buzzing. What's happening to me?" she muttered.

"What do you mean?" Gareth said, hovering over her protectively.

"I can't catch my breath."

"You gonna pass out?"

"What's happening to me?" she repeated. "Am I sick?"

He was silent.

"Gareth?"

He still didn't answer. She gripped his hands, looking up at him. Did he know something that she didn't? Why didn't he seem more worried?

"Easy, Mads, you're doing fine," he said.

"Fine? What does that mean?" she demanded, a frantic pitch to her voice.

"Stay calm. You're hyperventilating."

"Like hell—" she muttered.

A branch suddenly snapped behind them.

Gareth looked up. His eyes sharpened. He turned away from her to face the trees.

"Who the fuck are you?" he called.

Maddy stared past him down the forest trail. A figure stepped out from behind a large red pine tree. She released a breath. It was a middle aged man wearing a puffy orange jacket and a wool beanie. In his hands, he carried a pair of giant binoculars.

"Hey there! Sorry to startle you. Just bird watching." The man grinned. His grin was very wide, like a big curving moon across his skinny face. "Easy, big guy. That your girlfriend? She okay? She looks pale."

"None of your business," Gareth growled. "What are you doing way out here? Strange time of day to go bird watching."

"Oh, I'm staying at the campground."

"Campground's closed."

"Right. I'm just passing through. Staying there tonight."

The man's shit-eating grin never faltered. He looked very tan, like he spent most of his time outdoors. As he drew closer, Maddy caught a weird smell about him. It was bitter and noxious, unlike anything she had smelled before. It made her head feel worse. She rubbed her nose, annoyed by the stench. Her eyes started to water.

What is that? she wondered. She shouldn't be able to smell him at this distance, especially in the open woods.

Gareth took a step to the right, placing his body between her and the man like a shield.

"You two live in town?" the man asked.

"Like I said, none of your business," Gareth growled.

"Alright. I see I spooked ya good. Well, you both have a nice day. Hope your girlfriend feels better." He waved at them and continued up the trail.

Gareth watched after the strange man until he was gone. Then he looked down at Maddy.

"Can you walk?" he asked.

"Do you smell that?" Maddy grimaced. "Ugh. It *reeks*."

"Wolfsbane. That man was carrying it on him."

"Wolfsbane? Isn't that a plant?" Maddy's stomach churned.

"Yes, it's an herb. Also called monkswart. Supposed to ward off werewolves. It's very poisonous."

Maddy snorted. "Well that's just nuts." *Or maybe not,* she thought, sobering a bit. She had seen a big black wolf wandering around outside her trailer. Five men were dead from being attacked. Maybe this strange guy had the right idea. So what if he was a little superstitious?

"I guess it's close to Halloween, so you can't be too careful," she suggested with a bit of humor.

She had hoped to get a laugh out of Gareth, but he was quiet. He reached down and took her hand, then helped her stand up.

"Can you walk?" he asked.

"Yeah, I'm feeling better."

"Let's head back to the car," Gareth said. "I'll take you home. It's getting late."

They started back up the path. The playful mood was gone, and Maddy noticed how Gareth kept close to her side. He was a lot more watchful now than before. His head turned this way and that, surveying the trees. He wasn't jumpy, per se, but he was a lot more cautious than their initial run through the woods. He kept a firm grip on her hand and didn't let go until they reached the parking lot about twenty minutes later.

"Do you think that guy was dangerous?" Maddy asked as they approached the car.

Gareth relaxed as he unlocked the Camaro's passenger side door and opened it for her.

"Nah. Probably just camping out illegally. He'll move on now that we saw him. I'll report it to the ranger station. People shouldn't be camped out there."

Maddy shrugged. "I wonder if he really was birdwatching."

Again, Gareth didn't answer. She wondered at his unusual silence. It made her a little insecure. Had she upset him somehow? This was the second time she had gotten dizzy while they were together. At least this time she didn't faint. Maybe she was a buzzkill?

They climbed into the car. Gareth settled behind the steering wheel and stuck his keys in the ignition. As Maddy buckled her seatbelt, she lost her nerve.

"I'm sorry," she blurted out.

"What?" Gareth looked up with a bewildered expression.

"Sorry I got sick. I don't know what happened. We were running and . . . ." She vividly recalled the strange vision: she was a wolf running down the trail. *That's so crazy.* Her heart began to beat a little erratically. Why a wolf?

She thought of the strange man in the woods with the wolfsbane on his person . . . . Was it a coincidence? What could it mean?

Or was she finally having a mental break of some kind?

Maybe it was better not to explain.

"It's nothing. Nevermind," she muttered. She wasn't crazy, and she wasn't turning into a wolf.

"Don't worry about it. Shit happens," Gareth said, still watching her with concern from the driver's seat of the Camaro. He reached over. His big hand landed on her knee.

"You okay little girl?"

"I'm fine. Really."

"If you say so. We should get you home before dark. Probably better not to worry Dean."

"Like he cares if I stay out."

Gareth didn't reply. He started up the engine and the Camaro rumbled angrily to life, settling into a low growl. They drove away from the abandoned campground, merging onto Highway 20 as the sunset cast glorious golden rays through the mountain cliffs. Deep shadows settled between the canyons of the mountains, casting the forest in dramatic light. In another half hour, it would be dark. The sky was a symphony of color: gold, violet, peachy pink and indigo blue. Billowing towers of nimbus clouds soared across the sky. A few stars twinkled above the mountain's snow-capped peak.

Maddy gazed at the view. She didn't think she would ever grow tired of watching sunsets from the mountainside. The view looked like something out of a storybook.

"You know," Gareth said, "in big cities like Phoenix or Los Angeles, people pay a couple million dollars for a house on a hillside, and all they get is a bunch of dirt and a few trees. Can't even see the stars, there's too many buildings at night. But out here?"

He went quiet for a moment. Maddy glanced over at him.

"Out here?" she prompted.

"Ah. Well. I'm no poet, but these mountains are . . . some kind of majestic. Can't put a price on this view. And they say small towns like Black River are poor. But I don't think so. There's stuff you can get out here that you can't get in the city. It's all perspective."

Maddy considered his words as the Camaro flew down the winding highway. She didn't think much about the natural beauty of Black River. She was born here, and she didn't know anything else.

But now that she thought about it, she couldn't imagine living without the mountain towering over her shoulder, like a shield against the world. How did people survive in big smoggy cities, without a glimpse of a meandering stream, or a deer walking through their backyard? She imagined it was like living in a cage.

She glanced over at Gareth out of the corner of her eye, admiring the silhouette of his rugged face, his sharp jaw, the straight line of his nose and his firm lips. She couldn't imagine him living in a city. He seemed too big for it. Too full of vitality. The power of his presence filled the Camaro. It made her skin tingle whenever she was close to him. No. He couldn't survive in a cage.

She wasn't anything like him. He was all strength and confidence. And she was just a basket of insecurities.

Maddy remembered, suddenly, what Bea had told her yesterday. *Virgins are clingy, and guys hate it when you're clingy.* She didn't know where the thought came from, but it bothered her.

"Gareth?" she asked.

"What's up, buttercup?"

"Am I . . . clingy?"

Gareth raised an eyebrow. He didn't answer immediately. The question hung between them as he pulled in front of her driveway. He parked off the side of the road, behind a patch of trees where Dean couldn't see the Camaro from the trailer.

Gareth turned off the engine. The sudden silence was deafening. Crickets chirped. An owl hooted nearby. The dusky sky cast the forest in deep purple shade.

He turned in the driver's seat to look at her.

"Where did that come from?" he asked.

"I dunno. Something my friend Bea said."

"Oh? What's that?"

"She said virgins are clingy and guys hate that. Not that I should care, I guess, but she said most boys won't sleep with virgins because they get clingy. So like, am I clingy?"

It sounded dumb in her own ears. She glanced down at her hands, fiddling with the ragged cuff of her sweater. Then Gareth reached over and pinched her chin. His touch surprised her. She looked up.

"I'm not a boy, Mads. You can cling to me all you want."

Her stomach knotted at the sound of his deep voice. Her lips parted, breathless in the dark cab of the car. What was she supposed to say to that?

His hazel eyes flickered to her mouth. His gaze grew hooded.

"Damn you're cute," he murmured.

Was he thinking about kissing her? She waited, filled with anticipation. She shouldn't want this. Not after telling him to go slow. *We're just friends,* she reminded herself, but it was a flimsy little thought. Every time they were together, his body, his touch, *his kiss* was all she could think about.

"You got those big eyes . . ." he said, his voice a rocky rumble in his chest.

Golden heat filled his gaze. He leaned over the center console. His hand clasped her neck, and he pulled her close to him, his lips finding hers in the dark cab of the car, his tongue slipping into the cavern of her mouth. She felt the rough brush of stubble against her chin. She gasped. The scent of him filled her nose like an aphrodisiac, making her lightheaded. She felt her body respond to him with excruciating detail. First her pulse quickened, her heart fluttering in her chest. Then her breasts tightened beneath her sweater. Her stomach clenched sweetly. A wave of arousal traveled from her belly button up her body, leaving a wanton flush in her cheeks.

She couldn't hide her reaction to him. He watched her through half-closed eyes. He broke their kiss, his face hovering close to her own, his breath warm against her cool skin.

"I like that you're a virgin, Maddy," he murmured.

"You do?" Her voice was husky.

"I like the way your eyes get all wide when I say 'fuck.'"

"I do not . . ." she protested.

"*Fuck*," he said, and she felt herself flinch.

"Stop it!"

He laughed at her, loud and deep. Then he instantly became serious again. He captured her lips in another kiss. He pulled her across the center console against his broad chest. It was not the most comfortable position, but Maddy barely noticed. His lips stroked across hers, over and over, inviting her to play.

"We shouldn't . . . *I should go* . . ." Maddy stuttered, putting her hands against the cushion of his pectoral muscles and trying to push away. "What if Dean comes out and sees us?"

She tried to look toward the house, but Gareth's hand clasped the back of her neck.

"Fuck Dean," he growled.

Then his mouth claimed her lips again.

Maddy felt herself losing control. She couldn't think straight when he touched her like this. She felt her resistance melt away. She tried to return his kiss, but she was clumsy and unpracticed.

"Easy," he murmured when she used her tongue. "Soften your mouth. Good. Like this."

His hand held her jaw, his thumb grazing her bottom lip as he tutored her. A deep groan fought its way up her throat. He was a good teacher, warm and encouraging and patient. He instructed her with his mouth and his tongue. When the kiss ended, she was gasping for breath, her mouth swollen and buzzing. She gazed at him with glassy eyes, her body craving his heat.

"You want to keep going?" he murmured.

She nodded.

He reached down and adjusted the driver's seat, giving them more room in the cab of the car. Then he lifted and contorted her like a doll until she was sitting on top of him, her legs spread, their crotches touching through their jeans. Face to face. She stared into his eyes.

She felt vulnerable with her legs spread wide across his lap. She was intimidated by him. His age. His dominance. But her body was on fire. She could feel the hard bulge of his member between her legs. He was so big. She admired the dramatic angles of his face. His black hair falling down his shoulders. His muscular arms. His sensual lips. Her breasts brushed against his chest.

He started kissing her again. His mouth slanted across hers, capturing her tongue, devouring her. Every time she tried to take a breath, he brought her back.

"Take your shirt off," he whispered.

"Here?" Maddy asked. They were parked on the side of the highway. Night had fallen and there was no traffic. Still, a car could drive by at any time.

He grinned wickedly. "You scared?"

She wrinkled her nose at him. "Fuck that."

His teasing challenge made her both excited and nervous. She was tired of being "innocent virgin" Maddy. She drew up her shirt over her head, baring her pale stomach and her gray sports bra. Gareth's hands went to her back and ran across her skin, brushing over her scars. He traced them as though memorizing them.

Then she pulled off her sports bra. Her breasts sprang loose, heavy and swollen, her nipples pink and hard.

He groaned low in his throat. Or maybe it was a growl? His hand traveled up to her left breast. His calloused thumb brushed her left nipple, sending spirals of pleasure down her belly. Heat pooled between her legs. She ached for him.

He bent down and took her nipple into his mouth. He stayed there for a few minutes, making her groan and gasp at intervals. Then he switched his attention to the other breast.

"Are you getting wet for me?" he whispered against her soft skin.

She sighed, her thoughts feverish and hazy.

"*Are you?*" he prompted, nudging her.

"Yes," she murmured, shy.

He laughed low in his throat. She was soaking through her panties and he knew it. Her hips were grinding against him in small, automatic thrusts. She felt a throbbing emptiness deep inside, aching to be filled.

He started undoing the button on her jeans. She reached down to help him. He slid her pants off one leg, giving him access to the apex of her thighs. His fingers slipped up, stroking over her panties, then moving the cloth to one side. He ran his fingers along her wet slit, watching her face. Maddy whimpered, the little excited sound escaping from her throat.

Then his fingers slid deep between her lower lips. She gasped as he pressed into her folds, seeking entry.

"What . . . what are you doing?" she asked, her voice soft, her hands gripping his shoulders. This was different from last time.

"Relax," he murmured. "*You're so tight.*"

He changed his position, his arm snaking around her waist. His hand slid over her ass cheek, then under her panties, to probe her from behind. His touch sent little spirals of pleasure up through her belly. She didn't expect to feel pleasure like this. Maddy felt her breathing turn ragged.

His arms wrapped around her as his finger slid between her folds. This angle seemed to work better. She had never been touched this intimately before.

He pressed his finger deep inside of her.

"Ah!" she gasped.

She stiffened at his invasion. She was wet enough, but she was narrow and untouched, and it hurt a little. Her heart was hammering. She wondered if he could feel her heartbeat, they were crushed so close together.

Gareth pulled his finger out, watching her face, sensing her discomfort. Then without warning, his arms flexed. He was so strong, he maneuvered her easily in the tight space of the car, turning her and bending her across the front seat. Maddy found herself lying face-first down in the passenger seat, her ass boosted into the air by the center console, her legs tangled up in her pants.

"What are you doing?" she gasped.

She tried to turn around, but he threw his arm down on her back, pinning her. Then he kissed the round naked globe of her bare ass cheek.

"God, your scent," he groaned. "I'm gonna make you feel good, little girl."

Maddy squirmed. She thought she would die from embarrassment. He was right up on her ass. Wasn't it gross?

Then he pressed his mouth against the core of her.

Maddy lost all coherency. His big hands gripped her ass cheeks, holding her still as his tongue entered her. She moaned and sobbed into her arm as he lapped at her core. He inserted his tongue into her flesh, completely shameless, and moved it around. She made incoherent noises like a wounded animal. Then his lips found her clit.

She cried out, sobbing with pleasure as he pressed his index finger into her once again. She accepted it with a sigh of relief. He pushed his finger deep and she felt herself stretch. This was a lot more tolerable. Without thinking, she began to grind her hips back against his hand. Her body seemed to move on its own. His finger pushed in and out of her, in and out, as his tongue wetted her hole.

After a time, he changed positions, and she felt two fingers stretching inside of her. She nearly lost it, and she cried out in pleasure.

"You're so deep," she moaned.

He laughed. "I'm not even down to my knuckle, baby."

He switched his attention to her clit, and Maddy began to gasp brokenly. She felt so full. A tingling pressure began to build, and she thrusted back to meet him. She squirmed, trembling, dying for release. Her orgasm sprang upon her suddenly, violently. Her muscles contracted, clamping down on his fingers. Warmth flooded her body. The headrush made her dizzy. She moaned his name over and over as her muscles twitched and clenched.

He didn't withdraw his fingers until the last shudder swept through her. Then she lay across the seats, limp in the aftermath.

Maddy glanced back at him, her forehead sweaty, breathing hard. He gazed down at her, his eyes heavy with lust. He licked her juice from his fingers while she watched. He looked hungry, and she felt like a snack. He could have unbuckled his belt, taken out his member and fucked her right there.

"Do you want to keep going?" he asked.

His voice was so deep, she almost didn't understand him. She thought about it. Her entire body swam in an ocean of warmth and bliss. She wanted him desperately, she couldn't deny that. His fingers had probed deep. She could almost imagine what it would feel like with him inside of her, except that his cock was much larger than his fingers.

Then a car suddenly drove past. Maddy flinched as bright headlights flashed through the front windshield, illuminating the angles of Gareth's face and tousled black hair. If she had been sitting upright, her naked breasts would have been clearly visible. It was a sobering thought. She felt her head clear. Now that the heat of the moment had passed, her left leg was cramping up and she noticed the car was freezing cold.

"We should stop," she said, her voice hoarse. "Is that alright?"

"Yeah. Of course."

He helped her climb back into the passenger seat, which was surprisingly difficult. Her limbs seemed to have lost their strength. She felt uncoordinated and kept getting tangled up in her half-removed clothing. He fished out her sports bra and T-shirt from the backseat and she pulled them on, still shy despite everything he had just done to her body.

He seemed drawn to her shyness. As though sensing her withdraw, he leaned over and kissed her. She could taste her fluids on his mouth. It wasn't as unpleasant as she was expecting. Kind of sweet, actually.

She noticed the scent of her arousal filling the car.

"That's rank," she said, a little embarrassed.

"I like it," he said, licking his lips.

Maddy felt a twinge behind her belly button as his tongue glided across his lips. The muscles between her legs trembled sweetly.

"Wow," she muttered. "Um, yeah. That was . . . ."

They sat for a moment in silence, gazing at each other.

"So uh . . . is there uh . . . something I should do for you?" Maddy asked awkwardly. Blowjobs were a common topic of discussion among teenagers, but she hadn't realized a guy could do the same to a girl. She was *way* too innocent.

"We'll get to that later," he said. "Not tonight."

"*Later?* That's assuming a lot."

He grinned. It was more of a smirk. The look set her on fire.

"This doesn't mean anything," Maddy said defensively. "This doesn't make you my boyfriend. I'm not moving in with you. Nothing's changed."

"Sure thing, babygirl."

His confidence was maddening. Maddy reached for the car door, ready to go back inside. Dean would have noticed her absence by now, maybe, if he wasn't shitfaced.

"I should get going," she said.

"Hold up," Gareth said, stopping her. "Before I forget, I got you something."

Gareth reached behind his seat. When he straightened, he was holding a box of tea. Maddy took it from him curiously, turning the box over in her hands. The packaging was a greenish gray color with the brand "Harvest Moon" on it. She could smell the musty odor of mushrooms through the cardboard container.

"For your nausea and dizziness," he said. "My mom recommended it. She said it helps stabilize blood sugar."

"Wait . . . did you tell your mom about me?"

Gareth shrugged. "Maybe. Why, you like that? She said drink it in the evenings and it'll help."

Maddy took the tea from him. "That's super sweet. Thank you, Gareth."

"You're welcome. It's no big deal."

She leaned over and kissed his cheek.

"I think it's a big deal," she said.

"Hah! You're cute," he grinned.

Then Gareth reached past her with his big arm and opened the car door. The outside air was sharp and frosty. Maddy noticed the car windows were foggy, and she drew a smiley face on the window before climbing out of the car. She gave him a little wave before shutting the door.

The Camaro boomed to life. Gareth turned on his headlights and pulled onto the dark highway. Then he sped off toward town.

Maddy watched the Camaro disappear down the side of the mountain. She took a moment to enjoy the night air and collect herself. Her body was still glowing in the aftermath of her orgasm. She breathed out a deep sigh. Dang. She really needed better boundaries if she was going to keep up the "friends" thing. But she was beginning to suspect it was all a big fat charade. He wasn't treating her like a friend at all. It would be a lot easier if he wasn't so stupid hot.

Then she turned toward her house and started walking down her long gravel driveway, following the glow of lights from the living room window.

Chapter 21

"You were out late," Dean said as she came through the back door.

"I had work."

"No, you didn't."

Maddy felt a little chill go down her spine. She asked him, "What do you mean?"

Dean was eating peanuts in front of the TV, watching a sports game. He stank like he hadn't showered all week, which was true. He took a swig of beer and rinsed his mouth.

"I called your work, they said you weren't scheduled for tonight."

Maddy's heart raced. For a moment, she almost panicked. Then her eyes narrowed. Since when had Dean ever called her work? Sure, he could look up the number on the internet and dial it easily enough, but he was a lazy bastard.

"Who did you talk to?" she asked suspiciously.

Dean's smug facade crumbled. "Oh, uh . . . some gal. You know, one of the girls there." He glanced over at her, and she saw a flash of uncertainty in his gaze. Now he just looked like a drunk old man. He was full of shit.

Maddy relaxed.

"Right. Well, I was unloading boxes in the warehouse, so I don't know who you talked to, but I worked a long shift, and I'm exhausted."

"Right, okay, yeah, you look ragged as hell. Your hair's a fuckin' mess."

Maddy reached up and touched her hair. She hadn't even thought of that. It was probably tangled up from her makeout session with Gareth.

Dean watched her with narrow eyes. "You high?"

"Uh, no, why?"

"Your eyes look a little red."

"Like you're one to talk, you're smoking weed right now."

"Hah! Just fucking with you. You want a hit?"

"No, thanks."

Dean was still staring at her, taking in her appearance. Maddy fidgeted. She rubbed her nose on her sleeve. Her sense of smell had been excruciatingly sensitive this week. After everything Gareth had done to her in the car, she felt like a cloud of potent pheromones was following her around. The horrible thought crossed her mind that maybe Dean could smell it, too. *Ugh, gross.*

"Whelp, I'm going to take a shower."

"Hot water's out. I gotta call a repair guy."

"Great, didn't we just get that fixed?"

"Yeah, might need to replace it? I dunno."

How much did it cost to replace a hot water heater? Maddy felt her temples begin to throb. The warm afterglow of her orgasm vanished. Fucking bills. Fucking *life*.

Dean turned back to the TV and stuffed another handful of peanuts in his mouth. Apparently their conversation was over.

Maddy ducked down the hallway. She dumped her backpack in her room and grabbed a clean pair of sweatpants, underwear and a T-shirt. She stank of her own sex juices, and she was half-convinced Dean could smell it. *Yuck.* It made her cringe.

She entered the bathroom and turned on the shower. She couldn't get the water above lukewarm. Still better than ice cold. She gritted her teeth and stood under the stream and soaked down. Then she lathered up her hair with shampoo. As she adjusted to the warmish temperature of the water, her thoughts returned to the front seat of Gareth's Camaro. Her cheeks flushed at the memories. A familiar tingle returned to her breasts.

Maddy reached up and touched her hardened nipple, thinking of Gareth's warm mouth. She bit her lip, trying not to moan. Then her hand traveled down her flat stomach to the thatch of red pubic hair between her legs. She thought of Gareth's rough tongue teasing her cunt. Her muscles twinged deep behind her bellybutton, and she bit back a moan. No wonder sex was such a big deal.

What would it feel like to go all the way?

Maddy blushed, trying to imagine it. He said he was larger than average. She knew it would hurt, but on the other hand, maybe it would feel really good.

If she shifted her legs, she could feel a bit of soreness deep inside, where his fingers had stroked and played with her sensitive flesh. It was a new sensation, introducing her to places she hadn't felt before. It was her first time being penetrated like that.

She shivered.

What would it be like to take all of him?

She tried to imagine his cock. The bulge through his pants was pretty intimidating. One might even call it threatening. She glanced around the shower, trying to compare his size to her shampoo bottle or the facial cleanser. It wasn't quite right. She picked up the tube of facewash and gripped it in her hand. No, he was thicker than this. She hated to compare his dick to a summer sausage, but it seemed more appropriate. Or like, a meatloaf. A beef burrito?

She buried her face in her hands and laughed at herself. Good lord. How was something that large supposed to fit inside of her?

"Maddy, you're such a virgin."

She muttered quietly to herself.

A heavy hand suddenly knocked on the door, making her jump.

"Hey, are you done in there? I gotta shit."

"I'll hurry up!"

She turned off the lukewarm shower and grabbed her towel. She wrapped her hair up and pulled on her pajamas. Then she brushed her teeth.

Her phone pinged. It was resting on a little shelf below the bathroom mirror. She reached over and picked it up.

It was Gareth.

Just got home.

Everything good with Dean?

Seeing his text made her giddy. Maddy stuffed her toothbrush in her mouth and eagerly texted back.

Yeah he's fine, no problems.

"Hurry up, dammit, I'm gonna shit my pants!" Dean roared from the hallway.

Maddy spit out her toothpaste and shoved the toothbrush back in its tray. Then she yanked open the door.

"Bathroom is all yours!"

She ducked past Dean and shot across the hallway into her bedroom, firmly shutting the door behind her.

"Fucking teenagers."

Maddy listened until she heard the bathroom door shut and the fan turn on. A wave of relief swept through her.

Good, I'm safe, she thought. *He doesn't know.* Maybe Dean was suspicious, but he didn't have any proof that she had spent time with Gareth, so he couldn't get mad at her.

She threw herself down on her bed with a sigh, her red hair spread out over her pink pillow. She turned off the lights. Several clusters of green glow-in-the-dark stars dotted the ceiling. She remembered putting them up with her mom when she was super young, like sixth grade. Then she opened her phone's messages.

> *You in bed now?*

> *Yeah, I just took a shower, how about you?*

Her phone pinged. Maddy blinked. Oh jeez, he sent her a pic! Her phone's signal sucked, so it took forever to load. She waited with bated breath.

Then her heart did a little jump.

Gareth was standing in front of a foggy bathroom mirror. It looked like he had just taken a shower too. His wet black hair was parted down the middle and fell down his shoulders. The big scorpion tattoo stood out on his sleeve. A few strands clung to the gaunt angles of his face. In the bathroom mirror, Maddy saw the clear outline of his pectoral muscles and his chiseled abdomen, all the way down to the V-cuts that disappeared into the towel wrapped around his waist.

She rolled over, buried her face in her pillow and squealed. Holy fuck, where did this come from? Why was he sending her pics?

Then her phone pinged again.

> *Did it come through?*

> Yeah I got it.

> Why are you sending me nudes?

> Dang, you're like a model.

> Hah sure. Why else? So you send one back.

Maddy hesitated. Her cheeks were flaming. She had never sent a sexy pic to anyone before.

> I'm not photogenic.

> You're beautiful, Maddy.

She felt unexpected tears sting her eyes, though she didn't know why. It made no sense to get emotional over a text message. She wasn't bold like Bea, but maybe she could be? She didn't have any body confidence, but maybe a pic wasn't such a big deal. She trusted Gareth; she knew he wouldn't show it to anyone. She could send him something.

> Okay, I'll send you a pic.

Maddy laid back in bed and undid the towel from her hair. She opened her camera and tried to take a selfie. She took a few snaps, but the angle was bad. She tried brushing her bangs across her forehead and pursing her lips. Somehow, that made it worse. The lighting was all wrong.

She thought of the girls she saw on Picplace who took such beautiful photos. They always had their makeup done and their hair teased up.

As she messed with her camera, her phone pinged again. Another pic from Gareth? Her mouth went dry when she opened it.

Gareth's "casual" selfie could have been on the cover of Maxim magazine. He was lying back in bed on top of his gray comforter, propped up on his black pillows, his big left arm behind his head, his other arm raised up to hold the phone. He was shirtless. A lamp on his nightstand cast his impressive chest in a soft golden light. Maddy's eyes darted down to the little trail of hair beneath his belly button that disappeared into his pants.

She sucked in a breath. He was absolutely too fucking masculine. For a moment she didn't know what to say. She told herself to be chill. Play it cool. She texted him with nervous fingers, trying to be sassy.

> Are you trying to seduce me?

I thought I already did that . . . in the car.

Maddy groaned with quiet frustration. He had the upper hand again.

> This isn't fair. I told you I want to be friends. I can't handle a relationship right now

Okay. Let's be friends.

> You're not taking me seriously.

> Friends don't send friends pics like this.

Really. Then I have a question.

Can a friend give another friend an orgasm?

Maddy tapped her fingers against the phone, thinking. His question was ridiculous. Of course, friends didn't give each other orgasms unless they were "friends with benefits," and she didn't want to be like that with him. But she also didn't want to put an end to their little encounters. She was conflicted.

She texted back, rewriting her thoughts a few times before she hit "Send."

> Maybe sometimes it's cool, if both friends are consenting,

or if it doesn't ruin the friendship, you know?

Sounds good to me. I'm consenting if you are.

Maddy sighed. Yeah, she was more than consenting, she was diving head first down a water slide. If she refused to send him a pic, she knew he would understand. But after everything they had just done in the car, she was feeling a little frisky. This was kind of exciting.

She opened the first pic again, the one with him standing in front of the bathroom mirror after his shower, and used her fingers to zoom in on his abdomen, where those little V-cuts disappeared under his towel. A few more inches, and she would see his cock. She thought she saw a bulge. Did he have a semi? She couldn't really tell because of the towel, but she was filled with curiosity. She scrolled up to look at the deep indent between his pectoral muscles and the cuts in his broad shoulders. His tattoos. She squinted at the tiny phone picture, trying to see everything. Was she salivating?

It reminded her of that night when he pinned her down in his bed. She could almost feel the weight of his body on top of her own, his arms enfolding her, his massive cock pressed between her legs . . . .

Goddammit. Maddy closed her eyes for a moment.

He wanted her thinking about him. He was doing it on purpose; she wasn't that innocent. Now he was all up in her head, and she couldn't get the heat in her blood to cool off.

Two could play at this game. If he was set on torturing her with sexy pics, then she was going to send one back. She didn't really know how, but she was going to try, even if it made her squirm a little inside. It was just a little humiliating. But it was also kinda fun. She could be sexy, too. She just needed to find the right angle.

Maddy turned on the front camera on her phone; she took a few test shots. She didn't really like how she looked in her pictures. Did she smile? Did she pout? She looked tired and pale.

Maddy shrugged off her hoodie so that she only had her bra on. She snapped a few pics using her selfie camera. She looked cute-ish, but her bra wasn't anything special, just a plain sports bra, and it didn't really have the shock factor she wanted. She looked like she was going to the gym. She didn't really own any sexy underwear.

A naughty idea came to mind, and she played with a lock of auburn hair in indecision. Dare she? Was she bold enough?

Could she really send him a topless selfie?

She glanced down at her cleavage. It would definitely shock him. And that's what she wanted to do. Give him a little taste of his own medicine. Maybe this was her chance to finally break out of her shell a little.

She took off her bra. She thought back to a year ago, when she had first stolen his phone number from the hardware store. The thought had crossed her mind back then to send him a sexy pic, but at the time, she hadn't dared. She was too shy. But she had definitely imagined it.

She touched one of her nipples while thinking about his mouth, how he bit into her plump flesh like he was stuffing his face with a pastry. His rough tongue. His teeth. His strong hands. She pushed the little bruise beneath her finger, right next to her left nipple. It tingled. She could feel her breasts becoming sensitive as she felt more aroused. She felt a little flutter of excitement.

Yeah, this would be good.

She couldn't find a good angle lying on her back, so she sat up and tried to mimic some of the poses she saw female models use on Picplace. She remembered seeing a pic of a girl sitting by a pool with her legs tucked to one side in a cute bathing suit, sort of like that popular image of Ariel the mermaid sitting on a rock. She decided to go for something like that.

Of course, Maddy's breasts were so voluptuous that instead of Ariel sitting on a rock by the sea, she looked more like a curvy lingerie model tipping over a boat.

Alright, this was going to take a minute.

She finally figured out the best angle to fit her breasts and her face into the selfie cam. After a few pics, she started to enjoy herself. A little smirk grew on her lips. *Serves him right.* He wouldn't expect this—it was way out of her character. Her only regret was that she wouldn't see his expression when he opened it.

She finally picked the one she liked the most, where the lighting made her skin look all soft and smooth. Her eyes were big and sensual. A little pout framed her lips. She looked big-eyed and innocent and lusty. And her tits looked very round and bitable.

She hesitated, wondering if she was making a mistake. They were "just friends," after all. But somehow, that made it more fun; it seemed against the rules.

Besides, he started it.

She hit send.

She waited.

It took him a long moment to respond. She tried to imagine his face when he opened the pic. She wondered what he was doing. Why was he taking so long? Did he fall asleep? She had gotten a little carried away with the selfies, almost ten minutes had passed. What if he didn't respond at all? Maybe he was jerking off? She put a hand over her mouth and fought the urge to giggle. She liked that idea.

Then, finally, her stomach tying itself in knots, her phone pinged.

> *I see a bear in your bed.*

Maddy glanced down, and realized the little white bear that Gareth had given her was wrapped up in her quilt. She rolled her eyes. Damn, here she was, trying to be a seductress, but she had a child's toy next to her! Oh gawd, it was so cringe. Why was she so awkward? Maybe her phone would magically break so she couldn't text him anymore.

After squirming for a moment in silent humiliation, Maddy found the courage to text him back.

> *Oops yeah, that's embarrassing.*

> *Sorry, I forgot about that.*

Dammit, why was she apologizing? It's not like she did anything wrong. She bit her lip. He didn't respond again for a minute. She waited anxiously, questioning her life choices.

> *It's cute. Do you sleep with that bear?*

> *Yeah, of course.*

> *Good. I like that.*

Maddy was dying inside. She texted him:

> *Okay, but what did you think of the pic?*

> *I think you're playing a dangerous game, little girl.*

> *Maybe I should come over.*

Show you what happens when

you send a grown man pics like that.

Maddy's eyes widened as she read his text. She shivered; she could almost hear his voice. She could easily imagine him showing up in the middle of the night and knocking on her window. He would, too. She felt a little fearful.

No, don't, my dad's home. Please don't.

Okay, you got school tomorrow.

Guess the bear gets all the fun.

Maddy smirked and typed back,

Are you jealous of the bear?

Her phone started to vibrate. He was calling her. Oh no! Should she pick up? Her eyes darted to the door. Dean had left the bathroom already. He was back in the living room watching TV. If she kept her voice low, he wouldn't notice she was talking to anyone.

Maddy hesitated. She picked up the phone on the last ring.

"Hey."

"Hey there." She heard a grin in Gareth's dark voice. "Do me a favor."

"Okay?"

"Take that bear."

"Yeah?"

"I want you to brush it across your nipples and . . . *tease* yourself. Like I was there."

Maddy felt herself turning red again. She was in a constant state of blushing these days. "Are you serious? *For real?*"

"That's what I said. Do it now."

The command in his tone sent a sexy little shiver down her spine. Alright, so maybe she kind of liked it. Her hand trembled as she picked up the bear. She squirmed, feeling totally embarrassed, but she followed his instructions. It was a dumb little game, so how was he making her this wet? She rubbed the bear's soft fur across her skin, starting at her neck, then down her collarbone, across the skin of her chest, then over the mounds of her breasts. Her nipples were already two hard points from thinking about Gareth's mouth. When the fuzzy, slightly rough texture of the bear passed over them, she felt a tingle of warmth behind her bellybutton. *Oh!* Alright, so that was nice. It reminded her of the sandpaper feeling of his stubble, like how he had rubbed his face against her sensitive nipples in the car. Some of the tension in her shoulders relaxed. She tried to imagine him next to her in bed. Would he be doing this now to her, if he was there? Why was it making her so aroused?

"You feeling good?" he checked in.

"Yeah," she said, her voice catching. She sounded all sultry and breathy.

"Keep touching yourself. It's good for you." She heard some rustling, like he was lying back in bed. "So, you got something on your mind, little girl? Why'd you send me that pic?"

Maddy clutched the bear between her breasts and sucked in another breath. Her nipples tingled pleasantly. Thoughts of sex arose in her mind, but she was shy. She hadn't really talked about sex with anyone before, except Bea.

"Honestly?" she whispered.

"Yeah. Tell me."

"Um, I was thinking . . . how good it felt . . . in the car."

"Oh yeah? So that's what you were thinking."

"Yeah, and I was wondering . . . what sex might feel like, the first time."

His voice caught. He was quiet for a moment. *"Ah."*

Maddy waited. She imagined him running another hand through his long hair. Or maybe he was adjusting a giant boner in his pants. Hard to say.

To Gareth's credit, he didn't tease her. "Why, you scared?"

"Maybe a little? I think it's going to hurt, like, a lot."

"It will a little the first time, sure."

She grunted; she didn't want to hear that. She had hoped he would say something sexy and comforting.

In a low voice, Gareth added, "That's just the first time. It gets better after that. I'll be gentle."

"Wow, you really assume a lot," she laughed weakly.

"Yeah, I do." He cleared his throat, "So, in the car, that was new for you? How'd you feel?"

By the sound of his voice, she imagined him stretching out on his big gray comforter, one arm propped up behind his head as he talked to her. He sounded casual, like he was asking her about her favorite movies.

Maddy was having an entirely different conversation. Her anxiety made her want to squirm. Talking over the phone like this was intimate, but at the same time, it was kind of a relief.

"Yeah, that was new for me. It was different, but it felt really good," she admitted, keeping her voice low. "That place you touched. Um. It was intense. I came really hard."

"Good. That's your G-spot."

"Oh, okay."

"You heard of a G-spot before?"

"Yeah, wow, I'm not that dumb."

"Didn't say you were. Just asking."

Maddy rolled her eyes even though he couldn't see her.

She continued, "Um, it's a little sore? Is that normal? Do you think it's bruised?"

"You're just a virgin, Mads. Your body isn't used to the attention yet. It's all new. So you're going to feel some different things. Sex is like . . . how it felt with my fingers in you, just deeper. A lot deeper."

Maddy tried not to gulp. Her mind flashed to his member again. She still hadn't seen it.

"So, you're kind of larger than I expected," she said. "Are you, like, seven or eight inches?"

"More than that. You want a pic?"

"Uh, wow, a pic? For real?"

"You seem curious. I can send you one."

Maddy tried not to act shocked. She told herself to be cool, but her heart started to race. She dared herself to be bold.

"Sure, if you want to, you can send one."

He laughed, all gruff and low, at her reaction, though she didn't know why. His voice was like dark chocolate.

"Alright, give me a minute," he grinned over the phone.

Maddy put the stuffed bear over her face. She pushed her nose into its soft belly. Really? She had never received a "dick pic" before. A few guys had offered to send her one at the hardware store, which grossed her out. But the thought of seeing Gareth's cock made her stupid excited. She had come this far, so why the hell not? She wanted to see what kind of monster he intended to put in her.

The call went quiet as he took the picture. Or maybe he already had one saved to his phone? She kinda hated that thought.

Then she got a text notification. It took a moment for the pic to load. Maddy blinked. She sucked in a slow breath. *Oh wow, okay. Yeah, it's really big.*

The pic showed Gareth lying back in bed. The bedside lamp was shining in the background, the camera angled at his lower anatomy. His fingers gripped his shaft at the base; it was fully engorged and erect. From what she could tell, Gareth's cock had a nice shape to it. It was dark brown, girthy and thick. A few veins ran up and down its length. The head was flared out like a mushroom. Just as she suspected, the size intimidated the hell out of her. Past his thick rod, she glimpsed the tattoos on his arm, the indents of his six pack and the curve of his pectoral muscles.

"You got it?" Gareth's voice startled her back to reality.

"Yeah. Um. It's really big," Maddy said.

"So you still scared? Did I make it worse?"

"I mean, kind of? I'll be honest. I can't imagine that thing fitting inside of me."

Gareth laughed again. "There goes my ego. I'll teach you, babygirl. Don't you worry. We just gotta loosen you up first. You're very tight."

"Isn't being tight a good thing though?"

"Not for you, but we'll go slow. Get you nice and ready first. If you want it. You gotta masturbate more, babe. Otherwise, it's gonna hurt your first time."

Maddy felt a quiver between her legs as she imagined her first time with him. Her mind was flooded by sensations from just hours before. She was ready to take that leap; she knew it with certainty. Actually, she couldn't wait.

"Do something for me," he said.

"Okay?"

"I want you to slide your hand down. And rub your clit."

Maddy blushed. For real, right now? Dean was just down the hallway; it made her nervous, though she didn't know why. What could Dean do? He wouldn't barge into her bedroom.

After a short hesitation, she obeyed Gareth's command. She reached down and slowly started rubbing her clit through her panties. It was already swollen and sensitive. She released a shuddering breath as more tension left her muscles.

"You feeling less nervous now?" he asked.

"Yeah."

"Good. Keep doing that. Now tell me, how does it feel?"

"What?"

"Describe it for me. I wanna hear what you're feeling."

"Like, how do I do that?"

He growled low in his throat. "Why don't you try your best and imagine I'm there with you. What's your bedroom look like. What are you wearing right now."

Maddy took a shaky breath. Her voice was husky with arousal as she started to describe her comforter, her bed, her pajamas, then her panties. Gareth grunted occasionally as he listened to her. Then he started directing her to touch herself, telling her where to place her fingers. He asked soft, sensual questions in his deep voice. Did she like it? Did it feel good?

"You wet, baby?"

"Yes," she whispered.

"Good girl. Now slide your hand down between your legs."

Maddy put the phone down on the pillow next to her ear, so she could still hear him. In the dark, secret solitude of her bedroom, she searched for her hidden entrance. It was hard to find. She didn't feel as much when she tried to slip her finger inside. It wasn't like his penetration; her finger didn't reach very deep at all. Gosh, the opening was very small. She couldn't comprehend his size. She was starting to understand why he didn't take her virginity last Thursday night, after her first orgasm on his couch.

"How do you feel?"

"Empty," she breathed.

"*Ah,*" he groaned.

His voice caught again and she thought she heard him growl. Maddy was discovering a few different, new sensations as she massaged between her legs. She removed her finger and focused on the outside. She was finding it harder and harder to respond to him as her pleasure grew. He listened to her heavy breathing.

"Mm, good girl. Just think of me inside you, baby."

He encouraged her in his dark, delicious voice. Maddy's breath caught as she felt the pressure begin to build inside. She felt a little flutter behind her bellybutton. Was he going to make her come over the phone? He seemed to understand her vulnerable state. His voice deepened.

"Relax sweetheart . . . just enjoy yourself . . . ."

Maddy bit her lip, but couldn't hold back her whimper as a small orgasm rippled through her. Her back arched a little and her legs tightened up. She was breathing hard. She relaxed back in bed in a sweet glow, feeling warm and relaxed. It wasn't as intense as what she experienced in his car, or back on his couch, but she felt a sense of relief. Finally, she knew how to make herself orgasm.

She definitely wasn't going to tell him that was her first time successfully masturbating. In the past, she always got frustrated and gave up after a while, or Dean stomped around and her anxiety made her stop.

"How are you feeling now?"

"Um, super relaxed," Maddy murmured.

"Good. Wish I could be there to hold you, babygirl. I'd wrap you up with that bear until you fell asleep."

Maddy tried to suppress the deep sense of yearning she felt at his words.

"You'd probably break my bed," she said, trying for humor.

"No doubt."

Maddy fished around for something to say. He just made her masturbate over the phone and listened to her orgasm. She didn't know where to go from there, and he didn't seem eager to say anything. It was kind of sweet, how he just stayed on the phone with her, quiet and attentive. She wondered what he was thinking about.

"Hey, G?"

"Yeah?" he grunted.

"You ever think about when we met?"

"Yeah, sometimes."

"Like . . . I know before, you told me that story about being a wolf without a pack, but . . . Why do you like me?"

The sudden question with its blatant vulnerability seemed to take them both off guard. He echoed her words, *"Why do I like you?"*

She waited for his answer, feeling her toes curl a bit in anxiety. What if he didn't have a reason? What if he just wanted sex?

Gareth cleared his throat after a long pause. "Well, Mads, look, you're a young girl in a bad situation. Ain't nobody looking out for you, not from what I can see, anyway. So maybe I just kinda claimed you back then."

Maddy wasn't expecting that answer, and she wasn't sure how his words made her feel.

"Claimed me?" she prompted. He sounded so . . . territorial.

"Sure. *Claimed*, like I was gonna look out for you."

"You can't just claim people, Gareth."

"Why not?"

"Well, it's gotta be mutual."

"You saying you didn't claim me, too?"

Maddy's voice caught. She thought of her lowkey stalking over the years. Stealing his number from work. Snooping past his place. Yeah, maybe she did "claim him" a bit. Maybe she understood him more than she realized.

"Just think of yourself as under me, Mads. Ain't nothin' bad gonna happen to you so long as I'm around."

His words made her feel more *secure*, but they didn't really answer her question. Maddy wasn't sure how she felt. So, he just wanted to rescue her? That seemed a little offensive. She was more than just a "girl in a bad situation."

"For real? So that's why you like me? You 'claimed' me? What the hell, Gareth—"

"Maddy, wait. Hear me out."

"You just wanted to rescue me? That's so lame."

"No, it's more than that. I can't explain it, but . . . I think I was meant to meet you."

She allowed his words to soak in. She didn't want to admit it over the phone, but she felt the same way. A strange, gravitational force seemed to be drawing them together.

"Do you believe in fate?" she blurted out.

"I do."

Her heart gave a soft, sweet thump in her chest.

Gareth sighed. "Look, I think I met you for a reason. But we're taking it slow, baby. You don't wanna hear all that mushy stuff from me."

"Maybe I do . . . a little bit."

"Oh. A little bit?"

"Yeah."

She could hear his grin over the phone.

"When that day comes, I'll tell you everything. But not while we're just friends. In the meantime, I want you to relax and be yourself with me. I like you, Mads."

Maddy gripped the phone and pressed it against her ear. *Just be yourself.* What did that mean? She was always walking on eggshells around Dean. Or trying to fit in at school. Or wearing her facade at work. She didn't know who she was beneath it all. But maybe with him, she could begin to find out? Suddenly, she was reminded of something.

"Oh hey," she said, "This Friday, Bea invited me to go to Beaumont Farm's Haunted Manor and Fright Farm. I know it's last minute, but do you want to go with me?"

"This a date or a hangout?"

"Um." She didn't know how to answer, especially after what they had just done. She fidgeted with her blanket. She considered both options.

She couldn't deny her feelings for him; her crush seemed to have intensified, if that was possible. But she still wanted to take things slow. A date held a certain amount of expectation. It meant that eventually, if they continued down that road, she would have to revisit their conversation about moving out of the trailer. And she wasn't ready for that yet.

"Do we have to label it?" she asked, hearing the uncertainty in her voice.

"So a hangout, then."

"I guess so, yeah."

"Alright. I'll meet you there," he agreed. He didn't seem bothered by their unlabeled status, even after everything they had talked about over the phone. "I'm gonna ask Vin if he wants to go, too. Since it's *a hangout.*"

"Oh, sure, okay."

"When?"

"This Friday evening. I'm glad you're coming. I wasn't sure if haunted houses were your thing."

"Hanging out with you is my thing."

Maddy smiled and bit her lip, feeling a little butterfly tickle her stomach.

Gareth sighed; the deep sound vibrated over the phone. "It's getting late. As much as I want to keep you up all night, you gotta sleep, you got school tomorrow. Thanks for the pic, babygirl. I'll see you on Friday. Hey, do me a favor?"

"Yeah?"

"Hug that bear for me."

She grinned. "Alright. Goodnight Gareth. Um. Thanks for the driving lesson."

"No problem, Mads. Let me know when you want to practice again."

Practice. Did he mean driving lessons, or something else?

Then he hung up the phone.

Maddy rested quietly in her dark bedroom, staring at the glow-in-the-dark stars on her ceiling. She pressed the naughty white bear into her chest. She held it between her breasts, feeling the soft fur on her nipples. She thought of the day Gareth bought it for her. How heroic he had been after her panic attack at his house. Their date at Zippy's. Those intimate moments in the parking lot.

"I think I met you for a reason."

Maybe she was wrong last Friday night when she decided to stay at the trailer with Dean.

Maybe she should have gone back home with him.

She squeezed the bear. It wasn't that simple. But she wished it could be.

What am I doing? she wondered, asking him to hangout this Friday like she wasn't falling head over heels for him. Like she hadn't been obsessed with him since she was fourteen years old. *I'm an idiot. I have no idea how relationships work.*

He was still waiting for her to make up her mind and move out of her house. Every day, it was looking better and better. But she was still scared to make that leap.

At least for tonight, she could forget all those big complicated questions about their future, and just enjoy the memory of his kiss. Yeah. For now, that was enough.

Her phone pinged.

Goodnight, little girl.

She smiled at his text. She wished, for a painful moment, that she was falling asleep in his arms. She really missed him. A lot.

She texted him back:

Goodnight, G.

Chapter 22

Maddy survived Thursday by keeping her head down at school and her tail tucked.

During the midmorning Nutrition break, she saved Gareth's pic as the background on her phone, with his muscles all flexed and his smoldering gaze. Every time she saw it, she felt a little *zing*. He looked nothing like the boys she sat next to in class, who were gangly and baby-faced. His square jaw and strong neck, with the indent of an Adam's apple, was all man.

Shit. They were *just friends*, but she didn't know how to keep it casual. Especially after last night.

She checked her text messages again. He hadn't contacted her yet today. She wanted to reach out, but she didn't know what to say. Should she send funny memes? Talk about school? Maybe send him music? She hadn't asked about his favorite bands yet.

At lunch, she shared her favorite Phantogram playlist with him on her music app.

Thoughts? she texted after sending the link.

She skipped eating lunch and walked to detention, which was in the assembly hall near the Admin building. The auditorium was a big, square, brick building with majestic Greek columns framing the front doors. She was relieved to be anywhere other than the cafeteria, where the condom video was still circulating.

She recognized some of the kids sitting in the auditorium seats. Mr. Krozer, the Fine Arts teacher, made her put her phone away and gave her a worksheet.

"Thirty minutes of silent time," he said. "Complete this worksheet with a three paragraph essay. If I hear one word, you'll have to leave and finish another time."

Maddy nodded and took the worksheet, which asked her to write an essay answering the following question: "What have I learned from reflecting on my mistakes?"

She rolled her eyes to herself. *The audacity.* She hadn't done anything wrong.

She considered writing a snarky response, or crumpling up the paper and throwing it away, but then she thought better of it. *Just get it over with,* she thought. Her goal this year was to graduate, not get expelled. So she sucked in a deep breath and started explaining, in her own words, why she brought 100 rainbow-colored condoms to school. *It was all a joke,* she lied. Well, at least it sounded plausible, though she doubted anyone would read the essay.

What I learned was… what I learned was…. Maddy bit her lip. This was harder than she first thought. *What I learned is that condoms are not allowed on campus.*

After detention, when she checked her phone again, her text to Gareth still showed "Unread."

In Earth Science class, Maddy fidgeted with her phone discreetly under the lab table. She thought of texting Gareth again to check in, but she had already sent him two texts in a row. If she kept texting, she would look desperate. The strange anxiety stayed with her after 3pm, when school let out, then on her walk to the hardware store.

The rest of the evening dragged by. The hardware store was slow. She couldn't be on her phone at work. At 9pm, after her shift let out, she still hadn't received a response.

Maybe he was working late? He was probably super busy at the garage. Too busy to check his phone? What was he doing?

Whatever. Just forget about him.

Maddy got home on Thursday night after work to discover a new deadbolt installed on the front door. Dean was sitting at his usual place in front of the TV in a cloud of marijuana smoke. She looked from the deadbolt to the bullet hole in the wall. She didn't know if the deadbolt on the front door made her feel safer or more concerned. Was Dean expecting another break-in? The mysterious letters from Gelson's & Associates had disappeared from the coffee table. She couldn't ask Dean about them again. It would be useless to try. He wouldn't tell her anything. But she knew he was hiding something.

She crossed the living room to the kitchen and put on the electric kettle. She made a cup of tea from the box Gareth's mom had given her. Then she walked down the hallway to her bedroom. It was late, but she still needed to finish two homework assignments.

It was only a matter of time before Dean went off on another bender. Maddy was counting down the days. Then she would be alone in the trailer again, secluded at night in the dark woods, which had never seemed quite so terrifying before. What would she do if there was another break-in?

Maddy set down her backpack and took out her math book. She checked her phone. It was 9:30pm and Gareth still hadn't texted her. She bit her lip.

Thinking of last night made her excruciatingly shy. She cringed, remembering their intimate conversation over the phone. She couldn't believe she had actually sent him a full-on titty pic. And his cock! Oh god. Had she lost her mind? She deleted the photo in a moment of panic that morning, terrified Dean would grab her phone and see it. Now she kinda wished she still had it. She wanted to look at it again. What if she asked him for another one? That was as good as asking him for sex—again.

I blame temporary insanity, she thought. In the private darkness of her bedroom, she had felt bold and sensual. But now after a day of silence from him, she was shrinking back into herself. *I can't believe we talked about sex.* And they did a lot more than just talk!

The thought of seeing him on Friday was becoming more and more intimidating. His silence was unbearable. Did her text not send? How was she supposed to look him in the eye after all that?

Maddy finished her homework by 11pm. She drank the tea that Gareth's mom had sent her. It had a grassy, matcha type of flavor. Not bad. She wondered what Gareth's mom was like. Did she live in Arizona? Did she speak Spanish? She still hadn't asked Gareth about his family. There was so much about him she didn't know.

The TV blared from the living room, a dull murmur through the thin walls of the mobile home. Maddy climbed into bed and curled up under her blue comforter. She messed around on her phone. She checked her messages for the hundredth time. Gareth still hadn't contacted her. She wasn't sure how she felt about that. His sudden silence was unnerving. She wondered what he was up to. What the silence meant.

He's not my boyfriend, she reminded herself, feeling a little wistful. *So stop acting like a needy girlfriend.* She really needed to set better boundaries.

Maddy held the white stuffed bear against her stomach and breathed deep, trying to release the tight knots. Then she took a few puffs on her CBD pen. Still no texts. But she was too stubborn to text him first.

Gripping the white bear to her chest, she finally fell asleep.

***

Maddy arrived at school on Friday morning, exhausted yet full of nervous energy. *Calm down, dummy,* she told herself. But she could barely sit in her homeroom seat. Tonight, she would finally introduce Gareth to Bea. It was a big step. For five years, he had been her hidden crush, her midnight fantasy, and now she was *hanging out* with him. It felt surreal.

That is, if he didn't cancel. He still hadn't seen her text message. *What the hell.*

All day Friday she watched the clock, counting down the minutes until 3pm. She texted Dean at lunch, reminding him to feed Joker. She hadn't told him about the haunted house. She had kept her plans private.

Surprising her, Dean texted back:

> Are u staying out late?

Maddy fiddled with her phone, biting her lip. Did she tell Dean the truth? He would freak out if he knew she was seeing Gareth.

> I picked up an extra shift at the hardware store.

> since when do u work Fridays?

> since i had to pay your cable bill

> i paid it already dumbass

> Now they're gonna apply your check to the account

> Thanks for saving me money next month

Maddy felt sick to her stomach. The WaveTV bill was definitely pink. She wondered if Dean was telling the truth. If he was, then she had just mailed off $300 that could have been used to buy food or save for property taxes.

Did she just waste all that money for no good reason?

For a moment, she was blinded by rage. She sucked in a deep breath before texting back.

i'm just letting u know I'll be home late, so plz feed Joker

your shift gets out at 9pm

so i better see u home before 10

Maddy swallowed, hard.

I'll be out later than that

doing what?

I'm going to the Halloween Festival at Beaumont Farms with friends.

fuck no you're not. you're coming home.

I didn't say you could go to some carnival.

I don't want u hanging out with that cradle robbing fucker.

Maddy paled. She honestly didn't know what to write back. This was totally unlike her stepdad. He had never cared before if she was out late.

He knows, Maddy thought with a bit of dread. Dean was a bullshitter, so he knew when she was bullshitting, too. He knew she was lying about not seeing Gareth. She had been acting dodgy all week, avoiding Dean's gaze and being vague about her whereabouts.

She thought of Dean's threat: *"If I find out you're hanging around him, I'll knock you into next week. . . you understand, chickadee?"*

As she walked to her Earth Science class, her fear quickly turned to anger. Fuck Dean. She wasn't a little kid breaking the rules. She was a young adult. She deserved to date. Why did Dean make her feel like she was doing something wrong? She was over eighteen and she had a right to her own life. She needed to remember that.

She pulled her phone out of her hoodie and opened Dean's text messages. She grimaced at the words "cradle robber." She tried to suppress the rage that boiled beneath her skin. Then she started texting.

> I'm an adult, i can stay out all night if i want

> U can't tell me what to do

> sure i can

> Keep it up and i'll whoop your ass when u get home

> Show some fucking respect

Her shoulders stiffened. Fear slid down her spine like an ice cube. Dean texted again.

> You're still seeing that old guy. I knew it.

> U fucking him? U better not get knocked up

> I'll throw u out on ur ass

Maddy felt sick to her stomach. Was he threatening to throw her out? Was he really that upset? Or was he drunk and throwing a tantrum?

> u can't throw me out

> just watch me

> You are over 18

i'm not fucking anyone

I'm just seeing friends tonight

Maddy knew Dean was probably drunk if he was behaving this irrationally. He was overreacting. He probably didn't mean all that about throwing her out. He wouldn't do that to her. On the most basic level, he needed her to pay the bills. He was just trying to scare her.

She hung her head for a moment. Was this really her life? A tear threatened to slip down her cheek.

Her phone pinged again. It buzzed several times. Dean was sending her a lot of texts:

ur grounded

i don't care wat ur plans are tonight

ur not dating that fucker

someone's got to watch Joker tonight

I'm heading down to the casino

get ur ass home

Maddy paled. She tried to stay strong, but her hands were shaking.

Ok. I'll be home by 10pm.

She stood in the hallway, staring at the lie. The bell rang and a few kids ran past her into the science lab, their sneakers scuffing the wax floors. She was late, but she didn't move. She was defying Dean. She wasn't coming home by 10pm. She was going to stay out as late as she wanted, no matter what. And if Dean decided to punish her?

She swallowed hard. It was impossible to predict what he would do.

But her rage overpowered her fear.

"You can't force me to stay home. I'm not a child," she whispered to the phone. "If Joker tears apart your fucking couch, that's not my problem."

Dean didn't text her again. Maddy slipped into her science class, subdued, and sat at a stool at the back of the room. Today's lab was about examining different kinds of rocks and identifying them on a worksheet. Maddy partnered up with two other students and bent over her work. She tried to ignore the dread hanging over her like a little storm cloud. She never picked fights with Dean. It was too risky. He was unpredictable. It was stupid for her to provoke him. But she couldn't delete the text messages, and she wasn't going to change her mind or cancel her date—*hangout*—with Gareth. Oh fucking well.

After Earth Science class was Computer Lab, the last period of the day, which basically meant dicking around on the internet for forty five minutes. Bea sat at the front of the room and gave Maddy a little wave when she entered.

Maddy took her usual seat at the back row of computers, as far away from the teacher as she could get. Mrs. Lemony's perfume always bothered her nose. Today it seemed twice as pungent.

Finally, the last bell rang and school was let out. Maddy left the computer lab at a fast walk. She avoided Kaylee's group near the water fountain on her way down the stairs. Then she met up with Bea on the curb outside. The tiny Goth girl was already lighting up a cigarette. Her black witchy nails were decorated with little white spiderwebs and orange pumpkins. She was wearing a pair of high-waisted black cargo shorts. Her oversized Daft Punk T-shirt was tucked in at the waist. About a million black rubber bracelets covered each wrist.

She wasn't alone. Maddy was surprised to see two other girls mingling around Bea, checking their phones and chatting about school. Obviously Bea had her own little group of friends. Maddy felt shy, but forced herself to walk over.

"There you are!" Bea said, looking up as Maddy approached. "This is Andie and Rachelle. I wanted you all to meet. I've known Andi since seventh grade. Rachelle and I started hanging out last year."

Maddy waved a little. "Hi."

Andi waved back. "Hi! Bea said a lot of good things about you."

"Oh. Thanks. Nice to meet you," Maddy mumbled.

Andie was about as Goth Punk as Bea. She had black hair with two bright green bangs dyed on either side of her face. Rachelle was tall and a bit more colorful. The trend was "Light Goth." She wore a pastel purple sweater and black ripped jeans. Her hair was dyed bright pink, but she still had a nose piercing and dark eye shadow.

She looked a little familiar, but with her heavy eyeshadow and dyed hair, Maddy couldn't quite place her.

"Oh my god, Bea, I can't believe you're hanging out with . . ." Rachelle stopped. Then she cleared her throat. "Oh hey. You're the girl in the condom video, right?"

"Um, yeah."

"That really sucks to get pranked like that," Andie said in her soft voice. Her brown eyes got all big. She looked sincere.

"Don't people call you Porno Titties?" Rachelle blurted out.

"Rachelle, stop it," Bea said. "Maddy had a rough week. Anyway, we gotta get going. Meet you up later at Fright Farm?"

"For sure. We'll see you around 7 o'clock," Rachelle said.

"Yeah," Andie added, "Rachelle's mom is going to drive us. See you guys."

The girls waved. Then they turned and walked away. Maddy watched them go. So apparently Bea had invited several people to Fright Farm, not just her. That was okay. Just different from what she expected, and that made her anxiety worse.

As she watched the girls walk away, she saw Rachelle lean over and whisper something to Andie, who glanced back at Maddy over her shoulder. Maddy felt the hair prickle on her neck. She could tell they were gossiping. It made her uncomfortable. Black River High School was very small. She wondered how much Rachelle knew about her. Why did she look so familiar? She reminded Maddy of *someone*.

In sudden realization, Maddy recognized Rachelle from eighth grade. She was blond back then, but still taller than average. Maddy remembered her joining Kaylee's group just before she got annexed. Rachelle probably knew all about Maddy's drama with Kaylee, going all the way back to eighth grade. With a blush of shame, Maddy wondered what she was telling Andie.

Or maybe it wasn't such a big deal. It looked like Rachelle wasn't hanging out with Kaylee anymore. So maybe Rachelle would turn into an unexpected ally?

"Hey, let's get out of here," Bea said. "Come back to my place and let's get ready. Are you wearing that outfit tonight?"

Maddy glanced down at her secondhand sweater. The sleeves were frayed and she had worn little holes in the cuffs for her thumbs to fit through. She hadn't thought much about what to wear to Beaumont Farms Haunted Manor. She was more focused that morning on leaving the trailer while avoiding her stepdad.

Well, she was seeing Gareth tonight, so maybe she should try to look a bit more polished. Less like a Raggedy Anne doll, and more "fun and flirty."

"I didn't really think about what to wear," Maddy admitted. "Um, do you have any makeup I could borrow?"

Bea raised an eyebrow and blew out a puff of smoke from her cigarette.

"Do I have *makeup?* Girl, I've been waiting for this day. I can't wait to do your eyeliner."

Chapter 23

They reached Bea's house after about a twenty minute walk.

Bea spoke over her shoulder as she opened the front door.

"Have you eaten? Mom made spaghetti yesterday. Pasta is good for soaking up alcohol. Oh wait. Are you drinking tonight?"

Maddy shrugged. "I mean, probably not? It's not really my thing."

"Well, whatever. I'm bringing a flask."

Maddy followed Bea into the house. The open concept floor plan looked like any other craftsman-style home. They passed through a small living room with a broken-in couch and plasma TV. Then Bea led her into a wide, spacious kitchen. The appliances were outdated and heavily used, but the kitchen was clean and the dishes stacked neatly on a drying rack. Only two burners worked on the stove. The refrigerator door handle was duct taped on, and the microwave was broken.

"Who's that?" a boy asked from the dining room table. He was playing with a bowl of spaghetti and getting about half of it on the floor. He looked maybe six years old.

"That's Maddy, little dude," Bea said. "Be nice. She's cool. Maddy, this is my brother Joey."

The little boy blinked up at Maddy. "You're really pretty. You got a boyfriend?"

Maddy was shocked. "What?"

"Nevermind him. He thinks he's Don Juan," Bea said.

"You want some of my Halloween candy?" little Joey said.

"Stop, Joey, you already have three girlfriends, remember?" Bea said with a grin. Then she laughed at Maddy's expression. "You look traumatized! Jeez. Please ignore him. He doesn't really know what a boyfriend is."

"Yes I do!" Joey insisted. "A boyfriend is a hero who rescues girls. Like Iron Man."

"Yup," Bea said. "A boyfriend is like Iron Man. That's right."

Well, he's not completely wrong, Maddy thought, amused. "Are you going to be Iron Man for Halloween?" she asked.

"No, that was last year. This year I'm gonna be Beethoven."

"What?" Maddy asked again.

"He means the dog," Bea explained. "You know, that old movie with the St. Bernard? Nevermind. Let's go upstairs."

Bea made herself a bowl of pasta from a container in the fridge.

"You sure you don't want any?" Bea asked a second time. "I feel bad eating when you're not."

"It's okay. I'm full. Really. I had a big lunch." It was a lie. In truth, Maddy was too nervous to eat.

Bea picked up her bowl and motioned for Maddy to follow her. "Okay. Long as you don't feel bad while I stuff my face."

Halfway up the stairs, another boy ran past them. He was gangly and skinny, and Maddy guessed him to be closer to fourteen. He stopped when he saw Maddy. His eyes darted to her generous chest. He blushed. Then he looked up at her face.

"Oh hi," he said.

"Hi," Maddy replied.

The boy glanced around. "Oh hey Bea, did you do the laundry?"

"It's drying."

"I don't have any pants."

"What about the pants you're wearing?" Bea pointed out.

"They're like three days old."

"Gross. Get out of the way. Not my problem."

Bea shoved past her other brother. They continued up the stairs to the second floor.

"How many brothers do you have?" Maddy asked.

Bea rolled her eyes. "Like, four. There's Jack and Joey, who you met. Joey has a twin brother, Zach, who's at karate right now. Then the baby, Milo. He's with his dad while my mom's at work. Milo's my half brother."

"That's . . . a lot of kids."

"You're telling me."

Old brown carpet covered the stairs and upper floor. Maddy counted three bedrooms and two bathrooms branching off of a central hallway. Bea's bedroom was the last door at the end of the hall. The two other bedrooms belonged to her mom and her younger brothers. Maddy caught a glimpse of bunk beds and a very messy floor covered in laundry and toys.

Bea opened her bedroom door and dragged Maddy inside. "Come on, hurry up! Before those little punks ask me for something."

Maddy yelped as she stumbled into Bea's room, and Bea shut the door firmly behind them. Her friend propped a chair against the knob, because it didn't lock. Then Bea crossed the room to her dresser. She set down her bowl of noodles and started to rummage through the drawers, pulling out all sorts of brushes, powders, and palettes of eyeshadow.

Maddy stood in the middle of the floor and looked around. It felt like a large space, since her own room was barely bigger than a walk-in closet. Heavy blackout curtains covered the window. The walls were covered in posters of Bea's favorite bands: *Ghost, The Doors, My Chemical Romance, Fireflight.*

"You listen to Paramore?" Maddy asked as she looked at the different posters.

"I fucking love Paramore," Bea said absently as she pulled out even more makeup from the top drawer of her dresser. "I saw them in concert last Summer. I took a bus down to New York City. Can't believe mom let me go alone. I was seeing this guy off Tinder. I told my mom he went to my school but he was like, in college . . . ." She started rambling about how good a kisser he was, but after the concert, he wouldn't drive out to Black River to see her. So she dumped him.

Maddy stood next to the bed, inspecting a lava lamp full of green goop.

"What about you, Maddy? You ever been to a concert?"

"No," Maddy said.

"Did you do anything fun last summer?"

"Not really, just worked a lot. I had summer school," she said.

"That sucks. So what, you just work and pay bills? Doesn't your stepdad do anything?"

"Not really. I mean. He's kind of worthless. He just drinks all day."

Maddy bit her lip, realizing how that must sound. She glanced over her shoulder.

Bea stopped rummaging through her makeup and fixed Maddy with a pointed look.

"So, like," Bea started, "I didn't want to make you feel bad, but yeah, I've heard a few things about your dad. Pretty shitty."

Maddy felt her fists curl into little balls. If she were a wolf, she'd say her hackles went up.

Bea continued, "My mom told me a bunch of stuff. She feels terrible about your trailer getting broken into. She said your dad was a real piece of work. I guess my mom knows him pretty well. He's at the bar a lot. She says you're a survivor. Like, you've had it rough."

Maddy scratched her neck, a little self-conscious. Since Bea's mom was a bartender at The B Joint, she would remember when Maddy's mother overdosed on pills. She might even know some stuff about Dean from back in the day. It hit a bit too close to home.

Maddy felt tears stinging her eyes. Ugh. She didn't want to kill the mood.

"Dean's not all bad. Really, it's no big deal. Last summer I worked and I saved up a bunch of money." Maddy plastered a fake grin on her face. "I totally plan on traveling more this summer, after graduation."

"That's cool. Where do you want to go?"

"Um. Anywhere, actually."

Bea laughed. "I hear you. Come sit here on the floor. I'm going to do your makeup."

Maddy crossed the floor and sat down cross-legged in front of Bea's bedroom mirror. Bea sat down nearby with her pile of makeup paraphernalia. She put on a playlist and turned up the volume on her little tin-can Bluetooth speaker.

"Now hold still. I'm gonna make you look like a doll. When your sugardaddy shows up tonight, he's not gonna know what hit him. "

Bea was very focused as she worked. Maddy tried to sit still, her nose itched.

"So?" Bea asked as she worked. "Did you ever find out more about that Roxie chick? The girl on Picplace?"

"Um. We talked about it."

Maddy took a breath. It felt like weeks had passed since she last thought of Roxie, but it had only been two days.

"I guess she was just a hookup. He said he blocked her number," she explained.

"And you believe him?" Bea was skeptical.

Maddy shrugged. Honestly, she didn't have much choice. She knew she had trust issues. She was doing her best to take him at face value.

"I think we've gotten closer," she said. "So yeah, I believe him. I guess. I'd rather not make a big deal out of it. And, um, we're still figuring stuff out. Like for now, we're just friends, so I'd rather the other girls didn't know about us."

"What's to figure out? He's super hot and buys you groceries. I wouldn't turn that down." Bea laughed at Maddy's expression. "Don't worry. I promise your secret is safe with me. I'll be honest, I forgot to tell Becca about him, so my sister doesn't even know. But if he acts creepy or shady, or pulls any shit tonight, I don't care how pretty he is, I'll take him out."

Bea drew one of her long witchy nails across her throat.

Maddy laughed uneasily. She wasn't sure if Bea was joking or not. She was only five feet tall. *Still, it's the thought that counts.*

"Thank you," Maddy said.

"Of course, pumpkin. Now keep still while I do your eyeliner."

When she was done, Bea sat back with a victorious smile. "There you are!" she said proudly. "One sexy wonderbitch, as promised."

Maddy looked in the mirror. She almost didn't recognize herself. Her lips parted in surprise. Bea had used light powder and bronzer to contour her cheeks. Light brown pencil darkened her eyebrows. Merlot lipstick, smokey eyes, black eyeliner and mascara finished the look. A bit dramatic, but perfect for a covert second date.

"Dang," Maddy muttered. "I look . . ."

"Hot."

Maddy grinned. "You're really good at this," she said to Bea.

"Your expression is *so* worth it," Bea said, and snapped a few pics with her phone. "Don't worry, I won't post them. Just for my little collection. Did you want to borrow some clothes? I think I have some shirts that might fit you." Bea looked at Maddy's tits pointedly.

"Stop creeping me out!" Maddy laughed.

Bea stuck out her pierced tongue. Then she jumped up and opened her closet door. She yanked on a few shirts hanging up in the dark recesses of her closet and threw them down on the bed.

Maddy went to look through the pile. It was slim pickings. Bea was a short girl, thin as a wafer cracker, and her shirts hugged Maddy's curves in a lascivious way. Her breasts didn't fit in half of them.

"You sure you don't want to work at Sapphire?" Bea teased her.

Maddy rolled her eyes. Bea's shirts were so thin, the outline of her nipples was visible through her padded bra. Damn. Having large breasts was a pain in the ass.

"I really can't wear any of these," Maddy said in dismay. "The fabric is too thin."

"Here, try this."

Bea yanked down a cropped off ACDC T-Shirt from her closet and threw it at Maddy, who pulled it on. Her midriff was exposed, but the heavy T-shirt offered more coverage for her breasts.

"It has potential," Maddy allowed, though she wasn't used to her stomach showing.

"It's cute! You have a nice figure, Maddy. You should flaunt it more. Here, throw this flannel on. Perfect. Now this beanie. Alright. There. Gorgeous! I call this look Small Town Bonfire Sexy. Way better than the sweater you were wearing. I approve! Anyway, now it's my turn to get ready. I need to wash my face. I'll be right back."

Bea removed the chair from the bedroom door. Then she picked up her makeup bag and ducked into the hallway, heading for the bathroom.

Maddy remained in front of the mirror, turning this way and that, satisfied with her outfit. It was simple but perfect for a low-key "hangout" date. The glimpse of her midriff was provocative, just enough skin to tease the eye. Her makeup was on point. She couldn't wait to see the expression on Gareth's face.

At that moment, her phone buzzed. Maddy felt her heart do a little ba-dump.

She pulled out her phone. With a bit of relief, she saw Gareth's name. *Finally.* His long silence had messed with her head.

> Fright Farm still on?

Maddy felt a tiny butterfly tickle her tummy.

> yeah for sure

> just getting ready to leave now

> I got Vin with me

> Wat time?

> we are getting there like 7pm

> got it

> u eat anything today?

Maddy paused. She felt guilty. Honestly, she had been in too big a rush that morning to make food, and too anxious to eat when Bea offered.

> i'm fasting.

> what's that?

it's a new diet thing

you only eat one meal a day

u don't need to lose weight

What do u want for dinner?

I'll bring u something

Maddy fidgeted with her phone. She felt awkward asking him to pick up food for her. She needed to keep better boundaries. She shouldn't take advantage of his money.

no it's ok

Please don't, i'm not hungry

if u say so

But u should eat

See u soon

"Hey, you got a minute? I want to show you something."

Maddy jumped and looked up. Bea was standing in the doorway. The little Goth girl approached her with a sneaky smile and held up her hand. It was a condom.

"Why do you have that?" Maddy asked.

Bea handed it to her.

"Here. Better figure out how to use one *before* you need it."

Maddy's cheeks began to heat up. "I mean, I don't think . . ."

"Oh please. You keep saying you guys are 'figuring it out.' I know what that means. Look, it's gonna happen sooner or later. Go on! Unwrap it. Losing your V to an older guy is a way better experience. Trust me."

Maddy tore open the package and took out the rubber. It was gooey and wet with lubricant. She held it up with a grimace.

Bea laughed at her expression.

"I know, it's gross. Just wait until it's full of splooge. Here, you put it on like this."

Bea used her fingers to demonstrate. Maddy thought it looked simple enough. She thought back to Gareth's bathroom. *Magnum XL*. But these condoms weren't marked XL.

"Are these Magnums?" she asked.

"Hah! No. Magnums are for really big dicks. Why?" Bea's eyes narrowed. "Your sugardaddy uses Magnum?"

Maddy went pink. "Ah. Forget it," she muttered. She felt weird talking about Gareth's cock. She hadn't even seen it yet.

"You're so mysterious, Maddy."

Bea's phone buzzed. She checked it. "Speak of the witch, Becca's here! Are you ready to go? Shit, she's calling." Bea answered her phone. "We're coming down right now, I swear. We're ready. I said we're coming down! Okay, see you."

Maddy threw the condom in the trash and followed Bea out the door. They walked together down the stairs, across the living room and out onto the front porch.

Becca met them in the driveway. She was driving a black 2006 Range Rover. As they approached, Becca jumped out of the driver's seat onto the slick asphalt. Maddy thought she looked like an older, less Goth version of Bea, maybe 24 or 25. She was wearing camouflage cargo pants and a Metallica T-shirt.

"Little fucker, haven't seen you in forever!" Becca exclaimed.

"You know where I live," Bea pointed out.

"Don't be a brat. You know mom and I aren't talking right now."

"Yeah. Whatever. You guys are always fighting. Is that Levi in the car?"

At first Maddy thought she was talking about a dog, but then she saw a guy in a baseball cap sitting in the Rover's passenger seat.

"Yeah, it's about time I introduced him around," Becca confirmed.

"Are you still going to move in with him once your lease is up?"

"Yeah, I think so. It's cheaper. Plus he lives closer to campus."

"You've only been dating him four months, though," Bea pointed out. "That's kind of fast."

"I mean, it's going well," Becca said.

Maddy was surprised by this quick exchange. The two sisters talked like she wasn't even there. Maddy listened while her eyes darted back and forth. So Becca was moving in with her boyfriend? Four months didn't seem like a long time. But it was definitely longer than the week or so she had known Gareth.

Bea motioned to her. "This is my friend, Maddy."

Becca turned to Maddy and looked her up and down.

"Alright. I recognize you with the red hair. Bea showed me the condom video," she said. "You're a fucking rockstar."

Maddy froze up. She felt a little horrified. "Really?"

Becca gave her a serious look. "I'm gonna have a pinata full of condoms at my next birthday party. And you're invited."

Maddy laughed unexpectedly. Becca grinned too, her smile so wide that her eyes crinkled.

Becca rattled her keys and shooed them toward the Range Rover. "Come on, get in. There's going to be a huge line now! Forget the haunted house—the parking lot is the real nightmare."

The Land Rover was a big car. Maddy felt like she had to climb over a mountain to get into the back seat. Once inside, though, it was very spacious.

A man wearing a red baseball cap was sitting in the passenger seat. Levi turned around and gave Maddy a little wave. He had a narrow nose, a sensitive chin and stunning blue eyes. He wasn't her type, but she thought he was kinda cute. The blond scruff on his jaw helped. They made a cute couple.

Becca talked over her shoulder as she pulled out of Bea's driveway into the residential street.

"I heard about the break-in at your house, Maddy. It was on the News. Everyone at work was talking about it. You were a local celebrity for a few days, huh? I'm glad you're safe. Were those guys really killed by a wolf?"

Maddy shrugged. She had been asked that question all week. She still didn't have a solid answer. She didn't want to think about what could have happened in the dark woods on that night, if Gareth hadn't found her in time.

"Yeah, I guess so. That's what the police say. I don't really remember much. So where do you work?" Maddy changed the subject.

"Oh, I'm a dental assistant at Happy Smiles in the Davenport Mall. But who cares about work? Tonight is gonna be a wild time. Have you ever been to Fright Farm?"

"No, this is my first time."

"You're going to have so much fun! It's a good weekend to go. This is opening night. They got a corn maze, a wagon ride, a little train for kids, and like a whole fairground. The Haunted House is in the old Beaumont Plantation Manor. It's 18+ after 8pm."

"Like, is it very scary?" Maddy asked.

"It gave a woman a stroke last year," Bea said, her eyes bright with excitement.

"It wasn't a stroke," Becca rolled her eyes. "She had a panic attack. Or an asthma attack. Something like that. They probably made it less intense this year. I don't think they want a lawsuit."

Becca turned up the Bluetooth stereo and started blasting a song with heavy bass as they turned onto Highway 20. The chorus picked up to Rob Zombie's Dragula: *"Dig through the ditches and burn through the witches . . ."*

They all started to scream along at the top of their lungs.

Chapter 24

A little after six o'clock on Friday evening, Gareth sat in his Camaro in front of Vin's RV. Whimsical purple clouds filled the sky, outlined by the flaming orange sunset. For now the sky was clear, but the autumn wind was cold, and he could feel moisture gathering in the air. He didn't need to check the weather report to know a storm was brewing. It would probably reach them tonight.

Vin lived in a black and white camper parked on a wooded property on the outskirts of Black River. It looked like a three season camper; it made Gareth wonder what his plans were for the winter. Maybe he'd offer up the shop if it snowed. It didn't look like a weatherproofed kind of place.

Vin's rental wasn't as far out as Maddy's place, but still secluded, with a bit of acreage covered in fir trees, blackberry vines and wild grass. A ditch ran down the side of the property that connected to a storm drain in the street. It was a typical Black River kind of place. He saw a few broken down, rusty cars buried in the bushes. An old house stood way back from the road. It didn't look hospitable or welcoming. The windows were covered in sheets. Behind the house, Gareth glimpsed the side of a rotted-out school bus. He would have thought the property was abandoned, except for a big blue-nosed pitbull chained up on the front porch.

Gareth drummed his fingers on the steering wheel. He let out a long, slow breath. Then he read Maddy's text again. Fasting? The fuck. Why was she fasting? She needed protein.

Calm down. At least she is safe.

He checked out the playlist she sent him. He liked the vibe. Phantogram had a smooth, haunting electronica sound. It was a bit moody, a bit pop. He could see why Maddy liked it. He preferred Ghost or Metallica, personally, but it was a good mix.

After listening to a few tunes, he turned off his phone and slid it into his pocket.

"Jeezus, Vin. Hurry the fuck up," he muttered.

His mind wandered back to the day before. Thursday was a shitshow at work. It was a busy morning at Jack's Auto Repair, lots of customers picking up cars. They had several calls for a tow, which meant Vin was gone with the truck most of the day. Good for business, but that left Gareth alone at the garage to handle the customers.

He finally locked the doors around one o'clock for lunch and sat down at his computer with a sigh. Fucking needy people. The hardest part of the job was dealing with customers. The worst were the guys who knew just enough about cars to argue with him over the work. Pushy and entitled as hell. Second worst were the suspicious ones who thought he was trying to rip them off for extra services. It didn't matter how many five-star reviews he had on Yelp, there was always some detective trying to pull up dirt on his business, or complain enough to get a discount. He supposed some people just operated that way, like Mrs. Mackovich. Find the smallest thing to complain about, then don't let go until you get a coupon. That might work with big franchise places like McDonald's, but not a small business. They could fuck right off.

He almost threw a guy out that morning who accused him of up-charging for a whole list of services. The fucking audacity. But he had a full lobby and he couldn't lose it like that. He got out the guy's service agreement and took him through the work order. He pointed out a list labeled "Suggestions" with quotes good for 30 days. Then a separate list of actual work performed. Some people just didn't read.

Gareth sat back in his office chair with a deep groan and rubbed his temples. A burger and fries sat on his desk, untouched. He knew he should eat, but really he just wanted a nap. Fuck, what a day.

Instead of eating lunch, he opened up the browser on his computer. He had a folder of bookmarks for the different werewolf reddit boards online—the legit ones, not the goofy ones about Hollywood movies or Halloween. They were all closed communities; you had to show pack affiliation to get accepted. He'd been signed up for those boards a long time, since before Iraq.

He had a lot else on his mind other than work, which was adding to his stress. Since yesterday's driving lesson up on the mountain, he couldn't stop thinking about the Grayridge Pack. While he enjoyed spending time with Maddy, he regretted taking her so far into the wilderness. When they ran across that old, creepy birdwatcher, he realized the possible danger he had put her in. They were fortunate the guy was just camping off season, possibly homeless and just passing through. It could have been the Grayridge Pack waiting for them out there. Then Gareth would have had to fight them off without backup or an easy escape. He couldn't do that again.

He needed to find out more about their pack, their numbers, and their territory. It was pretty clear that they intended to spread into Black River, and he was in the way. The threat wasn't going to disappear. But how many was he up against? A dozen? A hundred? Wolf packs varied a lot in size.

He opened up the werewolf reddit boards and started searching different keywords: upstate new york werewolves, grayridge, gray-ridge, new pack, New England wolf packs.

He couldn't find anything recent. He had to go deeper.

Gareth opened up an incognito tab and entered a web address from memory. The webpage that loaded was black with a single login screen. It wasn't the kind of website that would show up on search engines like Google or Yahoo. But if you were a wolf, you knew about it.

He typed in his username and password and hit "enter." The webpage loaded a black userpanel with green text. On the home screen was a long list of countries and various states, regions and major cities. Under each major city was a list of topics and discussions. This was the wolf web—basically Craigslist for werewolves.

Under every major city was a subtopic called "Hunt and Play."

If you were a wolf, you knew what "Hunt and Play" meant. Basically, it was a list of invitations for meetups on the full moon, where wolves could run together, hunt, play, fuck shit up, kill large game, and other group activities not related to kickball or bar hopping. A lot of new packs formed that way. Not all wolf packs were full-on kingdoms like the Phoenix pack, which controlled the Sonoran desert up through Vegas. Some packs were just six or seven wolves who liked to hunt big game together on the full moon. It just depended on the size of the community in the area, and if an Alpha was in charge.

For whatever reason, packs always sprung up around Alphas. It tended to happen organically, and it was part of the mystery of being a wolf.

For whatever reason, packs always sprung up around Alphas. It tended to happen organically, and it was part of the mystery of being a wolf. Likewise, Alphas just seemed built for that business; they naturally took charge. It was in the blood. By all means, Gareth knew he should be starting a new pack of his own. He was almost thirty, so it was about that time. He was entering his prime as far as Alpha strength and vitality was concerned. It made him that much more of a threat to the Grayridge Pack. His lone presence out in Black River was an anomaly for their kind, just like his little wolf girl.

Gareth liked the way his younger brother Antony described Alphas using a videogame analogy. Antony was always into computer stuff; even as a kid, he was already a brilliant programmer. He remembered his brother's words from when they were in high school together, before Gareth went into the Army.

"Let's say you're playing an open world MMORPG. There's always a bunch of monsters roaming the map. You got your regular fiends and maybe a few high ranking beasts wandering around for extra XP. But every now and then, a super-boss monster spawns that's twenty levels too strong and impossible to kill, and if you defeat it, you get a lot of extra loot. And that's an Alpha wolf."

He grinned. Yeah, he was a boss monster, and some folks swore that Alpha parts—bones, teeth, pelt, blood, semen—had magic powers, good for spells or potions or whatever. He didn't know much about that, but he knew some eccentric people went after that loot. Just like there were werewolf forums, there were also hunters, but that was another world, nothing he ever dealt with before.

Wolves wanted to be safe, just like anyone else, so part of having a big pack was that added layer of security. Last he remembered, his brother Antony lived in Vegas and used his computer whiz powers to protect the Phoenix pack against local hunters. A lot of it was keeping their presence hidden and anonymous. It was a whole thing. Shit, he hadn't talked to Antony in a long time.

Gareth scrolled down the website to the section labeled "United States," then clicked on the New England postings, then the Upstate New York postings in his local area. He finally clicked on "Hunt and Play."

First result was for an auction. He scrolled past it. Of course, it wasn't labeled "Female Breeder Auction," but the context was obvious: *"Meet lusty females eager to mate... high stamina will keep you up all night...."*

Technically auctions were illegal, but that didn't stop them from happening.

A lot of postings on the wolf web were for sex. Wolf libido was a thing. Most of the ads were phishing schemes or dead links, but a few led to the real thing—secret auctions where female breeders could be purchased. Every wolf knew about it. It was almost assumed whenever a pair of bonded mates were encountered that the female was purchased, unless it was a human female. Of course, that wasn't very fair to female wolves; if they were lucky, they had a strong pack to protect them. Unlike Maddy.

He opened the search bar and typed in the keyword: Grayridge.

Finally, some results.

He found a handful of postings that went back about two years, when he found the earliest "Hunt and Play" meetup. Most of them were out of Niagara Falls, a little out of his way on the other side of Lake Ontario. But a few were closer to home. He saw a meetup posted two months ago in Davenport. Ah.

When he clicked on it, he saw an address for the River King Casino on the outskirts of Davenport. That was probably where Dean first encountered them. It wasn't hard to imagine Maddy's dad rubbing shoulders with the Grayridge wolf pack, especially considering their vibe. They were basically a bunch of petty thieves and glorified bar rats like Dean, from what Gareth could tell. Maybe their Alpha, Marquis, was more sophisticated, but he doubted it. Every wolfpack had a vibe, and that vibe usually followed its Alpha. So Marquis was just a drug lord operating out of Canada who had gathered enough followers to expand his territory. Great. He sounded like a pain in the ass.

Gareth clicked through a few more postings, trying to find any information on the size of the Grayridge pack, but mentions were sparse. Finally, he signed out and closed his browser. Well, at least he knew a bit more about their territory and history. They were fairly new, so they weren't very established yet. If he really wanted to confront them, he could always drive down to the River King Casino and bust some heads. But that seemed like a lot of gas to waste just to break a few jaws. And he had a business to run.

His eyes flickered down to his desk. He saw his phone light up with the name, "Brat."

Ah, what did his little wolf girl want now?

Gareth growled low in his throat, unaware of the sound.

He woke up with the taste of her still on his mouth. He'd been thinking about that tight little candy snatch all day. Fuck, she was sweet. He wanted to go again, lick all that sugary filling out of her. *Mmm*, he was hungry. Those pretty pink lips were gonna get a lot of attention, as soon as they got past this awkward "friends" thing.

Last night had been . . . . well, fuck. He didn't expect her to send a topless pic. That surprised him. He remembered gazing at his phone for a long minute, his eyes dilated and his jaw clenched. Damn. His innocent young mate was getting bold. Good. He wanted to see her get wild. He saved her pic to a folder on his phone, which he used that morning with enthusiasm.

A strange clunking sound from the driveway interrupted his thoughts, and Gareth put his phone down before checking it. At first he thought Vin was back with the tow truck, but then he heard a few voices talking. Another loud clang, this time against the garage door.

He stood up from his desk.

"What the hell?" he muttered. Then he called, "The fuck are you doing, Vin?"

No answer. A beat of silence. Then a loud *boom!* rattled through the garage. It sounded like someone had dropped a drain pan or a wrench or something heavy on the ground.

What the hell? Was there a customer somewhere in the shop?

With a growl of irritation, Gareth strode through the breakroom into the garage where two cars were up on lifts. He looked around, expecting to see Vin making a mess, but the garage was empty. That seemed extra suspicious. He paused for a moment, listening. Then he heard voices outside.

Moving at a fast pace, Gareth walked from the garage into the lobby, around the front desk and out through the customer entrance. The cold mountain air struck his face. It was a chill, cloudy day. The door to the lobby shut behind him with the little ding of a bell.

He exited the building just as a loud gunshot rang out. He started and ducked.

"What the fuck?" he demanded.

Johnny stood at the border of his property to his left. He had a shotgun in hand and a cigarette hanging out of his mouth. His face was stone cold.

"Looks like you got a pest problem, G," he spat.

Gareth's head swung to his right where two goons dressed in hoodies and N95 masks looked equally startled. Cans of spray paint fell onto the slick asphalt in front of his garage doors. By the looks of it, they were defacing the front of his property. The big garage doors were marked up with ugly red and black spray paint.

Gareth felt a surge of rage. It looked like the little punks had been going at it for a while.

"The hell are you two doing?" he demanded, pointing a big arm at them.

"You want me to bury some lead in their ass?" Johnny asked.

"Not on my property," Gareth said. "But thanks for the offer."

The two men looked between Johnny and Gareth. Then, in a mad scramble, they took off running across the parking lot.

Gareth charged after them, his boots slamming against the ground, kicking up gravel in his wake. *Fuck this nonsense*, he thought. If he caught the little bastards, he was going to drag them personally to the police station.

The two punks jumped the ditch at the side of his property and ran into the woods. Gareth flew over the ditch after them. He sprinted through the forest, relying on his wolf senses to follow after his prey. His pulse quickened, his eyes dilated—now he was on the hunt.

That's when he caught a whiff of their scent and it all made a certain kind of sense. These weren't just regular delinquents vandalizing his property. These were wolves.

Gareth felt his hackles go up. He would recognize that stench anywhere. It was the Grayridge Pack again. *The hell?* Were they taunting him? Trying to rile him up? Well, it was working. But why would they send two kids to vandalize his property in broad daylight?

Gareth sprinted through the woods, following the trail of the two wolves. He was gaining ground, fast. He knew this wilderness like the back of his hand. It was familiar territory. His territory. He often wandered this section of the mountain at night; it was a good place to hunt white tailed deer. He knew the location of all the streams, the deer trails and rabbit holes, the alder groves and the juniper bushes. The Grayridge Pack had a disadvantage; they just didn't know it yet.

Then Gareth's eyes discerned a strange dip in the ground before him. He leapt over it automatically. Light glinted. *There.*

Steel jaws snapped shut.

The shower of dirt from Gareth's passing set off the bear trap buried under a layer of yellow leaves. Luckily, his foot barely brushed it; he cleared it before the trap was sprung.

Gareth landed on the other side of the giant steel jaws. He stumbled forward a few feet. He came to a halt amidst a copse of dogwood trees and juniper bushes. He looked back at the trap. A flurry of red maple leaves fell down from above, shaken loose by the wind. Gareth listened to the whispers of the woodland; he didn't think anyone was nearby. But that didn't mean the two wolves wouldn't circle back to check on him, to see if he'd fallen for their trap.

Gareth walked over to the clamped metal jaws. A thick chain was buried under the layer of autumn foliage on the ground. The fucking thing would have snapped his leg in half. These fuckers were relentless. The Grayridge Pack was really starting to piss him off. Was this another assassination attempt? Maybe he should be flattered.

Gareth glanced around the woods again, considering his options, but he really wasn't in the mood to play cat-and-mouse with these fools. He decided to head back to the shop. He didn't see the point in chasing the two wolves deeper into the woods. Either they would try to lead him into another trap, or he would run into more wolves, and he had shit to do. The garage wouldn't run itself.

Gareth was a bit more cautious on his walk back to the shop. The woods stank of the Grayridge pack; it looked like they'd been circling around his property for a few days. If he wasn't so distracted by Maddy, he probably would have noticed them sooner. So they were watching him at the garage. Enjoy, motherfuckers. Nothing much to see except used tires and cranky customers.

As he leapt over the ditch that separated his property from the woods, he saw Vin climbing out of the tow truck, a bag of fast food in hand. He didn't see Johnny anywhere. The old Japanese man must have returned to the gas station. He would have to duck in later and apologize—he knew Johnny had his back, but he didn't like causing trouble for his neighbors.

"The hell happened?" Vin asked as Gareth approached. "I saw Johnny walking around with a shotgun. And what's with the tagging on the garage doors?"

"Vandals. I chased them into the woods."

"Did you catch up with them?"

"No luck. They got away."

Gareth paused next to Vin. The two men stared at the ruined garage doors. Gareth wanted to groan. Painting a building the size of his auto shop cost an arm and a leg, and he just got it done in a nice industrial gray color with red trim. The spray paint across the doors was gruesome. The threats didn't leave much to the imagination. *"Death 2 Alpha"* was sprayed across one door with a shitty caricature of a wolf skull. The second door read: *"We will mount your head."* They spelled "mount" like "munt."

Vin took out his vape pen and puffed on it, considering the rude letters across the front of the building.

"It's not even good," he said. "Like, there's graffiti art, and then there's just pissing on someone's turf. This ain't no art, boss."

"Yeah. I know."

"Like, I think someone's trying to threaten you."

"Probably," Gareth agreed. "You into street art, Vin?"

"Hell yes," Vin said enthusiastically. "I'm no Banksy but yeah, I paint. Mostly freestyle. I've got a few places I go to practice. Like out in the woods, there's a quarry down near the old Jefferson Bridge. Some train tracks run along it. Lots of kids tag out there."

"Right. You ever paint murals?"

Vin looked over at him. "I've done a few. Why?"

"Would you do one across the garage doors?"

"You serious?"

"Yeah." Gareth pointed at the crooked writing. "Just cover up this shit. I hate seeing this. Why don't you turn it into good art? I'll buy the paint, and I'll drop a bonus on your paycheck when it's done."

Vin stared at him with a spark in his dark eyes. "Okay. Cool. What do you want?"

"Something with a mountain. Maybe some trees. I'm not picky. Just make it good for the customers." Gareth started pulling off his bloody shirt. "Anyway, I'm gonna take a quick shower. Watch the front desk for me, will you? I still need to find an invoice for the green Honda."

Vin followed Gareth inside through the customer entrance.

"Oh, I got it up front," he said. "It's in the folder with the service agreements."

"In the . . . we have a folder for that?"

"Yeah, I made one."

Gareth sighed. "Well, now I feel dumb." Then he released a wry laugh. Dang. He should've asked sooner.

That was yesterday afternoon. Then last night, he had gone after work to check on Maddy's trailer. He had Changed into a wolf to scope out the property in the woods. His worst fears were confirmed when he found tracks from the Grayridge Pack at the border of her backyard. They were only a day old. It looked like several wolves had prowled unnervingly close to her house, which meant they were still coming after Dean.

It pissed him off. First, this was *his* backyard. As in, *his* territory. For five years now, he had come to this yard to keep an eye on her, to check on her, or just to be close to her. And now these fuckers were hovering around like solicitors leaving fliers on his doorstep. They even had the balls to threaten him at his own place of business. Attempted assassination, no less. It was fucking rude.

Sure, he was a lone wolf living far away from his family and the Sonoran pack. But he was still an Alpha, and he didn't like these new wolves invading his turf. Especially coming this close to Maddy. She could easily get caught in the fray if the situation escalated.

Fucking Dean, he thought. *What did you do?*

He didn't think the pack was after Maddy, per se. But whatever Dean had gotten mixed up in wasn't going away.

It must involve a lot of money, he thought.

Now here he was, Friday night, getting ready to go to a Halloween carnival. Not exactly lying low.

Gareth drummed his fingers on the steering wheel of the Camaro as he waited outside Vin's RV. He pondered the situation, his mind churning voraciously, looking at every possible course of action. He had to do something to keep the Grayridge Pack off his territory. But what? He didn't want to resort to calling his brothers. But did he have any other options?

Contacting his brothers was a big risk. They were Alphas, too, and they might take a liking to his territory. He would be forfeiting his hardwon privacy. Once his brothers came go Black River, he wouldn't be able to escape his family any longer.

Gareth groaned. There really wasn't a good solution. He couldn't wage war on the Grayridge Pack by himself. Could he? He had already killed their Beta. That was pretty much a declaration of war. He wouldn't be surprised if Marquis himself showed up on his doorstep next week, ready to blow his brains out personally.

"You ready to go, boss?" Vin asked as he opened the car door and slid into the passenger seat of the Camaro.

"Yup. You don't gotta call me boss, Vin. We're off work."

Vin shrugged. "Well, don't ask me to call you by your first name, cuz that's just weird."

"Mr. Delarosa it is, then," Gareth grunted. "Look, Vin, about yesterday—"

"Hey, it's cool," Vin said quickly. "But like, is there something you want to tell me? Like are you dealing drugs out of the garage? Is this a gang thing? Is Johnny in on it?"

"No drugs," Gareth reassured him. "And no, Johnny, our Yakuza friend, has nothing to do with it. A situation happened maybe a week ago. I think these guys want to sort it out."

"Sort it out? Like, by murdering you?"

"Sure."

Vin was quiet for a moment as he considered it. "So like, what is the situation? Did you get in a bar fight with the wrong crowd?"

"Something like that."

"That's shady as hell." Vin puffed on his vape, then continued, "Alright, so I was thinking about it. Why do these goons keep coming by the garage? I think because it's secluded. There'd be witnesses at your house, right? You have neighbors in town. But the garage is on the edge of the woods."

"There's still the gas station," Gareth pointed out.

"Old Johnny won't call the cops. That gas station would burn to the ground before he dialed 911."

"True," Gareth agreed, surprised that Vin had put so much thought into it. "You're right. Not gonna lie, Vin. They'll probably be back. You don't have to keep working at the garage if you don't feel safe."

"Fuck that. I like my job, and you're my boss, so I got your back."

Gareth grinned. "Alright. Then we're cool?"

"Yeah. You just tell me if you need backup."

"That's good to know. But I don't want you doing anything stupid. These guys show up with more guns, I want you out of the way. Don't risk your life. I'm serious."

"Alright. Sure."

Gareth put on his sunglasses. Sun was setting on the highway. He slammed the Camaro into gear and took off, burning rubber down Highway 20. He couldn't drive like this with Maddy in the car; it would spook her. But Vin appreciated it. The kid let out a whoop and rolled down the window as the Camaro's motor roared and raged.

Gareth found himself bearing his teeth in a grim smile. He still didn't have a plan. But next time they came at him, he would be prepared. No mercy. He might need to issue an Alpha challenge. Defeating Marquis might be the only way to put an end to their shenanigans. He would have to wait and see what they tried next.

Chapter 25

Fright Farm Haunted Manor was an old Victorian-era farmhouse built on Beaumont Farms, where Fruitdale Road met Old Route 99. The house was no longer used by the Beaumont family and preserved as a historical landmark. At different times of the year, it was rented out for weddings and special events. During Halloween, the old Victorian farmhouse and the twenty acres surrounding it were converted into a fairground.

The Hallowen carnival drew crowds from all over Jefferson County, from Davenport to Whitehaven.

"It's packed," Bea said as they trudged across the parking lot.

"It's opening weekend," Becca pointed out. "I told you it was going to be crazy."

A long line of cars spilled into overflow parking. Maddy's group walked almost half a mile through gravel and mud to get to the front entrance of the fairground. The front gates to the old plantation were built of brick and mortar, with big decadent archways from the Greek revival period. The gates were sixty feet wide and about fifteen feet deep. There, a long line of people waited for bag checks and ticketing before entering the fair.

"How old is this thing?" Maddy asked, gazing up at the brick front gates.

Surprisingly, it was Levi who answered. He was holding a flier for the fair in one hand. He read from it: "*Fright Farm Haunted Manor began as The Beaumont Harvest Festival when the farm saw its first profitable year in 1866.*' Dang, so that's more than a hundred years ago."

"And before that, this land belonged to the Native tribes," Becca said.

Maddy glanced over at Becca and Bea. She thought of Bea's grandmother and her connection to the mountain. There was something sacred about this land, she had no doubt.

Rachelle and Andie were waiting for them in front of the big gates. Andie saw them and started waving. Bea waved back animatedly.

Maddy shoved her hands in the pockets of her heavy flannel jacket. The sky turned a vibrant shade of blood-orange as the autumn sun disappeared behind the mountains. Overhead, the darkening sky was already filling up with stars. Laughter, carnival music, and spooky sound effects drifted on the chill autumn air.

Bea noticed the anxious look on Maddy's face as she scanned the parking lot.

"Has he texted you?" she asked in a whisper.

Maddy glanced at her phone for the tenth time since they got out of the car. "No. Not yet."

"It took forever to find a spot. They're probably parking," Bea said.

They reached Rachelle and Andie. Both girls looked eager to enter the carnival, but Bea stopped them.

"Let's wait outside for a few more minutes," she suggested.

"Why? Who else is coming?" Rachelle asked.

Maddy didn't answer right away. She shared a look with Bea.

"Um, Maddy invited someone," Bea said.

The group stood quietly for a moment, looking at Maddy in expectation.

Finally Becca asked, "So, who did you invite?"

Maddy felt a spike of anxiety. She hadn't mentioned Gareth to anyone, and now she didn't know what to say. They weren't really dating, and she was a little nervous about introducing him to her new friends.

"Uh . . . my . . . neighbor," Maddy mumbled.

Becca folded her arms. "A neighbor? Okay, well, maybe we can go inside and they can meet us up later."

"Yeah, I need to find a restroom," Levi added. "Empty the tank, you know. We were stuck in traffic for a long time."

"Yeah, let's go in, I'm tired of waiting around," Rachelle agreed.

Andie didn't say anything, but she glanced over at the gate longingly.

Maddy didn't want to hold up the group, but she was still hoping Gareth would materialize out of the crowd. She glanced back at the parking lot.

"Maybe I'll wait just a few more minutes?" Maddy suggested.

"I'll wait, too," Bea added.

Becca glanced between them and shrugged. "Okay, if you want. Text me when your neighbor gets here. We'll head in first."

Then Becca and Levi strode through the front gates of the fairground with Rachelle and Andie in tow. Bea and Maddy remained outside the entrance.

"Your neighbor?" Bea asked with a raised eyebrow.

"I'm an *idiot*," Maddy groaned.

"I think you're adorable," Bea laughed. "Just remember, Becca is kind of a watchdog. She's not going to like it that you lied to her. She takes stuff pretty seriously."

"Oh, um, right. Sorry."

Maddy felt a little bad, but it was too late to amend the situation, so she turned to stare at the parking lot. The sky was darkening from vibrant orange to purple dusk. Groups of people walked between the cars, shadowy and indistinct. That evil little voice in the back of her mind taunted her, *"He's going to ghost you. He bailed. He's not coming."* She tried to ignore it, even as her anxiety grew.

Fifteen minutes passed. As the sky darkened, the air cooled, and Maddy's bare midriff was covered in goosebumps. She folded her arms, a little cold.

Finally, Bea tugged on her arm. "Maddy, I hate to say it, but I'm getting cold. Let's go inside and get some hot chocolate."

Maddy felt herself deflate. She checked her phone one more time. Gareth still hadn't responded to her text from almost an hour ago. Maybe he was driving. Or maybe he wasn't coming.

"Yeah, okay, let's go inside," Maddy agreed. She avoided Bea's sympathetic look. She kept glancing over her shoulder as they passed through the front gates of the fairground, but no use. It seemed like Gareth wasn't coming after all.

Once inside the Halloween festival, Maddy was dazzled by all the bright lights and noises. Rows of carved pumpkins and hay bales lined the entryway. Orange and black streamers crisscrossed the main corridor through the fairground, with a big banner that read, *"This way to the haunted manor!"*

The sheer volume of people was overwhelming at first. Maddy's eyes dilated as she looked around, her heart quickening in her chest. Her hearing and sense of smell seemed excruciatingly keen. Bells rang, horns blared and people shrieked with laughter. Actors in costume, dressed up like vampires, zombies and spooky clowns, strode around the fairground, teasing and taunting different guests. A fellow dressed up like a scarecrow wandered around on stilts.

Just inside the entrance to the fairground, a greenhouse had been decorated to look like the candy-themed cottage from the German fairytale, "Hansel and Gretel." A trio of ladies in extravagant witch costumes, complete with brooms, wigs, capes and big warty noses, stood in front of the candy house. A line of kids with their parents waited their turn to take pictures. A vendor sold bags of homemade fudge out of the witch's house. It looked pretty cool. Giant gumdrops framed the door, man-sized lollipops decorated the garden, and the chimney was a strawberry cupcake. Maddy was tempted to get in line, but the wait was a half hour long.

The scent of popcorn, churros and frier grease made Maddy's mouth water.

"Becca's at the food trucks," Bea said, checking her phone. "Let's go meet up with her. I want a bag of kettle corn!"

Bea caught her hand and surged ahead, dragging Maddy through the fairground.

***

It was opening weekend at the Halloween festival, and the lines were long for all the food vendors. Maddy and Bea stopped by Becca's table first to say hello and check in. Becca and Levi had already gotten food and were sitting at the picnic tables. Rachelle and Andie were standing nearby taking pics with their phones.

An outdoor stage was set up at the far end of the eating area. Under bright stage lights, Maddy saw a group of people standing about. An old lady wearing a yellow dress and a white bonnet was speaking into a microphone. She was dressed up like a historical pioneer woman. Maddy tried to hear what she was saying, but even with the help of the mic, her voice was too soft and wavering to reach the back tables.

"What's all that about?" Maddy asked, pointing.

"Oh, there was a livestock competition," Andie said. "They hold one every year. They're handing out all the awards and medals now. The cash prizes are pretty sweet."

"You raise livestock?" Maddy asked.

"Yeah. You know White Meadows Blueberry Farm?"

Maddy couldn't place it in her head. She didn't have a car, so she didn't leave town very often, but there were a lot of little farms in the area. A little ways downriver, heading away from the mountain, was a wide valley with lots of ranches and horse properties. The hardware store where Maddy worked catered to the downriver farming community, though originally Black River was a mining and forestry town. All the mines were closed on the mountain long ago and boarded off, but the old forestry roads still existed. A labyrinth of trails and switchbacks sprawled across the mountainside. The number of lost roads, hunting shacks, abandoned firewatch towers, mysterious alcoves and strange burrows on the mountainside were innumerable.

As for the downriver farming community, Maddy rarely traveled in that direction, unless she was heading into Davenport.

"White Meadows Blueberry Farm? I might have heard of it," Maddy said slowly. "Sorry, I don't know."

"It's okay. Our farm is about twenty minutes outside the town limits. We have cows, chickens, sheep and some ponies. I used to compete in the junior livestock competition when I was younger. Anyway, it looks like the Higgins family won this year. They got the blue ribbon."

"Who's that old-fashioned lady handing out the prizes?" Bea asked.

"That's Granny Beaumont," Rachelle said. "I'm surprised she's doing the awards this year. She had a stroke over the summer. We were all worried about her."

"Is that your grandma, Rachelle?" Becca asked from her seat at the picnic table. "I thought you looked familiar. I didn't recognize you with the pink hair."

"Hah! Yeah." Rachelle blushed a little. "That's my grandma. She's been handing out the livestock awards for forty years."

Maddy felt a bit of shock. "Wait. You're Rachelle Beaumont?" she blurted out. "So then . . . is this like . . . *your* Halloween festival?"

"That's funny. Um, not really? My cousins own the land and the town runs the festival," Rachelle said, looking even more bashful than before. "Like, I got a free ticket. But that's about it."

"So you live in Elk Haven?" Maddy asked.

"Yeah." Rachelle shrugged. "It's no big deal."

Maddy didn't respond, but . . . it was kind of a *big* deal.

The Beaumont family was one of the founding families of Black River. They lived in Black River back when it was a post office and a general store. They owned most of the land the town was built on. Elk Haven used to be their private campground before they converted it into vacation homes.

So Rachelle was something like Black River royalty, and her excessive show of humility only made it more real.

"That's wild," Bea said. "We've been hanging out all summer and I had no clue you were a Beaumont. Well, I feel dumb."

"It's really no big deal. I didn't want to bring it up. People get weird when they find out," Rachelle said.

Maddy could understand why. She was starting to feel uncomfortable. She thought of her secondhand clothes and all the hours she put in at the hardware store just to keep the electricity on. Rachelle lived in a different world.

A brief, awkward silence fell over the group as Maddy searched for something to say to Rachelle. *So, what's it like owning half the town? Do you get discounts?* Nope, she should bite her tongue. Rachelle seemed like a good person. No need to be snarky.

Then a haughty, high-strung voice came from behind her. The familiarity of it made her cringe.

"Oh! Rachelle! Hello my dear. It's good to see you here."

"Hello, Mrs. Mackovich," Rachelle said.

Maddy half turned and caught sight of Mrs. Mackovich standing behind them. Her stomach sank. *Oh god.* Where did she come from?

She looked Mrs. Mackovich up and down. The woman's hair fell past her shoulders in a sleek wave: a glossy, expensive looking peroxide blond. She wore a red-and-white checkered dress with a very low V-cut neckline. The look seemed a bit too young and flirty for a woman her age, like she was trying a bit too hard. An impressive pushup bra supported her breasts, and a big gold cross dangled between her breasts.

Maddy thought of Mrs. Mackovich hitting on Gareth at the car garage. She felt a little grossed out. Maybe the divorce wasn't just a rumor, and Mrs. Mackovich really would be Ms. Banner soon.

"Mom! Can I have money for the carnival games?" came another cringeworthy voice.

If possible, Maddy's stomach sank a little lower.

There, prancing through the crowd, came Kaylee. She looked beautiful, of course. She was wearing a blue denim romper with spaghetti straps. Her blond curls were tied back in a perky ponytail with cute little tendrils falling around her face.

Kaylee glanced at Maddy. Her eyebrows arched up like she smelled something unpleasant. Then she turned back to her mom, who was pulling a hundred dollar bill out of her wallet.

"Here you go, honey. Remember we have dinner reservations at the cider house in an hour. The mayor will be there. We don't want to be late."

"I know mom," Kaylee said.

Mrs. Mackovich turned back to Rachelle. "Will you be attending the banquet dinner as well? Your grandma is giving a little speech on the history of the town, like she does every year. I'm glad to see she's recovered from her stroke."

"She's doing a lot better," Rachelle agreed. "I'll probably be there, yeah."

A beat of silence passed.

Maddy glanced back and forth between their two groups, wondering at the tension. Mrs. Mackovich was obviously brown nosing. Rachelle seemed uncomfortable with all the attention. She and Kaylee were not acting friendly toward each other. Were they still friends? Maybe Rachelle had a falling out with Kaylee's group?

Mrs. Mackovich briefly met Maddy's gaze. Recognition flickered in her eyes, and her lips turned down in displeasure. She glanced over Maddy's crop-top, flannel jacket and ripped jeans. Was it just her imagination, or did the woman stare at her tits for a second too long? Mackovich pursed her lips again.

Then she looked away as though Maddy didn't even exist.

"It's been a while since you came over to our house, Rachelle," Mrs. Mackovich continued. "You should come by sometime. We're just up the street, you know. I'm sure Kaylee would love it."

"Mom, stop," Kaylee grumbled. "Rachelle's got other things to do."

"Nonsense, Kaylee. You and Rachelle go way back. We just love the Beamont family. You're all such fine people." Mrs. Mackovich gave Rachelle a plastic smile. "'Birds of a feather should flock together,' I always say. You know, not everyone in this little town has a bright future ahead of them. Careful you don't fall in with a bad crowd."

Maddy felt numb. She only heard half of Mrs. Mackovich's words. Her anxiety was making it hard to focus, and she dropped her eyes to the ground.

Bea, who was listening, looked furious.

"What is that supposed to mean?" Bea demanded.

Again, Mrs. Mackovich acted like everyone but Rachelle Beaumont was invisible.

"We're late to the awards ceremony. I hope to see you at the cider house later, Rachelle. We'll save you a seat. Come along, Kaylee."

Then Mrs. Mackovich turned toward the stage and the judges' table. Without another word, she flounced off through the picnic tables with Kaylee in tow. Kaylee stuck her nose in the air as she walked past, mimicking her mom. She looked like a pedigree show dog prancing along after her master.

"Thanks for standing up for me," Maddy said to Bea once they were out of earshot.

"No problem. I hate Mrs. Mackovich. Ugh. She's such an almond mom."

"A what?" Maddy asked.

"One of those typical 'skinny bitch' moms."

"Yeah, she's awful," Rachelle chimed in. "I used to feel sorry for Kaylee, but now I think she's just like her mom. You know what I think? I think Mrs. Mackovich knows what Kaylee gets up to, and she uses her influence on the school board to protect her. I think that's why Kaylee gets away with all the shit she pulls."

The group was quiet for a moment, considering that.

"Weren't you part of Kaylee's group last year?" Maddy asked Rachelle.

"I was, until I realized she's a stuck up bitch. My grandma hates their family. She thinks they're all con artists who moved up here from New York City." Rachelle glanced at Maddy. "Kaylee really hates you, by the way."

Andie put a hand to her mouth. "Rachelle, that's too blunt!" she gasped.

Bea was listening with a pissed off look on her face. "I think the whole school knows that by now," the spunky Goth girl said.

"Yeah," Maddy shrugged, trying to be nonchalant. "She tortures me."

"She used to talk shit about you all the time when we hung out," Rachelle said.

"That's kinda psycho," Bea pointed out. "She's obsessed. I don't get it."

"Her mom started it," Rachelle explained. "Like back in Middle School. I think her mom thought Maddy's family was . . . like . . . ."

"Trash?" Maddy suggested.

Rachelle winced. But she didn't deny it. "Mrs. Macko*bitch* told Kaylee to stay away from you because of your mom and the drugs. She said it was bad news when your mom overdosed and you got held back for a year . . . um, I'm sorry, Maddy. I didn't mean to say it like that."

"It's fine." Maddy shoved her hands in her pockets. She felt her pulse quicken as her anxiety spiked. Those were painful memories. "Look, it wasn't drugs. It was sleeping pills. My mom took too many, or mixed them with wine, or something like that. It was an accident."

"A tragedy," Bea added.

"I had no idea, Maddy!" Andie rushed to say. "I'm so sorry. That must have been terrible for you!"

"Yeah, well, shit happens," Maddy grumbled, uncomfortable. She sounded like Gareth just then: *shit happens. That's just life.* She didn't like talking about her mom. It always left her with a confusing mix of shame and grief.

Rachelle continued, "So that's how it all started. And I think the bullying has gone on this long because Kaylee's jealous of you."

Maddy scoffed. "What? That's ridiculous. Why would anyone be jealous of me?"

Rachelle raised an eyebrow. "You really don't know?"

"No. I have no idea."

"Trace Reynolds."

"Huh? What are you talking about?" Maddy was genuinely confused. "I thought they broke up in ninth grade."

Rachelle agreed. "They did. It was epic. I'm pretty sure Trace was her first. Like, she told me they 'did it' in the tree house in her backyard. They broke up like three times after that, because she found out he was talking to other girls on Picplace."

"I can't imagine losing my V in a tree house," Bea snorted with laughter.

Rachelle continued, "Trace was so popular, I think he was cheating on her the whole time. He was always talking to other girls. But Kaylee denies it. She still talks about him.

Anyway, she tried to get him back after they broke up the third time. Then she found pics of you on his phone."

Maddy almost choked on her own saliva. "Wait. Huh? Pics of me?"

"Yeah. I was there for it. I guess he took a bunch of pics of you at some football game. Kaylee stole his phone and we went through it at her house."

Maddy suddenly remembered the event. It was early Sophomore year. She was on the color guard for a hot second before she had to quit extracurriculars and focus on work. She was a year older than everyone else on the team, and her tits had just made their big debut. The color guard uniforms were snug and form fitting. After the game, she remembered Trace Reynolds coming down from the bleachers to hang out. She remembered him standing very close to her. But they didn't talk.

It made her feel strangely violated that he had taken pictures of her on his phone without her consent.

Rachelle continued, "He admitted to all of it when Kaylee confronted him. I guess he wanted to ask you out. But he didn't, because . . . ."

"Because I'm trash?" Maddy asked sarcastically.

Rachelle looked uncomfortable. "Look, Maddy, I don't think of you like that. Just, people are awful."

"Yeah, people suck," Andie agreed. She had been quietly listening for most of the conversation. "Don't feel bad, Maddy. I didn't know half of this stuff, either. Not everyone thinks badly about you. Like I just thought you were Bea's new friend. And Trace Reynolds is a total creep. I don't care that he's hot. He always makes me feel uncomfortable."

Maddy didn't know what to say. She appreciated Andie's reassurance. But she still felt bad. Not even a playboy creeper like Trace Reynolds wanted to date Crazy Porno Titties. She had a reputation, and now half the school thought she was a prostitute, all thanks to Kaylee Macko*bitch*.

"For real?" Maddy muttered to herself. "Kaylee's held a grudge all this time over that?"

Rachelle shrugged. "I mean, yeah, Trace said some really shitty things to Kaylee when she confronted him about it. He said you were way hotter than her, and nicer, and that Kaylee was a slut. He said she had BO."

"BO?" Bea laughed. "Oh, that's hilarious."

Rachelle cracked a smile, too.

"So of course Kaylee couldn't let that slide. That's why she's always targeting you, Maddy. Anyway, I'm sorry, for what it's worth. I never wanted to bully you. It took a while to figure out what she was doing. We were all pretty dumb. And just a heads up, that group is still under her spell."

"What made you leave?" Bea asked.

Rachelle sighed. She looked back to the stage where they were handing out second place ribbons to the contestants.

"My grandma had a stroke last summer. It was a pretty big deal. The whole family rallied around her. I couldn't go camping with Kaylee and the rest of the group for her birthday weekend. And like, she threw a fit. She would not let it go. She's just . . . a spoiled brat." Rachelle was quiet, and then, "I wish I'd left the group earlier. I feel bad for the way we treated people. Kaylee really acts like she owns the school."

"Well, I'm glad you figured that out," Maddy said, shoving her hands in her pockets and glancing at the ground. She felt a little awkward. It wasn't exactly pleasant to be reminded of her reputation as a black sheep. Maybe Rachelle was right; Kaylee would never be held accountable for her bullying as long as her mom was around to protect her.

Andie yawned and stretched. "I want to check out the livestock that won the competition," she said. "Rachelle, do you want to go with me? We can say hi to your grandma."

"Yeah, good idea."

Rachelle and Andie linked arms and started through the crowd. Maddy watched them walk away. She messed with the buttons on her flannel jacket as she digested the past twenty minutes. That hard knot of anxiety in her stomach had returned. She thought back to Middle School and everything that had transpired in eighth grade after her mom died. That was the hardest year of her life. If it hadn't been for Gareth, she might have jumped in the river. She couldn't believe Mrs. Mackobitch had told Kaylee to end their friendship. It seemed like something that hateful woman would do. But it had made Maddy's life a living hell.

Trace Reynolds taking pictures of her on his phone was unnerving. Maybe even illegal? She didn't have any classes with him this year. Actually, he might have graduated already. Would it be weird to seek him out and confront him about it?

"That was some bullshit," Bea muttered as she lit up a cigarette.

"Yeah," Maddy said. "Totally."

"How do you feel about Rachelle?" Bea asked.

Maddy hesitated. "I don't really know her. But she lives in Elk Haven."

"Yeah," Bea agreed. "That's another world."

They stood in companionable silence for a moment as Bea puffed on her cigarette. Then the wind shifted and a spicy scent caught Maddy's nose. She sniffed the air. Her heart quickened. Suddenly, she felt a warm clench in her stomach.

She half turned, searching the crowd. She didn't see him anywhere, but every fiber of her being told her that he was nearby.

Then Bea said, "Oh my God, Maddy, is that him?"

Maddy turned around.

Chapter 26

Maddy's mouth went dry as the crowd parted. She caught sight of Gareth standing maybe a dozen yards away. He hadn't spotted her yet. He was turning in a slow circle, his dark eyebrows low and focused, his eyes narrowed like a hawk. He was looking for her, she could tell. She wondered how he knew she was at the food trucks. For an insane moment, she thought maybe he could smell her, too, like a wild animal. But that was crazy.

He stood almost a head taller than the crowd of fairgoers. His long black hair was tied at the base of his neck. He wore a black leather bomber jacket over a gray acid-wash T-shirt. The sleeves of his jacket were pushed up, revealing his muscular, tatted forearms. A silver watch and a variety of leather bracelets adorned his left wrist. From the waist down, he wore dark blue, distressed jeans and black leather combat boots. His shirt was loose and casual, so she couldn't tell if he was wearing a belt or not. It really didn't matter. He looked casual but polished; a little rugged, a little sleek. She couldn't stop staring. Honestly, he looked . . . *delicious.*

His leather bomber jacket didn't hide his thick shoulders or the indent between his chest muscles. Her heartbeat tripled in her chest. Her mind flew back to Wednesday night, to his low voice over the phone as they talked in her bedroom:

"That's just the first time. It gets better after that. I'll be gentle."

"Wow, you really assume a lot."

"Yeah, I do. "

Fuck. He basically told her he was going to be her first. This manbeast planned to take her virginity. She felt a twinge below her bellybutton at the thought, and placed her hand over her bare midriff.

She remembered asking about his size:

"So what is it like . . . seven or eight inches?"

"More than that. You want a pic?"

"Uh, wow, a pic? For real?"

"Yeah, you seem curious. I can send you one. "

She felt her cheeks growing hot. How could she be so bold over the phone? She was a total coward in person! How was she supposed to look him in the face, knowing she had seen his dick and sent him a nude?

"Oh my gosh, he's wearing a leather jacket," Bea gushed.

"What?"

"It's a leather jacket, Maddy."

"Yeah, I see that. So what?"

"Guys *only* wear leather jackets on dates."

Maddy felt a spike of anxiety. Really? She glanced down at herself, feeling more and more self-conscious. Bea called her outfit "small town bonfire sexy," but now Maddy wasn't so sure. With a heavy plaid jacket, cropped ACDC T-shirt and beanie, she looked dressed for something between a bonfire and an underground punk rock show. Very young and cute and spunky.

Gareth's outfit was simple, yet somehow, he looked way more sophisticated.

"Go on!" Bea nudged her. "Go say hi to him!"

"You think I should?"

"Duh! He's looking for you, isn't he?" Bea took a drag off her cigarette. "I'll hang here with Becca for a moment and keep her distracted."

"Alright."

Maddy sucked in a nervous breath and started through the crowd, wondering if he'd turn around and see her. But he didn't look in her direction. His eyes combed the lines at the food trucks, his back halfway turned to her.

When she was a few feet away, she cleared her dry throat and forced herself to speak up.

"Oh, hey, um," she said. Jeez, why was her voice so tiny?

He turned instantly and looked down at her, his eyes sharpening. She thought, maybe, he looked shocked. The angles of his face seemed to grow gaunt as his eyes swept over her from head to toe. He looked focused and intense, like he wasn't expecting to see her standing right behind him. His eyes swept over her a second time, more slowly, allowing her to feel the weight of his gaze. His expression changed, becoming less hawklike, more sensual as he drank her in. A smirk curled on his lips. His gaze lingered on her bare stomach, then flitted up to her face.

"You're wearing makeup," he said in a deep growl.

"Oh, right," Maddy said. She had almost forgotten about that.

"You look good."

He crossed to her side in two strides and slipped his arm around her bare waist, his hand landing on her lower back. Maddy found herself suddenly pressed into his large body. The musky scent of cologne clung to his leather jacket, but Maddy barely noticed it. She was overcome by *his* smell, all spicy-pepper-woodsy, that made her want to sink her teeth into his chest. She inhaled deeply, letting all those potent, masculine pheromones rush to her head. She felt her breasts swell pleasantly against the rough fabric of her bra.

The warmth from his palm against her lower back seemed to radiate up her spine. His other hand gently clasped the nape of her neck as he wrapped his arms around her. She felt some of the tension leave her shoulders. After a minute, she returned his embrace, looping her arms around his waist. They stood like that for a long moment, just feeling each other's warmth.

"You eaten yet?" he asked, his voice low and husky.

"No," she admitted, "not yet."

"Alright. Let's get you something to eat. Then let's meet up with your friends."

Maddy pushed away from him with a reluctant sigh.

"It's fine, I don't really have the money to buy food here."

"I offered, I'm buying."

"Gareth . . . this is a hangout, not a date."

He challenged her with a stern gaze. "So what?"

"So you shouldn't pay for stuff for me. Otherwise that makes it . . . ."

Maddy's voice faded at his look. Yeah, it was pretty dumb, insisting on the "friends" thing after asking him for a dick pic last week. *It's . . . re-dick-ulous.* Maddy almost placed her face in her hands with a sigh. After everything they'd talked about on the phone Wednesday night, they definitely weren't "just friends." It wasn't going to work out like that, she already knew.

A playful glint entered his eye.

"So you're saying . . . a friend can't buy *a friend* a turkey leg?" he asked.

Maddy blushed. Damn, it was like he could see right through her. He laughed deep in his throat.

"Come on, babygirl, let's get you dinner."

His big hand wrapped around her wrist, his arm entwining with hers as he walked with her into the crowd. Maddy felt like a leaf caught up in a big river. She couldn't resist him. He was too big, too dominant. He pulled her along to a nearby food truck and got in line.

"Where's Vin? Didn't you say he was coming with you?" Maddy asked.

"He went to get some hot wings," Gareth said. "He's around here somewhere."

Gareth stood close to her in line and kept her hand clasped in his. Anyone looking would definitely assume they were a couple. He wasn't acting casual at all. Maddy worried her lower lip as she stood next to him. Maybe Bea's comment about the leather jacket was true. She wondered if Gareth had planned it all out: get to the fair late, sweep her off her feet, turn the whole night into a second date. Whatever his game, his tactics were working.

With this in mind, Maddy gave herself permission to lean into his large body, seeking his warmth. His big arm settled protectively around her shoulders. His hand brushed her waist. Maybe it was the leather jacket, his scent, his closeness, or his possessive little touches, but it felt like he had cast a spell over her.

The line moved quickly at the food truck. Maddy kept glancing over her shoulder, trying to catch Bea's eye, but the picnic tables were too far away. Hopefully Bea and Becca wouldn't wander off to check out the fairground quite yet. Maddy was gathering her courage to introduce Gareth to her friends. It was going to be . . . interesting.

Gareth went up to the counter to order. He didn't release her hand until he reached for his wallet. She stood quietly by his side, watching him pay for their meal, feeling a little flustered.

He glanced down and caught her gaze. He gave her a little half-smile.

"Something on your mind?" he asked.

"Oh, I, uh . . . ."

He pocketed his wallet, then he slipped his arm around her shoulders again. "You like what you see, huh?"

He dipped his head down and pressed a soft kiss to her lips, like the flutter of butterfly wings, and for a moment her heart stopped.

When he straightened, he dropped his arm and turned back to the vendor, who was handing them their order. He passed one of the smoked turkey legs to Maddy with a little flourish, like he was handing her a bouquet of flowers. Maddy grinned and took it from him. The rich smell of meat filled her nose and saliva filled her mouth. Suddenly she was ravenous. She took a big bite out of the turkey leg without thinking and groaned at the smokey flavor. Fuck, she was really hungry. How did he know?

When she looked back up, Gareth had a satisfied glint in his eye. They didn't say much after that. Both of them stood at the side of the food truck near a trash can and devoured their turkey legs.

After she was finished, Maddy tossed her bone in the trash and licked the grease off her fingers. She felt a lot better.

"That was really good, thank you."

"No problem, babe."

"So my friends are over at the picnic tables," she said to Gareth. "Do you want to meet them?"

"Yeah, but hold up a minute, I see Vin over there. Let me grab him and I'll meet you at the tables. You go ahead."

Maddy nodded. "Okay, cool, see you soon."

She turned away from Gareth and pushed through the crowd. She crossed the food court back to the picnic tables, weaving between the rowdy groups of people, until she spotted Bea and Becca's table. She headed in that direction.

Bea looked up as she approached. The short Goth girl looked relieved when she saw her. She stood up from the table and crossed the short distance to Maddy's side.

"There you are! For a moment, I thought you ditched me!" Bea exclaimed. "So? Where is he? Don't tell me he left already."

"He's coming, see? Over there." Maddy pointed at Gareth, who was approaching them from the food trucks, his hands shoved casually in his pockets.

"Oh, wait, who's that guy with him?" Bea asked, her voice dropping low.

That's when Maddy noticed Gareth's shadow. She recognized Vin coming up behind him, wearing an oversized yellow-and-black flannel jacket and a black beanie. He was carrying a paper plate full of sauced-up hot wings.

"That's Vin. He works with Gareth at the garage," Maddy said.

Bea's interest was too obvious. She went up on her tip-toes to get a better look. It was adorable.

"He is *also* hella fine," Bea muttered. "Is he single?"

"I think so. Maybe you should add him on Picplace," Maddy suggested.

"Maybe. It will depend on his music tastes."

Maddy glanced down at her tiny friend. Lining the two up next to each other, with their various facial piercings and similar aesthetic, Bea and Vin looked like a matching set.

As Gareth and Vin approached them, both Becca and Levi stood up from the picnic table.

"Hi! Are you Maddy's neighbor? I'm Becca. Sorry we didn't wait for you at the parking lot."

"Neighbor?" Gareth said, glancing at Maddy with a raised eyebrow. He looked amused. "Yeah, sure. That's right. We're *neighbors.*"

Maddy turned away, avoiding his gaze. Oh shit. She had forgotten to give him a heads up, and now it was hard to meet his eyes, or even look at his face. *Neighbors. I bet he loves that.* Maddy was so busy staring at her shoes, she didn't see Gareth cross the distance between them. Then his arm snaked around her waist and he pulled her firmly into his side. A little gasp caught in her throat. What was he doing?

Becca noticed the tension between them. She squinted up at Gareth and then at Maddy, then at his arm around her, obviously assessing the nature of their relationship. Maddy felt her cheeks turning pink. She dropped her eyes to the ground again, staring resolutely at her sneakers.

"*Are* you neighbors?" Becca asked again.

Gareth flashed her a grin. "Yeah, we're neighbors, but this is a date-slash-hangout. I own Jack's Auto Repair up on Highway 20. It's near her house."

"Oh. I know that place," Becca said, looking him up and down again. "So you own it?"

"I do. I'm Gareth Delarosa. And this is Vin. He works with me."

"Hi Vin," Bea cut in with a wide smile and a little wave with her witch nails. "Is that a Depeche Mode T-shirt?"

"Uh, yeah," Vin straightened up.

"I *love* Depeche Mode."

"Oh? It's a limited edition T-shirt. Got it off their official online store. What's your name again?"

"I'm Beatrice. You can call me Bea."

Bea launched into a conversation about Depeche Mode, a band that Maddy hadn't heard of.

Becca turned her attention back on Gareth.

"So how'd you guys meet? I bet it wasn't at a bar. Maddy's not old enough to drink."

Maddy almost choked. She forced herself to speak up, "We, uh, met at the hardware store. Sorry I wasn't more honest," she squeaked.

When Gareth spoke, he sounded cool and collected. "Maddy invited me to the fair. It sounded like a good time. Why?"

Becca folded her arms, a frown hovering around her lips. She definitely looked like a protective older sister. Maddy got the feeling that she did not approve of their age gap; she was Bea's big sister, and Gareth was older than all of them by a good amount of years. Becca pursed her lips. It seemed like she had something to say.

At that moment, Levi swooped in.

"Babe, chill," he said. "Look, he just came to hang out, it's no big deal." Then he shook Gareth's hand. "I'm Levi, Becca's boyfriend. So do you guys want to check out the carnival games?"

"Sounds fun," Gareth said.

Becca hooked Levi's arm and they took the lead, strolling through the crowd toward the carnival music and clanging bells. She looked sassy and uptight, a perfect compliment to Levi's low-key demeanor. Maddy noticed Becca looking back at her at Gareth through the crowd with a little frown and pursed lips. She sighed inwardly. She should have been honest from the beginning. In a moment of panic, she'd introduced Gareth as *her neighbor*. Now she was on Becca's bad side, and that made her uncomfortable.

I didn't mean to lie, but it was supposed to be just a hangout, she reminded herself. To be fair, Maddy hadn't planned on Gareth sweeping her off her feet with a turkey leg and a leather jacket.

Bea and Vin followed after Becca and Levi. Bea was already clinging to Vin's arm. They had only been chatting for twenty minutes. Maddy watched her little Goth friend with some amusement. *Is this what they call a "meet cute?"* she wondered.

She noticed Gareth seemed distracted; his eyes kept scanning the crowd again. Was he looking for someone? She couldn't tell. Maybe he was feeling nervous? No, that didn't seem like him. Whatever his reasons, he seemed extra alert and unusually tense. Maddy wondered what had him so worried. She wanted to reach out and touch him somehow, but she couldn't find an excuse.

"Did you have a good day at school?" he asked, noticing her little glances.

"Yeah. It was school, so you know, whatever."

Gareth flashed her a grin and she felt herself blushing. *Those eyes.* They glinted the color of honey. There was something intimate in his look. She felt a delicious little twinge somewhere behind her bellybutton. Damn, his look alone made her blood hot.

A large family with a bunch of kids cut in front of them. For a moment, she and Gareth were isolated from the rest of Becca's group. He leaned in close to her. His hand slid beneath her flannel jacket and brushed over her bare waist. Maddy jumped.

"Is that shirt meant to torture me?" he growled close to her ear.

Maddy flushed. "Uh, yeah, actually."

"That's not very neighborly of you," he teased her.

Maddy knew he meant to tease her, but she still felt a little embarrassed about the whole thing.

"Sorry, I really didn't know what to tell Becca about our . . . uh . . . situation."

"So you told them I was your neighbor?"

"Yeah, um, sorry, did that bother you?"

He was quiet. Yup. It definitely bothered him.

Maddy started to feel bad. Not only had she been dishonest with Becca, but she had hurt Gareth's feelings, too, something she hadn't thought possible. She had really made a mess of things. She needed to set things right. She slowed down, pulling him a little out of the flow of traffic.

"I'm sorry," she said, searching his eyes. "I kind of panicked. I didn't know how to introduce you, and it was confusing. I'm sorry if that hurt you."

"Yeah, well, I'll be honest, this whole week's been a little confusing."

She didn't expect him to say that, but she couldn't deny the truth. She knew what he meant.

"Look, I didn't mean to lie to anyone, and I didn't handle the situation well. I've never introduced *anyone* to my friends before."

"I'm not just anyone, Mads, or is that how you feel?"

She caught his stern gaze; he wasn't teasing her anymore. He was calling her out, and Maddy didn't know what to say.

Gareth pulled her closer to him, taking her hands in his own, and said, "I know you want to go slow, but after Wednesday night, I think we need to figure this out. I don't want you sending pics like that to anyone else."

"Oh, um, I'm not," Maddy mumbled.

"Yeah? Well how do I know that, if you're calling me your neighbor?"

"I thought we're still sorting that out . . . ."

"Then let's sort it out now."

He leaned down. His lips brushed her earlobe. He lingered there, sucking gently on her ear, fully aware of the sweet pleasure caused by his mouth on her tender skin.

Maddy couldn't move; she felt like a hare caught in the jaws of a wolf. His hot breath on her neck sent chills all the way from her head to her toes. A blissful little tingle shot down her spine. So that's what he meant to do—*sort it out.*

"I don't know how to be in a relationship, Gareth," she finally said, pushing away from him.

"Well babe, I hate to break it to you, but I think we're in one."

"You mean, us?" she murmured, her voice fading in her throat.

He raised an eyebrow. "You tell me."

Suddenly a large group of college kids passed by. The boys stumbled back and forth, loud and boisterous. Gareth straightened up. He pulled her into the shelter of his body, his arm wrapping around her. Then he guided her away from them, shielding her with his large shoulders. As they continued through the carnival together, Maddy felt totally under his power.

It seemed like their short, intense conversation was over. Maddy was secretly relieved, but his words stayed with her: *I think we're in one.* Yeah, well, if she was being very honest with herself, she kinda felt like his girlfriend, and she had felt that way for a long time.

Even years ago at the hardware store, she had felt like she had dibs on him. But he wanted her to make some big changes in her life that were difficult to face.

"I didn't hear from you yesterday," Maddy said.

"Yeah, sorry about that. Garage got busy. Hey so, I was meaning to ask. Any people come by your trailer yesterday? Anything unusual?"

Maddy glanced up at him questioningly, but his hazel-gold eyes were scanning the crowd again.

"No, just Dean bringing over some friends. Why?"

"No reason. Just do me a favor. Tell me if anyone comes by who you don't recognize."

"I will." Maddy didn't like his tone of voice. It set her on edge. "Um, well, Dean installed a bolt on the front door. Not sure if that means anything."

"Sounds like added security."

Maddy didn't exactly agree. A new bolt on the front door didn't feel like much protection. Especially when half her troubles lived inside the trailer with her. Dean himself was more of a threat to her than a gang of strangers.

She thought back to her text message exchange with her stepdad earlier that day. Dean had forbidden her from going to the Halloween carnival, and he didn't want her staying out late. She wondered if Dean would retaliate when she got home tonight? Should she be worried?

Her hand fumbled with her phone in her pocket. She wondered if Dean had said anything else since she arrived at the fair. She put his texts on mute so she didn't get his notifications. She held her phone in her pocket for a long minute, wondering if she should check his texts. She knew it was a bad idea, but curiosity finally got the better of her.

Maddy slipped her phone out of her pocket and unlocked the screen. She opened up her texting app. Well, shit. What did she expect? Two missed calls. Twelve unread text messages. *Twelve?* Her eyes widened. Damn, Dean never blew up her phone like this. He was having a total freakout.

Her thumb hovered over the screen of her phone. If she opened his texts, the little "Seen" box next to his messages would show up. If she was smart, she wouldn't look, but she was filled with morbid curiosity. She wanted to know what kind of trouble she was in.

With a little cringe, Maddy opened his texts and scrolled through them quickly. She instantly regretted it.

Alright, so Dean had really called the hardware store this time. He talked to Mr. Hawkins and he knew she wasn't scheduled to work. He was pissed. He was going to tan her hide when she got home.

He wanted to know if she was banging that old guy.

Was she at the carnival?

Get your ass home right now.

She was grounded.

He was going to confiscate her phone, her laptop and every paycheck from now until the end of the school year.

The last text was the real kicker:

> If you want to bang some old men, I'll set you up with a gig at Sapphire.

> Maybe then you'll make some decent money.

> I'm gonna beat your ass when you get home.

> You're fucking grounded "like, for real."

Maddy read his texts twice, her face going pale. Her steps faltered.

"You got quiet," Gareth said as they slowly stopped walking.

Maddy was so focused on her phone, she barely noticed the crowds of people pushing past her, or the flashing lights of the carnival games. Gareth guided her to the side of the thoroughfare so they didn't get trampled. She couldn't feel her feet move. What was she supposed to do now? Honestly, the thought of going back to the trailer seemed worse than the haunted house. Dean was unpredictable, especially if he was drinking.

"What's wrong?" Gareth prompted.

"Dad's throwing a fit."

"Does he know you're out with me?"

Maddy paused. Her little hesitation told him everything.

"Mads . . . ." Gareth murmured.

"I told him I was going to the Halloween festival."

"Then why's he mad?"

The silence stretched. Gareth waited a few beats, then he sighed. In a quiet voice, he reproached her, "I don't like you sneaking around and lying to your dad. If he doesn't want you seeing me, then I'll talk to him."

"He's just being a jerk. I don't know why he gives a shit if I'm with you."

"So he *really* doesn't like me."

"He hates you. I think he's scared you're going to come in and change things. He said if I ever hang out with you, he'll—" Maddy stopped. Realizing what she was about to say, she held back her words. She didn't want to make the situation worse.

Gareth's tone changed. "He said he'd do what? Did he threaten you? Wednesday night, did he do something? Did he hit you?"

"No, no! Jeez. Stop it. You're overreacting. He says all sorts of stupid stuff when he's drunk. I just ignore him half the time."

Gareth grabbed her wrist. He was fast. He smoothly slipped her cell phone out of her hand. Maddy jumped after it with a cry, but he raised the phone over his head, out of her reach. He kept a firm hold of her arm to stop her from tackling him. With his other hand, he held her cell phone up high as he scrolled through Dean's text messages. He frowned as he read them.

Maddy's face flushed with shame. Oh no. She didn't want him reading all that! It was humiliating.

"Gareth! That's not fair! Give me back my phone!" she exclaimed.

Gareth was dangerously quiet as he read through Dean's messages.

Then, with a voice thick with rage, he asked, "So which one of these crazy threats is real? Is he going to beat your ass? Are you grounded? Or is he gonna whore you out for money?"

Maddy flushed. "He says dumb things like that when he's drunk. He's overreacting."

"No excuse. This guy's an asshole. No one should treat you like that, Mads. I'm done waiting for this shit to shake down."

"No! What are you doing? Don't!"

With a few swipes of his thumb, Gareth pulled up her phone's front camera. Before Maddy could react, he snapped a photo of them together. Then he sent it to Dean. He texted something after the photo and sent that, too. Then he deleted the message before she could read it.

"What did you send him? What did you say?" Maddy demanded.

Gareth handed her back the phone. "I just invited him out."

"You invited him . . . here?"

"Yeah. Like I said, I want to talk to him."

"What the hell! Why did you do that? You're way out of line. I didn't say you could text him!"

"I didn't ask your permission, sweetheart."

Maddy felt her legs wobble. She clutched at Gareth's arm, a wave of anger and fear rushing through her. Oh no. This was a really bad idea. Gareth was declaring war on her stepfather. Now she would have to deal with the fallout. Would Dean actually come out to the carnival? If he showed up, what would he do? And what about afterwards, when she went home? How was she going to face Dean back at her trailer?

"What's wrong?" Gareth asked, noticing her trembling lip.

"I'm really scared, Gareth."

"Don't be. Whatever happens, we'll deal with it together."

Maddy met his gaze, stern and steady. He was serious. He wanted her to rely on him. She just needed a little courage. But her courage always failed her when it came to Dean. He made her feel like a helpless little orphan anytime they fought.

Gareth reached out and took her hand. "Trust me, Mads."

She nodded. She felt sick to her stomach. But she squeezed his hand. She hoped beyond hope that her stepfather was passed out drunk, or down at the casino in Davenport, and the text message would never reach him.

"We should get back to the group," Gareth suggested. "Before they suspect we're more than just neighbors."

Maddy snorted with unexpected laughter. Shit. For real? After all that, how could he act so nonchalant?

"You're not going to let me live that down, huh?" she asked.

He grinned. "Nope."

Then they continued through the crowded, noisy carnival.

Chapter 27

They met up with Bea, Vin, Becca and Levi at the ticket kiosk, where they could buy tickets to play the carnival games. It was pretty cheap. Fifty bucks got them more than enough tickets for the whole night. Gareth paid without saying a word, and refused when Levi and Vin offered to pitch in.

"Nah, I got it," he said.

First they went to a dart game. Levi was super enthusiastic about darts. With a cup of frothy pumpkin ale in hand, he followed Vin and Gareth up to the game booth, talking animatedly about the tournaments at a local bar near his apartment.

Maddy hung back with Bea and watched Gareth interact with the two younger men. He wasn't as talkative as Levi, but he had a strong presence, and when he laughed, his deep voice boomed across the fairground. Vin was like a little shadow by his side.

Gareth was obviously the leader of the group. Maddy didn't know when it happened; it's not like the men pulled straws. But she noticed that whenever Gareth stopped walking, the other two men stopped too. And when he approached the game counter, the other two men flanked him like satellites, chatting and drinking their beers.

Gareth didn't drink, which she found unusual. She recalled him not having any alcohol in his house. Maybe he didn't like the taste of beer?

A few sprinkles of rain fell on Maddy's head, distracting her from her thoughts. She glanced up. It looked like a layer of clouds was beginning to cover the starry night. She could feel moisture in the air. She hoped it didn't start raining. The fair would be a lot less fun if it all turned to mud.

Bea hooked Maddy by the arm and dragged her after the men, heading to the tent with the darts.

"Gosh, you're like an old lady, you're so slow. Come on Maddy! I want to see them play."

"You mean, you want to see Vin play," Maddy said with a little smirk.

Bea gave her a cheshire cat grin.

The dart game was pretty straightforward. Contestants needed to pop ten balloons to win a prize. The prizes ranged from bags of candy to little stuffed pumpkin bean bags, to fancy cinnamon-scented candles.

Becca joined the three men at the booth, and the dart throwing quickly became competitive. Balloons popped like crazy. Becca howled when she missed her last throw.

Surprisingly, Vin came in first place. He won a bag of Halloween candy. Maddy watched out of the corner of her eye when he offered his candy to Bea. She wasn't an expert at romance, but it seemed like a good sign.

"I'm surprised you didn't win," she said to Gareth with a little teasing grin.

He quirked an eyebrow at her. "Can't win every game, Mads, then you won't make any friends."

"Oh, is that right?"

"Yup. That's how it works."

She laughed.

Next they played High Striker, the classic strongman game with a hammer and a twenty foot pole. Maddy held Gareth's jacket as he picked up the big hammer, which was almost as long as she stood tall. Her mouth went dry as she watched his muscles ripple across his wide shoulders. He brought the hammer down with a two-handed swing on a loaded platform. The force of his swing sent a little metal puck sailing up a twenty foot pole, where it hit the bell at the top. A bunch of orange lights went off, and a group of college kids started cheering nearby.

Vin and Levi looked a little intimidated as they took the hammer from Gareth. They each gave it a swing, but they couldn't get past the ten foot mark.

Bea waggled her eyebrows at Maddy, who blushed.

"Those are some loaded guns," Bea whistled.

"Huh?" Maddy asked.

"His arms."

"Oh, yeah." Maddy laughed weakly.

The prize for winning the strongman game was a little enamel pin that read "Beaumont Farms" and two vouchers for free pumpkin ale, which Gareth gave to Levi. He and Becca looked excited, and they headed for one of the drink stands that dotted the fair.

Maddy wondered at that. She felt a little self conscious. Maybe Gareth wasn't drinking because of her? Even Becca was having a hard cider. She noticed Bea sipping discreetly on a little metal flask she slipped out of her black jacket. She watched her pass the flask to Vin.

When Gareth joined her side, Maddy felt the need to say, "Hey, just thought I'd let you know, I don't care if you drink. You can have a beer if you want."

"I know," he said.

He swept up her hand in his own, surprising her. He raised it to his mouth, sucking briefly on her knuckles. Maddy gazed up at him in shock; she felt a pleasant tingle at his touch. Gareth flashed her a devilish grin, then he started walking down the long row of carnival games at a leisurely stroll, holding fast to her hand. In his other hand, he carried his leather jacket slung over his shoulder.

Maddy fell into step next to him, a little flustered.

"I mean, don't hold back from drinking just because I'm underage or whatever," she said.

"Or whatever?"

"Yeah, or for other reasons . . . like my dad."

"Ah." Gareth glanced down at her with a bemused expression. He didn't answer her right away. They walked in silence for a minute, then he said, "Actually, I'm sober for other reasons."

"What? Really? So you don't drink at all?"

"Naw, I don't drink."

She gave him a suspicious glance, unable to keep the worried look off her face. He noticed her expression and laughed.

"Don't look at me like that," he said. "I wasn't hiding it from you. It just never came up."

"Alright, well, I noticed you didn't have any alcohol around your house, so . . . did you quit drinking? Like, were you a heavy drinker before?"

"Nope. I got an allergy."

"Are you serious? You have an allergy to alcohol?"

"Yup. Dead serious."

Maddy bit her tongue; she found that hard to believe, but maybe she shouldn't be skeptical. She reasoned some people must be allergic to alcohol, just like people were allergic to strawberries or peanuts. She thought about that for a moment. She didn't know a lot about drinking besides her dad's habit. She didn't have any personal experience with hangovers or different kinds of alcohol.

Then she asked Gareth, "So, how bad of an allergy? Do you break out in hives or something?"

He bared his teeth in a wide grin. "I turn into a wolf."

Maddy groaned. "Not the wolf thing again."

"For real. I get all hairy and crazy and howl at the moon."

"Stop! Oh my god, you're embarrassing me."

"I know. You're cute."

He leaned down suddenly. Maddy gasped, her lips parted, and he captured her mouth with his own. She felt his tongue gently brush against hers, but he kept the kiss brief and chaste for her sake, sensing her shyness. She wasn't used to kissing him in public. She liked it, but she also wanted to hide.

As he broke away, his lips grazed the tip of her nose. A swarm of butterflies filled Maddy's stomach.

"Hey!" Bea interrupted them. "Get a room, you two!"

Maddy pulled away from Gareth with a laugh. She looked over at Bea, who was standing with Vin across the aisle between two different stalls. The tiny Goth girl was smoking a cigarette while Vin puffed on his vape. She made a little cat paw at Maddy with her long nails. Maddy grinned sheepishly, and Bea stuck out her pierced tongue.

"Don't forget the condom I gave you," Bea called to her.

"Oh, um . . . ." Maddy thought she would disappear in a little poof of steam, her cheeks were so hot.

Gareth watched her drown under a debilitating wave of shyness. With a husky laugh, he wrapped his big arm around her shoulders and pulled her into the shelter of his body. Thankfully, he didn't ask her about the condom. She leaned into his warmth as he led the way through the carnival.

***

Together in a group, they tried the ring toss, ax throwing and mini basketball. Bea and Vin got tipsy off their shared flask, while Levi and Becca drank another round of spiced pumpkin ale. After that, Levi and Becca wandered off to look at the costume competition. They promised to meet up later at the haunted house after 9pm.

After waving them off, Maddy turned to smile up at Gareth.

"What game should we try next?" she asked.

He gazed down at her for a moment longer than necessary. Her cheeks were flushed and her eyes bright after winning a candy bracelet from the mini basketball game. His look was fleeting, but Maddy noticed how his eyes lingered on her face.

Then he straightened up and looked around. He raised his tatted arm and pointed to a big white tent at the end of the row.

"Let's try that one next," he suggested.

A banner hung off the side of the tent that read: *Wild Wild West UFO Shootout! Hosted by Upriver Community Paranormal Podcast (UCPP.)*

Bea's eyes lit up when she saw it. She grabbed Vin's arm.

"Upriver Paranormal Podcast? I love that show! Bigfoot Carl is the best host ever. I heard he lives off grid somewhere up on the mountain, but he's super mysterious about it."

"Wait, you also like UCPP?" Vin said enthusiastically. "Yeah, Bigfoot Carl talks about his crib in Season 3, episode 27. He's got a container house with wind generators, a water catchment system, composting toilet, everything. He even built his own kiln out of naturally sourced fire bricks. Did you listen to his podcast about growing mushrooms in his garden shed?"

"Oh my god yes!" Bea gushed. "I tried to start my own mushroom shed, but my mom wouldn't let me use the one in the backyard. I didn't know UPCC had a booth here. What's a UFO shootout?"

"I think it's a shooting gallery," Vin said and puffed on his vape.

Maddy listened curiously, watching her two friends rant about their favorite podcast. She didn't have a great internet connection at home, so she didn't go online a lot, and she didn't listen to any podcasts. She watched Bea's face light up. Her friend's eyes genuinely sparkled as she talked with Vin. Maddy liked seeing her like that. Vin seemed like an interesting guy; he was surprisingly smart. With his vape hanging out his mouth, Maddy thought he looked kind of like a punked out Sherlock Holmes.

Vin and Bea started wandering over to the UPCC tent.

"You like paranormal stuff?" Gareth asked.

"Oh, no, not really. I mean, I haven't listened to the podcast or anything. I guess I don't really believe in that stuff."

"Gotcha."

"What about you?"

"I've seen some things, but nothing like UFO's," Gareth said, a little vague. "Let's check out this shooting gallery."

He walked with her over to the white tent, their hands clasped together.

Strands of bright bistro lights illuminated the inside of the tent, where a cowboy-themed shooting gallery was set up. Maddy heard the toy guns popping before they reached the front entrance. A bunch of men holding cups of beer stood around the front of the shooting gallery. By the look of the crowd, the booth was popular with the local hunting community, who liked guns, and the New Age hipsters who followed the podcast. The two groups were divided on either side of the tent. A bunch of guys in camo were hanging out in one corner, talking about different kinds of ammo and favorite spots to go shooting. At the next table, a woman wearing a purple turban whipped out her tarot deck for an impromptu reading.

Maddy followed Bea and Vin up to a counter built out of wooden pallets, where a guy dressed up like an astronaut was handing out prizes. A big sign hung above the counter explaining the rules. It looked pretty straightforward. Two shooters went up at a time. The stage was decorated with a scene from the wild west, with a cardboard saloon, cactuses and barrels of whiskey. Cardboard aliens popped out from behind the different props on little springs. Each player had thirty seconds to clear out all the aliens.

The shelf behind the counter was packed full of prizes: T-shirts, hats, sunglasses, cheap electronics and stuffed animals.

"You want me to win you something?" Gareth offered.

"Oh, uh, sure, if you want to." Maddy felt a little uncomfortable. "No pressure, I don't expect anything."

"No pressure, huh? Well now I have to."

Gareth stretched his big arms up behind his head, and for a moment, Maddy almost thought he was showing off. She noticed a few guys glance over at him, sizing up the competition, then their eyes traveled to her. Actually, a lot of guys were leering at her and Bea. Maddy self-consciously pulled her flannel jacket over her bare midriff.

Vin joined Gareth's side and handed over a wad of tickets to the fellow running the counter.

"Count me in, too," he said. "How many rounds is this?"

"Three rounds for you both. Here you go," the astronaut said, handing over a pair of wooden guns. "No firing off stage, just at the targets, you got it?"

"Yup," Gareth said.

"For sure," Vin echoed.

They waited for a few minutes as the last team finished their round, then Gareth and Vin approached the stage. A loud bell rang, signaling the start of their session. The two men barely had a moment to raise their guns before the game started. A variety of aliens on little levers started to spring up from behind the saloon and different prop cactuses. The artwork was pretty good. Some of the aliens were pretty big, almost the size of a small dog, while other cutouts were smaller and harder to hit. It was impossible to predict where each alien would pop up, and they only appeared for a few seconds at a time. Maddy gasped and started each time an alien jumped onto the scene. She cheered and clapped right alongside Bea as the two men shot down their targets.

Then a prop alien bounced up right in front of the stage. Maddy jumped back a few inches and Bea grabbed her arm. The two girls laughed.

Maddy had never seen Gareth shoot before. Vin was pretty good, but Gareth was on another level. Even if it was a toy, he wielded the miniature rifle with ease. Some of the outdoorsmen noticed it, and roared their approval when he cleaned out all the aliens.

"Wow, he's really good," Bea said, a note of admiration in her voice.

Maddy felt a flush of pride, but she was more than a little intimidated by his skill. She reminded herself that he was an NCO in the Army. She wondered if he had ever killed anyone in battle. She deflated slightly thinking about that. She wondered if she would ever have the courage to ask him about his time in Iraq.

After the first round, Gareth and Vin took a minute to reload their toy guns as the props reset. The second round was about to start.

That's when Maddy felt her phone vibrating in her pocket. She took it out.

Shit, it was Dean.

"Is that your dad? What does he want?" Bea asked, looking over her shoulder. "He's blowing up your phone. Maybe it's important?"

Maddy gnawed on her lip, staring at her phone screen. In all the excitement, she had almost forgotten about the text Gareth sent her father.

"Go on, answer it," Bea encouraged her. She shooed Maddy toward the entrance of the tent. "The second round is starting. Don't worry, I'll let them know where you went."

Maddy hesitated, torn. She had no idea what Gareth had texted her father, but maybe if she talked to Dean first, she could get him calmed down and he would leave her alone for the rest of the evening. Her only other choice was to ignore him, and that would be like throwing gasoline on a fire. With a sigh, she turned around and headed out of the tent. A wave of anxiety was already building inside of her. She really didn't want to deal with this right now. Dean always had the worst timing.

Behind her, a bell rang, signaling the start of the second round. The violent sound of popping air rifles filled the tent.

Maddy walked outside into the cool night air. She took a deep, steadying breath. Then she picked up the phone on the last ring.

"Hey dad," she said.

"Where are you?"

Dean's words were a little slurry, a little muffled. He sounded pissed, as she expected. Maddy tried to stay calm. She didn't want to fight with him.

"I'm at the fair."

"Is that guy with you?"

"Um . . . ." Well, she couldn't deny it; Gareth had sent Dean a picture of them together. "Yeah, he's here, but . . . he's kind of busy."

"Too busy to talk to your old man? Well I got that fucking text message and I'm here. Jim gave me a ride from the bar. We're in the parking lot."

Maddy paled. "You're in the parking lot?"

"Yup. That asshole you're with said he wanted to talk. So I'm here. Let's talk. Man to man."

Maddy's hands were starting to tremble. Shit. So Gareth invited Dean to the fair for a little chat. Why? What did Gareth want to talk about?

Maddy could take a few guesses: probably the text messages Dean sent to her phone, or maybe he was tired of tiptoeing around her stepdad. Either way, a confrontation between the two men sounded like a terrible idea, especially after Gareth got all warmed up at the shooting gallery. A lot of men around Black River carried firearms, and she knew Jim kept a shotgun in the bed of his Silverado truck. She didn't want a real shootout going down in the parking lot.

"Um, look, he's not with me right now, but I can be out there in five minutes," Maddy said, trying to keep the tremor from her voice.

"Fine. Good. We're out front."

Dean hung up. He sounded a little slurry, but he seemed coherent. Maddy sighed and stared at her phone for a moment. Gareth's text must have reached Dean while he was at The B Joint drinking with Jim. He must have finished a few more rounds before deciding to drive down. He was definitely pissed. She didn't know what she would say to him, but she needed to smooth things over somehow.

She texted Bea: *My dad's in the parking lot. I need to go talk to him about something. I'll be right back.*

Then she started through the game booths. The wind was brisk and chill. Silvery moonlight filtered down through layers of inky black clouds. The sky looked dark and bruised, ready for a storm. She avoided two actors dressed up like zombies who were jump-scaring people. It was almost 9pm and the fairground was packed full of excited fairgoers. It was a little disorienting, trying to navigate the carnival with so many people jostling her back and forth. A few times she got turned around, but thankfully, wooden signs directing people to different areas of the fairground were posted all over. The signs pointed to the food trucks, haunted house, restrooms, etc. Maddy followed the signs that pointed back to the entrance.

Maddy walked with her head down at a fast pace. When she reached the main entrance of the carnival, the road widened significantly, and the crowd became more spaced out. She jogged the rest of the way through the front gates.

"Are you coming back in?" a lady asked as she passed through the exit line.

"Yeah, I think so?"

The lady stamped her hand with an orange pumpkin before waving her through.

Chapter 28

Maddy's eyes scanned the parking lot. Traffic in and out of the fairground was just as crazy and chaotic as it had been earlier that day. It took her a moment to spot Jim's familiar Silverado truck parked a few hundred yards from the front entrance of the fairground, out toward the corn field. She saw Dean outside of the truck, leaning on the cab with his burly arms crossed over his potbelly. His wispy blond hair was a slicked back mess from driving with the window open. He looked red-faced and scowling, just as she had envisioned him over the phone.

Maddy felt a spike of anxiety at the sight of his angry, red face. Her hands curled into little fists. She didn't expect their conversation to go well, but she had to try.

"Hey dad," she said as she approached the truck.

Dean pushed off the passenger-side door and opened it.

"Get your ass in. We're going home."

Maddy hesitated a short distance away. She was taken aback. Really? He wanted her to leave, just like that?

"Dad, I came out here to talk to you," she said, crossing her arms nervously over her chest. "So . . . um, is everything okay?"

Dean looked furious. His mouth clamped shut and he glared at her.

Inside the truck, Jimmy Manner leaned over the center console from the driver's seat. He gave her a little wave. Maddy felt a bit better seeing him. Jim was tall and lanky. He had a big handlebar mustache and warm brown eyes. He was that type of easygoing guy who was friends with everyone. He and his wife weren't bad people. Actually, his most toxic trait was that he was friends with Dean.

"Hi Maddy, good to see you," Jim called in a neighborly fashion, like she wasn't having a confrontation with her father in the middle of a muddy parking lot. "How's school? Did you get our birthday card?"

"Yeah, I did, thanks," Maddy said. "School's fine. Thanks for asking."

"Good, good, that's good," Jim said.

"Right, Jim drove all the way out here to pick you up," Dean growled. "So get your ass in the car. We're leaving. We can talk when we get home."

Maddy turned back to her father.

"Dad, I'm not going home with you. I just came out to see if you're okay."

"Oh, you're checking to see if *I'm* okay? I'm fucking dandy. Now I owe Jim a tank of gas. You gonna waste my time and my money on a Friday night?" His voice darkened. "*You lied to me, chickadee.*"

Maddy felt a shiver of fear at her dad's tone. Would he take a swipe at her here in the parking lot? She wouldn't put it past him. But she wasn't getting in that truck. Once he got her alone back at the trailer, she didn't expect things to go well.

"Look, I'm sorry I screwed up."

"Yeah, right. You're grounded, so get your ass in the truck."

"Grounded? You can't ground me. I'm nineteen."

"Hah! Nineteen. You're a fucking kid. You'll obey my rules so long as you live under my roof."

"I pay half the bills, anyway," Maddy glowered.

"Yeah? Well maybe you'll change your tune after I throw you out on your ass!" Dean pointed a sausage-like finger in her face. She could tell he wanted to smack her; she could see the tension in his hand. "Nobody disrespects me. I told you to stay away from that old fuck. You've been lying to me all week. I had a good long chat with your manager at the hardware store. I know you were out Wednesday night, too. So yeah, you're grounded. Now get in the fucking car."

"No, I'm not going home."

"Get in the car. Now. Before I knock you into next week."

Dean reached for her arm and Maddy ducked away. He reached again and grabbed her jacket, dragging her close enough so he could catch her elbow in a crushing grip. Maddy whimpered, half-expecting a blow across the face. Dean pulled her so hard, she thought he would dislocate her shoulder.

"Hey, Dean!"

At that moment, a fist came flying out of nowhere and connected with Dean's jaw. Maddy watched his head snap back in slow motion. She gasped. Dean released her arm with a groan and fell back against the truck.

"Whoa!" Jim yelled from the driver's seat of the truck. "Holy fuck! You okay, Dean?"

Gareth grabbed Maddy and pulled her behind him. He placed his body protectively in front of her. She stared at his broad back in awe. Where did he come from? Then she glanced around. A few curious people were glancing in their direction. She wondered if someone would call for a security guard.

Her stepdad looked like a fallen humpty-dumpty against the side of the Silverado truck, all potbellied and angry. He stared up at Gareth, his face bright red. Blood leaked down his chin from a split lip. He seemed unaware of the injury.

"Oh, here he is, here's the guy!" Dean yelled to Jim in the car, pointing his finger at Gareth. Jim didn't look eager to get out of the truck. Then to Gareth, Dean said with a glower, "You're the asshole who's fucking my daughter!"

"Yeah, I am."

Maddy's mouth dropped open. Technically they weren't having sex yet, but Gareth didn't seem concerned about that detail.

"Glad you could make it out, Dean," Gareth said, "cuz I got some words."

Gareth slung his big arm around Dean's shoulders in the most intimidating way imaginable, then started walking with her father away from the Silverado truck.

Maddy gave Jim a little wave, then followed after them.

"You want me to wait?" Jim called.

"Uh, yeah," Maddy said. "Can you?"

"Sure thing, hon."

Maddy trailed after Gareth in a strange sort of daze. They walked up the side of the fair in the opposite direction of traffic, moving away from the front entrance and the busy parking lot, away from the bright headlights and crowds of people. It looked like Gareth was leading her father to a more private, secluded corner near the back fence of the fairground.

When Gareth seemed satisfied with their location, he shoved Dean bodily away from him, sending him stumbling into the wooden fence.

Dean sputtered at Gareth furiously, but he seemed at a loss for words.

"Alright, so let's talk, Dean. I saw your texts. I got a problem with you threatening my girl."

"That's *my* daughter. I can talk to her however I want!" Dean sputtered.

"Yeah, well she's my girl now, and all that's gonna change," Gareth said.

Maddy felt a shiver at his words. *My girl.*

Dean gathered himself up and pointed at Maddy. "You think you can fuck my daughter, come 'round and start telling me what to do? Fuck off, man. Actin' like some hero. You're just after those big tits and tight pussy."

Maddy didn't see Gareth move, but suddenly her stepfather was on the ground. Gareth was standing over him, his fists clenched, poised to strike again. Maddy's heart started to race. By the looks of it, he had punched Dean square in the mouth.

Dean groaned and spit out a tooth.

"Last Thursday, some bastards broke into your trailer," Gareth said in a low growl. "Scared Maddy real good. I don't like it when my girl's scared, Dean. Turns out you owe them money."

Dean groaned and dragged himself into a sitting position.

"What? Huh? I don't know anything about that," he grumbled.

Her stepdad didn't sound very convincing. Maddy watched his bravado slowly drain away. His narrow, bloodshot eyes flickered back to the Silverado truck. He looked like he was thinking of running.

Gareth planted himself firmly between Dean and the parking lot. He folded his big arms across his chest. Hell, he was intimidating.

"I've had these assholes show up twice at my shop this week. They won't get off my ass, and it's your fault, Dean. You fucked up. So you're gonna tell me what kind of shit you stepped in."

Maddy watched, her mouth gaped open. She had never seen her stepfather shrink down so low. He looked like a worm.

"Alright alright," Dean buckled. "I took out a loan. Just a small amount. Had to pay back some debts at the casino. But then I couldn't pay the loan back, so I struck a deal with these guys to move a few bricks. Just a few bricks. Not a big deal . . . b-but I lost them—"

"Bricks? Of cocaine?" Gareth asked.

Dean's eyes flashed. "Bricks of dirt for all you care."

"Alright. So you lost 'em?"

"Yeah, they went missing."

"They went missing or you used them?"

Dean grimaced. He spit red at the ground from his bleeding gums.

"I ain't done that," Dean barked. "The bricks went missing and that's the end of it."

"Yeah? Well these fuckers don't think it's the end. They want their money, Dean. What're you gonna do?"

Dean gave Gareth a wild look. "Why do you care? You working for them? Holy fuck. You're one of them, aren't you? You're one of those bastards. I shoulda seen it sooner.

Look, man, just stay the fuck away from me. I'll get you the money, I just need more time."

"I don't give a shit about your money. But I give a shit about your daughter. It's nice of you to finally tell her the truth." Gareth grabbed her stepdad under the arms and dragged him to his feet. Then he gripped him by the shirt and forced him to look at Maddy. "Now apologize."

"What?" Dean sputtered. "What for?"

"For putting her in danger. For shitting all over her life. Apologize for being a worthless parent and a piece of shit."

Maddy dropped her eyes at first, feeling embarrassed. But she couldn't deny her anger. Her stepfather's confession was shocking, but it made too much sense. All those letters from Gelson's & Associates were for a delinquent loan, just as she suspected. So he tried to sell drugs to pay off his debt, but he "lost" the cocaine. *Sure. Right.* She very much doubted those bricks of cocaine "went missing." The friends he brought over from the bar weren't exactly discreet. She recalled seeing plenty of baggies over the last year. Her dad loved a good party. She was pretty sure even Jim had bought an eightball off him.

Steeling her nerves, Maddy forced herself to raise her head and look Dean in the eye.

"Well?" she said. "Don't you have anything to say to me?"

Despite being pinned against a fence post in a cold, dark parking lot at night—Dean still looked petulant. By his expression, Maddy could tell that he didn't really want to apologize.

Holy shit, she thought. *He really doesn't think he did anything wrong.*

Gareth shook him by the nape of his neck.

Finally, Dean stuttered, "I-I-I'm sorry, Maddy. So now you know the truth. Anyway. Yup. Sorry about all that, with the trailer and the drugs and stuff."

It was a pathetic sort of apology, but Maddy knew it was as good as she was going to get. Her fists tightened. She hesitated for a moment as her rage built up and her pulse throbbed in her neck. Then she stepped up to Dean, crossing the space between them, and slapped him open-handed across the face. *Crack!*

The sharp sound of her open palm striking his cheek rang out through the air. Maddy's heart raced. She was shocked at herself. She had never thought she would have the guts to do that. Even Gareth looked surprised.

She shook out her wrist. Then she backed away from the two men. The smack was supposed to make her feel better, but instead, she felt kinda numb.

"I'm sorry, Maddy," Dean repeated.

"It's fine, dad," she mumbled.

Of course it wasn't fine, but there didn't seem to be much else to say.

Then Gareth released him. Dean stumbled a few steps forward, recovered his balance, then started limping back to the truck. Stringy wisps of blond hair stuck to his sweaty face. He looked in pretty bad shape, his face flushed, his nose bright red, a dribble of blood leaking from his swollen bottom lip.

Maddy followed after him. She stood at the side of the parking lot as Dean climbed into the cab of the Silverado. Jim helped him buckle his seatbelt, then he rolled down the driver's side window as Gareth circled around the truck. Maddy watched curiously, wondering what Gareth was going to do. He pulled out his wallet from his back pocket and riffled through it, then he handed Jim a large bill. Maddy didn't see exactly how much money he handed over, but it was enough to fill the gas tank, she was sure. She leaned forward, trying to catch Gareth's words as he spoke to Jim, but his voice was too low.

Jim laughed unexpectedly. Then he said, "Hey, shit happens, no worries. I'll take him home. Thanks for the gas money."

Gareth tapped the side of the truck as the Silverado kicked forward. Jim pulled away from the curb and guided the big truck into traffic.

Maddy watched the truck roll away until it disappeared in the long row of cars headed to the exit. Gareth rejoined Maddy's side. He stood next to her in silence, his hands shoved casually in his pockets, as they both gazed after the Silverado.

"Hey Gareth?" Maddy said.

"Yeah?"

"Thank you."

"Anytime, babygirl."

On sudden impulse, she turned and wrapped her arms around his waist. She buried her face in his chest. She felt tears sting her eyes. Fuck. She didn't want to cry, except here she was, crying. She hadn't realized all the tension she was holding inside. She had never seen anyone stand up to Dean like that before, not for her sake. She was overwhelmed with emotion.

Gareth's arms encircled her. He pressed her into his big, hard body. They stood like that at the side of the parking lot, embracing for several minutes. Maddy couldn't hold back; she was a complete mess, sobbing and sniffling, ruining his cotton shirt in a downpour of tears. He rested his chin on the top of her head, holding her firmly, rubbing a gentle hand across her back.

Finally, her tears slowed down to a few hiccups. Gareth glanced down at her face. His thumb wiped a damp trail from her cheek. For a moment they stood like that, pressed together as Maddy regained her composure. She felt warm and safe in his arms.

"I'm really sorry," she finally mumbled into his chest.

"For what?" Gareth asked.

"For not letting you do that sooner."

Gareth grinned.

"Yeah, well, now you know. You got a problem, you come get me. Alright?"

She nodded into his shirt. "Right," she said, her words muffled by his jacket.

"Hey," he said.

"What?"

"You got a minute? I want to talk to you."

Maddy felt a little shiver of trepidation, though she wasn't sure why. What did he want to talk about? She didn't think she could handle another scolding after all that. But maybe he didn't mean it like that.

"Yeah, okay," she said in a small voice.

"Come on. Walk with me."

Gareth released her from his firm hug. He took her hand and started walking along the side of the parking lot, back toward the entrance to the fair. She walked next to him, wondering what he wanted to say. He guided her to an empty, secluded spot under a maple tree, somewhat removed from the onrush of people. There, he paused. He turned to face her.

Maddy took a deep breath to steady herself. Then she looked up at him, meeting his eyes, reminded of his height and his imposing presence. The clouds broke apart at that moment. Silver light illuminated Gareth's face. Maddy gazed up at him, entranced by his golden eyes. He looked exotic and mysterious, just like she remembered him from the mountain.

Unexpectedly, he pulled something out of the pocket of his leather jacket. She glanced down. He was holding a stuffed brown bear from the prize shelf at the shooting gallery.

"Did you win that for me?" Maddy gasped.

"Yeah."

"Oh, wow, it's adorable," she said, reaching out to take it, but he stopped her.

"Wait, first, Maddy," he said, "there's a question I gotta ask you. You ready?"

She nodded, her mouth going dry.

"So, I understand you want to go slow, but I think we both agree the 'friends' thing is getting a little old," he said.

She nodded silently. She felt the same way, she just didn't know what to do about it.

"So, if we're gonna keep this up, I think we gotta be real with one another. I'll always be your friend, but I want to be more, and I think you want that, too. So . . . will you be my girlfriend?"

"Oh . . . well . . . ."

Maddy chewed on her lip. She wasn't good at talking about her feelings with people. It was much easier to throw a tantrum or run away. But she couldn't run away from him anymore—and she didn't want to. After the way he confronted Dean, it didn't make any sense to pretend to be "just friends." But . . . getting into a relationship with him was a little scary. He was older than her, intimidating as hell, and there was this feral, wild side to him that she didn't really understand. But no one had ever treated her with so much loyalty and respect. She knew he really cared for her, genuinely and truly, and she cared for him, too.

He raised an eyebrow. He seemed so confident, yet at her hesitation, his eyes flickered with uncertainty. That flash of vulnerability made her heart melt.

"I mean, yeah, duh, of course I'll be your girlfriend," she finally said, trying to act nonchalant, but she sounded super awkward to her own ears. Damn, why couldn't she be cool and smooth like him?

Gareth released a big sigh, like he had been holding his breath.

"You got me all nervous," he laughed.

"I make *you* nervous?" Maddy asked with irony.

"More than you know, little girl. Anyway, here's bear number two. Looks like we're starting a collection."

He handed over the stuffed bear to her with a grin. Maddy squeezed it with her fingers. It was a little larger than the white bear he bought her at Zippy's. It had brown curly fur, and it was dressed in little green overalls.

"You gonna name it?" Gareth asked.

"Jeez, I'm not a kid," Maddy scoffed. Then, with a sly grin, she added, "Yeah, probably."

He laughed and offered her his arm, which she took. Then they started back toward the fairground. Maddy felt like a heavy weight had been taken off her shoulders, though she wasn't sure why.

"Um, so, if I'm your girlfriend, does this mean I have to move out of the trailer?" she asked.

"We'll see," Gareth said.

It wasn't really an answer, but Maddy wasn't worried about it anymore. Dean's confrontation with Gareth had been a turning point, though where that road was headed, she couldn't guess. Whatever happened next, she and Gareth would figure it out together.

Then Maddy's phone pinged. She checked it.

"Looks like Bea and everyone else is headed to the haunted house," she said. "We should hurry up and meet them."

"Sounds good, babygirl. Should we tell them we're not neighbors anymore?"

Maddy snorted with unexpected laughter. Jeez, after all the drama with Dean, she had almost forgotten about the neighbor thing. It was pretty dumb.

"Yeah, I mean, I guess they've already figured it out," she said.

She messed with the buttons on her flannel jacket. To be honest, Maddy felt a little nervous about telling the group about their new relationship status. She and Gareth were finally going "official." No more hiding in the shadows, or darting forbidden looks around the hardware store. It would be a whole new world.

She expected Bea to be happy for her, but Becca seemed a little disapproving. She hoped Becca's attitude toward Gareth didn't make the whole night awkward.

"Hey, come here," Gareth growled, noticing the little frown of concern on her face.

With a gasp, Maddy found herself pulled into Gareth's arms one more time. He leaned down and captured her lips with his own. His hand brushed her hair back from her face as he kissed her, slow and wet and sensual.

Maddy wasn't used to kissing him in public. She couldn't really appreciate it fully, she was too distracted by the crowds of people. She felt the urge to pull away after a minute, but he took a few steps forward, pushing her back up against the plaster facade of the fairground's entrance. He pinned her there between his big body and the front entrance of the carnival. Crowds of people pushed past them, coming and going from the fair, but he kept her sheltered with his broad shoulders. He focused on her mouth, passionately kissing her over and over, swallowing her little sighs, sliding his tongue down her throat, until she forgot where she was standing. Fuck, he was relentless. She started to feel a growing wave of arousal; her skin felt hot and flushed. Her breasts tingled pleasantly, aching to be touched. She could easily imagine abandoning the fairground, going back to his car, and finishing what they had started in the backseat of his Camaro.

When he finally released her, Maddy felt drunk. Her eyes were hooded, her lips beestung and swollen from his passionate kisses. She gazed up at him, her arousal written plainly on her face. He grinned at her wanton expression. Then he licked his devilish tongue across her lower lip.

"You ready for this haunted house?" he asked.

Maddy nodded, speechless.

"You can grab onto me if you get scared."

Maddy wanted to grab onto him *right now*. He noticed her heated look and leaned in to nibble at her chin. He softly bit the side of her jaw.

"I'll be fine," she managed to say in a breathy voice.

"Alright, but you got that anxiety thing, so I brought a CBD pen just in case."

"For real?"

"Yeah, cuz you keep forgetting the one I bought you."

"I still have it," Maddy protested, trying not to melt into a puddle from his gentle caresses. "I use it before I go to sleep at night."

"Good. Glad to hear it. But if this haunted house is too much for you, just say the word, and we can bail."

"No, let's go. I'm ready for it."

"Alright, if you say so."

His hand brushed between her legs just for a moment, sending a jolt of electricity through her body. Maddy gazed up at him, warm and throbbing from pent up desire. Then he straightened up, leaving her bereft, the night air cooling her flushed skin. He slung his arm around her shoulders and led her back into the fair.

Chapter 29

The line for the haunted manor wrapped around half of the carnival. Maddy and Gareth found Bea and the rest of their group about halfway down the long line. The people on either side of them were pretty tipsy. Nobody said a word when they cut in.

As the hour grew late, families with young kids headed home while more and more college kids showed up, already drunk from pregaming in their cars. The fair took on a different kind of energy: rowdier, darker, a bit more chaotic, if that were possible.

Bea looked relieved when she saw Maddy.

"Oh good, you're still here! So how's your dad? Is everything okay?"

"Yeah, he's fine," Maddy said. "There was a misunderstanding, so, um, I just had to sort out a few things."

Becca turned to look at her with a questioning gaze. She glanced between Maddy and Gareth. Then her gaze landed on the stuffed bear in Maddy's arms.

"Where'd you get that?" Becca asked Maddy. She looked up at Gareth. "Did you win that for her?"

"Yup," Gareth said. "She's got a collection going."

"It's cute," Becca said, her voice a little strained. "So what does your dad think of Gareth, Maddy? Has he met him?"

"Oh yeah, we've met," Gareth said. His tone didn't invite more questions.

The line moved forward. They approached the front entrance to the Haunted Manor. Maddy's gaze traveled over the restored Victorian house. It looked like a spooky dollhouse: a decadent porch, bay windows, a steeply pitched roof and whimsical, twirling little finials. The front yard was littered with fake headstones and plastic skeletons. A slew of creepy old props, straight from a grandmother's attic, covered the wrap-around porch. The eaves were covered in cobwebs, and strings of neon lights wrapped around the banisters.

Their host, a college-aged actor, stood at the front door of the haunted house. His face was painted white like a zombie. He wore a butler's uniform with a velvet tophat. Fake blood spattered his white cravat and dress shirt. He wore a mic clipped to his lapel and entertained the long line of guests with a little bit of haunted history about the manor.

Maddy listened with some interest. It sounded like a daughter of the Beaumont family had gone insane while living in the house. The young woman claimed to be possessed by a demon, which made her do atrocious and violent things, like attempting to murder her younger sibling. So the Beamont family locked her in the attic of the house. One day, a maid found the young woman hanging from the rafters of the ceiling. It was a tragedy. The young woman had hung herself using her own bedsheets.

It was a haunting story, to be sure. Bea was all about it. She even made a little note in her phone to look up more history on the Beaumont haunting.

Maddy wasn't all that interested in ghosts. Sure, hauntings were spooky, but not as scary as an unexpected property tax bill.

Their vampire concierge allowed groups of 10 people at a time to enter the haunted house. Once inside, a small legion of actors and volunteers ushered people through the manor, room by room, where they were subjected to all kinds of horrors. A siren blared every time a new group was released into the house. Maddy assumed the 5 minute wait between groups was for the "monsters" to reset their positions.

Suddenly, a piercing scream emitted from somewhere inside the manor. The hair on Maddy's arms stood on end. The people in line all jumped, then started talking excitedly.

"Oooh man! That was a good one!"

"They really outdid themselves this year. It's my second time going through. Totally worth the wait."

"I hope I don't piss myself, I drank a lot of beer . . . "

"I don't know if I can go in. It looks scary!"

Maddy tried to look brave, but it was hard to do in a crowd of nervous drunk people.

"You sure you're up for this?" Gareth asked, glancing down at her.

Maddy nodded. She tried to keep her cool. She wanted to be a badass, but in truth, the scream unnerved her.

Bea pointed at one of the windows high up on the side of the house that might have been to the attic.

"Look there! I saw a face in the window!" she shouted.

A few people turned to look, including Maddy. She didn't see anyone up there, though. The window was covered by gauzy white curtains. It was pretty small. The people standing in line around them grumbled and looked away, unimpressed.

"Really, I saw someone," Bea said to Vin.

"I believe you. I bet there's an actress up there playing the role of the crazy Beaumont daughter."

"Yeah, probably," Bea said, though she had a doubtful frown on her face.

The line inched forward, a certain tension lingering over the guests. Everyone was excited to go into the haunted house. Maddy kinda wanted to get the whole experience over with—rip it off like a bandaid. Waiting for the line to move was a special kind of torture.

"So Gareth," Levi asked, probably to pass the time, "You said you owned that auto shop up Highway 20? Where did you learn to work on cars?"

"Started up in Alaska when I was eighteen, after I joined the Army. I've been doing it a while."

"Oh wow, so you're a soldier?"

"Yup. I'm a vet."

"That's pretty neat," Levi sounded impressed. "My dad was in the Army. Thank you for your service. You know, we're always hiring good people down at Jepsen Industries. What kind of engines do you work on?"

"Just auto and diesel," Gareth said.

They started talking more about machinery stuff. It sounded like Becca's boyfriend was also a bit of a car guy. He worked at a manufacturing plant called "Jepsen's" outside of Davenport. The plant employed a good chunk of Jefferson County. Gareth answered his questions politely, but he didn't seem interested in a job.

"So like, how much do you make as a mechanic?" Levi asked.

Becca elbowed him. "Babe, that's rude."

Levi flushed and scratched the back of his neck. "I'm just curious. Jepsen pays its mechanics good wages. Especially supervisors."

"No worries," Gareth says. "I own the shop, so it's more than average. We're doing good this year. Take home is over six figures."

Maddy's ears perked. *Over* six figures? That was . . . a lot of money. Maybe she had misheard him? She gazed up at Gareth, a little shocked. He wasn't looking at her. He stood in a wide stance, his arms folded as he chatted amicably with Levi. She hadn't thought much about his salary, considering the rusty Camaro he drove around in. But restoring a classic car wasn't cheap, even if he was doing most of the work himself.

Levi seemed equally surprised. "Is that above average?"

"Oh yeah. Most of it's from the summer rush," Gareth explained. "Lots of RV's with issues and cars breaking down on road trips. We were working 7 days a week, huh Vin?"

Vin and Bea were having their own private, mumbled conversation a little ways away. Vin glanced up.

"Yeah. Summer was nuts. I basically lived at the shop. It was worth it, though. Got a nice bonus."

"Summer's really that busy, huh?" Levi asked, a hand to his chin, thinking. "I guess that makes sense with all the tourists driving through the Adirondacks, heading back and forth from Canada."

"We get a lot of big trucks coming over the mountain during the summer," Gareth explained. "Chains break down. Wheels fly off and axles get bent. The tow back to the shop can cost a couple grand. That's just getting them to the garage. Then overnight parking fees. It adds up. It all gets billed to their company, so the guys don't care."

"Nothing like a midnight call to tow a truck off the mountain," Vin said with a groan.

Gareth clapped him on the shoulder. "Yeah, but you always showed up."

"He pays doubletime on night tows," Vin explained.

"Well shit, maybe I should work for you," Levi laughed.

Bea was listening with some interest. She poked Vin in the ribs. "So is he your boss?" she asked.

"Yep. I'm just a maintenance tech right now, but Mr. Delarosa is training me to become a mechanic."

Maddy caught Bea's look. Her friend's face clearly said, *"Mr. Delarosa?"*

Maddy blushed. She didn't really know how to react.

"Line's moving!" Becca exclaimed, interrupting their conversation. "Finally!"

The siren sounded above the door to the haunted manor, shaking Maddy from her thoughts.

The vampire concierge unleashed a malevolent laugh, very theatrical, and said in a spooky voice, "Are you ready for a *scary* good time?"

"Oh god," Bea groaned. "Bring it on!"

The vampire undid the red velvet rope barring the door. One by one, their group filed into the haunted house. The front door creaked loudly as it opened and closed behind them with a loud slam.

Immediately, a blast of cold air struck them in the face from a fan positioned above the doorway.

Maddy yelped and almost dropped her stuffed bear.

"Oh!" Bea gasped. "Wow, I didn't expect that."

"They get you right on the first step, huh?" Becca said.

Their party of six filtered through the foyer of the old house.

"Honestly, the restoration is kind of cooler than the decor, huh?" Levi pointed out, looking at the antique chandelier hanging above them, and the handcrafted wardrobe near the front door where coats and hats might have been hung up by a stuffy, antebellum butler. "I think these are the original floors. Look, they put down plastic over the wood so it doesn't get damaged."

"That's great, babe. But have you noticed the murder scene?" Becca pointed out.

The walls of the manor were covered in fake blood. It took Maddy a moment for her eyes to adjust to the low lighting. A recording of fake screams and haunting music played over a sound system. It was pretty good. As Maddy looked around the murky room, she saw a bunch of dismembered fake body parts strewn about. A pair of fake legs were stuffed into the dumbwaiter, suggesting the murderer had tried to stash a body inside. The windows were blocked off by black drapes, so no glimpse of the carnival outside could ruin the ambiance. With the red lighting, fog machine and spooky soundtrack, it was almost like they had stepped into another world.

Access to the upper floors was roped off. Bea went to the edge of the staircase and peered up it with an intense frown, like she was looking for someone.

"Do you think these stairs lead up to the attic?" she asked.

"I think they lead to the second floor," Becca said. "Come on, we're supposed to go that way. We should get moving. They're going to send in another party soon."

A very clear path lit by red string lights led from the foyer down a hallway, deeper into the house. The hallway was very dark. Maddy thought she saw some glow-in-the-dark cobwebs hanging from the ceiling. Vin started down the hallway first. Then Bea dragged Maddy behind her by the wrist. Gareth followed them. Becca and Levi brought up the rear.

Levi walked behind Becca with his hands on her shoulders. He kept turning her toward the scary props, a stupid grin on his face.

"Don't you dare tickle me or pinch me!" Becca gasped, smacking his arm the third time he did it. "This place is scary enough without you teasing me!"

They passed through a haunted tea room. Actors dressed like Victorian zombies were drinking from an antique tea set. One actress played the part of a grieving widow; she wore a black dress and veil. Maddy guessed the other actresses were supposed to be the corpses of her dead family, or maybe her daughters, or something like that. Maybe it tied into the story of the young woman who went insane? She wished she had paid more attention to the vampire concierge out front.

Fake rubber rats covered the settee and the little ornate tea tables. Antique damask wallpaper gave the room a creepy dollhouse feeling. The electric wall sconces flickered ominously.

"I think this is the original wallpaper," Levi said, reaching over a rope barrier to poke at the wall. "Or maybe they scavenged it from another local site. Hard to say."

"That's really interesting, babe," Becca rolled her eyes.

"This is *so* my vibe," Bea said, looking at the velvet settee and the widow in her Gothic dress.

Maddy's group walked through the drawing room, following the path outlined by red lights on the floor. A barrier of rope stopped people from wandering too far off the pathway. When they reached the far end of the room, Bea stepped on a strange panel duct taped to the floor, and a trap door sprung open in the ceiling. A shower of little plastic spiders fell on them along with a cloud of fake cobwebs.

Becca screamed, fighting off the cobwebs with wild hands. "Oh my *fucking* cheese and crackers!"

Maddy gasped too, and took a few steps backward. She stumbled into the solid wall of Gareth's chest; his big hands landed on her shoulders. She was startled, but luckily she wasn't scared of spiders. She was used to walking through the woods at night, so she recovered quickly. When she glanced up, she saw a big grin on Gareth's face.

"You good?" he asked.

"I'm fine," she grumbled, brushing the little plastic pests off of her jacket.

Next, they entered a cobweb covered library full of musty old bookshelves. Flickering red lamps lit the room. Levi almost immediately left the path and started leaning over the rope barrier, trying to get a look at the old books that lined the shelves.

"Do you think these are real collector's editions?" he asked.

"No, babe, I really don't," Becca said.

"Oh cool, they're all horror novels. Look, it's Braham Stoker's *Dracula,* and I see *Hound of the Baskervilles* by Sir Arthur Conan Doyle. That's Sherlock Holmes, in case you didn't know. Oh, and there's Edgar Allen Poe. Did you know that Poe wrote the first mystery novel? Well, it was a short story, 'The Murder in the Rue Morgue' in 1841."

"Did you learn all that in college?" Becca asked.

"No, it's on this plaque over here. Kinda hard to read in this lighting, though."

Suddenly, a very convincing vampire leapt out from behind a bookshelf.

"Bwahahaha! I am Dracula!" the actor screamed with an evil laugh. "I will drink your blood!"

Becca almost attacked the vampire. Levi dragged her away. The actor hissed and clawed at Becca with gnarly monster hands. Beneath the red light, his costume looked pretty convincing. Maddy and Bea stumbled into each other, laughing.

"Beware what lies ahead!" the vampire cried from the other side of the rope barrier. "Beware Hell's Kitchen!"

Maddy and Bea exchanged a glance.

"Hell's kitchen?" Bea asked.

"Sounds interesting," Maddy grinned.

Next they walked through a spa-sized bathroom with a big clawfoot bathtub.

"Oh wow, this is nice," Becca whistled appreciatively.

The floor was covered in little thumbnail sized tiles. Stained glass windows lined the eastern facing wall. The clawfoot bathtub took up most of the space in the bathroom. The water inside the tub was dyed red and looked convincingly like blood.

"Oh gross," Bea said, pointing. "Look at that!"

A headless corpse was lying in the tub. It looked gruesome. One limp arm dangled over the porcelain rim. Maddy stared at the discolored arm, fascinated, then forced herself to look away. She had to walk pretty close to the tub to exit out the other side of the bathroom. She cringed slightly as they walked by.

At first she thought the corpse was just a prop, but as she passed by the tub, the "headless" actress reached out and grabbed her leg.

Maddy screamed bloody murder.

She jumped a foot in the air and bolted. She flew through the bathroom, out the second doorway and into the dark hall. There, she got tangled up in a blackout curtain that was covering one of the windows. The curtain tripped her up and she fell, yanking it off the rings. She fell down with a cry. Orange neon light from the carnival outside flooded the hallway.

Gareth followed on her heels. He reached her in the hallway, knelt down by her side and started untangling her from the black drapes.

"Fuck!" Maddy cursed. "Dammit! What the heck. Get this thing off me!"

"Hey, easy," he said. "Calm down, I got it, here we go." He finally got the curtain untangled from her legs and helped her up to her feet.

Maddy groaned as she looked down at the bundle of drapes on the floor. Then her eyes traveled to the window. It looked like they were at the back of the manor. Through the branches of a skeletal tree, she could see the distant line for the haunted house weaving through the fairground.

"Fuck," Maddy groaned. "Oh my god!"

Bea and Becca both came to check on her. Bea was laughing.

"I don't feel like such a dumbass now!" she said. "Are you okay, Maddy? They got you good!"

Fuck, this is terrifying, Maddy thought. Adrenaline pounded through her veins in a hot rush. She felt like her senses were heightened. Becca's perfume was stifling in the small space. She imagined she could hear Bea's pulse from a few feet away. *I need to calm down.* But her heart kept racing. She was ready to fight.

Maddy took a deep breath and coughed. Actually, everyone's B. O. seemed excruciatingly potent and distinct in the stuffy hallway. Not only could she tell apart their separate deodorants, but underneath all the soap and bodywash, she could discern an earthy mix of sweat. Levi particularly stank of fear, even though he was trying to hide it for Becca's sake. Maddy was amazed at herself. She felt like she had stumbled across a hidden superpower. She could actually smell Levi's fear. Instinctively, she knew what the metallic, tangy odor meant. What in the world? How could she *smell* emotions?

She glanced at Becca, using her super-sharp nose and tuning in. Becca was . . . angry? At Levi? Or maybe it was a fear response?

Bea smelled aroused. She was very attracted to Vin, and Vin was high. His vape juice contained THC.

Holy shit. How could she tell all that with a few sniffs?

Then her eyes turned to Gareth. His scent was different from the rest of the group. And not just because he smelled utterly delicious. His scent wasn't anything like Levi or Vin, or the other girls. He seemed like a completely different animal.

She stared at him, fascinated by this new awareness, as the rest of their group sauntered past down the hallway, giddy and excited.

Gareth noticed her look. He met her gaze. They faced each other across the narrow hall, half illuminated by the neon orange lights outside the window. He didn't move. Just watched her silently, waiting.

Maddy didn't understand it, but she found herself stepping forward. She sniffed the air like a cautious puppy. Her eyes traveled up his tall frame. Why was he so different? His scent meant something to her. Her bones sang with the knowledge . . . but . . . it was like she had amnesia. She couldn't remember . . . .

Gareth crossed his arms and leaned back against the wall.

"You . . . ." Maddy hesitated.

"Yeah? What?"

He gazed at her expectantly. His eyes dared her to continue. To be bold.

He knows something. He's waiting for me to figure it out. What is going on? Am I losing my mind?

Maddy lost her nerve.

"Nevermind," she shrank back. "We should catch up with the rest of the group."

She started to walk away, but Gareth caught her arm as she passed by. She looked up at him in surprise.

"You feeling alright?" he asked, searching her face.

She nodded, a bit pale and sweaty. "Yeah."

"You dizzy? Nauseous? You been fainting in class or anything?"

"No, I'm okay. Really. Your mom's tea helps. I've been drinking it."

"Good."

He searched her face again, like he was looking for something specific, then he released her arm. He seemed reluctant to let her go. Maddy felt a little unnerved. She suddenly felt like something altogether *'other'* was walking at her back, something predatory and inhuman. She couldn't explain it, because of course Gareth was just a man.

It's the haunted house getting to me, she thought.

Together, they walked down the hallway into the next room, where they met up with everyone else. Their party of six stood outside a set of heavy oak double doors, propped open. The room beyond was lit with spooky purple and blue lighting. It looked like a big hotel-style kitchen, with several workstations and a long central island. Pots and pans hung from racks along the far wall. A ghastly soundtrack played over the speakers mounted in the corners of the room.

"This must be Hell's Kitchen," Becca said as they entered through the wide doorway.

A big fat lady in a white apron was hacking away at a pile of raw meat in the center of the kitchen. It was probably raw pork, but under the glowing purple lights, it looked convincingly like a human leg. The meat made a nasty, wet thwacking sound every time the giant cleaver swung down.

The path of red string lights along the ground led them right past the wicked cook's workstation. As they passed by the butcher block countertop, the gluttonous actress turned toward them with a snarl. Her makeup was gruesome. It looked like she had boils all over her face.

"Who's trespassing in my kitchen?" she screeched. "I'll put you in my stew!" She rattled the butcher knife threateningly.

"Run!" Becca screamed.

They bolted. The nasty woman chased after them, running down the other side of the long kitchen island, swinging her meat cleaver above her head. She howled threats and obscenities through the kitchen. She even hurled bits of fake raw meat after them. Some of it stuck to the back of Levi's sweater.

"Ugh, gross!" Becca laughed, trying to pick the goo off of him. "I think it's dyed cabbage, not real meat."

"It better not be real meat!" Levi exclaimed.

At the other side of the kitchen, Becca and Levi crashed through another set of double doors into an empty dining room. Maddy caught a glimpse of a long banquet table covered in fake cobwebs, pewter plates and antique candle holders. Vin and Gareth followed after them.

Bea grabbed Maddy's wrist and dragged her in another direction. She went off the path, under the rope barrier, then dashed to a smaller door on the left side of the kitchen. It looked like this door led into a separate part of the house.

"Bea, what are you doing?" Maddy gasped.

"Shh! Just follow me!"

Bea dragged Maddy through the second exit. She didn't stop running, but pulled Maddy through the next hallway, making random turns. Maddy didn't hear anyone following them; the kitchen actress must not have noticed their sudden departure in the wrong direction.

This part of the house wasn't decorated for Halloween. Maddy got the terrible feeling that they were trespassing on a part of the manor closed off to guests. But Bea didn't seem to care. The little Goth girl ran along, keeping a surprisingly strong grip on Maddy's arm. She dragged Maddy through room after darkened room.

Then Bea found a staircase and started up it.

"Bea, what are you doing?" Maddy panted, following behind her. "Where are we going?"

"To the attic."

"What? Are you crazy?"

"Maybe." Bea looked back at Maddy, her eyes illuminated with a fierce glow. "I saw something in that window, Maddy. I swear I saw a woman. *She waved at me.* I want to see if there's an actress in the attic, because I think I saw a real ghost."

Maddy felt a cold shiver run down her whole body.

"Oh no, Bea, that's a bad idea, we should get back to the group—"

"Fuck it, Maddy. I have to go look!"

They reached the top of the narrow staircase. Both girls stopped on the landing to catch their breath. They were on the second floor of the house. Maddy leaned against the wooden banister. She wiped the sleeve of her heavy flannel jacket across her sweaty brow. With all the lights and electric equipment running downstairs, the manor's second floor was stiflingly hot and humid.

Maddy looked back down the staircase behind her. They were in a separate part of the house, removed from the walkthrough for the haunted manor. Below the staircase, the first floor was obscured by deep shadows. From this vantage point, she could hear the distant strains of haunting music and spooky sounds from the themed part of the house. It felt like she stood inside a labyrinth of dark shadows, closed doors and weird little hallways. She had no idea how they were going to get back to Gareth and the rest of the group.

Maddy turned and looked around the second floor. She couldn't see much in either direction. Then Bea turned on her phone light and flashed it around. A black-and-white photograph of the Beaumont family hung above the landing for the second floor. Maddy's eyes looked over it. She didn't know enough about the family to identify any of the figures in the painting, but she saw a woman, two children and a stern looking father posed on a settee. The father had a wide handlebar mustache that grew past his lips, and the mother wore her hair up in a proper bun. They were dressed in Victorian fashion, with clothes buttoned up to their jawlines and big puffy sleeves. The younger children wore what looked like lace dresses.

"Do you think that's the crazy daughter who killed herself?" Bea asked, pointing at a young, morose looking woman who stood at the back of the photo.

"I don't know, Bea," Maddy said. "I don't see a plaque or anything. Maybe it is?"

Bea looked fascinated. She stood up on her tiptoes, trying to get a better look.

"She looks kind of like the girl I saw in the window," she said.

Maddy felt another chill run down her arms. "Are you sure you're not just fucking with me?"

Bea glanced over at her with intense, dark eyes. "No, I wouldn't do that. I swear. I wouldn't lie about this. You know my grandmother was a shaman, right? She saw spirits all the time. She could dreamwalk and everything."

Maddy felt another horrible shiver of foreboding. She had thought to humor Bea by following her up to the attic, but now she felt a little tendril of fear slide down her neck. Had Bea actually seen the Beaumont ghost?

"Alright, I'll go with you to the attic to check it out," Maddy sighed. "But just for the record, I think this is a terrible idea."

Bea gave her a cheeky little grin.

"Fuck yeah. I knew you'd make a good sidekick."

Maddy turned away from the creepy photo. She looked up and down the second floor hallway. They could choose between two directions: right or left. She saw a few paintings hanging from the wood paneled walls, and several closed bedroom doors. At the far end of the hall, Maddy saw a window and another staircase leading higher up. It probably led to the third floor. Then above that would be the attic.

Shit, was she really doing this? She didn't want to see a real ghost. Even though she didn't really believe in the supernatural, there was always a slim chance, right? And Bea's grandma was a shaman. What if she really saw something?

Together, the two girls started walking down the dark hallway of the hundred year old house. The floorboards creaked eerily beneath their feet. Bea held out her phone in front of her like a flashlight, illuminating the hallway in front of them, but it wasn't really enough to see much. Maddy flinched at every groan of the old house.

After a few minutes, she pulled her cell phone out of her pocket, intending to use the screen for more light. But then her phone pinged in her hand. She started, then she rolled her eyes at herself.

It's just your phone, silly, calm down.

She checked her messages. Of course, it was Gareth.

> **Where are you?**

She felt a sense of relief. It was easy to feel completely isolated in the dark house with Bea. She was already on pins and needles from the jump scare in the bathroom, and the cook in Hell's kitchen. But this was another level. All of the lights were off and the hallway was totally dark. It was super creepy.

Maddy started to text Gareth back, but Bea stopped her.

"Is that your sugardaddy? Don't tell him where we are! He'll ruin it for sure."

"What? No he won't."

"Yes he will. He'll tell Becca and she'll be up here in two seconds."

Maddy bit her lip. She saw Bea's point, but she didn't want to lie to Gareth. They were in a relationship now. She was trying to turn over a new leaf.

Boyfriend, she thought. *He's my boyfriend.*

So what would a girlfriend do? Dang, relationships were hard. She wasn't good at this. If he was her boyfriend, shouldn't she tell him where she was?

"I have to text him something," she said to Bea. "What if he gets worried and tells the staff we're missing?"

"Alright, then tell him you dropped something and we went back for it. Tell them to keep going and we'll meet up outside. Just tell him not to worry, alright?"

Maddy was kind of annoyed at Bea's bossy tone, but she understood her friend's tension. This was a ghost hunt, after all. And they were breaking all the rules. The second floor was off limits. She really didn't want to get caught by any of the staff working at the manor.

She started texting Gareth back.

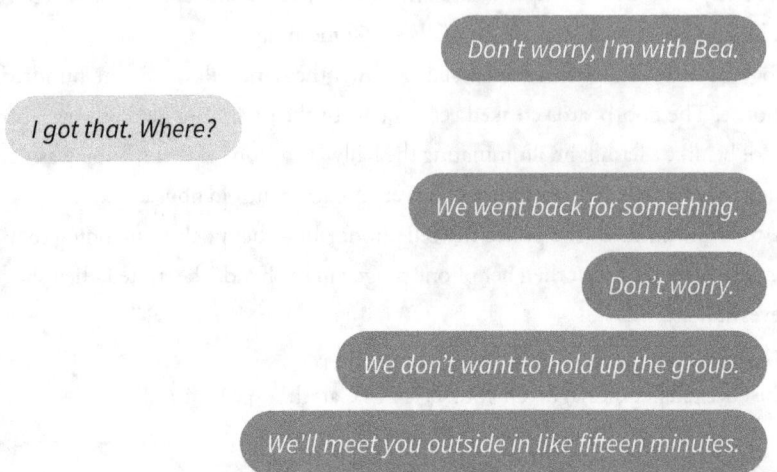

Don't worry, I'm with Bea.

I got that. Where?

We went back for something.

Don't worry.

We don't want to hold up the group.

We'll meet you outside in like fifteen minutes.

Maddy felt pretty good about those texts. It was vague enough that she wasn't lying, so she didn't feel quite as guilty for ditching him. She went to slip her phone back in her pocket, but it pinged again. Gareth had texted back.

I'm coming to get you.

No, don't . . . .

Maddy stopped herself mid sentence before hitting send. What should she say? She hesitated before typing out her text message. How did he intend to find her? He sounded like he knew where she was going, but that was impossible. Maybe he meant to track her through the haunted house somehow, like he had special skills from the Army? She really didn't know.

Then her phone started to ring.

"Ugh, for real? He is totally smothering you," Bea grumbled.

"He's just worried. We kind of took off without telling anyone. I'm surprised Becca hasn't called you."

"She has. I ignored it."

Maddy bit her lip. She felt a little uncomfortable.

Bea sighed. "Fine, answer it, I'll wait."

Her little Goth friend stood with her arms crossed and her weight on one hip, looking sassy and annoyed in the middle of the dark hallway. Maddy felt flustered. All this cell phone business was ruining the vibe. She could see the disappointment on Bea's face and she felt bad. She could tell this was really important to Bea, even if she didn't really understand it. Maybe Gareth was being a little overprotective? Did she really need to pick up his call?

After a long hesitation, Maddy rejected the call and put her phone on silent. She texted him back.

We'll just be a few minutes. See you outside.

Then she pocketed her phone. She didn't look to see his reply; she didn't want to get cold feet.

"Alright, let's go quick, before they come looking for us," Maddy said.

Bea looked surprised. Then a mischievous grin crossed her face. The little Goth girl turned up the screen light on her phone. She flashed it around the dark hallway, then they continued toward the stairs.

Chapter 30

The third floor of the Beaumont Manor was totally empty and silent. It was pretty stuffy, too. The air smelled like dusty old linens and mildew, and the strong tang of furniture polish.

Maddy stopped briefly to peek outside at the fairground and the long line wrapping around the haunted house. She didn't think the old wooden windows could open. Thin lace curtains covered the window at the top of the staircase, and she pushed them aside to see out.

Bea came to join her. "Wow, the line is twice as long as when we got here," she said.

"Yeah, it must be an hour wait," Maddy agreed.

"The park closes at midnight. They're going to have to close off the line soon, so this is probably the last call," Bea said, like she knew something about how theme parks worked.

Maddy cast her little friend a side glance. Bea was fiddling with a lock of her long, glossy black hair. It was straighter than straight and fell down past her waist in a black curtain. It kind of reminded Maddy of Morticia from The Addams Family, a look she could see Bea emulating. She looked a little nervous. Bea always sounded like she knew what she was talking about, but maybe her friend's boisterous confidence was all a facade.

"Alright, let's find this attic," Maddy suggested, turning around.

Bea turned up her phone light and fell into step next to her. The two girls locked arms and started down the gloomy hallway together.

Despite her initial misgivings, Maddy felt a little zing of forbidden excitement. Sometimes she liked breaking the rules, if nobody got hurt. The risk of getting caught made her feel a little naughty, a little bad in a good way. She caught Bea's eye and the two girls shared a mischievous smile. Okay, so this was kind of fun. Hopefully they could find the attic, take a look around, and make it back downstairs without getting caught. With any luck, they would *not* encounter a ghost. The thought of running into a security guard was more intimidating to Maddy, but so far so good. The upper floors of the house were empty.

Then Maddy tripped over a little narrow table with a vase on it. She caught the vase before it fell to the floor.

"Nice," Bea whispered. "Like a ninja!"

Maddy rolled her eyes. Shit, that was a close call. She would have to be more careful.

They searched up and down the dark hallway, but there didn't appear to be any more stairs leading up to the attic. Maddy was ready to give up, but Bea pointed to the row of closed doors.

"It's probably behind one of these," she whispered. "Let's check!"

Then Bea started testing knobs and pulling open different doors. She shined her phone light into each empty room. Maddy wondered how her friend got so bold; personally, she had never been more freaked out in her life. She braced herself each time Bea turned a handle, because behind each door, she didn't know what they would find: lonely, empty mattresses; little narrow bathrooms with dusty mirrors; linen closets full of wicker baskets and unlabeled wooden boxes. Maddy felt like she was playing a horror videogame and a zombie might jump out from behind any corner.

As they hunted for the missing set of stairs, Maddy became less convinced there was an actress in the attic, and more concerned that Bea had seen a real ghost. Was it possible?

"Was your grandma really a shaman, Bea?" she whispered. She didn't know why she was whispering. The third floor was abandoned.

"Hell yes," Bea stage whispered back. "She had all sorts of powers. I swear I saw her levitate once."

"Oh, wow. That's pretty intense. So . . . you really think you saw a ghost in the attic, then?"

"I think that's what we're about to find out," Bea said victoriously, as she yanked open the last door at the end of the hall. There, a narrow set of stairs led up into a very dark, shadowy destination.

"Yes! We found it!" she gushed, and pumped her fist in the air.

Maddy gazed up the dark staircase. She felt all of the hair on her arms and neck stand on end.

"Um, why don't I stay here and keep watch while you check it out?" Maddy suggested.

Bea snorted. "No way. You're coming with me. I'm not going up there alone."

She grabbed Maddy's wrist and dragged her up the narrow staircase. It wasn't wide enough for two people to pass through shoulder to shoulder, so Maddy huddled behind her small friend as they climbed up the dark passageway.

Then the ceiling widened out above them. The staircase emptied directly onto the dusty attic floor. Maddy noticed how there wasn't a banister or any railing to stop people from tripping down the staircase in the dark. She would have to remember where the steps were and be careful when they came back down.

The two girls huddled close together and looked around the spacious, open room. The ceiling was about ten feet high, crisscrossed by solid wood beams. The attic of the Beaumont manor spanned almost the full length of the house—larger than Maddy's trailer. It was full of boxes, wood pallets and old furniture covered in white sheets. Maddy saw a grand piano standing in the far corner of the room. Little porthole windows looked out onto the fairground. Some light from the carnival outside filtered into the room, casting the oblong furniture in strange shades of orange, green and purple. But most of the room remained in deep shadow.

In the light of their cell phones, Maddy spotted a mouse trap under a chair nearby. Ugh. She cringed inwardly. Far worse than a ghost in her opinion, she hated rats. Sometimes, they showed up under the kitchen sink in her trailer. Maddy shuddered at the memory of waking up in the middle of the night to the sound of scratching and skittering. It was enough to drive anyone crazy. Luckily they hadn't had a rat infestation in a while, not since their neighbor got a big tomcat. But Maddy remembered the summer of her fifteenth year—the same summer she had fallen on that broken handle of rum—they had a bad infestation from all the trash Dean left around the trailer. It made her skin crawl.

Maybe that's what happened to the Beaumont daughter—the rats drove her insane.

"Okay, looks like the attic is empty, I don't see anyone," Maddy said, satisfied with their brief investigation. "Let's go back down now."

"Just wait, I want to check out that window," Bea said, pointing across the length of the attic. "That's the window where I saw the face, I'm pretty sure."

"But . . . ." Maddy hesitated, her eyes traveling to the trap on the floor. Bea followed her gaze, waving her phone light around.

"What's that, a mouse trap? Oh my god, are you kidding me? You're scared of mice? They're tiny!" Bea scoffed at her, and Maddy rolled her eyes. Bea had obviously never dealt with a rat infestation.

"Alright, but just imagine them jumping on you, or falling from the ceiling," Maddy said. "Maybe I'll wait here while you check it out."

Bea looked uncertain. "It's pretty dark. I don't want to go alone."

Maddy sighed. She was done with the attic, but when she gazed at Bea's hopeful expression, she felt bad. She couldn't let Bea wander through the attic all by herself. And the little Goth girl looked super excited to see a ghost. They had come this far, was she really going to bail now?

With a sigh, Maddy took Bea by the hand and they started together through the creepy room. Occasionally, the light from the carnival outside would shift, making the shadows move across the ground. It was easy to imagine someone hiding between the piles of boxes and abandoned furniture. The floorboards creaked loudly; it almost sounded like a third person was walking behind them. Maddy told herself it was a trick of her ears, even as her pulse quickened.

She reached into her pocket, fishing around for Gareth's CBD pen, but she didn't have it. Didn't he give it to her outside? Actually, no, he had kept it in his pocket. Well, damn. What good was that?

Okay, she needed to calm down before her nerves ran away with her. Maddy tried to pretend she was in a forest at night. She imagined the open sky above her, the soft scent of pine trees and wet earth. If a dark forest didn't scare her, then an attic should be no big deal. A mountain lion was way scarier than a ghost.

At last, they reached the far window through the maze of junk. Maddy peeked outside. Yup, this looked like the right window. She saw the line leading to the front of the haunted manor, and she recognized the place where they stood down below. She watched the fairgoers for a long moment, just a bunch of bored people milling around. It wasn't very exciting.

"Alright," Maddy said, straightening up. "This is it. I don't see any ghost, Bea. So I think we should head back downstairs before Becca gets too worried."

Bea didn't answer her.

Maddy looked over her shoulder. Bea was standing behind her, but she was turned toward the corner of the room, her spine rigid, her shoulders stiff.

Maddy followed her gaze, but she didn't see anything, just a pile of boxes, and a dusty corner where the slanted roof met the floor.

"What is it?" Maddy asked. "Is it a rat?"

Bea didn't answer, but her eyes got all wide and her face looked sickly pale, even under her makeup. She kept staring at the empty corner of the room. It was so melodramatic, Maddy was half-convinced she was faking it. She considered grabbing her friend's arm and dragging her back downstairs.

Then she felt a gust of cold air strike her feet, and a strange smell touched her nose.

Maddy sniffed the air. Was it . . . perfume? Maybe. There was something sickly and pungent about the smell, like a moldy bouquet of old flowers. It was unusual. Where was it coming from? She had never smelled anything quite like it.

Maddy frowned and sniffed the stale air again. Could it be . . . she was *smelling* the ghost?

"Maddy," Bea whispered.

"What?"

"Maddy, it's . . . it's right next to you."

"What is?" Maddy said, turning around and taking a few steps back. She raised her phone's flashlight, but she didn't see anything.

She felt that cold brush of air again, and that weird smell of old flowers filled her nose.

"Maddy, she's real. The ghost is real!" Bea gasped.

"But I don't see anything."

"I do!" Bea grabbed Maddy by the arm and dragged her into a run.

Something loud fell over behind them–*bang!*

Maddy jumped. She almost fell, but kept her footing, running after Bea through the cluttered attic. It sounded like someone had slammed shut a window, or dropped a heavy book on the floor. The sound rang out through the silent attic.

Then something went flying past her head to shatter on the ground—a wine glass? A picture frame? Maddy couldn't see it clearly. She yelped and ducked her head. The sound of footsteps behind her was unmistakable.

Chills ran over her whole body. Instantly Maddy was taken back to the night of the break-in, when the gunshot flew past her head. Her heart lurched into her throat. A wave of sickening adrenaline washed through her. She glanced back, and out of the corner of her eye, she saw the lurching shape of a woman running after them.

"Run! Don't look!" Bea screamed, sprinting through piles of old boxes and covered furniture.

Their phone lights bobbed wildly back and forth, flashing around the dark room. It reminded Maddy of when the men had chased her through the woods. She felt sick to her stomach, like it was happening all over again.

They almost fell headlong down the attic stairs. Maddy caught her balance just in time and skidded to a halt. She dragged Bea back from taking a fatal plunge down the staircase.

"Careful! You'll break your neck!" Maddy cried.

"Go, go, go!" Bea screamed.

Tripping over each other, the two girls flew down the attic stairs and slammed through the door into the third story hallway. Maddy didn't know if the ghost was following them, but she didn't want to stop and find out. The two girls sprinted down the pitch black corridor, Bea's phone light forgotten. Maddy's foot caught the little end table she had bumped into earlier, and the wobbly vase went crashing to the ground. It shattered across the floor behind them. She didn't stop to look at the damage. She barely registered it.

Maddy pulled ahead of Bea, her arms pumping, her breath heaving in her lungs, her heart racing so fast she thought it would leap from her mouth.

"Fuck, you're a fast runner!" Bea panted behind her, trying to keep up.

Maddy dashed down the staircase to the second floor, practically flying. As she circled the banister, she ran headlong into a towering shadow.

Wham!

"Oh!" Maddy gasped, half grunt, half shout. She felt all the breath leave her lungs from the impact. For a moment, she was stunned.

Then Bea slammed into her back. "Ouch!"

The short girl fell onto her ass on the ground with an *oof!*

Maddy thought she had run into a door. Panicked, she tried to shove through it, but a pair of strong hands slid under her jacket to grip her bare waist. She wasn't expecting the touch. She squealed in terror.

"Let me go!" she yelped.

"Calm the fuck down!" Gareth said.

He lifted her off her feet and slung her easily over his shoulder. He smacked her solidly on the ass, surprising Maddy. The sharp sting snapped her out of her hysteria.

"You're a fucking brat, you know that?" he growled. "What the hell are you doing?"

"Put me down!" Maddy gasped, kicking her legs uselessly. "Gareth!"

"Not until you tell me why you're up here."

"We . . . uh, we were . . . ." Maddy stuttered, returning to her senses. How did she explain? She tried to speak, but it was hard to pull in a breath, her heart was racing too fast. She couldn't seem to calm down.

"We went to see if there was a ghost in the attic," Bea cut in, dragging herself back to her feet. "I wanted to check it out. It was my idea."

"And that noise just now? Did you break something?" Gareth asked.

Bea went quiet.

"Well, shit," Gareth grunted.

"Yeah, maybe best not to go back up there," Bea said.

Maddy squirmed a bit, trying to slide her way back to her feet, and he smacked her ass again for good measure.

"Fucking stay still," he growled.

"Don't be mad at us!" Bea exclaimed. "I swear we saw the Beaumont ghost. It even threw a picture frame at us. It was real. There's a ghost up in the attic. That's why we were running; it chased us back down the stairs."

Gareth didn't sound impressed at all.

"Yeah, well you're not supposed to be up here, it's called trespassing. Your sister is worried sick about you; she might already be talkin' to security. Why don't you call her and tell her you're on your way down?"

A brief silence descended on their group. Bea stared up at Gareth with wide eyes.

"What about Maddy?" she finally asked.

"She's got this anxiety thing. I'll stay with her. Now you go call your sister."

Bea wasn't immune to Gareth's commanding presence. She nodded speechlessly. Then she took out her cell phone, a little sheepish, and started scrolling through her contacts. As she dialed, she walked down the second floor hallway to the staircase. Her steps were a little wobbly. After a moment, she started speaking to her sister over the phone.

"We saw a fucking ghost!" Bea said in a stage whisper, a hysterical edge to her voice. "*A real ghost in the attic! I told you I didn't imagine it, Becca. It's just like grandma said, it had an aura and everything, it looked fucking gruesome—*"

Maddy watched the whole exchange while slung over Gareth's shoulder. She wished she could appreciate the moment, because it was kind of funny and more than a little bizarre, but her heart was racing. She didn't like being carried. She felt like she couldn't breathe.

"Gareth," she panted. "Please put me down!"

Gareth swung her down from his shoulder and placed her gently on her feet. That's when Maddy discovered that her legs had no strength. She collapsed onto the floor, her arms and legs shaking. She leaned back against the wall, utterly spent.

"Careful," Gareth said, kneeling down next to her. "Alright, it's over now. The hell got into you? You really think it was a good idea to go looking for a ghost?"

Maddy heard the words he didn't say—*with your anxiety?*

"I can't . . . ." Maddy started shaking all over uncontrollably. "I can't breathe . . . ."

Maddy felt hot and sweaty. Her heart was still pounding. It refused to let up. Her sense of smell was excruciatingly keen. The stale air was stifling. She imagined she could smell the mold behind the walls of the old house, even the rat droppings beneath the floorboards. It made her want to gag.

Gareth took something out of his pocket. It was the little brown bear he had won her at the shooting gallery. Maddy had forgotten all about it. She must have dropped it back on the floor when Bea dragged her away from Hell's kitchen. He pushed the little brown bear into her chest.

"Breathe, Mads," he murmured.

Maddy gripped the teddy bear in her arms and tried to take a deep breath, but she couldn't. Her heart was racing too fast. Fuck. It would be nice to have a hit off Gareth's CBD pen about now, but she couldn't even do that. She was hyperventilating.

"Hey, is she okay?" Bea asked, coming to stand next to them. It looked like she had finished her conversation with Becca on the phone.

"She's got this anxiety thing," Gareth murmured.

Bea stared down at Maddy, looking shocked. "I didn't realize it was this bad. If I'd known, I wouldn't have asked her to come up here with me."

"It's . . . okay," Maddy wheezed as she tried to catch her breath. She wanted to reassure Bea, but her chest hurt; she felt like she was choking on air.

Gareth knelt in front of her, his big hands resting on her knees. She stared at the gaunt planes of his face and his exotic golden eyes. She hiccuped and gasped, struggling to calm her racing heart. Even with the hallway empty, she felt claustrophobic.

"Breathe in through your nose, out through your mouth," he instructed with a low, soothing voice.

She did so, clutching the bear to her chest.

"Is she having a panic attack? Do we need to call an ambulance?" Bea asked in concern.

"Naw, it'll pass. She just needs a minute," Gareth said, his hands resting on Maddy's legs. He reached over and took her wrist in one hand, his thumb pressing against her pulse. Maddy realized he was checking her heart rate. He waited calmly, watching her breathe.

Bea's dark eyes traveled from Gareth to Maddy, glancing back and forth between them. A little knot formed between her eyebrows.

"So . . . you're more than just her sugardaddy, huh?" she asked.

Gareth glanced up at Bea. He looked surprised and possibly amused.

"I'm her boyfriend."

"So you're official, then?"

"Yup, as of . . . two hours ago."

"Alright, I didn't realize." Bea sounded a little taken aback. "Like, I might have gotten the wrong impression before, I didn't think you were all that serious about her."

"Well, I am."

Bea looked between them again, watching how Gareth leaned forward protectively over Maddy's body, shielding her with his big shoulders, and how he ran a soothing hand down her arm. The affectionate touch seemed to make her uncomfortable.

After a long moment, Bea glanced up and away.

"Well, Vin is probably outside with Becca," she said. "I should get going. I told them I'd be down in a minute. Will you two be okay if I leave?"

"Yeah, I'll stay with her until we can walk out."

"Okay." Bea leaned in close to Maddy and said loudly, like she might be deaf and not having a panic attack, "I'll be right outside with Becca, so call me if you need me. We won't go far. There's a gift shop behind the haunted house, so we'll be over there, okay?"

Maddy gave her a little thumbs up. It was kind of adorable, how Bea didn't know what to do with herself. The little Goth girl gave them an awkward wave, then took out her phone and turned on the bluish-silver screenlight again. She started back down the hallway by herself and disappeared downstairs to the first floor.

With Bea gone, a new kind of silence filled the hallway, this time much more serene. Gareth's calm energy seemed to fill the whole corridor from wall to wall. He remained kneeling in front of her on the floor, holding her wrist, feeling her pulse slowly return to normal.

"There we go," he murmured as her breathing became easier. "Alright, so, you got all the way up there and you saw a ghost. How'd it go?"

"I didn't see it . . . but I think I smelled it?" Maddy said in a breathy voice. "It threw something after us. I think it broke a picture frame on the floor."

"Well, that's one hell of a thing," Gareth said, but somehow he didn't sound surprised. Maddy wondered if he believed in ghosts. He certainly wasn't scoffing at her story.

Maddy dragged in a deep breath, finally able to fill her lungs. She felt wrung out and exhausted from the adrenaline rush, and her sense of smell seemed excruciatingly keen. Gareth's spicy scent was particularly noticeable, it almost made her hungry. As the layers of panic dissolved, she felt her body awaken to a different sensation altogether: heat.

Shit, for real? Was she really getting turned on right now?

She didn't know if it was her fear, his scent, the adrenaline or the physical exertion that made her blood suddenly hot. Gareth was kneeling very close to her. She became deliciously aware of his large body hovering above her own. She sat cross-legged on the hardwood floor, sandwiched between his mountainous shoulders and the wall. *Traitors,* she thought to her tits, which were hardening into little points beneath her jacket. A layer of goosebumps covered her midriff, but she wasn't cold. She met his gaze and blushed; she saw a spark of fire in his hooded eyes. Like he could see right through her.

He leaned forward, positioning his body between her legs. His hand slid under her jacket to rest against her bare waist. Her heart quickened, but not from fear.

Then he pressed his lips against her forehead.

She released a breath as the tension left her shoulders.

"You got freaked out good, huh?" He brushed her long red hair off her face, tucking it back behind her ear. Then he cupped her face with one hand. He kissed her forehead again, then her nose, then each cheek. He didn't kiss her lips. His touch was gentle and reassuring.

"Yeah . . . yeah, but I'm okay now." Maddy's voice was hoarse. She took a deep breath, overwhelmed by his potent scent. "God, why do you smell so good?"

"I don't know, because you like me?"

"No, I'm serious. . . there's something *different* about you. "

"Naw, babygirl, I'm just some old guy you're dating."

Maddy half laughed, half wheezed. She was starting to feel more normal. His steady voice grounded her.

"You ready to get out of here?" Gareth suggested.

Maddy nodded, and he pulled her up to her feet. With one arm around her waist to steady her, he walked with her through the quiet hallway to the staircase. Together, they continued down to the first floor. Gareth seemed to know his way around the dark house with an unusual amount of confidence. He led her from room to darkened room until they found their way back to "Hell's Kitchen" and the spooky dining room.

"The exit is through there," he explained, pointing to a door on the far end of the dining room. "We can finish out the haunted house if you're game, or we can bail and take the emergency exit. What do you want to do?"

Maddy stood at the edge of the staged dining room. It seemed like a good place to stop for a minute and consider their options. She held the stuffed brown bear between her hands, squeezing it subconsciously.

"Just one more room, then the exit?" she asked.

"Yup, right through there."

"Well, that doesn't sound too bad. It's probably faster than looking for another exit."

Maddy steadied her nerves. She had come this far, even encountering a real ghost with Bea in the attic. One last room didn't seem like that big a deal. This would be the final stretch of the haunted house. How bad could it be, after everything else?

"I think we should finish it out," she decided. "Let's go."

Gareth raised an eyebrow. He leaned up against the long oak banquet table, his big arms crossed over his chest. He looked a little skeptical.

"You sure?" he asked.

"Really, I'm good, I can handle it. Nothing can possibly be scarier than that attic."

He studied her determined face. "Alright, but I'm going first."

She nodded.

"Remember, it's just actors in costumes, it's not real."

She nodded again.

"You want to close your eyes?" Gareth asked. "I can carry you."

Maddy gave him a horrified look. That sounded super embarrassing—she definitely didn't want that.

"No, I'm okay," she insisted. "I'll follow you through the rest of the house. It's really no big deal."

"If you say so."

Despite her bravado, Maddy hid behind Gareth's back as they entered the next room. It looked like the servants' quarters. He reached back and grabbed her hand, locking it in his firm grip. His warm, dry palm dwarfed her own. She felt a little silly. How could she ever be frightened with this man beast ready to protect her?

They followed the path outlined by red string lights. Through the servants' quarters, a second door led into the cellars. Here, Maddy hesitated. Down a short staircase, she saw flickering red lights illuminating the underbelly of the house. The basement was probably the perfect place for a jump scare. Yeah, maybe this wasn't such a great idea.

Gareth led her down a short staircase under the house, then through a maze of wine barrels. The lights in the room kept flickering on and off. The spooky soundtrack was ramped up to double volume. For Maddy's sensitive ears, it was an absolute nightmare. She started shaking. She grabbed Gareth's arm with both hands and clung to his side, trembling. At any moment, she expected some horrifying murderer to leap out at her from behind the barrels. She could feel her lungs beginning to constrict painfully tight.

"Gareth," she said, gripping his arm. "Gareth, I don't feel good."

"Yeah? Too much?"

"I can't catch my breath."

Someone in a baggy robe and a mask jumped in front of them. Gareth grabbed Maddy and pressed her face into his chest, the fuzzy bear squished between them. He stopped walking and held her like that while she trembled. His deep voice rumbled through her cheek. He was speaking to someone.

"It's too much for her. No, she's okay, it's just too much for her. Thanks. Yeah, I'm going to walk through, where's the nearest exit?"

Holding her firmly in his arms, he walked her backwards with his big body, keeping her face shielded against his chest.

"Just keep your eyes closed, babe," he said when she tried to look around.

She never got to see who he was talking to, but someone led them through the rest of the wine cellar to the exit. The cellar door opened, and Maddy felt a burst of cold night air. They climbed up a short staircase. Then the heavy door slammed shut behind them.

Gareth released her. Maddy sucked in a deep breath, then she looked around. They stood on the back deck of the Victorian manor. A roped-off pathway led them across the deck and down a wide staircase. Then the path wandered through a garden decorated with glowing jack o'lanterns, happy scarecrows and blow-up ghosts. On the other side of the garden, the path led directly into a tented gift shop. Little strings of pumpkin lights dangled from the rim of the tent. Inside, she saw kitschy produce crates stacked full of T-shirts, mugs, magnets, postcards, bottles of cider, and all manner of Fright Farm souvenirs. Since the haunted manor was the main event at the carnival, the gift shop looked packed with people.

Cheerful music was playing from the gift shop, completely at odds with her terrifying sojourn through the manor. It took Maddy a moment to adjust to the change of environment. She turned around and looked back up at the old Victorian house. From the outside, it didn't look half as scary. It really was just an amusement park attraction.

"Gareth?"

"Yeah?"

"Do you think . . . do you think I might have an anxiety disorder?"

He reached into his pocket and offered her the CBD pen. "Maybe. I think you run a little anxious. Nothing wrong with that. It's a haunted house, Mads, it's supposed to be scary."

Maddy took a puff on the vape and coughed a little, then she tucked it into her pocket. She wasn't sure if the CBD was working or not, but she felt better being outside. She let the quiet night wash over her. The air was moist, clean and refreshing after the humid wine cellar.

Fuck, that was terrifying. She felt like she had gotten her fill of Halloween, and it wasn't even the end of October. They still had another two weeks to go.

Gareth reached over and snagged her hand. He held their clasped hands up, looking at her fingers threaded through his own. Then he flashed her a wolfish grin.

"You're fine. Just hold onto me, yeah?"

"Okay," she murmured.

He started walking with her through the garden toward the souvenir tent. He escorted her across the back deck, then down the wide staircase and across the yard toward the gift shop. He acted like some sort of Victorian gentleman, walking at a stately stroll with his leather jacket and tattoos. Maddy felt herself blushing again; she couldn't keep the stupid smile off her face. Damn him for being so fucking charming.

"So . . . you really smelled a ghost?" he asked, all nonchalant.

Maddy snorted with laughter. It sounded totally ridiculous. She remembered the glass breaking on the floor, but now she wondered if she hadn't knocked over a picture frame or a vase while sprinting through the room. Already, the incident in the attic was fading into a hazy sort of dream. It was easy to explain away the whole ordeal as a sort of Halloween-induced hallucination.

"Well, I don't know, maybe," she admitted.

"What did it smell like?" Gareth asked.

"It smelled a bit like moldy old flowers," she said. "It seemed pretty real at the time, but do you think I imagined it?"

"I don't know, but it sounds legit. That's exactly how I imagine a ghost would smell."

Maddy laughed again.

"I'm a little surprised, Mads. You almost made it through the whole haunted house. I thought you'd quit after that girl grabbed you in the bathroom."

"Yeah, I'm tougher than I look," she said, grinning.

"No doubt."

Chapter 31

About a half hour later, their small group huddled around one of the outdoor tables behind the gift tent. Everyone seemed a little winded and disoriented from the haunted house. At first they all rushed up to Maddy, eager to check on her and relay their adventures through the wine cellar. Vin puffed on his vape while Bea lit up a cigarette. Becca swore she had seen a real dead body. Vin assured her it was a sack of straw in clothing—he went up to the prop and checked.

Then the topic turned to the two girls' misadventure in the attic. Bea recounted their journey through the Beaumont manor, with Becca scowling in disapproval the whole time. Maddy chimed in on occasion, adding dramatic details. Both girls swore up and down that they had encountered a ghost in the attic, but Maddy couldn't tell if the group believed them. She hardly believed it herself.

Then, as their energy drained out, they all sat around the table scrolling on their phones. Maddy looked around their little group. She couldn't keep the smile off her face. It had been a wild night. She couldn't remember ever having this much fun before. Even with Dean showing up and almost having a panic attack, it felt like the perfect evening. She felt like any other normal teen. Better than normal. She felt *good*.

Their picnic table was located at the very back of the fairground. The haunted manor stood behind them on a slight incline, overlooking the rest of the Beaumont property. A little downhill from their table, past a split rail fence, several acres of cornfield spread into the horizon. Beyond that, Maddy discerned the dark outline of a forest.

She watched the quiet night, appreciating the view. Light from the half-moon broke through the heavy cloud cover, casting the landscape in a silver glow. It was kind of romantic.

Maddy squinted into the distance for a long minute, then she pointed.

"What's that big hill over there? Is it part of the mountains?" she asked.

A large mound of earth rose up beyond the line of dark forest. It wasn't quite large enough to be considered a cliff. Maddy thought it looked like the shell of a giant tortoise sleeping under the moon.

"Wow, you can see that?" Levi said, squinting. "You have good eyesight. I think that's Beaumont Hill." He slapped his fair pamphlet down on the table between them. It was a bit crumpled from being in his pocket all night. "This flier doesn't say much about it, but I guess it was the location of the original Beaumont farm before they moved it over here."

"It's a local landmark," Becca explained. "It's technically part of the Beaumont property, but our grandma used to call it Cloud Hill. She used to hike up there all the time."

"That's pretty cool," Maddy said.

"Yeah, she was a weird one, old nana." Becca exchanged a glance with Bea.

Maddy didn't know what the two sisters had shared regarding the ghost. She had overheard a bit of Bea's conversation on the phone back in the haunted manor. It sounded like seeing spirits had something to do with shamanic powers. But again, she wasn't sure how she felt about all that stuff. It was easy to write it off as her imagination. She knew Bea's family believed in spirits; it was part of their religion. But Maddy wasn't sure if she believed in anything. Maybe she believed in the mountain.

When she looked up, she saw Gareth watching her with an unreadable expression on his face. She wondered what he was thinking about when he gazed at her like that. He stood at the end of the table, his arms crossed, like he was guarding their little group.

"You want a cup of cider?" he asked Maddy.

Before she could respond, Bea answered, "That would be great. Get me one too?"

Gareth blinked at her. Then Vin stood up, followed by Levi.

"I got it," Vin said.

"I'll go with you," Levi added. He sounded tired. "Babe, do you want cider?"

"Sure," Becca said. "Thank you."

The men walked away, leaving the three girls at the table. Becca watched the men get in line at the cider stand. She messed with the charm bracelet on her wrist. Then she turned to Maddy.

"So, about your neighbor, I have to ask," she said, "are you guys dating?"

The question took Maddy off guard. She stuttered for a moment under Becca's accusing gaze.

"Well, I mean . . . yeah."

"So this was a date, then?"

"I mean, initially, no. I invited him to hang out. But after we went to the parking lot to meet my dad, we had a longer conversation." Maddy shrugged, wondering why she felt the need to explain herself in such detail. Becca's tone made her feel like she was in trouble. "Anyway, yeah, we're dating now. So he's my boyfriend. Sorry I wasn't upfront about it. I didn't mean to lie to you."

"You should have just told me in the beginning," Becca said reproachfully.

"I know. I'm sorry. I didn't mean to mislead you. I just . . . didn't really know how to introduce him."

"Yeah, well, he's been hovering around you all night. It's pretty obvious he's into you," Becca pointed out.

Maddy blushed. She looked over at Bea, but her friend was posting a video of the haunted house to her Picplace account and didn't seem to be listening.

"So how old is he?" Becca asked bluntly.

"Twenty-eight."

Becca was quiet. She looked over at Gareth again. A frown creased her brow.

"Well, I can definitely see the attraction. He's smokin' hot, and he doesn't seem like a bad guy. But I'm gonna warn you, cuz you're Bea's friend. I think he's too old for you. He's almost thirty. Guys get a power trip from dating young girls. I think you should be careful around him. Or better yet, break it off and find someone your own age."

Becca's advice was blunt. Maddy felt embarrassed, but she had expected Becca to say something eventually.

"I know what it looks like—" Maddy started.

"Do you?" Becca raised an eyebrow. At that moment, she definitely looked like Bea's older sister. "Because from where I'm sitting, it looks . . . well, it doesn't look right. He might be handsome, but he looks a lot older than you. What do you have in common with a guy like him? Think about it. He lives in a totally different world. Owns his own business. Probably has a house, too. You're just graduating high school, Maddy. You don't even know who you are yet. What about college? Or traveling? You have plenty of time to date. I just don't want you to get taken advantage of."

Becca was starting to sound a bit like Dean, ironically. A much more reasonable and sober Dean. Her advice was well intentioned, but her words stung. Maddy glanced down at her hands. She didn't know how to explain herself. Becca had a point—Gareth was too old for her. She didn't have anything to offer him as a partner, just juvenile problems. She felt that way. She really didn't know why he was into her. He said all the right words, but part of her doubted he would stick around forever. He would get tired of her young adult issues eventually, she had no doubt.

Besides running into each other on the mountain at night, or at the hardware store, what did they have in common? A fun date at Zippy's? A fondness for the outdoors? They might have known each other for five years, but only a week had passed since they officially "met." She hardly knew anything about Gareth, except that he liked cars.

But . . . Becca also didn't understand Maddy's life at all. Sure, she was young. She was still in high school. But she wasn't like other teens. She paid all her own bills. She took care of the trailer by herself and cleaned up after Dean's mess. Her stepdad left her for weeks on her own sometimes. No one was looking out for her. Gareth was the first person to actually care about her life. Not only that, he was the first person to stand up for her. He actually made Dean fess up and apologize. When had Dean ever apologized before?

The more she thought about it, the more she wondered . . . what did a boy her own age have to offer? She didn't want to date someone living at home with his parents. She liked that Gareth was a homeowner. It meant she could tell him about her broken water heater and he might know what to do. She could complain about property taxes and house projects, bemoan her job at the hardware store and the endless onslaught of bills, and he understood her stress.

More than anything, she was tired of people judging her life.

"Mind your own business," Maddy said flatly.

"What's that?"

"I said mind your own fucking business, Becca," Maddy snapped.

Becca stared at her.

Bea looked up from her phone and glanced between them. "What did I miss?" she asked.

Becca shrugged. "Right. Okay. Forget I said anything."

Bea rolled her eyes. "You always turn into a cranky bitch when you're tired, Becca. Are we going home soon? It's almost midnight."

"Is it really that late?" Becca groaned. "I gotta work tomorrow."

The men returned with drinks in hand. Maddy took the cup of warm cider that Gareth offered to her.

Becca stood up from the table. "Levi, it's time to head out."

"Seems about that time," Levi agreed.

"Oh, you're leaving?" Vin said. He sounded bummed.

"Yeah, the park's closing soon anyway . . ." Bea glanced from Becca to Levi, then back to Vin. "Hey, I got an idea. Becca, why don't we go to the Black Bear Diner? It's 24 hours. Maybe Vin can come too?"

Becca pursed her lips. She looked annoyed. Then Levi chimed in with his usual cheerfulness.

"A burger after a haunted house sounds really good," Levi said. "Maybe a slice of pie? Hm? You hungry, babe?"

Becca sighed. "Alright, fine. I guess some pie and a cup of coffee sounds good."

"Vin can come with us!" Bea suggested. "He can fit in the back seat. Then we can give him a ride home. Do you live in Black River, Vin?"

"Yeah, off Mohen Road."

"I know where that is," Becca said. "Sure, we can drop you off . . . well, maybe not. The seatbelt for the center seat is broken. I don't want to risk getting a ticket. They'll be pulling people over tonight for sure."

The group fell silent. Maddy felt awkward. She didn't have money to go to a diner, and it was almost midnight. She really needed to get back home.

Right. Home.

She suddenly felt cold.

Am I really going back to the trailer?

Maddy glanced down at her hands, picking at her fingernails in thought. Honestly, she didn't want to go back to the trailer and spend the night alone with Dean under the same roof. Not after all that drama in the parking lot. Shit, she had actually slapped him. She felt like they both needed some space to let things cool down. Dean might be afraid of Gareth, but if he was blackout drunk, he might still try to retaliate or assert his authority somehow.

But the carnival was closing, and she needed to sleep *somewhere*.

Maddy felt the noose tightening around her neck. She didn't know what to do. It seemed a bit late to ask Bea if she could sleep over. Her eyes traveled to Gareth.

"You want to ride with me?" he asked.

After some hesitation, she nodded.

Becca opened her mouth, then paused. It looked like she was going to disagree with Maddy, but she didn't say anything.

"I don't really feel like going to the diner anyway," Maddy said. "I'll ride with Gareth. Then Vin can go to the diner with you guys."

"Are you sure?" Bea asked.

"Of course I'm sure."

It seemed like everything was decided. Vin looked relieved. The group walked back across the fairground together. The big crowds had dispersed, and the carnival was empty except for a few groups here and there and the janitors.

Bea and Vin paused outside the front entrance to say goodbye.

"Have a good night, Maddy," Bea said. "Text me when you get home safe, yeah?" She wrapped Maddy in a tight hug. As she leaned in, she whispered, *"Don't forget to use a condom."*

Maddy gasped and shoved her off. "You're such a ho!" she laughed.

Bea stuck out her pierced tongue. Then she turned and walked after Becca and Levi across the gravel parking lot. Vin fell into step behind her.

Maddy watched them depart. Then she joined Gareth's side. They started walking in the opposite direction, toward the overflow parking.

"So?" Gareth asked as they walked leisurely across the dark parking lot. "How did I do?"

"What do you mean?"

"Your friends. Did I pass?"

"Oh. Yeah, I think so. Definitely neighbor material."

Gareth let out a deep guffaw in his big, baritone voice.

Maddy added, "Well, Becca thinks you're too old for me. But I can tell Bea liked you. She definitely liked Vin. I'm going to be checking Picplace tomorrow to see if Bea updates her status."

"Status?"

"From 'single' to 'dating.' You can do that on social media."

"Right. Well. Not my thing."

"Not your thing? How else do you make a relationship official?"

Gareth caught another laugh in his throat. He looked bemused. "We're as official as it gets, babe. But I stay off that social media crap. I like my privacy." He reached over, grabbed the hood on her flannel jacket and playfully dragged it over her head.

"Hey!" she exclaimed.

"Let's get you home, little girl."

Home? The thought of going back to her trailer left a cold pit in her stomach. *Yeah. Home.* Where Dean was likely waiting for her.

"Um, about that," she said hesitantly. "Can I . . . stay over at your place? I just think it's probably safer after what happened earlier . . . ."

"Yeah, of course. Maybe I should've been more specific. You want to come home *with me*, little girl?"

He caught her eye. Maddy couldn't keep the smile off her face.

"Yeah," she agreed. "I'd like that."

As they walked, a thin veil of mist crept over the parking lot. Maddy shivered. She regretted her choice in clothing. Her bare midriff was covered in goosebumps. Gravel crunched under her Converse sneakers. It was pitch black outside the fairground. The parking lot was wide and long, close to empty, and lit by a row of unreliable solar lights. The lights kept flickering on and off. It was a little creepy.

Maddy was relieved when she saw the sleek outline of the Camaro near the far end of the overflow parking lot. Soon they would be back at Gareth's house, snuggling up on his couch in front of the TV. She felt a delicious little shiver. Yeah, she couldn't wait for that. She was more than ready. Maybe this time, he wouldn't hold back when things got too heated. They might go "all the way."

She felt a nervous little zing. Was she really bold enough? Was she planning on sleeping with him tonight? She cast him a little side look, wondering if the same thought was on his mind, but his eyes were focused on the distance. His jaw was set in a firm line. It wasn't the sort of easygoing expression she expected to see. Actually, he looked worried.

Maddy looked back at the parking lot, trying to see what had caught his attention. Then she frowned. At first she thought she was imagining it, but as she approached Gareth's car, she saw several shadows materialize around the vehicle. A cold, ominous feeling gripped her.

"Gareth," she said, "who are those people?"

Gareth stiffened. His heavy footsteps slowed on the gravel.

"Mads, get behind me," he said.

The wind shifted and Maddy was hit by an unfamiliar stench. Her sense of smell was still painfully keen after the haunted house. These men smelled *different*. Not like the sweaty mix of B. O. and soap from the fairgoers. These men smelled more potent, but in an unpleasant way. More primal. The animal stench called to a deep part of her that she couldn't explain. It seemed oddly familiar. She felt her pulse quicken.

Although it didn't make any sense, she began to feel afraid. It seemed like these men were not human *at all*. They seemed predatory. Threatening. She shrank instinctively behind Gareth's back.

"What do you want?" Gareth called to them.

"I think you know why we're here," their leader replied.

One fellow stood in front of the rest. He wore a thick gray coat. Maddy couldn't make out his face in the dark. But he smelled pretty rank, like a dog after a good run; instinctively, she knew that meant he was physically strong and primed for a fight. The hair stood up on the back of her neck. *How do I know that?*

"You killed our men," the leader said. "This is blood for blood. Nothing personal."

Gareth placed his body between Maddy and the group of thugs.

"Stay back, Mads," he warned her. "Don't come any closer."

"Gareth, what's going on?" she whispered. "They said you killed someone? What does that mean? Are they serious?"

"*I said, stay behind me,*" he growled.

Maddy felt like she had stepped into a nightmare. She was completely confused and disoriented. Who were these men? What was going on? It seemed these threatening strangers were also curious about her. A few of the men started to notice her hiding behind Gareth's back.

"Who's the female?" a shorter, scrawnier fellow said.

"Mind your own fucking business," Gareth replied.

The scrawny guy walked a little closer, circling around to their left. Gareth remained motionless, but tracked him with his eyes. A scruff of gray stubble covered the fellow's narrow face. Maddy thought he looked like a wiry old jackal. He shot her a wicked grin and sniffed the air.

"I smell wolf blood," he leered.

Something deep inside of Maddy shuddered. She remembered the night those men came to her trailer, when they ripped open her shirt and held her down. This jackal-looking fellow reminded her of those men. Was this the same gang?

"She's a *female*?" another man echoed.

The group shifted, turning toward her and changing positions. Maddy felt a wave of new attention focus upon her. She crept closer to Gareth's back, wishing she could disappear.

The little jackal man tapped his pointy nose with a long forefinger.

"Oh yes. A young female just beginning the Change. My nose never lies. Looks like our rogue Alpha is hiding a secret."

Maddy didn't follow half of what the little man said. She was bewildered. *What's an Alpha? What do they mean, Change?*

"Gareth, what are they talking about?" she whispered.

He didn't answer her. Instead, Gareth called out to the little man, "You want to touch her? Just try it, shit-sniffer. I'll rip off your face."

Silence. The men sized him up again. The tension grew in the darkness. Maddy felt like a bomb was about to explode.

Then their leader said, "Bring her here, boys. I think we found ourselves a treat."

"Maddy, *run*," Gareth said.

"What? Why—"

"Just do as I say!"

Gareth grabbed her arm and shoved her away from him, almost causing her to fall in the mud. Maddy stumbled across the parking lot, clumsy and uncoordinated. *What the hell is happening?*

Then Gareth faced off against the pack of men. He shrugged off his jacket and tossed it on the ground. Then he pulled something out of his back pocket. He slipped it around his hand. Maddy's eyes went round. A pair of brass knuckles gleamed in the dim solar lights that lined the parking lot.

She stared. Brass knuckles? Really? Was that his only weapon? *This isn't a kung fu movie!* No wonder his tattoos read "*lobo loco.*" She watched in horror as the pack of men converged on Gareth. There were so many! She couldn't get a headcount in the darkness, but she estimated around ten or twelve thugs were ready to pounce.

Maddy pulled out her phone to dial 911. Her hands were shaking and her palms were sweaty and slippery. *Shit shit shit. Keep it together, Mads!* She fumbled with her phone, trying to call the emergency line, but she didn't notice the man sneaking up behind her. Suddenly someone grabbed her from behind, knocking the phone from her hand. A meaty fist went over her mouth to muffle her scream.

Maddy kicked and fought. She bit down on instinct, sinking her teeth into a dirty, fleshy pad. She tasted blood.

"Fuck! Dumb bitch!"

The man dropped her.

Maddy took off running the moment her feet hit the ground. Gravel flew under her sneakers. She sprinted across the parking lot, pumping her arms, gasping for air. Her mind raced. Where was she going? She had two choices: head to the fairground, which was far away across an empty lot, or run into the cornfield. At least in the field, she could hide.

She picked the cornfield and ran as fast as she could.

Chapter 32

Maddy didn't expect to stumble into a maze. She plunged through the tall stalks of corn, her arms held out in front of her to fend off spider webs and wide, wet leaves. Within thirty feet, she fell into an open corridor between the rows of corn. She stopped in her tracks, thrown off guard.

What the heck? Suddenly, it felt like she had entered a Stephen King novel.

She remembered, vaguely, Becca mentioning a corn maze at the Halloween carnival, but she hadn't realized the maze was in the field next to the parking lot. The corn field ran alongside the parking lot all the way to the fairground, then wrapped around its east side. So yeah, maybe this was it.

Secretly, she was grateful. Running through corn was no joke, and she couldn't see a damn thing over the ten-foot stalks. It would be much easier to run through a maze. Even if she didn't know where the heck she was going.

Maddy turned and sprinted down the corridor of mud and trampled corn husks. The maze was totally empty. A few strands of LED solar lights illuminated the pathways through the field, but the lights were barely visible against the vast darkness of the night. Every time the wind blew, a dry, rustling wave swept through the corn. It sounded like dozens of children running through tall grass next to her. It was unnerving.

She couldn't tell if the men were behind her, or still stumbling through the field, or if she was being pursued at all. With all the panic, it was difficult to tell how much time had passed. It felt like she ran for hours, though more likely, it was no more than a few minutes. Thoughts of Gareth filled her mind. Was he alright? Was he dead? *What did they mean, this is blood for blood?*

She wondered if she should go back to the parking lot. What if he needed help? Then again, what could she do? She couldn't fight off a dozen men. She didn't even have her cell phone. She was terrified.

The path split in front of her, breaking off into two different directions. Maddy began to slow down. Which way led deeper into the maze? Or did she want to head toward the fairground? The corn was too tall. She couldn't see the horizon; she had no sense of direction. She didn't know which direction to turn.

Suddenly a loud *boom!* split the night. A gunshot.

Maddy's blood went cold. She whirled around, staring back the way she came. Was that the direction of the parking lot? *Shit. Oh shit.* What happened? Was Gareth okay?

Then, out of nowhere, a dark shadow lunged out of the corn. Maddy screamed.

The man tackled her to the ground, and she fell into the mud. She kicked her legs and lashed wildly about, but the man was too strong. He was almost as big as Gareth, and he easily overpowered her.

After a short wrestling match, Maddy found herself on her back in a wet, sticky mud puddle, with dirt all up in her hair and smeared across her face. Her captor sat on her chest and laughed.

"Hey Stevie! Cristo! Found her! She's over here!"

She heard more rustling in the corn. Then two lumbering brutes appeared through the shadows. She couldn't make out their features clearly, but their size alone made them scary AF.

"Little bitch got pretty far," one of them said. "She runs fast, huh Logan?"

"She's a wolf girl. What do you expect?" Her captor, Logan, pointed at their shoes. "Cristo, give me your shoelaces. Hurry the fuck up. You're gonna tie her wrists while I hold a gun to her."

Maddy felt tears streaming down her cheeks, though she didn't know why, because she wasn't crying. She stared up at the guy sitting on her torso. He looked around 40 years old—a very fit and muscular 40. His weight crushed her and she struggled to breathe. He had a medium length beard and a handlebar mustache. Biker or hipster, she couldn't tell. In either case, he was an asshole.

Maddy couldn't fight against the three grown men. She felt a rising wave of helplessness and terror. What were they going to do to her? What about Gareth? She remembered the roar of the gunshot. Was he dead?

They grabbed her by the arms and none-too-gently forced her into a sitting position, tying her hands behind her back with Cristo's bootlaces. The rough lace cut into her wrists painfully. As they tied her, Logan pressed the cold muzzle of his gun against her midriff, just below her belly button. Maddy wished she hadn't worn a crop top. He slid the gun across her navel suggestively, watching her face with a sneer. She shuddered as his dark gaze traveled over her body.

"A little wolfgirl," he sneered with an accent that might have been British Canadian. "Well you're a snack, aren't you, hon? We're gonna take you back to our Alpha. Otherwise I'd have you to myself."

What the hell is a wolfgirl? she wondered. More slang for girls with big tits?

Maddy spat at him, but her mouth was too dry to summon any saliva. He laughed at her. She wanted to kick him in the face, but she couldn't struggle with the gun pressed against her belly and his weight pinning her down.

Maddy didn't consider herself "easy to lift." She wasn't a tiny, waiflike girl like Bea. But after her wrists were tied, Logan stood up, grabbed her bodily and threw her over his shoulder. She shrieked again, scared that she would fall onto the ground and break her neck. But Logan's big hands gripped her firmly by the waist. He smacked her hard on the ass. Then he guffawed.

"This ain't so bad, is it sweetheart?" he laughed. "Come on, let's get her back to the van."

Van? They had a van? *What, did they carpool here?*

The three men started running through the field with Maddy flung over Logan's shoulder, like she was nothing more than a sack of potatoes. They left the wide corridor of the maze and cut through the tall corn stalks. Stevie led with his phone out, using his phone's flashlight to see the ground. Cristo brought up the rear. Maddy tried to come up with an escape plan. Her only hope was to take them off guard and make a run for it. But where the hell was Gareth?

Blood for blood, she thought again. Whoever these thugs were, they came to kill him. He might be dead already. She could barely wrap her head around it. What the hell was going on? The night had turned into a bonafide horror movie. *How is this happening right now?*

Her head throbbed trying to figure it all out. One thing was certain: she couldn't let them put her in a van. That was like Abduction 101—you never get in the van. She didn't know how she was going to escape, but she wasn't going to let them take her.

The wind blew, and with it came an eerie shushing sound through the corn.

"This is spooky as fuck," Stevie said. "I keep thinking someone's behind us."

"Someone's gonna be if we don't hurry," Logan grumbled near her head. "Are we going in the right direction? This bitch is heavy."

Fuck you too, Maddy thought.

"I think so. The parking lot is over that way."

"If that's the parking lot, then what are all those trees?" Cristo complained from the back. "There ain't nothin' out here but more corn. It don't seem right. Fuck, this was a bad idea."

"Too late to quit now," Logan said. "Keep going."

Suddenly, they stumbled out of the cornfield into a fifteen-foot circular clearing, with a metal pole at its center and a little flag on top.

"I think this is one of the corners of the maze," Stevie said, flashing his phone at the flagpole. Some trash littered the ground at its base.

"I don't remember this on the way in," Cristo said. "I think we're lost."

"Fucking fine. Stevie, call them," Logan snapped.

Call who? Maddy wondered. *More backup?*

Stevie turned off his flashlight and tapped at his phone. He held it up to his ear. It rang for a moment. Then he said into the phone, "Hey, can you hear me? Look, we got lost in the corn maze. . . . *Fuck you*, you try finding your way around in here. . . . I don't know what happened to the Alpha. We left them in the parking lot. I'm sure Enzo took care of him. He had a female with him . . . yeah, a real live breathing . . . sure I'm sure. Fuck. I'm not dumb." He looked at Logan and rolled his eyes.

Logan urged him, "Tell them to bring the van around and come get us."

Stevie relayed the order into the phone. Then he listened for a moment. "Alright, we'll stay put. See you soon." He hung up. "They're gonna come meet us. Might be a few minutes. I guess they left to get coffee."

"Goddammit," Logan groaned.

He swung Maddy to the ground and set her ass down in the mud. *Squelch.* She grimaced. Her arms were wrenched at an uncomfortable angle. She was losing feeling in her fingertips from the shoestring around her wrists. She knew she should be more scared, but all she could think about was escaping. If she was going to panic, she would do it while running for her life.

Alright, think! So they had to wait for the van and reinforcements to show up. Now was the perfect time to slip away into the corn. But she needed a distraction . . . and to free her hands somehow.

Another gust of eerie wind blew across the corn field, followed by that creepy, ominous rustling sound. Maddy sniffed. A familiar scent caught her nose.

Stevie looked around. "You smell that?"

"Yeah." Logan reached into the nook of his back and drew out his gun.

The men all turned and looked at the corn field behind them. Maddy's heart jolted in her chest. Maddy heard something thrashing through the corn field; it was like a real monster was about to emerge from the darkness.

"Fuck, what is that?" Stevie yelped.

"I told you that asshole was gonna be a problem!" Logan roared.

Then a big, black shape leapt out of the corn nearby and tackled Logan to the ground. The gun went off. *Boom!* The sound made Maddy jump. If she wasn't already sitting, she would have fallen to the ground. Her ears rang.

Terrified, she rolled away from the two men wrestling for the gun on the ground. She came to a halt at the edge of the corn field. There, she lay like a possum playing dead. She slitted open her eyes, filled with cold trepidation.

Gareth pinned Logan beneath him. His wild black hair was unmistakable. Fuck. A wave of relief swept through her—*he's alive.*

The two men were grappling over the gun. Maddy had never seen two grown men fight before—it was brutal and shocking. Gareth's hair was unbound, falling down his back, and he had lost his shirt. She stared at the bloody gashes trailing down his muscular shoulders, like he'd been mauled by a mountain lion. He finally ripped the gun free from Logan's hands and flung it across the clearing into the corn. Then he punched Logan across the face. Blood spattered across the corn stalks. Logan slumped back on the ground, unconscious or dead, she couldn't tell.

Gareth's eyes glowed yellow in the night. He looked like a true-to-life demon. The sight terrified her. He stood up and faced off against the other two men. He cracked his knuckles.

"You don't want to do this," Cristo said, his voice laced with panic. "You ain't got no pack out here. The girl's coming with us. Better back down or you'll be dead."

Gareth lunged. Maddy squeezed her eyes shut. When she squinted them open, she saw Gareth slam into Cristo. Gareth's knuckles connected to the man's temple and Cristo dropped to the ground.

Stevie had a knife out. Gareth slammed into him, too. He grabbed his arm and twisted it behind him, breaking his wrist. The man howled in agony and collapsed in the mud. Then he struggled back up to his feet and took off running into the corn.

Gareth looked like he wanted to give chase, but he didn't. After a tense moment, he turned toward her. He crossed the clearing with long strides and knelt by her side. Maddy was shaking. She was terrified by the violence she had just witnessed. She flinched when he reached for her, but he ignored her reaction. His hand went to cup her jaw, turning her face toward him. She stared up at him, wide-eyed. She saw a few cuts and scratches along the side of his face. He was bleeding profusely from a gash on his shoulder. His black hair was slick with sweat. He looked . . . savage.

Her mouth went dry. She couldn't think of what to say to him.

"You alright?" he asked in a thick, guttural voice. He brushed some of the mud from her cheek. "You okay? Can you walk?"

"Yeah. Yeah, I'm okay," she murmured. She felt shaky and pale. "I-I-I don't understand what's happening."

He cut the bonds on her wrists using Stevie's knife. Then he lifted her to her feet.

"Rub your hands," he said. "Get the circulation going."

She did so, trembling.

He raised his head and looked around the clearing with the metal pole at the center. Maddy watched him warily. She felt like she stood next to a complete stranger. Nothing about him seemed familiar. She had never seen such brutality. *Who the fuck is he?*

"Are they dead?" she stuttered, looking at the three men on the ground.

"Fuck I hope so," Gareth muttered. "We need to get back to the parking lot."

He grabbed her wrist and started to pull her across the clearing toward the corn field. Then he froze.

"Shit," Gareth cussed.

As the word left his mouth, five more men emerged from the corn fields and fanned out, blocking their path forward.

Maddy went ice cold. "They called for backup," she mumbled, her words small, almost inaudible.

"Stand behind me," he ordered, and she obeyed.

Gareth planted himself between her and the new threat. By this point, Maddy had fully accepted her new role as a damsel-in-distress in a B-rated horror film. Not her ideal role. These men looked human, but she was convinced they were something else. They just . . . weren't right. Their eyes glowed eerily in the dark. Even if they looked like thugs, dressed in oversized T-shirts and tatted up like billboards, they stank like animals.

The biggest man stepped forward. He had a tattoo of a ram's skull on his neck. Maddy stared at it, wondering what it felt like to get a neck tattoo.

Ramskull pointed at Gareth aggressively. "Hand over the girl and we'll let you walk away."

"No," Gareth answered flatly.

Maddy cringed. Why were they so focused on her?

"You think you can fight us all?" Ramskull chuckled. "A loner without a pack? We'll keep coming after you. Where you gonna hide? Give us the girl, and we'll let you leave Jefferson County with your life."

"Sounds like a shit deal. How about I kick your ass instead?"

Ramskull sneered. "You really think you're tough shit, huh."

"Fuck around and find out."

A dangerous tension fell over the group. The wind shifted, and the men glanced around at each other. Maddy saw one of them cringe away slightly, the equivalent of tucking his tail. Then she realized, despite Ramskull's threatening words, they all looked nervous. That was a good thing. She was fucking terrified of Gareth, too.

In a low voice, barely audible, Gareth murmured to her, "Once this shitshow starts, run into the corn. Go left. You'll reach the woods. Just keep running. I'll find you."

"Okay," Maddy whispered, barely able to make her throat work.

Then Gareth turned back to the group of thugs. He adjusted his grip on the brass knuckles. Without further warning, he lunged. He nailed the first guy in the stomach, then clipped his jaw with an uppercut, dropping him to the ground. A second thug rushed him, a knife glinting in his hand. Gareth jumped back, but the blade grazed his side, slicing along his ribs. Maddy gasped, swallowing a cry. Then Gareth twisted away, putting distance between himself and the knife. Her heart pounded in her chest. She couldn't bear to watch, but she couldn't look away.

"I'm bored with this fight," Ramskull growled. "Let's kick it up a notch."

Ramskull raised his left arm and made a little "circle up" motion with his hand. Suddenly, the rest of the men dropped to the ground, crouching down on all fours. To a bystander like Maddy, it looked like a strange sort of dance. But then it got weirder. As she watched, the men began to . . . change. At first they seemed to shrink, but then they seemed to grow sideways, becoming long and narrow. Fur replaced bare skin, fangs pushed out teeth. Muscles bulged. Claws sharpened. Snouts lengthened.

Maddy's mouth dropped open. She couldn't believe her eyes.

Within a minute, five gray wolves faced Gareth in the corn.

Wolves.

These men were . . . werewolves?

Maddy felt a terrible urge to start cackling with laughter. What the fuck? *This isn't real. Am I dreaming? Wake up! Wake up!*

***

Gareth couldn't fight off five werewolves in his human form. He had no choice but to Change as well.

Shit, this was not how he wanted to break the news to Maddy.

He glanced upward at the sky, seeking the moon through the dark clouds. He allowed the fire of the Change to sweep through his body. The Alpha wolf was always lurking just beneath his skin. His wild blood coursed through his veins. Strength surged through his muscles. The world stretched around him, growing wider and darker as he fell onto all fours. His snout stretched. His Lycan instincts became sharp and cold.

He must protect his mate, no matter the risk to his life. It went beyond duty. It was survival.

As an Alpha wolf, he was almost twice the size of his opponents. It really wouldn't be a fair fight.

With a bloodthirsty howl, he leapt upon the other wolves, his fangs long and gleaming.

Chapter 33

Maddy watched the confrontation with wide, terrified eyes. It was amazing how adrenaline could sharpen the senses. She could see the individualized patterns in each wolf's coat as they converged in the darkness, growling ferociously. Fur literally flying. The leader of the gray wolves was a little larger than the rest, his coat a deep gunmetal gray. The other wolves were built smaller and lankier. Their colors ranged from sleek silver to a tarnished, rusty brown. They fanned out around the clearing inside the corn maze.

Maddy could scarcely believe her eyes.

These wolves used to be men.

She was shocked. Within a matter of minutes, all five men had collapsed onto the ground, their bodies contorting into grotesque shapes, becoming four-legged and hairy, their clothes falling off their limbs. She watched them . . . *change*.

Gareth was no exception. In fascination, she watched him undergo the same transformation. He seemed ready and primed for it. He popped his neck and rolled out his shoulders, then stretched each arm like he was about to do some heavy lifting. She stared, unable to look away.

As he rolled his shoulders, his spine began to lengthen. His arms flexed unnaturally forward. He fell into a crouch, his limbs contorting, his neck thickening, his skull lengthening until a big black wolf stood in his place. It was larger than the rest. A lot larger. And she recognized it. The size of the beast was unforgettable. Dear god, she had seen that wolf before. Its sleek black pelt shimmered under the moonlight, a deep blue-black. His fangs were white and gleaming like ice. His hackles raised, his fur bristling, the monstrous creature snarled at the other wolves.

The size difference between the black wolf and the other grays was noticeable. The black wolf towered over the rest, a behemoth of a beast, a nightmare of fangs and claws.

Maddy thought the smaller grays didn't stand a chance. They were half the size of the big black monster. Then again, wolves were known to take down large game like moose or elk, if they hunted in a pack. Maybe they would overcome Gareth with their numbers?

The wolves jumped on each other with thunderous growls.

Maddy could only stare in equal parts awe and horror as the clearing became a blood-bath. She stumbled back a few steps, sinking into the corn. Far from screaming, every nerve in her body told her to duck down and be quiet. She hovered at the edge of the field, hidden behind a screen of wet leaves and corn husks, unable to look away from the battle under the moonlight.

The big black wolf pinned down a smaller gray one. Fangs flashed and blood sprayed. When the black wolf released the gray, the smaller wolf limped off into the darkness, wheezing and whimpering, bleeding profusely from a wound on its neck. The black wolf could have killed the gray, but he didn't.

Then a second gray wolf darted in from his left, this one scrawny and mangy. Gareth's jaws caught the wolf's leg and crushed it. The beast collapsed on its belly and wormed away through the mud, unable to stand up.

Maddy was afraid to blink. The wolves were so fast that, within a few minutes, two grays were already out of commission. Then Gareth faced off against the big gunmetal gray wolf, the leader of their group. This match looked a bit more even. Maddy couldn't say for sure, but she thought this wolf might have once been Ramskull. He was flanked by his two remaining cronies. They looked ready to pounce.

Then some movement at the border of the corn caught Maddy's attention. She turned her head. Unexpectedly, she saw two silver shapes prowling along the edge of the corn field toward her, one to her left and one to her right. Two more wolves? Where did they come from? They must have been hiding in the field all this time. Their glowing yellow eyes were trained upon her. These grays might not be as large as the black wolf, but compared to a human woman, they were very big. Maddy became acutely aware of the two hunters stalking toward her. She was their prey.

A terrible chill went down her spine. Then her feet moved on their own accord.

Maddy turned away from the clearing and darted into the cornfield, sprinting as fast as she could through the slippery mud. The two wolves gave chase. Heavy bodies crashed through the stalks of corn and wet leaves behind her. One of her pursuers raised its voice to a bone-chilling howl. Somehow, she knew what that howl meant—the hunt was on.

She ran headlong through the corn toward the dark line of pine trees beyond the field. Her arms pumped at her sides. Her feet flew over the ground. She could hear the wolves in hot pursuit, their bodies crashing through the corn behind her.

Somehow, she made it to the other side of the field. She shot into the woods like an arrow, darting through pine, fir and aspen. The trees were spaced far apart, without much underbrush in between, which was a small blessing. She lengthened her strides, her breath heaving in her lungs, her long hair streaming out behind her. She didn't need to glance over her shoulder to know the two gray wolves were right on her heels. She could hear their paws thrumming on the ground, snapping twigs and spraying dirt in their wake. The corn had slowed them down a bit, but now they were gaining ground.

Suddenly, the trees parted before her, and a sheer cliff of solid rock emerged out of the darkness.

Maddy skidded to a halt, her eyes searching up the rock ledge. It wasn't quite vertical; she could climb it, if she was ambitious. She thought, maybe, she had reached Cloud Hill. Becca said her grandmother used to hike here, but it didn't look like an easy climb, and she didn't see any friendly trails circling around the cliff.

It would be dangerous to attempt such a climb in the dark. The ascent was almost vertical, but Maddy was desperate. She didn't see any other choice. Either she went straight up, or she became dog food.

Maddy threw herself at the rock wall and started climbing. Adrenaline fueled her strength. Her hands and feet naturally found footholds and handholds between the stones. Her instincts led her upward. She didn't have time to be afraid.

She heard the wolves break through the trees and enter the little clearing below her. She heard them jump up and scrabble at the rocky cliff, but they couldn't climb like she could, their paws couldn't grip the rocks. They fell back down, howling and snarling in frustration. Then they leapt up again, snapping at her heels like dogs after a treat, but she pulled her feet out of the way, steadily climbing upward.

The two gray wolves circled and snarled down below her. They paced back and forth through the dry autumn leaves. Maddy risked a glance over her shoulder. She wasn't very high up, maybe around fifteen or twenty feet, just out of reach. Two sets of yellow eyes glinted in the darkness below her. The wolves looked ferocious. They seemed larger from this angle, their long narrow bodies taut with muscle. They circled eagerly, staring up at her with dripping fangs, waiting for her to slip up.

Maddy regretted her decision to climb up the rocky ledge. She was only halfway to the top, and her arms were burning. Her hands were covered in scratches from the rough stone. She didn't have the upper body strength to make it to the top. She could see a ledge above her that looked relatively wide; maybe she could rest there a moment? She reached for it, trying to pull herself up, but her foot slipped. She fumbled. No, no, no! Terrified, she felt herself sliding backward as she lost her grip on the rough stone. She battled for a moment, fighting for balance against the vertical wall, but gravity won out.

With a shriek, Maddy fell backwards. Her arms pinwheeled—she didn't have anything to grab onto. Then she plummeted to the ground. It was a short drop. She landed on her back in a moldy pile of leaves, the wind knocked out of her. Fuck, that hurt.

The gray wolves were on her. One of them pounced on her chest, pinning her down with a big paw. A gust of rancid, warm breath struck her face. She heard a ferocious growl. *I'm gonna die!* She was dog food after all. She threw her arms over her head and shut her eyes. She anticipated the pain of teeth ripping into her flesh.

Then, with a truly monstrous roar, a black shadow came flying out of the darkness, lunging at the wolf on top of her. Maddy barely clocked it. The big black wolf smashed into the smaller gray one, sending it toppling through the leaves. Then the black beast stood over her body, a low growl rumbling deep in his chest. She stared up at its shaggy underbelly, its thick black coat covered in scratches and teeth marks. It stood over her protectively, its hackles raised, teeth bared.

She gazed up at the black beast in awe. Her body started to tremble. For a split second, she thought the savage brute would lower its head and tear into her. But it remained focused on the two grays, which circled around them, snarling.

Then one of the grays lunged.

The black wolf met the gray wolf head on. They locked together a few feet away from where Maddy was lying. With a shriek of fear, she curled into a protective ball. The black wolf's jaws clamped down on the gray's neck. With a mighty twist of his head, the monster snapped the smaller wolf's neck and flung the ragged corpse across the clearing.

Holy shit. Maddy watched, curled on the ground in a pile of fallen leaves, frozen in fear.

The second wolf was faster than the first one. It fought against the big black monster in a tornado of claws and teeth. Maddy listened to a thunderous storm of growls, snarls and snapping fangs as they darted between the pine trees. Then the fight broke apart.

The second wolf fled into the night, limping and yowling in pain. It wasn't walking right; it looked like its back leg was broken, or maybe a hip. It vanished into the shadows of the night.

Maddy stared after the gray wolf, her heart hammering against her ribs. Was the fight over? She stared into the dark forest with dilated eyes. She waited for more wolves to appear, her blood pounding in her ears, her breath loud and raspy. She strained to hear any sound above her own racing heart. Was she safe?

A breathless minute passed. It felt like an hour. Then she slowly uncurled from her fetal position on the ground. Mud and fallen leaves clung to her clothes. Her hair was a wild tangle around her face. Her eyes combed the shadows between the pine trees. Where was the black wolf? Had it gone after the last gray?

A cool wind brushed her cheek, passing through the woodland. Slowly, the midnight creatures began to stir; she heard an owl hoot somewhere nearby, and a rustling sound that might have been a possum. The chorus of crickets started up again. It seemed like the danger had passed. Silver moonlight filtered down through the canopy overhead. It was . . . soothing. She pulled in a deep breath. She could smell blood in the air. She thought, maybe, the fight was over.

Maddy gazed up at the rocky ledge from where she had fallen. She was lucky she didn't crack her skull. Then she wondered if there was an easier way to climb up. From the top of Cloud Hill, she could get a clear view of the forest and the surrounding farmland, and find her way back to the Beaumont manor.

So . . . what now?

She didn't have time to formulate a plan. Something moved in the shadows between the trees to her left. Maddy's heart lurched in her chest. Then something very large loomed over her.

Maddy cringed back as the monstrous black wolf approached her through the trees. She started trembling again, shrinking back against the ground. It was the same beast she had seen outside her house. The one who had led her home that day in the woods, when she got lost with Joker. It was probably the same wolf to save her from those men who broke into her trailer.

The beast stood over her. She felt small and puny, completely at the mercy of those long fangs and powerful jaws. Maddy couldn't control her shaking. Her lungs constricted and her breathing came in short bursts.

"G-Gareth?" she asked.

The beast before her began to change shape. It hunched over, its limbs bending and contorting. Most of the gruesome transformation was hidden by the deep shadows between the pine trees. A small mercy—she didn't think she could stomach seeing it again.

Then a human man was crouched before her. He slowly uncoiled and stood up. Rolled out his broad shoulders. Cracked his neck. Shook out his long black hair.

Maddy could scarcely believe her eyes.

Gareth gazed down at her with unnerving intensity. He might have changed back into a human male, but he still resembled a nocturnal beast. His eyes glowed like twin lanterns in the dark, filled with the light of the moon. Slick with sweat, black tendrils of hair stuck to his forehead and fell past his shoulders in a wild mess. He looked utterly primitive, his tattoos almost tribal, like a caveman from days long past.

He was completely naked.

"Gareth?" she asked hoarsely.

As she watched, he raised a hand to wipe the blood from his mouth.

"Mads," he said, his voice dark and deep in his chest.

"Oh fuck no," she said.

Maddy sprung to her feet like a frightened deer and took off through the woods. This was so much worse than a haunted house.

Fuck this nightmare, she thought. *I want to wake up! This can't be real. This isn't real!*

She heard Gareth curse behind her and give chase.

No way was she going to let him catch her.

Adrenaline made her eyes keen and her senses sharp. Sounds were crisp and clear. Smells stung her nose. She navigated through the unfamiliar wilderness. She didn't know this area like she knew the trails around her house. It was brand new territory. She found a deer trail, almost invisible in the underbrush, and sprinted along it. She leaped over fallen logs. Shoved her way through brambles and thickets. She had no idea where she was going, but that didn't matter. She had to escape from the monster behind her.

The gruesome vision of the men changing into wolves played over and over in her head.

It can't be real. It isn't real.

Shit, it's real!

She raced on through the dark forest, aware of Gareth only a few yards behind her. He was bigger than her with longer strides. She felt him closing the distance between them. He reached out, trying to snag her jacket, and she twisted around, barely slipping from his grasp.

She skidded down a short, grassy slope and plunged into a stream at the bottom of it. She gasped as her head almost went underwater—the stream was much deeper than she anticipated. The water was ice cold mountain runoff. She struggled against the strong current as she waded across the black water, submerged up to her chest.

A heavy body entered the brook with a splash, just as she pulled herself up the rocks on the opposite side. Fuck, she was exhausted. But she had to keep going.

Running wasn't so easy now. Her shoes were wet. Her waterlogged clothes clung to her skin. She pushed ahead through the ferns, shivering as exhaustion weighed her down.

In her distraction, Maddy's foot caught on something hard and square. She fell face-first to the ground. She clutched at her ankle, biting her lip in agony. Fuck. It felt like her whole leg was on fire. She clenched her jaw, trying not to scream in frustration.

She tried to climb back to her feet, but promptly collapsed again. This was bad. Her ankle was bruised. It wouldn't hold her weight.

She looked around. What had she tripped over? In the thin light of the moon, she picked out the pattern of a half-built house. It looked like an old homestead. Only one wall was left standing. The ruins must have been a hundred years old. In the darkness, she could barely make out what looked like an old hearth. She had tripped over a clay brick the size of a cinder block. Just her luck.

On her hands and knees, Maddy scrambled through the ancient foundation of the house, then beyond that, through a tunnel of moist, leafy ferns. There, on the opposite side of the clearing, she reached the trunk of a toppled pine tree. The dead tree was massive, an ancient mother of the forest, the base at least ten feet across. She half dug, half forced her way under the trunk, hiding in the soft earth like a fox in a hole. She lay on her belly under the tree, the cool earth against her stomach and her chest flattened to the ground, sheltered by a screen of leafy ferns.

Maddy bit her lip, trying to keep her breathing calm and quiet. Her heartbeat was so loud, it felt like a drum in her chest. She was surprised it didn't echo through the whole forest.

She heard the sound of thrashing branches and rustling leaves. From her hiding place, she watched Gareth enter the old ruins of the homestead. He emerged from the trees at a full run, charging headlong through the clearing. He easily leapt over the pile of rubble where she had tripped.

She hoped he would pass by her hiding place and continue through the woods. Then he slowed down. He came to a stop between the trees, the old homestead to his back. He turned, the profile of his face and shoulders silhouetted by moonlight.

Maddy bit her lip. She pressed against the earth, struggling to breathe silently as her heart threatened to choke her.

Under the moonlight, Gareth's hair was wet, loose and wild, falling in tangled waves across his shoulders and down his broad back. Every muscle looked taut and distinct. He stood perfectly still, surveying the forest, his head turning left and right.

As Maddy stared at him, her cheeks grew flushed.

He was . . . very naked.

Damn.

Despite her adrenaline, or perhaps because of it, she couldn't help but admire his herculean physique. The moonlight revealed his godlike body in mesmerizing detail. Her eyes trailed over his broad shoulders, his muscular chest, his tattoos, down to his chiseled abdomen. Then her eyes found the thatch of dark hair between his legs. She was shocked to see his member fully erect. Fuck. Even in the darkness, she could see its impressive size.

Something clenched deep inside of her at the sight. The wind shifted and she caught his warm, spicy scent. Dark, primal feelings stirred within her.

Oh no. Was she . . . aroused? How? Why? There was absolutely nothing sexy about being chased through the woods at night. Still, she drank in the sight of him as a tendril of desire curled within her belly.

He turned. His eyes fixed upon the ancient tree trunk where she huddled near the ground, screened by a curtain of leafy ferns. She was pretty sure she was hidden from sight, yet his eyes passed over her little alcove again and again.

"I know you're hiding from me, Mads," he said.

She bit her lip. Maybe he could see her. Maybe not. She wasn't going to answer.

He took a step closer to the fallen tree. Her heart lurched in her chest. His bright yellow eyes searched through the shadows, like a hound seeking a rabbit in the brush. He didn't look human at all, more like a monster from a fairytale.

"I know you're scared," he said. "But you can trust me."

Like hell, she thought. *What are you?*

"That was pretty wild, huh? Men turning into wolves. Like nothing you learned about in school, I bet. I'd be freaked out, too." He kept talking as he slowly circled around the clearing and the crumbling homestead, his voice low. "I wanted to tell you sooner, but I was waiting for the right time. When's the right time? I don't know, Mads. You had a lot going on. Didn't want to dump more on you. But I didn't want you to find out like this. You deserved to know sooner. I hid it from you. So yeah. I'm the bad guy."

Now he was walking away from her, away from the fallen tree. She listened to his footsteps grow more distant. Some of the tension loosened in her stomach. Maybe, if she stayed very quiet, he'd wander off and leave her alone.

Maddy's eyes darted back and forth. Shit, she lost sight of him. He had left the clearing and now she didn't know where he was.

Suddenly, his voice came from directly behind her.

"But you know," he said, "I saved your life twice. So maybe that's alright."

Maddy yelped and turned around. Gareth was kneeling on the other side of the tree trunk behind her. Before she could react, he grabbed her by the hood of her jacket, like he would scruff a kitten, and pulled her out of her hiding spot.

"Easy does it," he said, "watch your ankle."

"Get the fuck away from me!" Maddy rasped, her voice hoarse from panic.

"Mads, calm down."

"No!"

"Let's talk."

"Let me go!"

She tried to squirm free of her jacket, but his hand went to her arm. His grip was like iron.

"Fuck you!" Her heart thundered in her ears. "Those men turned into wolves. *You* turned into a wolf. You're a freak! *Let me go!*"

She shrieked the last words into the night. They echoed through the trees. She stared up at him, wild eyed.

His lips were set in a firm line. She almost thought he looked . . . hurt.

"They were going to kidnap you, Mads."

"Why? Why were they going to kidnap me? Who were those people?"

She was on the verge of hyperventilating. Her eyes were fully dilated. Maybe she could still run. Her ankle throbbed, but adrenaline made her feel superhuman. She was ready to fly into the forest the moment he loosened his grip on her arm.

"What the fuck are you?" she demanded. She felt a little unhinged.

Gareth studied her, so calm. How could he act so nonchalant at a time like this?

"I'll explain," he said levelly, "but we should get out of these woods. Look, you hurt your ankle. Let me help you back to the car. Then I'll tell you everything."

"My ankle's fine!"

"It's not fine. You can't walk."

"Fuck you, I can walk!"

"Calm down, Mads. I'm not going to hurt you."

"How do I know that?" She felt like she was going to have another panic attack, just like in the haunted manor. "You turned into a . . . a . . . ."

"A wolf. I did it to protect you."

She stared at him. How could he sound so rational?

"You're going to climb on my back and I'm going to carry you to the car," Gareth said.

"Fuck that. You're naked. I can't climb on your back."

His eyes glinted. "Oh yeah? You want to climb on something else?"

Maddy was shocked. She went to slap him—pure reflex. He raised his other arm, blocking her, then grabbed her by the wrist. Now he held her with both hands.

"How dare you!" she seethed.

His face was gaunt, his jaw firm. His eyes glinted down at her, full of heat.

In a low voice, he growled, "Go on, lie to me. Tell me you don't want me, Mads. I can smell it on you."

She opened her mouth. Her gaze swept over his naked body. Fuck, she couldn't.

"You're not carrying me back to the car," she repeated.

"Fine. Let's stay out here in the woods then. I'm game. We'll camp here next to this tree. But your clothes are wet. We should get those off you. Don't worry, I'll keep you warm."

"Shut up!"

He quirked an eyebrow, his grip powerful on her arms. He pulled her toward him. She resisted. Then, with a firm yank, he dragged her against his chest. He caught her jaw in the palm of his hand and angled her face upward.

His lips claimed hers without asking for permission. She was helpless as his tongue entered her, pushing deep inside. His hand controlled her jaw. His golden eyes glowed down at her, half-hooded, as he devoured her mouth. Wolf eyes. A reminder that he wasn't human.

Maddy felt completely swept up in his power. His kiss was like fire. Her body, fueled by adrenaline, ignited in a wave of lust.

He was a monster. She shouldn't want this. It was wrong.

But the way he took control . . . .

His hand cupped one of her large breasts. His calloused thumb started rubbing her nipple through her wet shirt. She shuddered, weakening under his firm touch.

He pinched her, a bit rough.

"Ah!" she gasped into his mouth, more surprise than pain.

He didn't stop. He rubbed her nipple again, massaging her breast with a strong hand. His touch wasn't soft and patient like before, but filled with urgency. Maddy felt a thrill of excitement.

He pulled her jacket off. Then his hands went up under her shirt, under her bra. He dragged off her wet clothing without a word and tossed her bra and shirt into the woods. Cold air hit her breasts. Then he leaned down and took her left nipple into his hot mouth. He sucked hard enough to bruise her pale skin. She moaned as tendrils of pleasure shot from her breasts to her bellybutton, then down to her clit.

She looked down at his face as he sucked at her nipple. His cheeks were gaunt, his gaze stern, focused, full of sharp intensity. He looked like a man with a powerful craving.

Maddy leaned forward, taking a step closer to him. Without meaning to, her hand brushed over his rigid member. He flinched, glancing up at her, his eyes gleaming in the dark. She blinked, equally surprised by the graze of flesh on flesh. Their eyes caught again. Some sort of electricity passed between them—the air seemed charged with it.

He released her breast. He watched her sink down before him, kneeling before his rigid cock. She couldn't explain what she was doing. Feeling emboldened and a little wild, Maddy settled on her knees on the soft earth, gazing up at his anatomy. She had never seen his cock like this before. It stood fully erect, hard as rock, thick and girthy. The length was impressive. The head was smooth and shiny, flared out like a mushroom. She hesitated, then she reached out to touch it. She couldn't wrap her hand around its thickness.

Her fingers traveled up his swollen shaft, exploring. Her thumb grazed over the wide head, feeling its silky smooth texture. Then her hand slid down its length to the thatch of pubic hair at its base. After a pause, she explored lower, feeling the rough skin of his testes between his legs.

Gareth groaned deep in his throat. "Mads . . . ."

Her hand rested on his engorged member. She felt insanely aroused.

She leaned down. Her hand stroked his hard cock. Then her lips brushed the head of his member, placing a gentle kiss upon its glistening tip.

Gareth's hand sank into her hair.

"Mads, what are you—"

She took him into her wet, soft mouth.

Chapter 34

There in the woods, surrounded by ferns and the scent of pine needles, she sucked on him. She had never done anything like this before. She stroked him with her hand as she teased him with her tongue, timid at first, then growing bolder. She tasted his sweat for the first time.

Gareth growled, just like a wolf. Then his growl turned into a deep groan. It was the manliest sound she had ever heard.

He stood with Maddy kneeling before him, her mouth wrapped around his cock. His hand tightened in her hair. He pushed himself deeper into her mouth, holding her head still, until she felt his cock touch the back of her throat. She almost gagged, but kept her reflex under control.

Keeping a firm grip on her hair, he used her mouth to pleasure himself. He thrust his thick length down her throat, over and over again. She struggled to keep up. He was dominating. Powerful. His scent filled her head with potent pheromones. Fuck, she was so aroused. She felt herself growing drippy and wet down below.

She gazed up at him with wide eyes, watching the pleasure on his stern face. His dark eyebrows were drawn close together. His lips remained firm, his jaw clenched. She had never seen anything so erotic.

She felt his shaft swell as he neared his climax. She whimpered as he pressed himself deep down her throat, burying his long cock to the hilt. She had no choice but to accommodate him. His cock twitched and jerked, then his hot seed exploded into her mouth, tangy and salty. She gulped it down, swallowing so she didn't choke. He groaned and panted as he ejaculated, coating her mouth and throat with his thick, sticky cum. It was a lot. She couldn't keep up. It overflowed past her lips and dribbled down her chin.

He stared down at her, his eyes never leaving her face as he filled her mouth with his cum. It was the most sexual thing she had ever experienced.

After he finished, he pulled her up from her kneeling position. She gazed at him with wide, doll-like eyes. He placed his hand reverently along her cheek. His thumb brushed her swollen lips, wiping his juices from her chin. Then he leaned in close. He didn't kiss her, but licked his tongue over her lips, shamelessly cleaning off her mouth.

"I don't know why I did that," she mumbled.

"Because I'm your Alpha."

"What?"

Then he caught her lips in another deep kiss.

Maddy gasped and moaned. She felt so weak. She trembled in his arms. His member, which had softened briefly after the blowjob, was standing swollen and engorged once again. Maddy found that hard to believe. How was he still erect?

Gareth's hands went to the button on her jeans. He started undoing her pants and sliding them down over her round hips. He hooked her panties and pulled them down her legs, too.

"Gareth, what are you doing?" her voice hitched.

"You want me to stop?"

Their eyes caught. Maddy realized what he meant. What he intended to do. After a breathless moment, she shook her head.

"No," she whispered. "Don't stop."

He finished pulling her pants off and tossed them into the pile with the rest of her clothes. Then he placed his hand on the back of her neck, guiding her down onto a bed of soft earth and moss. He settled down first, then pulled her up on top of him so that she sat astride his hips, their crotches pressed together. He gazed up at her, his eyes traveling over the heavy mounds of her breasts, her swollen pink tits, her vulnerable face. She saw the lust in his burning golden eyes. He looked hungry. Like he would eat her up.

Then he reached his hand between her legs and slid his fingers between her moist lips. Maddy went up on her knees as his fingers explored her body, seeking an opening.

"You know, werewolf cum is an aphrodisiac," he murmured.

She blinked. "Werewolf? You're a . . . a werewolf?"

He grinned up at her like he was baring his fangs. "What else would I be, little girl?"

Maddy felt a flutter of trepidation in her stomach. So, it was all real. She had half-convinced herself this night was a dream.

"Really?" she murmured, wondering at her intense arousal. "An aphrodisiac?"

"Sold on the black market. Guess we'll find out if it's true."

His finger found her tight entrance. Maddy gasped as his middle finger pressed up into her, down to his knuckle, sliding firmly into her tight, virgin core. He stroked her hidden flesh, tickling the sensitive spots buried deep inside her. She gasped, staring at him helplessly as he played with her body. Fuck, she wasn't used to this at all. It was uncomfortable at first, but as the seconds slid by, she felt a burning heat growing between her legs. Her skin tingled. Her breathing became heavy. She began moving her hips with tentative little thrusts against his hand.

"Good girl," he growled deep in his throat, his teeth clenched in a wolfish half-smile. He flicked his finger back and forth as she grew wet and creamy. Then he withdrew his finger. He gripped his thick shaft and rubbed his head up and down along her slit. Her pulse tripled. Fuck, it was so intimate.

"Feel that, babygirl? Why don't you rub yourself on me like you want to?" he murmured.

She bit back a whimper. Shit, this was really happening. They were going to have sex. Here, in the middle of the forest, after the most terrifying night of her life. She almost lost her nerve. But she was too aroused to stop. Whether her arousal was caused by drinking werewolf cum or by sheer, crazy adrenaline, she didn't care. She began to undulate her hips back and forth, sliding her wet lips up and down his shaft, coating him in her juices. He raised his hips to meet her. She ached inside, craving his fullness. She could still taste his salty cum in her mouth. She wondered what it would feel like to have him ejaculate inside of her.

They moved like that for a while as Maddy learned his rhythm, every inch of her tingling as she rubbed herself along his thick shaft. Then he reached down and angled his cock against her opening, encouraging her to slide down onto it. She lowered herself on top of his shaft. He was very wide. She couldn't imagine how he would fit inside, when she could barely accept his finger.

She tried to settle onto his thick head, but her entrance was too narrow. She tried a few times, feeling clumsy and a little awkward. She bit her lip, frustrated to no end.

"I-I don't know what to do," she admitted, her voice hitching with embarrassment. *Fuck, this is impossible. There's no way.*

Discouraged, she started to squirm away, but he caught her wrist.

"Let's try a different position," he murmured.

Then he rolled her onto her back. She felt the soft moist earth press against her bare ass. The ground was cool and comfortable. He layered himself over her with a deep, contented groan, like he was settling down to business.

"You know how many times I've thought about this?" he murmured, pausing to brush a casual kiss over her left nipple.

She shivered, sweaty and weak, unable to summon words.

He gathered her up in his tattooed arms. His chest was so wide, he blocked out the sky. He kissed her forehead tenderly. She was completely compliant and docile, overcome by his large body. She felt his weight settle on top of her.

Fuck, she thought. She was ruined.

He casually hooked her legs over his shoulders, spreading her wide open beneath him. She felt the head of his cock nudge between her drenched lower lips again. He rubbed his cock up and down along her slit, teasing her, rubbing her juices over his thick head. He seemed to find an angle he liked. He began to push into her.

Maddy gasped. He was so wide. She felt a twinge of pain as he began to enter her for real. So big. *Too big.*

She tensed up, her hands gripping his biceps.

"Ah!" she whimpered.

"Relax, little girl . . ." he murmured.

He held her in his powerful arms, unremitting as he pressed into her. She felt her body opening in a way she couldn't prepare for. He watched her face intently. His hand brushed the hair back from her forehead. Despite her sounds of distress, he kept pushing his cock deeper, his shoulders and biceps fully flexed, his abdomen tight.

"It's gonna hurt, babygirl," he coaxed her softly, biting her cheek, then her neck. "Grab onto me. Yeah, it hurts, I know. That's just how it is. But after this, I'm gonna make you feel so good."

The sensation was overwhelming. Maddy lost control of her voice and started moaning like a small animal, gripping his biceps, digging her nails into his skin. Her flesh resisted him, but he didn't let up. He was so large.

A tear slipped down her cheek. She stared past him up at the trees, up at the moon hovering in the cold sky. She had a flash of memory—of meeting him in the woods the first time. Somewhere in the darkness on the mountainside. She was so much younger then. And so innocent.

Now here he was between her legs. Pushing inside. Inch. By. Inch.

Somehow, she had always known it would be *him.*

His hips finally settled against hers. He paused, no longer moving.

"Are you . . . all the way in?" she asked, her voice small.

"I'm in enough, babygirl. Let's just feel this for a moment," he groaned.

He gathered her up in his big tatted arms and licked her cheek. He rested his full weight against her, pinning her with his hips, his thick rod filling her virgin core.

Maddy felt utterly helpless. So he wasn't all the way in yet? How much more? She felt skewered. It didn't hurt as long as he kept still. She willed her muscles to relax, to accept him. She was fully impaled and filled to the brim. The head of his cock was pressed against her cervix deep inside, a sensation she had never experienced before. His engorged length touched every sensitive bundle of nerves, every inch of hidden flesh. She had never felt anything that deep.

Maddy realized she was breathing hard. She was scared to move. But. The pain was slowly receding. It was alright. She was okay. He began kissing her gently, softly, caressing her lips. Kissing and kissing. Running his tongue along the edges of her mouth. Her chin. Her neck. She felt a spiral of new arousal as he nibbled and licked her ears. She moaned softly, moving her hips without thinking, then gasped when she felt him slide an inch deeper.

"Ah," he groaned. "There it is. Fuck, you're wet. I'm going to move now. You ready?" She nodded.

"Alright, little girl."

He withdrew by half, then thrust into her. She gasped, and he took her little sounds of pleasure into his mouth, kissing her deeply. She gripped his arms. She didn't want him to stop. In the beginning, he was so gentle and sensual. She was deep in the forest, lost in his passion. Pine needles tickled her back, moss cushioned her head, as she gazed up at his dark expression. Her legs were spread wide beneath him, his cock anchoring her to him, soothing her, comforting her. It felt like he meant to tie her to him permanently. He held her locked to his chest, his head resting above hers protectively as he pumped into her.

Fuck, he was strong. Holding her pinned, he began to thrust into her with more speed. The pain subsided, replaced with growing pleasure as her clit rubbed against his pelvis. His cock reached a spot deep inside that made her toes curl. She felt the most exquisite tickling sensation behind her bellybutton. It kept growing with every rhythmic thrust. She didn't expect to feel pleasure so deep. She stared up at him, overwhelmed by the feeling, her mouth slightly open, her eyes wide and glassy. She was growing very wet.

He fucked her with long, deep strokes. She shuddered beneath him as his cock touched every sensitive nerve in her body. Weak and mindless, she moaned, unable to control the sounds oozing from her throat.

"Aaah," she moaned. *"Ah!"*

He kept moving at a mind-bending pace, steadily driving her insane.

The friction against her clit was something else. The pleasure grew into a wave. She started to gasp, but he was holding her so tight, she couldn't breathe. Was she going to faint? She felt like she was losing her mind. The pressure built until she couldn't take it anymore.

Fireworks. She cried out, widening her legs, grinding her hips against him over and over as the wave took her. It was a completely different feeling, gripping down on his thick cock as he massaged her insides.

"Gareth!" she cried. "Gareth! Ah!" Jumbled up with her incoherent moans, she might have uttered, *"Oh fuck, daddy!"*

"Yes," he murmured, holding her tight like a doll. He pushed deep. "Say it again."

"Aah . . . daddy . . . ah . . . please . . ."

Maddy collapsed in his arms as the orgasm passed, her body a pool of syrup.

His hand went to her neck where he gripped her lightly.

"Hmm . . . am I your Alpha, Mads?"

She gazed up at him, utterly devastated. How could she feel this shy with his dick inside of her? She nodded, her lips parted. Fuck. She was so broken.

"Hmm," he growled.

He tightened his hand until she felt her airway restrict. A little submissive shiver shot through her. He watched her reaction with a sexy half-grin. Then he began to rock her body gently with his hips, pumping in and out with sensual slowness. His thumb feathered over her jaw.

"Look at you, all calmed down. Not so scared of me now, huh?" He grinned down at her. *"You just needed a grown man's cock to feel safe . . ."*

Maddy was so humiliated, but so aroused. He seemed to enjoy watching her squirm. He pulled all the way out, then sank into her again, the wide head of his cock kissing against her cervix, teasing that sensitive bundle of nerves that was her G-spot. She whimpered. He stroked in and out, in and out, letting her feel every inch of him filling her flesh.

He whispered into her ear, "Maybe I shoulda tried this sooner. Got you alone in the hardware store . . . *slipped your panties down . . . pushed in just the tip . . . then a little more . .* ." He mimicked his words with his dick, pulling out and pushing in again slowly, training her tight lips.

"I should've tied you up in my bedroom . . . kept you for my pleasure . . . fuck, maybe I'll do that now . . . ."

He kissed her forehead, then licked her sweat, then trailed kisses down her temple until his lips pressed against her ear. He began to grind his hips against her. He was going to make her orgasm again.

"No . . . no, it's too much . . ." Maddy whimpered.

"You wanted this big cock, little girl," he said. "I'll decide when you've had enough."

Maddy felt pressure building again. Something fluttered deep inside. She couldn't handle another orgasm. It was too much, too soon.

Her next orgasm was so strong, she forgot how to breathe for several seconds.

"Say it," he murmured into her lips.

"Daddy... oh fuck...."

"That's right, little girl."

From that moment, it seemed to become his personal mission to make her orgasm as many times as possible. The pain of losing her virginity was quickly forgotten in the waves of intense pleasure ravaging her body. He worked her clit expertly until she was so sensitive, she couldn't bear to touch it. Her body hummed and quivered. She was sticky with sweat and her own juices. She lost count of how many times he brought her to her peak.

At one point, she realized he was pounding into her forcefully, taking his own pleasure, trapping her against his body with his big arms. He fucked her hard, pumping his full length in and out, their bodies resting in a pool of sweat and sex juice. She gazed up at his face, stern and hard with passion, his eyes dilated and lustful. He fucked her on and on, taking her like an animal, his gaze full of dark, primal passion.

Maddy felt her mind break as she orgasmed, quivering and crying. She ground her hips against him as he thrust deep inside. She didn't know what manner of words poured from her lips. It was an incoherent mess of moaning and pleading . . . .

When the pleasure subsided, he kissed her nose, gazing deep into her eyes, her face slick with sweat and her cheeks flushed. Whatever he saw there brought a seductive smile to his face.

"Your cunt is so tight. It's gonna be so full of my cum."

She shuddered. *"Ah . . . Gareth . . . ."*

"I'm gonna cum in you now, babygirl. I know you want me to. You're getting so wet."

She shuddered, her breathing hoarse. She felt him swell up bigger inside of her, preparing to spill his load. She whimpered, her face flushed, helpless in his firm arms. She could hear her broken voice floating between the ferns and hollow logs, as his cock filled her in the forbidden dark.

"Gareth . . . ah . . ."

She felt him swell inside of her. Then he shuddered. With a deep thrust, he spilled his hot seed into her womb.

Feeling his climax unleashed an orgasm so powerful, Maddy blacked out for a few seconds. Her whole body clenched down on him, milking his cock deep inside. She screamed and writhed and flexed against him. He caught her in his arms and pumped into her flesh. It took a full minute for him to unload into her womb. Her muscles shuddered and twitched as he filled her with his warm seed, each spurt accompanied by waves of sensual pleasure.

Then Gareth collapsed. He lay across her, their bodies stuck together by sweat, saliva and juices. His scent filled her lungs with each breath. He didn't pull out immediately but kept himself tucked, warm and semi-erect, inside of her sweet canal. They laid like that, their bodies tied together in the aftermath.

Maddy was unaware of herself for a few blissful minutes. Her mind floated, immersed in a glowy, warm daze. As she slowly settled back into her body, she became aware of his weight on top of her and his cum dripping down her leg. Her entire body was vibrating. She could feel her pulse through her clit, she was so sensitive.

Then Gareth stirred. He pulled out with a sigh, his cum spilling out around his cock. Then he rolled off her. Maddy was so spent, she couldn't move. He grinned when he saw her face, and he kissed her tenderly on the forehead.

"You're a puddle, huh?" he murmured. "Sexy girl. I guess that means I did a good job."

She released a deep, long breath. She gazed up at him, dazed. She felt like she was coming out from under a spell. Her body was still humming with arousal. Maybe it was true what he said. Maybe werewolf cum really was an aphrodisiac.

Werewolves. Right.

"You're a wolf," she said softly.

"Yeah."

"Say it," she repeated.

"I'm a wolf, Mads."

She had the sudden urge to giggle. She had seen him shed his human skin and transform into a beast. She couldn't deny what she had witnessed with her own eyes. And now, she had fucked him. Her first time. With a werewolf. *Monster sex.* She lost her virginity to a monster.

This is some kinky shit. Bea will never believe me.

Gareth had always seemed a bit more feral, more wild, than the average man. He belonged in the woods. That's where she always found him. And that's where he had claimed her body.

"Gareth?"

"Hm?"

"I'm not really into dads," she mumbled, a blush rising to her cheeks.

"Hah!" he grunt-laughed. His hand stroked the side of her cheek. "Did that embarrass you?"

"Um," Maddy blushed.

"Yeah, it did. You gush when you're embarrassed."

"Wh-what?"

"Inside. You get wet, babygirl. I could feel you. Deny it all you want, your body don't lie. I think you like a little humiliation."

Maddy gasped. "I do not!"

He grinned like the devil. "Sure, baby. I think you got a kink, is all. It's fun. I'll play."

Then he climbed to his feet, brushing leaves and bits of grass off his toned body.

Maddy pushed herself up into a sitting position.

"A kink? What's that?"

"What's that . . ." Gareth paused and glanced down at her. "Ah, right. You're innocent. Well, maybe not so innocent anymore. A kink, Mads, is like . . . domination. Sadomasochism. Roleplay. Shit people do to each other in the bedroom to get off. Makes sex spicy. It's normal. Don't worry about it."

Maddy didn't know the first thing about any of that. She wondered if he had any kinks. She wondered how she could tell.

Shyly, she asked, "Did you mean that . . . about tying me up in your bedroom?"

He paused. He didn't answer immediately. She grew more concerned.

"Gareth?"

"Naw. Well, maybe."

It wasn't an answer, and that was a little frightening. She chewed on her bottom lip for a moment. She couldn't imagine what that would be like, having sex with him multiple times a day. He was too large. He would destroy her.

"Would you really do that?" she asked again.

"Maybe. Fuck, Mads, I don't know. That's a hard question. You want the man's answer or the wolf's answer?"

She gaped up at him. Her cheeks turned bright pink. Holy shit, was he serious? She decided to back down—she didn't really need to know.

"Alright, nevermind then, forget I asked. Um, so . . . does that mean the sex was okay?"

Gareth looked shocked. Then he grabbed her and pulled her to her feet next to him. Her legs wobbled a little. He planted a firm, wet kiss on her mouth.

"It was fucking amazing, Maddy," he said. "I will cherish it. Always. What about you? Are you okay? I was a bit rough at the end."

Maddy nodded wordlessly. "Yeah, I'm fine," she said.

Then she took a step forward and gasped. She felt a deep ache in her core, like every muscle was bruised and sore. Her hand traveled between her legs, where his semen was dripping down her thigh. Damn. So this was it. Her first time. It had been . . . nothing like what she expected.

"Easy," Gareth said, supporting her by the arm. "I knew I got carried away. Shit."

He started to pick the leaves and moss off her back and out of her hair. She was covered in dirt and little scratches. Maddy shivered, folding her arms across her bare tits. She hadn't noticed how cold the night was before now. It was autumn in the mountains. She was freezing cold.

"We're crazy to be out here naked," she pointed out.

"We should head back to the car," Gareth agreed. "Can you walk?"

"I . . . I don't think so."

"Alright. Let me help you."

He helped her pull on her damp clothes. Then he straightened up and turned away from her, briefly looking around the forest, his keen eyes discerning the best path through the woods.

That's when Maddy got a clear view of his bare back. Her mouth gaped open. Deep, bloody gouges covered his shoulders and upper back.

"You're injured," she said, shocked.

"Don't worry about it."

Her heart lurched. Did he really make love to her like that? She felt terrible. She hadn't thought about his wounds, but now she remembered seeing his cut-up back earlier in the corn field. She wanted to help him somehow, but she wasn't sure what to do. The gashes looked pretty gruesome.

"Those aren't just scratches," she said. "It looks really bad, Gareth. Did the wolves claw you? Are those teeth marks? What if they get infected? Maybe we should go to the hospital."

"It's nothing. I'll take care of it. Let's just get back to the car."

"Put your arm around me," she insisted. "Let's walk together."

"Not with that ankle. I'll carry you."

"My ankle is feeling a lot better. I can make it back to the car just fine. Really."

With a low growl, Gareth slung his arm under her legs and lifted her against his chest. Maddy yelped as her feet left the ground.

"Gareth, no! Your back!"

"I said don't worry about it."

His tone of voice was final. Maddy knew it was futile to argue with him. He wasn't going to put her down. Still, she could feel his exhaustion. It was going to be a long walk back to the parking lot. But they could make it.

He really is an Alpha, she thought. She didn't know what that meant, exactly, but it was obvious who was in charge.

Then without a word, Gareth started through the woods. His presence was steady and powerful. The wind shifted and she caught his scent. Masculine. Potent. Familiar. She found something soothing about his smell, something she couldn't describe.

He carried her through the underbrush, six-foot-four-inches of towering muscle. He was still very naked. She clung to his neck, her breasts pressed against his wide chest. She could feel the heat rising from his body. His seed was still dripping between her legs, making her all slick and tingly. It was very distracting.

Moonlight filtered through the trees, illuminating the forest floor as they walked in silence. Through some heightened sixth sense or intuition, Maddy felt a million little tree spirits watching them from between the pine bows. If she listened to the wind, she could almost hear their murmured laughter, watching the two lost souls wander through the dark.

Chapter 35

As they walked, a curtain of heavy clouds swept in from the north and covered the moon. It started to rain. The raindrops pattered on the field in a soothing rhythm. It was almost meditative. Maddy's mind drifted back over the events of the past few hours. She could scarcely believe what she had witnessed. But some things were too strange to imagine.

Gareth was a wolf. He was *her* wolf.

He had a lot of explaining to do.

But first, she just wanted to get back to the car.

It took them probably a half hour to reach the corn field, not as long a walk as Maddy imagined. Gareth carried her out of the forest, then back to the clearing in the maze with the metal pole.

Gareth set her down gently inside the clearing.

"Wait here. I gotta find my pants."

He crossed to a pile of wet clothes and started pulling on his muddy jeans.

Maddy stood in the rain and waited. She kept flinching at the slightest rustle in the corn. Because of the storm, the whole field sounded full of werewolves, but she didn't see any signs of life. She and Gareth were alone.

The rain washed out any evidence of the fight, but her memories were still vivid. As much as she wished it was all a bad dream, she knew it was real. Her imagination wasn't that original. As she thought back over the events of the night, more details began to emerge. She gnawed on her bottom lip in thought. Actually, she had a lot of questions.

She recalled the jackal-looking man creeping up on her in the parking lot, his nostrils flared: *"I smell wolf blood . . . a young female just beginning the Change. My nose never lies. Looks like our rogue Alpha is hiding a secret."*

Now that the night was calm, she was recalling more of the chase. *A little wolf girl,* they called her. Like she was a prize.

She clutched at the edge of her damp shirt, her stomach tying itself into knots. *Wolf girl?*

Gareth returned to her side, wearing a pair of muddy jeans belted at the waist. His shirt and shoes were missing. His eyes swept over her. Checking her. Assessing her. He noticed the thoughtful frown on her face.

"What is it?" he asked.

"Those men who tried to kidnap me . . . . Why did they come after me?"

"Ah." Gareth paused. He looked at a loss for words. "That's gonna be a complicated conversation, Mads. We should sit down and talk, but let's get out of these corn fields first."

"Can you just answer my question?" she asked, her voice trembling.

Gareth gazed down at her, his eyes gold in the darkness. He reached out and lightly caressed her cheek. She leaned into his touch instinctively, seeking comfort.

"Trust me, Mads. I want to explain everything to you. But let's get somewhere safe first. Then we'll talk, I promise."

She nodded. Yeah, they were standing in the middle of a muddy field, drenched by pouring rain. This really wasn't the ideal place for a deep conversation, no matter how much she wanted to strangle all the answers out of him. She had a feeling whatever was coming would knock her on her ass.

Gareth handed her something in the darkness. It was the sopping wet bear from the shooting gallery.

"I tried to get all the water out," he said apologetically. "But we should run it through the wash. Sorry, babygirl."

"It's fine. I still like it."

She clutched the bear to her chest. More comfort. She suddenly wished she could turn back the clock. Go back a few hours in time to the haunted manor, hanging out with Bea and Vin. She wondered if Bea had made it home alright, or if Vin invited her back to his place. Now that Maddy thought about it, it seemed pretty obvious that's where their evening was headed.

She wanted to text Bea everything, but she wondered if her new best friend would be able to handle all this. Werewolves? Really? Would Bea believe her?

Well, they had seen a ghost together in the haunted manor, and Bea believed in a lot of weird stuff. Why wouldn't she believe in werewolves, too?

Maddy reached for her jacket pocket, then stopped. "Shit, my phone," she said.

"You dropped it in the parking lot," Gareth said.

"You're right. I remember now. Fuck, it's probably long gone."

"Naw, I threw it in the car."

Maddy blinked up at him. "Wait, really? You grabbed it for me?"

"Yeah. Come on, let's go."

He turned away from her, scanning the corn field for a path that would lead them back to the parking lot.

Gareth moved at a steady pace through the corn. The rain was pouring down harder, turning the field to a muddy mess. It drenched their clothes until Maddy felt like a drowned rat. Gareth was silent, his jaw clenched tight with pain. He didn't bother with the maze but cut straight through the rows. He didn't seem lost at all.

It only took them twenty minutes to reach the other side of the field. Maddy breathed a sigh of relief when the corn fields fell behind them, and they entered the open air. The parking lot resembled a miniature lake. It was all water, gravel and mud. Gareth carried her through the giant puddle toward the Camaro. It was the only car in the lot. He set her down next to the passenger side door.

He leaned against the side of the car as he fished his keys out of his pocket. He almost dropped them.

"Gareth, let me help you," Maddy said again.

"There's nothing you can do."

"I can drive."

A stubborn look passed over his face, but Maddy ignored him.

"Give me your keys," she said, and held out her hand. "You look like shit. What if you pass out on the road?"

His jaw clenched, but he didn't argue with her. After a pause, he tossed her the keys.

Maddy unlocked the door and got him into the passenger seat. Then she circled around to the other side of the car and got behind the wheel. She took a moment to adjust her mirrors and her seat, like he had taught her. Then she took a deep breath. With a little prayer, she put the key in the ignition and turned it.

"You gotta hit the brakes before you put it in drive," Gareth reminded her.

"I know," she grumbled, but she was quietly thankful he said something.

Luckily, it was after 1am and the lot was empty. She pulled forward and circled her way slowly around the giant puddle, following the signs that pointed to the Exit.

"Turn on the high beams," Gareth said.

"How do I do that?"

"It's on the knob next to the steering wheel."

Maddy didn't know what he meant. She fumbled around for a moment, accidentally turning on the windshield wipers and her blinker. Then she finally found the headlights. She turned them all the way up. She guided the car onto the highway. The rain poured down and she turned her wipers up on high. *Fip fip fip.* Still, she could barely see out the windshield.

She looked in both directions. There was no traffic this late at night. She turned onto the black road through the farmland.

Maddy drove carefully, holding her breath, her knuckles white on the wheel. She guided the Camaro down Fruitdale Road, away from Beaumont Farms. Every mile between her and the corn maze made her feel better. As she drove, she took quick, anxious glances at Gareth in the seat next to her. He leaned away from her, his elbow propped up on the door and his hand bracing his forehead. His eyes were closed. He was sweating profusely.

"Are you in pain?" Maddy asked.

He grunted. "Keep your eyes on the road. You're doing good."

He pointed at an upcoming intersection, and she turned where Gareth instructed her. She was totally lost. She wasn't brave enough to go over 35mph, even though the speed limit was 55. It was pitch black and her high beams didn't reach that far. The farmland was full of little backroads. Every time she reached an intersection, she found herself slowing down and squinting through the rain, looking for street signs. The country roads ran off into the darkness, disappearing into hills and fields.

Maddy felt like she had entered another nightmare. *God, when will this horrible night end?* She couldn't see a damn thing out the windshield. She prayed to the gods she didn't drive into a ditch. On a rainy night like this, all manner of things could go wrong, including mudslides and flooding as the river swelled up.

"Turn up here," Gareth instructed.

Maddy bit her lip. She turned onto a ramp and merged onto Highway 20. She felt a bit of tension ease away. As she entered the highway, she saw a green sign that read "Black River - 15 miles." At least now she knew where she was going.

She felt more confident on the empty highway, and the Camaro picked up speed. Fifteen miles passed in the blink of an eye. Maddy barely registered the drive. She gazed out the front window in silence as the windshield wipers flipped back and forth. *Keep it together. Almost there.* She knew she was heading into some strange state of shock. But she couldn't seem to pull herself out of it.

Gareth pointed to the exit she should take. Then he directed her through the silent streets of Black River. He made her drive a short stint down Main Street. They passed a cop car parked at the side of the road, which was the scariest moment, since Maddy didn't have her driver's permit with her.

"Calm down, it's fine," Gareth said. "Cop has no reason to pull you over."

"They need a reason?"

"Sure they do."

Then she was driving past her school and turning between streets of residential houses. The neighborhood looked familiar, though everything was a little different behind the wheel. Then suddenly she was pulling in front of Gareth's house. A miniature river flowed down his driveway into the storm drain in the street. It reminded her of the little streams and waterfalls she saw sometimes running down the mountainside through the forest. She didn't see any other cars or people outside at this time of night. The house was dark and the street was silent.

"Good job," Gareth said. He was bracing himself against the dashboard, his jaw tight with pain. "Don't turn off the car yet. Let's park the car inside. Don't want anyone seeing we're here."

"Right. Okay," Maddy said nervously.

Maddy pulled into his driveway and stopped, the engine idling at a low rumble. Gareth opened the car door and stepped out into the rain. Then he walked up to his garage where he unlocked a padlock and slid up the door. In the headlights of the Camaro, she got a good look at the cuts running up his back. Shit.

Maddy waited behind the wheel on pins and needles as he unlocked the garage door and slid it open. Then he waved for her to pull forward. Bit by bit, he guided her into the garage. The motion detector lights flipped on automatically. Maddy blinked, her eyes dazzled by the sudden brightness. She eased the Camaro forward, holding her breath the whole time. Gareth's garage was filled with cardboard boxes and workout equipment. A bike hung from the wall. An unplugged freezer was buried under a tool box and a stack of totes. She didn't want to accidentally hit anything.

Gareth motioned for her to stop after she had cleared the entrance by a few feet. Then he closed the garage door behind her and locked up.

Maddy rested her forehead against the steering wheel and took a deep breath. Fuck. Her muscles were so tense from the drive, she felt her shoulders cramping. Her hands trembled a bit. She wanted to throw herself out of the car. *Almost done with this nightmare.*

Maddy pulled the keys out the ignition, but they were stuck.

"What the hell," she muttered.

She tried to yank the keys out a few times, but they were jammed solid.

"Stupid piece of junk!" she cursed. Fuck, she was about to lose her mind.

Gareth opened the driver's side door. He noticed her struggling and quickly assessed the situation. Then he leaned past her, threw the car in "Park," and pulled out the keys.

"You gotta put the car in park first," he said with a slight grin.

Maddy stared up at him, tears of frustration shimmering in her eyes.

"Oh," she said stupidly.

"It's alright. You did a good job, babygirl. You got us home safe. Now let's go inside and get cleaned up."

Maddy felt dumb. After all that, she had forgotten to put the car in park? She almost started laughing. Fuck, she hated driving.

Gareth slipped his keys into his pocket and undid Maddy's seatbelt. Then he helped her out of the car. At the last minute, she remembered to grab the little brown bear from the backseat. Maybe it was a little juvenile to carry a stuffed bear around with her. But after all the panic and terror, it was a small comfort.

Security bear, she thought. *I must be five years old.*

"So, what now?" she asked.

"Now? We shower. Then first aid. Then fucking sleep. We'll keep the lights off and the door locked. I don't think the Grayridge Pack will come after us here. Not tonight, at least."

"The Grayridge what?"

"Pack. Wolf pack." He gave her a searching look, taking note of her pale skin and hollow eyes. Then he brushed a strand of hair from her face and tucked it behind her ear.

"Nevermind. You look pretty shaken up. How about walking? Can you walk? Let me look at your ankle."

He tugged up her pant leg, revealing her swollen left ankle. Maddy winced looking at it. The injury hadn't bothered her much in the car, since she didn't need her left foot to drive. But in the white halogen lighting of the garage, her ankle looked bruised and nasty.

Gareth hissed when he saw it. "We gotta get your shoe off."

Maddy flinched when he touched her foot. Just the brush of his finger sent a stab of pain all the way up to her knee.

"Is it broken?" she asked.

"Maybe. We're gonna find out." He loosened the laces on her Converse sneaker and tried to take it off, but stopped when she whimpered. "Well shit. Maybe we'll hold off for now."

Gareth straightened up. He scooped her into his arms without warning. Then he carried her across the garage. Maddy didn't try to resist. She was exhausted and didn't feel like hopping around on one foot.

Gareth seemed concerned that the Grayridge gang . . . or *pack* . . . might follow them to his house. That bothered Maddy. She tensed up as Gareth unlocked the door that connected the garage to the house.

"Are we safe here?" she asked warily.

"I don't think we're safe anywhere at the moment, baby. But we're probably safer here than most places. I got plenty of guns. There's a small arsenal at your disposal." He grinned at her, and she almost laughed.

"I can't believe you're joking right now," she said.

"I'm dead serious. There's weapons all over this house."

Then he unlocked the door and pushed it open. A warm gust of air hit Maddy's face, along with the familiar scent of Gareth's house.

"Home sweet home," he said.

Chapter 36

As Gareth and Maddy stepped inside, the heater turned on somewhere in the dark house. The sound was strangely comforting and normal. Maddy recognized the hallway, the doors to the bedrooms and the old brown carpet. The familiar smell of Gareth's home filled her nose: a bit like old spice and vanilla air freshener. She immediately relaxed. She knew this place. It was safe and warm.

Across from her, an open door led to the laundry room, and Gareth carried her in that direction. Maddy was exhausted. She wanted to take a hot shower and go to bed. But that wasn't going to happen immediately. They still had a lot to talk about. She sensed the tension running through Gareth's shoulders. His jaw was tight. Was he worried? In pain? Annoyed at her? Or just exhausted? She could feel his mind churning. A heavy conversation loomed before them.

Gareth flipped on the lights in the laundry room and set her down on the linoleum floor. Maddy held onto his arms for balance, favoring her left foot. Then she froze. She stood inches away from Gareth's broad chest. Under the fluorescent light, her eyes traveled over his tattoos, up his shoulders to his masculine neck. She thought she saw steam rising from his muscles, he was so fucking hot. Had this man really taken her virginity?

A wave of desire rushed through her. She wanted him. Badly.

Maddy closed her eyes as her mind flew back to the forest, where he had bedded her among the moss and ferns, their bodies wrapped together in the rich earth. She could feel him entering her all over again. They had mated like wild animals, totally primitive, his powerful body dominating her own. Now she craved the comfort of his body. She wanted to feel secure in his arms.

Her blood simmered. She smelled like sex. She smelled like *him*.

Gareth noticed her wanton gaze. He leaned down and kissed her lips, his mouth warm and soft, his stubble grazing her chin. She reached up and touched his face, deepening the kiss, leaning up on her tip-toes as much as her bruised ankle would allow. He hooked her pants with his fingers and dragged her against his body. He pressed his hips against her, and she felt the unmistakable bulge of his erection.

"You want to go again?" he teased in a low voice.

"Wait," she mumbled. "We need to talk."

"We can talk tomorrow," he murmured.

She was in his house, in his arms. It would be so easy to say yes. She kissed him for a long minute, heat pooling in her belly.

Then Gareth murmured, "First thing's first. You're soaking and we both stink. We need a shower, so let's get these muddy clothes off. I'm gonna get the water going. Then I'll help you."

Maddy looked at him skeptically. "I'm not decrepit. I don't need help taking a shower."

"With that ankle? I'm not gonna risk you falling, babygirl. I don't got railings. Now get naked."

He flashed her a devilish grin. Then he stood up and left her in the laundry room. After a moment, she heard the shower turn on. A cloud of hot steam started to seep into the hallway. Maddy appreciated the moist heat in the air. It was kind of pleasant. It felt a bit like a sauna.

Maddy pulled her muddy clothes off for the second time. It felt good to remove the damp, cold, dirt-smeared T-shirt from her body. She tossed the shirt in the washer. Then she untied her Converse sneakers. She pulled off her right shoe. Then she gingerly tugged off the left shoe. She undid all the laces and pulled the tongue out to loosen it up. She finally got it off, biting her lip so hard it bled. *Ouch, that hurts!*

Then she stripped off her wet socks. She unbuttoned her pants and peeled them off. She threw all of her wet clothes into the washing machine along with the toy bear. Then she sighed. She felt like she had accomplished something.

A little metal stool stood in the corner of the laundry room. Maddy sat on it, totally naked, and waited for Gareth to come get her. She heard his shoes come off, then his pants drop to the ground. The heavy clunk of his wallet and keys. The shower curtain rustled.

As she waited, she checked between her legs with her fingers. For the past hour, sticky fluid—his semen—had been dripping into her underwear. It looked a little pinkish. Was that her virginity? Some girls bled their first time. Did she bleed? She hadn't noticed anything in the woods. Then again, it was very dark. She felt a little bruised up inside, in a delicious, naughty, sadistic way.

I had sex with a werewolf.

Oh god.

Was it wrong? Right? *What the hell am I doing?* She had stopped asking that question a while ago. She felt like she didn't know herself anymore.

Maddy hunched forward on the stool, her head almost between her knees. This was not how she had imagined the end of her evening.

Gareth's shadow fell over her a minute later. He was naked except for a black towel around his waist. She didn't know if she felt relieved or a little disappointed. He tossed his dirty clothes in the washing machine, then added a cap full of soap from the bottle of detergent on the shelf. He switched the knob to "heavy duty" and started the load.

Then Gareth knelt down in front of her. "You doing alright? You look a bit pale."

Maddy indicated her ankle. "Um. Do you think it's broken?"

He gently took her swollen foot in his hands. Maddy cringed. She hated being touched when she was injured. Her anxiety spiked as she tried to pull her foot away.

"We had a lot of foot injuries in the desert," Gareth said. She realized he was referring to Iraq. "Lots of potholes and uneven roads. Do you feel any tingling? Numbness?" He gently began pushing his thumbs into her swollen flesh. "Any sharp pain?"

"No . . ." When he got up to the ligament around her ankle, Maddy flinched. "There. Stop."

"Alright, I'm stopping," he said, and set her foot back down. He put his hands on his knees and looked up at her with a reassuring smile. "Likely just a sprain, little girl. Let's wrap it up and ice it. But first, let's get you in the shower."

She bit her lip and nodded. She still wasn't used to being naked in front of him, especially under the harsh light of the laundry room. It was a bit intimidating. Gareth stood up and helped her to her feet. Then he picked her up and carried her to the bathroom.

The shower was running and the entire room was steamed up. The heat felt good on her sore muscles. The chill of the rain was beginning to leave her bones.

Gareth set her down inside the stall under the flow from the showerhead. He entered the shower next to her, towering over her body. She raised her arm to shield her tits from his gaze, though due to their generous size, it was futile.

"So modest, Mads," he said. "It's cute. Now stand still. I want to take a look at you."

"I'm fine. Just my ankle is sprained."

"Let me see you," he repeated.

Maddy didn't know why, but when he used that voice, so firm and patient, she felt an instinctive urge to obey. His hand landed on the indent of her waist, and he turned her. He brushed her hair over her shoulder to get it out of the way. His hand gently trailed down her back.

"You got a few scratches here. Probably running through the woods," he said, his hand sweeping across her shoulder blades. "A few bruises. That was probably me. Sorry if I was rough."

Maddy sucked in a slight breath as he ran his hand down the gentle slope of her spine. His palm settled on the lump of scar tissue above her left hip from long ago. He touched her with confidence, like it was his right. Despite herself, she felt a twinge between her legs. Her body remembered him. It responded easily to his touch. Her nipples swelled pleasantly.

She waited, submitting to his inspection. She didn't know what else to do. When he turned around to grab the shampoo bottle, she caught sight of the bloody scratches all over his muscular back. She flinched at the sight. She felt her mouth go dry.

"Gareth . . . your back . . . ."

"It's fine. It'll heal up on its own."

"It's not fine! Those cuts are *huge.* Were you stabbed with a knife? We should go to the hospital."

"No knife," Gareth said, rubbing a bit of shampoo between his hands. "Just big claws. They'll look a lot better in the morning."

"But your back looks like . . . like torn up tissue paper!"

He grinned ruefully. "You're forgetting something important, babe."

"What?"

"I'm a werewolf."

Maddy went silent. Her left hand curled into a fist and she dropped her eyes. Right. A werewolf.

This is insane, she thought again. But here she was, rolling with it.

Gareth started lathering the shampoo into her hair. She didn't question why he was washing her. And she didn't protest. He massaged the shampoo into her red locks, then rinsed out her hair, then applied the conditioner.

When he was finished with her hair, he lathered up a washcloth using a bar of soap. Then he ran it over her skin. Her back. Her shoulders. Around her stomach. He spent a long time washing her between the legs, then around her ass cheeks, his hands massaging her smooth skin, making her squirm. Then he rubbed the rough cloth over her tits. His fingers played with her nipples, pinching and teasing her, and her cheeks flushed. She felt herself growing slick and creamy between her legs. She rubbed her thighs together, a little embarrassed. Why was he being so persistent? Was he teasing her?

She expected him to shut off the water and help her out of the stall. But he didn't. Instead, he placed his hand over her abdomen, beneath her bellybutton, close to her crotch. His face grew serious.

"How do you feel?"

"You mean, from . . . ?" She searched his eyes, realizing he meant their lovemaking in the woods. "Sore," she admitted, "but really good, like . . . *so* relaxed."

Gareth kissed her again. His warm lips quickly became the focus of her world. She closed her eyes, feeling the caress of his soft mouth. Then he dipped his head down and took one of her swollen nipples between his teeth. He teased it with little bites. She felt a jolt of pleasure all the way down to her clit. When he released her breast, she saw hickies covering her pale skin from his mouth.

With a gasp, Maddy felt his stiff member press into her soft belly. He reached between her legs and began to rub her clit. The sensation wiped all thoughts from her head. She was instantly aroused.

"You wanna go again?" he growled low in his throat.

She nodded, unable to summon words.

"Turn around," he murmured. "Put your hands on the wall."

Maddy obeyed without question. She found herself bent forward with her ass flared out. Her hands found the tiled shower wall.

She felt his hard cock probing her from behind. Her breath hitched. She could feel the thick head of his shaft kissing her sore lower lips. He rubbed himself in her juices. She was a little bruised and tender down below, but she ached to feel him again.

"Gareth . . ." she moaned.

"Relax, babygirl. I'll go slow."

One hand rested on her hip. With the other, he pressed his cock into her slippery canal. His engorged rod impaled her a second time, fitting snugly inside her flesh. Maddy gasped, leaning forward to get away, but he gently pulled her back, impaling her on his cock.

She bit her lip. It felt totally different from this angle.

He slid out and she sighed, bereft. Then she cried out as he sheathed himself to the hilt in a single, long, deliberate thrust.

"Ah! Gareth!"

Gareth grabbed her ass cheeks in his big hands, squeezing her flesh. Maddy tightened, feeling her muscles quiver around his cock. He pinched her playfully and she whimpered in surprise. Then he bent her over more, so she was almost horizontal, her hands braced against the shower wall.

"What are you . . . *ah* . . . doing . . . *ah* . . . to me . . ." Maddy panted.

"Going slow, sweetheart," he said with a wicked grin.

With long, slow thrusts of his hips, he began to fuck her from behind, holding her firmly by the ass. His penetration felt totally different from this angle. Maddy found herself gasping in pleasure as his cock stroked the sensitive bundle of nerves around her G-spot. He kneaded the soft flesh of her ass cheeks in his hand.

He bent forward, folding himself over her and pushing himself deep. Maddy moaned loudly, her legs almost giving out. She cried and whimpered, his hands bruising her hips as he picked up the pace. She could feel the brush of his fat head against her womb, he was so deep. Her muscles began to close around him. Her orgasm came upon her in a wave. Her legs almost buckled, but his arms kept her from falling. Fluid dripped down her legs. She might have peed. She couldn't tell. It was too overwhelming.

Then he groaned. His shoulders stiffened. She heard his breathy growl and felt his cock swell bigger inside. She whimpered as he unloaded into her a second time, spilling his hot seed into her womb. Maddy sobbed. She felt his cock twitch and throb down her canal. The sensations were vivid and exquisite. She started to orgasm again as the warmth of his seed filled her.

When he pulled out, a lot of cum leaked down her leg. She swooned forward. Her body was filled with a warm, buttery glow. She leaned against the shower wall. He gently grabbed her arms and pulled her into his body, holding her up so she didn't fall. Then he kissed her forehead.

"You alright?"

She nodded. "Yeah . . . it was good, but . . . now I'm really sore."

"It'll hurt the first few times," he said, "until you get used to me."

She felt the possessiveness in his words. He owned her. He knew it. A delicious shiver traveled up her body, making her sensitive tits tingle. She didn't mind being his woman. She was totally okay with that.

Chapter 37

Maddy was delirious by the time he finished his play. He cleaned her up, wiping down her body gently. He washed himself again as well. Then he turned off the shower. He toweled her off in the bathroom like a pet, refusing her attempts to do it herself. Then he lifted her into his strong arms and carried her into the bedroom, where he laid her down on his King-sized mattress.

Maddy hardly remembered leaving the shower. She slowly became aware of her surroundings as she lay in bed, floating back into her tender body. She was sore from head to toe. The skin on her thighs was chaffed. Damn. Parts of her ached that she had never felt before.

Outside the window, a thin strip of silver light was beginning to appear on the horizon. Jeez.

The comforter was soft and cool on her skin. Maddy thought she would fall asleep the moment her head hit the pillow, but she found herself lying awake, sore and uncomfortable from the long night. She waited, listening as Gareth closed up the house and returned to her side.

She tried to sit up when he entered the room, pushing against the mattress for balance. Her arms shook with the effort. Her core muscles ached. She had no strength.

"Hey," Gareth said. "Careful." He turned on the bedside lamp. Then he helped her sit up. He handed her a cup of water and two ibuprofen.

Maddy laughed at the sight. She felt like an old lady. Fuck, this was embarrassing.

"What time is it?" she asked, exhausted.

"4am," he said.

He climbed under the comforter next to her. Then he pulled her against his clean, naked body. He smelled fresh from the shower. His big tatted arms encircled her, and he cradled her head against his chest. She found herself snuggled against him, their legs entwined, her entire body buzzing. Lying against his naked body made her heart flutter. Unexpectedly, she felt shy. She had never cuddled naked with a man before, and Gareth wasn't just any man. The smooth feeling of his warm skin made her breathless. God, how many times had she orgasmed that night? She couldn't count them all.

"How do you feel?" he asked.

"I'm so sore," she murmured. "I can't move."

"Sorry, babe. I kind of lost control . . ."

"Kind of?" she muttered. "You almost killed me."

"I'll take that as a compliment."

Maddy half laughed, half groaned. How was she supposed to survive this kind of sex? It was totally earth shattering.

"I might be a little scared of your cock," she admitted.

He snorted. "There goes my ego."

"How about you? How do you feel?"

"Like I could do it all over again."

Maddy stiffened. "Gareth . . ."

"Yeah. I'll wait. Maybe an hour. Let you catch your breath."

"No, I mean, I'm sore . . ."

"I'm kidding, Mads. Take your time, baby, rest up. I know I wrecked you."

She snorted with laughter, then winced as her abdomen ached.

"Full of yourself?" she asked.

"You screamed 'daddy' a dozen times. I call that a gold fucking medal."

"Don't you ever tell anyone about that," she grumbled, a stupid smile on her face. Then she rested her head against his chest.

As she lay next to him, her mind wandered over the events of the past day. It felt like years had passed since getting ready at Bea's house for the haunted manor, agonizing over what makeup and which outfit to wear. She thought back over their wild night: meeting Rachelle, Andie and Becca, encountering Dean, seeing Gareth win all the fair games. It all seemed perfectly right.

Everything after the haunted house, however, belonged in a 1980's B-Horror movie. Like for real, she might need therapy after this. She could still hear the vivid sound of bones popping and flesh contorting as the men turned into wolves. It made her gut churn. *Holy hell.*

She and Gareth had a lot to talk about. Her body might be exhausted, but her mind was spiraling with questions. She didn't think she could sleep without getting some answers.

"So, you're a werewolf," she said, testing the waters.

"Yeah?" he asked. He sounded drowsy but still awake.

Maddy felt a little awkward. Talking about werewolves sounded strange to her own ears. Like they were little kids making up a fantasy world. But this was real.

"So, do you have extra stamina? Like more than a regular person?"

"Yup. Got plenty of that."

Maddy grew more curious. She rolled onto her stomach and propped her head up on her arm, gazing up at him. He glanced down through his dark lashes. Gareth was laying back on his bed, one arm propped behind his head, the other around her shoulders, looking very relaxed.

"Have you always been a werewolf?" she asked. "You weren't like . . . bitten as a baby or something?"

His eyes flickered over her with some amusement.

"I was born like this. The bite thing is a myth. You gotta inherit the gene."

"Oh." Maddy thought for a moment. "So last weekend in the woods, I got lost with Joker . . . there was this big black wolf in the woods . . . uh, seems kinda obvious, but I was wondering . . . ."

"Yep. I came by to check on you."

She felt a little chill. Her guardian wolf.

"Alright," Maddy said, slowly piecing together the events of the past week. She felt like she had a fresh perspective on everything. "Then, those thugs that got attacked by a wolf outside my trailer . . . the wolf I heard in the woods . . . that was you, too?"

"Yeah. That was me."

"Oh." It was crazy to think about. "So you killed those men."

"They were werewolves. Lycanthropes. It's not the same, Mads. But yeah, I did."

Maddy felt a twinge of anxiety. "So that's like murder."

Sensing her discomfort, Gareth shifted and wrapped both of his big tatted arms around her bare shoulders. He stroked a hand through her long red hair.

"Our kind has different laws," he explained. "They were going to rape you, Mads. It was justified. And I'd do it again in a heartbeat to protect you. Werewolf law permits this kind of killing. A wolf has a right to protect his mate."

Maddy fell silent. She took a moment to digest that. Werewolf law. So werewolves had their own laws? That was difficult to imagine. Then he really belonged to a different world.

She spoke slowly, piecing it all together: "So back in the parking lot at the fair, when those men said it was 'blood for blood,' that's what they meant? They wanted revenge?"

"Yeah. Pretty much. That was the Grayridge Pack. They're the ones who broke into your trailer. They've been harassing me all week. Fucking bastards. They're new to the area. I haven't seen them before."

"What about you? Do you have a pack?" she asked.

He gazed down at her, his hand still playing with her long red locks.

"Naw. I'm out here on my own. I'm a lone wolf," he said.

"Are wolves territorial?"

"Yes, Mads. Very territorial."

So he was a lone wolf living in Black River, and this was a new pack in the area. It all made a certain amount of sense. They wanted him off their turf, but he was there first. But maybe that was a lot to assume. She really didn't know much about his world.

She thought of the men who had attacked them in the parking lot. Wolves fighting against wolves. Gareth said killing those thugs outside her trailer wasn't the same as murder. But it scared her a little. He wasn't human. He was a beast. His existence defied everything she understood about "real life."

Then she asked, "What do you mean, 'a wolf has a right to protect his mate?'"

Gareth stared into her eyes, willing her to understand. Maddy felt her mouth go dry as her thoughts circled back over the night.

"Those men in the corn maze called me a wolf girl," she said slowly. "They called me . . . *a treat.* They said I was starting to change."

She hesitated to say more. She had a feeling his answer would completely change her world. They stared at each other for a silent minute, a bit of tension rising between them. She didn't want to ask her next question, but she pushed forward anyway.

"Gareth, why did those men try to kidnap me?"

"We don't have to talk about this tonight, Mads. I know you're exhausted."

"Fuck that, Gareth. How am I supposed to sleep with this hanging over me? What if they come back?"

"You're safe here," he reassured her. He picked up one of her hands and held it, his thumb running over her palm, his fingers intertwining with her own. "Mads, I don't really know how to tell you this. I've thought about it a lot. I even practiced a damned speech. But now here we are, and I don't know what to say."

He seemed uncomfortable. Maybe even nervous? Maddy stared up at his face, trying to understand his expression. He almost looked bashful.

Maddy felt the corners of her mouth lift into a grin.

"Are you . . . are you getting shy?" she asked, amazed.

Gareth's eyes darted away. His dark eyebrows instantly lowered. "Aw shit, Mads."

"You are! You're embarrassed!" It was disarming, seeing him like this. She wanted to wrap her arms around him in a big hug. She teased him playfully, "Why are you so nervous? Is it about the 'mate' thing? You're acting like you're about to propose to me or something."

He cleared his throat.

Holy shit?

"Right, so, you've asked me before why I'm always helping you," he said. "Why I came to you that night five years ago, when I found you on the mountainside. Do you remember asking me about that?"

Maddy's eyes widened. "You said you felt like you were meant to meet me. You told me that story about being a lone wolf on the mountain without a pack. And you found a lost little wolf in the woods. So you meant what you said?"

"Every word."

"So then . . . ."

"You're my lifemate, Mads. And you're a wolf, too."

His words struck her. *There it is.* The bomb she'd been waiting for. It fell on her like Hiroshima. Maddy stared at Gareth with wide eyes, her mouth hanging open.

Then a laugh fought its way up her throat. It was a forced sound, pure nerves.

"Hah! Alright. Sure. I'm a werewolf. But that's impossible because I've never turned into a wolf or anything. So you must be mistaken."

"I wouldn't lie to you, Mads."

"You're wrong. I'm the opposite of a werewolf. I'm a total sheep. Or like, a deer. You know, just some average girl."

Maddy could feel her heart racing in her chest. She closed her eyes tight and avoided his penetrating gaze.

Gareth explained patiently, "You haven't gone through the Change yet, Mads. So of course you wouldn't know that you're a werewolf. But that's gonna start soon. You're showing all the signs."

"What signs? What 'change?' I'm totally normal. I'm just a girl living in a shitty trailer in the woods, trying to graduate high school."

Maddy wanted to push him away. The whole idea was absurd. This conversation was supposed to be about *him*—how *he* was a wolf. This was his problem. Not hers!

But she couldn't help but look back over the strange events of the past week. Her fainting spells. Her sharpened senses. That vision in the woods, when she had actually imagined she was a wolf. It seemed so real.

Maybe she was grasping at straws. Maybe she was losing her mind.

"No!" Maddy said firmly. "It's not possible."

"It's the truth, Mads."

"Nope."

"It doesn't matter what you think, little girl. It's happening now. This is real. You saw everything tonight. Don't deny it."

"I'm not denying werewolves exist. That much is obvious. But *I'm* not a werewolf. And I'm definitely not your lifemate, whatever that means."

Gareth sighed. "Yes, you are. I was going to tell you eventually, but I wanted you to get to know me first. I wanted you to trust me." He studied her face, trying to read her expression. "Don't be scared. It's just new. That's all."

"So what's a lifemate, then?"

"It's a bond. It's like . . . two wolves destined to meet. It's part of our survival. It's . . . instinctive."

"How can I be your lifemate? We only just had sex."

He stifled a laugh. Then he grinned like she had said something cute.

"Sex is just sex, Mads. Lifemates are different. It's some mystical shit, like two lost souls coming together by fate. There's some special power involved. I don't know how it all works myself, but maybe we can figure it out together."

"Two lost souls brought together by fate?" Maddy echoed, a little shocked by those words. She really didn't want to consider it could be true. But how many times had she thought of Gareth and herself that way? How many times had she been lost up on that mountain, and how many times had he guided her home? It was like they were destined to meet.

Oh god, was she actually buying into this? Maybe the lifemate thing was real? Maybe it was *their* thing? She didn't believe in fairytales. It was really hard to swallow.

"I don't know, but I can't rush into this," Maddy said. "This is a lot, Gareth. I don't think I'm ready for it. I mean, werewolves? I just want to be a normal girl. My goal this year is to graduate high school. After that, I thought I'd travel a bit. You know, take a bus down to the city and be someone else for a while. I don't want to be a werewolf."

"You can still do all that, wolf or not." Gareth considered her for a long moment, his hand thoughtfully running through her hair. He searched her eyes. Then he sighed. "Alright, sure Mads. It's a bit too much for you right now, I get that. So maybe you're not a wolf. Maybe I'm wrong. You got a point, you haven't undergone the Change yet. So maybe it won't happen for a while."

"Maybe it will never happen. Maybe I'm not a werewolf at all," Maddy pointed out.

Gareth's eyes flashed. "If you want to believe that, I'll play."

"I don't *want* to believe anything. I'm just pointing out the facts. I love the idea of being your lifemate. But I have to be realistic, it's not like I'm growing a tail or sprouting fur out my ears. So maybe we shouldn't assume anything yet."

Gareth studied her with a dissatisfied frown. Maddy knew he wasn't pleased with her attitude. But he couldn't argue with her. Her logic was sound. She *knew* werewolves existed, she couldn't deny it. She had seen him change form before her eyes. But that didn't mean she was a werewolf, too. Maybe some strange coincidences happened this past week, but she couldn't jump to conclusions.

She really, really just wanted to be a normal girl.

"Alright," Gareth agreed. "Have it your way. Let's forget all this lifemate stuff for now. Maybe it's all a big misunderstanding. Like you said, how do we know you're a wolf for sure until you Change?"

Maddy felt relieved. She knew he was just saying what she wanted to hear, but it gave her a sense of control. She needed that comfort. She didn't think she could function otherwise.

"But I gotta say this," Gareth continued. "After tonight, we're not just friends. I won't fight off a wolf pack for 'just some girl.' So it's official. You're my girlfriend. I'm your boyfriend. Got it?"

Maddy pretended to give it some thought. She scrunched up her nose. "Well . . . ."

Gareth groaned. "Well what? Am I gonna have to fuck you into submission?"

Maddy's mouth dropped open. Gareth's head dipped down and his tongue entered her mouth, startling her. The kiss turned hot and heated as he slid his tongue boldly across her own. Heat flared between them. Maddy felt her sore muscles quiver between her legs, an achingly sweet sensation. Then without warning, Gareth rolled over, his tatted arms landing on either side of her head. The bed dipped. His shoulders blocked out the ceiling. Oh shit. Maddy's body flooded with anticipation. She felt sore but definitely willing.

He gazed down at her with hooded golden eyes, and she realized what he intended. He wasn't joking. He meant his words. That smoldering look kicked up a storm of butterflies in her stomach. With a vulnerable expression, Maddy reached up and laid a hand against his masculine face. She felt the prickly brush of his stubble against her palm.

"Yes," she said, "*Yes, yes, yes*, Gareth. I'm your girlfriend."

A tenderness overcame his face that was difficult for her to describe. It was endearing to see his gaze soften. Then he bent his head down and planted a firm kiss on her lips.

"Good. Now I think it's time for bed, babygirl."

Their conversation was finished. Gareth reached over and turned off the bedside lamp. Then he resettled onto the mattress and pulled her close to his side, snuggling with her under the soft comforter. A silver glow was visible through the blinds of his bedroom window. The sun was coming up. It had been a long night.

With a sigh, Maddy laid her head against his strong chest. She could hear his heartbeat and the rhythmic hush of his breathing. She found herself matching his breath without thinking about it. Their conversation was . . . *illuminating* . . . but for now, she felt drunk with exhaustion. Her thoughts moved in lazy spirals, on the fringe of falling asleep. She found herself thinking of Gareth's passionate lovemaking.

She rolled closer to him, resting her head on his chest. No more "just friends." That word, *girlfriend,* stuck with her. She felt a little twang in her heart. She wondered if this whole week had been some sort of game. He had played along the whole time, waiting for her to sort out her situation with Dean, but he never stopped taking care of her. *Just friends? Yeah, right.* She was a fool to believe they could be anything else but lovers.

Maddy sighed in contentment. The sound of his heartbeat beneath her ear was the last thing she remembered before she fell asleep.

Wolf Girl Running

Continue the story with Book 2!

Deep in the Five Ponds Wilderness of the Adirondack mountains, a few miles outside the town of Black River, New York, an abandoned hunting cabin was located. The lonely cabin stood at the end of a long, potholed forestry road, lost in a thicket of red spruce and ancient dogwood trees. The peaked roof was ten feet tall, and the cabin's main room was open and spacious. Built of hardwood logs, designed with meticulous craftsmanship, it stood strong as a fortress against the elements, showing hardly any signs of decay even after years of disuse.

The spot was recommended to Kevin Montgomery by a local member of the hunter's guild. Kevin didn't know how long the cabin had stood empty. With a bit of TLC, it could be rehabilitated into a proper home, he reasoned, as he piled firewood into the ancient brick fireplace. Too bad he was just passing through.

A few years ago, he might have considered purchasing a little place like this, somewhere secluded out in the woods, far away from society. Nowadays, he didn't see the point. He didn't stick around one place long enough to set down roots. For a man of his proclivities, the nomadic life was more convenient. This cabin would serve as temporary housing, a place to hole up for a few days, while he worked out his kill zone. He liked the darkness of abandoned places. It was a vibe, a mindset. Monster hunting didn't belong in the daylight.

He finished stacking firewood next to the hearth, then went about unpacking his bags. A black duffel bag contained two guns for hunting big game. The first was a 22" bolt-action rifle with a nice satin walnut finish. The second rifle was a semi-automatic in camo colors. His two smaller bags were full of magazines. The guns were specially designed for hunting big game, like tigers and lions down in Africa. He just so happened to use them for a different kind of hunt.

He set the guns down on the table at the side of the room beneath a single square window. Someone had thoughtfully cleaned the cabin before his arrival. They even left a pile of canned goods and a sleeping bag for his use, a stash of emergency candles, lighter fluid, a little gas burner, some pots and pans for cooking, and a towel. He saw a handful of yellow wildflowers in a vase on the windowsill. A feminine touch.

As the thought crossed his mind, his phone rang. It was a Boost Mobile prepaid flip phone, a little burner phone he used on jobs. He recognized the number. He took a seat in the chair next to the fireplace. Then he picked up.

"Oh, hi, hello," a woman's voice said nervously into the phone. "I didn't mean to disturb you, sir, just wanted to check if you found the place."

"I did."

"Oh good," the woman said quickly. "I left some supplies for you. Supposed to be a big storm blowing in. Just wanted to make sure you were comfortable. Is there anything you need?"

"Nope." There was a silent pause. Kevin realized the woman expected a little more from him. With a sigh, he added, "The place looks nice. Thanks."

"Oh, you're very welcome. It's an honor to have someone of your . . . er, *standing with the guild* . . . come to a little town like Black River. You're one of the best. Anything I can do to help. I can show you around town tomorrow, if you like, if you're free."

Kevin listened to the woman babble into the phone. It sounded like his reputation had preceded him. Twenty years of werewolf hunting had gained him the Hellstrom Medal for excellence in the field. Mostly, it was a little "Achievement" badge next to his screen name on the guild's job boards. It marked him one of the top tier werewolf hunters in the world. It was a niche community. It didn't get him a tax exemption, but it definitely got him laid.

Kevin wondered how big the woman's tits were and if she smelled nice. Maybe a night in a small town motel wouldn't be a bad thing.

He was fifty-six years old, and he had learned a lot about women over his lifetime. They liked fantasy better than reality. Some played Sims Online and struck up affairs with imaginary characters. Some became penpals with murderers and serial killers in prison. Werewolf hunters had their own little group of fangirls. Seemed like this woman had a thirst.

"Sure," he said. "Tomorrow's fine. How about we grab a drink?"

"Oh yes, I'd love to. There's a bar in town with great burgers. I wouldn't recommend the onion rings, though. They roll them in pancake batter. It's a little bready. But the sweet potato fries are good."

"Sure. I like burgers. Text me the address, and I'll meet you there tomorrow. By the way, did you get the pictures I sent over?"

"I did." The woman hesitated over the phone. "I don't recognize the man. But the girl looks . . . um, well, she looks a little like someone I work with. But I find it hard to believe she would be involved with this."

"Werewolves come in all shapes and sizes," the man grunted. "Let's talk more over a drink. I want to learn more about this girl. Maybe you can arrange a meetup this week."

"I don't really know her that well, but . . . maybe, if it's for the guild. I'll see what I can do."

"Good. Great."

The woman went quiet, waiting for him to say something else, but Kevin was tired after a long day on the mountain, and he didn't have the bandwidth to make smalltalk. He cleared his throat a few times and stared into the fire, waiting for the woman to give up.

It didn't take too long. After about a minute, she said, "Well, I should get going. I was just checking in and I'm sure you're tired. Have a nice night."

"Yup. Goodnight." Kevin hung up the phone.

One of his dogs growled from the floor next to the fireplace. His biggest boy, Bruce, barked twice. It sounded like the low huff of a bear. Kevin grinned at the dog, displaying a missing incisor on the left side of his jaw. Three massive hounds lay on a pile of mats on the floor beside the fire. The lion-like dogs were a special breed imported from Russia: a mix of Caucasian shepherd, Rhodesian Ridgeback and a bit of real wolf. The dogs all weighed more than a hundred pounds, with wiry double-coats and thick ruffs to resist werewolf jaws.

Kevin had selected and raised all three puppies for the sole purpose of werewolf hunting. For years, he had been adding wolfsbane to their food and water, so that even their blood and flesh had become poisonous to werewolves.

The two boys and one girl were from the same litter. The biggest male, Bruce, was bulky like a little bear, with a dark brown coat and beady black eyes. The smaller male, Colt, was more wolf-like in appearance, with a masked face and long snout. He was the fastest runner and the best for tracking prey through the woods.

Sitting by Kevin's feet was his pride and joy, Rosie, the only female in their little pack. She might be smaller than her brothers, but she was smarter and a lot meaner. She was a real wild card in a fight. The bitch sat near his feet while the boys piled next to the fire. She was the leader of their little pack.

He reached down and scratched his girl behind her cream-colored ears. She let out a little love sigh.

"Don't be jealous now, sweetheart, you're still my number one," he said.

Rosie whined up at him, her affection apparent in her honey-brown eyes. Her intelligent gaze almost seemed human. Kevin didn't have a daughter—but he considered Rosie better than a child. He loved his dogs; he wouldn't be one of the best hunters in the world without them. A human couldn't pace a werewolf on foot, but his hounds could track a wolf pack through the Catskill Mountains for a solid week before cornering their prey. Once they got the scent, they didn't quit.

Kevin stood up from his chair with a groan, stretching out his sore back. Then he kept unpacking his bags. Night was falling. Time to get settled in.

On the west facing wall of the cabin, he pinned up a bunch of bird photos printed out on glossy computer paper. Northern New York was a great area for birding. The list was extensive: red-winged blackbirds, swamp sparrows, Northern cardinals, warblers and waterfowl, house wrens, great blue herons, black-capped chickadees, blue jays and raptors of all kinds. Just a few days ago, he had captured a macro shot of a white-breasted nuthatch. The little sparrow-shaped bird was hanging almost upside down from a tree branch. Its startling silver wings sparkled in the sunset. Magic hour. He had already sold twelve downloads of the photo from his stock photography account online.

Next to his plethora of bird photos, Kevin pinned up a picture of his latest obsession: an Alpha wolf he had spotted on the mountainside just a few days ago. He could hardly believe his luck. Finding a lone Alpha in the wilderness was nothing short of an anomaly. It was an auspicious sign. This might just be his retirement staring him in the face.

The photo showed a large man on a hiking trail, partially obscured by foliage and pine bows. Behind him, a smaller red female crouched on a log, hidden behind a screen of green hobblebush leaves.

Both wolf shifters were in human form, but that's why Kevin kept wolfsbane on him. The fellow's little girlfriend had almost passed out from the smell. Only a werewolf would react like that to the herb. He wasn't interested in the female, though. She wouldn't gain him much of anything. But the big male oozed Alpha vitality.

Only a week ago, the job posting had gone live on the guild's board about a possible werewolf attack outside of Black River, NY, a little mountain town lost in the Adirondacks. The posting mentioned the mysterious deaths of five men outside a trailer in the woods. The police suspected a wolf attack due to the teeth marks on the bodies, even though gray wolves were not active in upstate New York. The guild member who posted the job was worried about possible werewolf activity in the area, and Kevin agreed. He had just finished up a gig in Maine and was looking for a new assignment. So he took the job on a whim.

He didn't expect to encounter an Alpha the same day he arrived in town.

Kevin ran his thumb over the smooth, hooked fang hanging from a chain on his neck. Then he tucked it under his dirty plaid shirt. It was a trophy from his first Alpha kill, almost sixteen years ago now. It had kicked off his career, but he hadn't encountered another Alpha since. This upcoming hunt might just be the capstone of his career.

Kevin stood back and crossed his arms, thoughtfully gazing at the photo pinned to the wall. Unfortunately, he hadn't gotten a clear shot of the man's face. His features were blurry and obscured by trees. The redheaded girlfriend was a lot more recognizable. Red hair would be easy to spot around a small town like Black River, and she looked young, maybe early twenties. If he tracked her down, she would lead him straight to his prize. His contact in town sounded like she recognized the girl. If that were the case, then this hunt might go a lot faster than he first thought.

After he killed the Alpha, he could sell the loot on the black market. The pelt alone was a novelty item; certain shamans and wizards would pay top dollar for Alpha fur and claws. Werewolf blood was used for all sorts of potions and elixirs among the underground paranormal community. Almost every part of the body would be salvageable, from the testes to the teeth. If he played his cards right, he was looking at a six figure bonus. And he didn't have to split it with the guild or nobody else, because the guild didn't need to know.

The guild had its own code, its own way of doing things that were "humane" and "fair" to these monsters who paraded about as men. Werewolves were a menace, but they were still part-human, with families and lives of their own. So the guild came up with a hundred and one codes and bylaws to prevent unconscientious killing. Hunters weren't murderers, after all. They followed a creed. A code. That made it all a lot more justified. The main three rules were this:

First, hard evidence must be acquired to confirm the subject was a werewolf.

Second, it had to be proven the wolf was a danger to the community.

Third, the hunt couldn't take place man-to-man. The werewolf had to be Changed, in wolf form, for the killing to be considered ethical.

About a hundred laws followed the main three: the wolf couldn't be killed in his own home, it had to be out in the woods. The body couldn't be skinned or dismembered for parts. It couldn't be sold on the black market. No trophies could be taken or kept as evidence of the kill. The hunter had to obtain a hunting permit in the local area, the gun had to be registered, and it all had to be above board.

It was a lot, so Kevin kept a healthy lack of visibility between himself and the guild. It's not like anyone was really policing them. The guild's laws were more of a formality, really. Official law enforcement and society at large didn't know anything about werewolves.

His next step would be to locate the Alpha and his mate. He liked the chase. The rush of cornering his prey. The battle of wits, the bloodplay. Yeah. In another world he might be considered a serial killer, but this was different. This was monster hunting.

Chapter 1

Black Bear Diner was located on Highway 20 just off exit 206, about halfway between Black River and Davenport. It was famous to the upriver community for its chicken and waffles. A big sign above the entrance advertised "Breakfast All Day!" and the gravel parking lot was always full.

Beyond the Black Bear Diner, a winding country road passed by a gas station, a little Baptist church, a fruit stand and a blueberry farm. Past that blip of civilization, the road continued on through cattle ranches, horse properties, farms, patches of wetland and dense woods, before disappearing into the Adirondack mountains.

On this gloomy Sunday morning, heavy rain poured down from an overcast sky. Thick curtains of mist clung to the mountains and gathered between the dark pine trees, casting the forest in a ghostly, haunted shroud. It seemed appropriate for October in Northern New York.

The parking lot of the Black Bear Diner was full, and the front of the restaurant was packed with families waiting to be seated. Maddy put her name on the waiting list and looked for a place to sit down. Several groups of people milled about the entrance of the restaurant, grumbling about the wait and the lousy weather. There really wasn't much space to sit or stand in the lobby. Maddy felt a little claustrophobic.

Gareth took her by the hand and pulled her outside. A wooden carving of a black bear stood at the entrance of the restaurant. Seeing the statue reminded Maddy of the stuffed brown bear Gareth had won for her at Beaumont Farms. He got a perfect score at the shooting gallery. She remembered him clearing out the rows of cardboard aliens with relative ease, as the local hunting community cheered him on from the sidelines. It was pretty cool, and a little frightening, to see how good he was with a toy gun. He was an Army vet, but she didn't know much about the time he spent in Iraq.

His arm slipped around her waist, interrupting the memory.

"Come on, let's stand out of the rain," he said.

Maddy shivered at the sound of his low voice. She followed him to the side of the building, where the roof's overhang provided a few feet of shelter from the rain.

Gareth wore a white T-shirt under a gray flannel button-down, with a black weatherbreaker and dark jeans. Even the layered look couldn't hide his muscular shoulders and the two little mountains across his wide chest. His long black hair was pulled back into a casual bun at the base of his neck, accentuating his firm jawline and angular cheekbones. His black eyebrows gave his face a stern appearance. Long dark lashes framed his hazel eyes, which today were a greenish brown color, though sometimes they glowed yellow or gold. He looked like he belonged on the cover of GQ Magazine, modeling a new line of Fall fashion, not hanging around a backwater little burg like Black River.

Maddy still wasn't used to being together with him in public.

He leaned against the side of the building and pulled her against his body, positioning her between his legs. Her cheeks flushed pink.

Gareth was . . . a bit older than her.

And a lot more experienced.

Actually, until a day ago, she had been a virgin.

Maddy remembered waking up just a few hours ago to the sound of rain thrumming against the bedroom window.

She was alone and naked in Gareth's bed.

She rolled over. The clock above the bedroom door said it was almost 9am, but it felt like midnight. The room was dark and murky, like a little cave. Gareth's gray comforter, bedsheets and walls added to the effect. The clouds outside the window were black and ugly. Sheets of rain fell from the sky, spilling over the metal gutter that lined the roof. It felt like an angry god was determined to flood the world.

It was the day after the harrowing events at Fright Farm Haunted Manor.

The wind whipped the trees back and forth in Gareth's backyard. He owned a little postage stamp of property near the middle of town. Through the bedroom window, Maddy saw a line of pine trees and raspberry bushes running along the back of his half-acre. The side of his neighbor's blue house was barely visible through the trees and torrential downpour, then beyond that, the mountain.

Maddy gazed at the snow-capped peaks for a moment, hazy through a layer of rain. Today, the mountain wore a cloak of fine white mist about its shoulders, and a silver crown of storm clouds upon its head. It loomed, solemn and foreboding, above the town.

Maddy lay for a moment in bed, feeling the weight of the previous night settle over her shoulders. The onslaught of memories seemed as relentless as the storm outside: the haunted house, the corn field, the woods. Losing her virginity. The long drive back to Gareth's house in the rain.

Werewolves.

Holy shit.

Gareth is a werewolf, she thought. *Lobo loco,* just like his tattoos said. He was a crazy wolf.

Her memories were too vivid to be a dream. In technicolor detail, she remembered the sight of the Grayridge pack shifting into their wolf forms. The faces of the men had melted—*literally* melted—as their skulls elongated and their bodies shrank. Fur sprouted.

Teeth turned into gnarled fangs. The sight was more gruesome than any concocted effect in a movie.

Gareth was no exception. She remembered the sight of him Changing into a wolf in the corn field, the sound of his bones popping and flesh contorting. She remembered his dagger-like fangs, hooked claws and sleek blue-black pelt. He was twice the size of the other wolves; he tore them up with his massive jaws. He was a fucking monster, and he had saved her life.

It was absurd. Werewolves didn't exist. It was impossible. And yet, she couldn't deny what she had seen with her own eyes. She recalled the big black Alpha standing above her in the forest, protecting her from the smaller gray wolves. Close enough for her to reach out and touch his fur.

When he shifted back into "Gareth," she had run from him. He chased her down in the woods. And then . . . .

I lost my virginity to a werewolf.

Was monster sex different from regular human sex?

She didn't have anything to compare it to.

What the hell was I thinking?

Well, that's the thing, she wasn't thinking at all. In the dark forest, after the most terrifying night of her life, an inferno of passion had consumed her. But now, in the gray morning light, she felt very sober.

Maddy felt a twinge behind her bellybutton at the memory of her first time. Gareth was . . . very large. Her muscles were tender from his deep penetration. She placed a hand on her lower belly with a wince. Somehow, she had expected the pain to be worse. She sort of liked it. The tenderness reminded her of their lovemaking.

Her hand traveled down between her legs. His seed stained her thighs where it had dripped out during the night. She pressed her fingers into her bruised flesh. She was moist and warm. A little tingly. When she pulled her fingers out, they were sticky with his seed.

This is wild, she thought. It was totally primitive. Their scents were mingled together.

She remembered him unloading into her body for a full minute. She had orgasmed twice from that feeling alone. His thick seed had overflowed down her leg into a sticky puddle on the ground. The size of his cock had kept them pinned together for a long while as he finished. When he finally slipped out, she felt fully sedated, almost drugged.

She didn't know how much a normal man ejaculated, but it seemed like Gareth's load was very large.

He isn't human, she reminded herself. *He's a werewolf.*

The more she thought about all of it, she began to feel overwhelmed. She kind of wanted to run away. Find a safe place to hide and process everything that had happened on Friday. But she was in his house, in his bed, and eventually, she needed to get up.

With a sigh, Maddy threw off the comforter and set her feet on the carpet. She stood up. She felt self-conscious walking around his house naked, despite all the intimate ways he had touched her body. She dragged on a big hoodie and sweatpants from his closet. The scent of him washed over her, all woodsy and peppery, making her skin tingle.

She frowned as she moved around the room. Then she paused, glancing down at her feet. She noticed her ankle wasn't sprained from the night before.

She wiggled it around a bit. *Okay, that's weird.*

She felt a twinge when she rotated it, but nothing terrible. The skin was a little discolored, but the bruising and swelling was mostly gone. She did a little one-two hop to the left. All good. Had she imagined busting up her ankle? Maybe the injury wasn't as bad as she remembered? Or maybe she had slept for six weeks instead of six hours?

It was super mysterious and freaky.

Swimming in his oversized clothes, Maddy walked down the hallway to the bathroom. Her thighs and core muscles were a little sore. She felt like she had done a thousand sit-ups the night before. She grimaced when she caught sight of her reflection in the bathroom mirror. Her long auburn hair was a rat's nest. She had dark circles under her eyes. She looked like shit.

Ugh. Maddy groaned at her reflection. Then she flipped the light switch on, but nothing happened. She tried the switch again a few times. The lights stayed dark. Then she turned on the sink, but the water didn't run.

The wind howled outside, reminding her of the storm.

Shit, the power must be out.

Gareth's house was probably on a well system like her trailer—not all the houses in Black River were hooked up to the city's water reservoir—which meant the well pump was out, too. The storm must have blown over a few trees downriver. It wasn't anything she hadn't dealt with before, but the timing wasn't great. It was annoying, but not a surprise.

She left the bathroom and walked through the house looking for any sign of Gareth. The hallway emptied into a living room with a big leather couch, recessed lighting and a 60" TV hanging above the fireplace. The wood-paneled walls and red brick fireplace gave it a definite 70's vibe. The floor was covered in thick brown carpet. With the lights off and the curtains drawn, the house felt similar to the bedroom: like a cool, dark cavern.

It was soothing. She stood for a moment in the living room. The dull background hum of the refrigerator and the electronics was silent. It was kind of nice.

She didn't see Gareth anywhere.

She walked from the living room into the kitchen. She passed by a big stainless steel sink and a brand new refrigerator with an ice maker. The square floor tiles were cool on her bare feet. On the other side of the kitchen, a door led through a little mudroom into the backyard. She wondered if Gareth was outside. Maybe she should check?

Just as she reached for the handle of the back door, it opened. Gareth stepped in from the rain, his black weatherbreaker drenched and dripping, an irritated scowl on his face.

He slammed into her.

"Oh!" Maddy yelped.

With a grunt, he grabbed her arms. His eyes flashed over her, widening. Then he looked again, his gaze sweeping over her from head to toe. Maddy felt self-conscious. Her long red hair looked like a crazy bird's nest. She was drowning in his hoodie, and his sweatpants ballooned around her hips, comically large. She didn't consider herself a small woman, but Gareth towered a few inches over six feet and stood as broad as a door frame. His clothes fit her like a tent.

Gareth, on the other hand, looked . . . well, stern and a little irritated, for one. But even drenched with rain, his black hair loose and tousled by the wind, she didn't think it was possible for him to look anything less than 9/10 on the hotness scale. The dramatic angles of his face were drawn into a frown; his sensual lips were pressed into a straight line. His high cheekbones gave his face an exotic appearance, and his dark tan skin was deliciously smooth. His jaw was strong and firm, with a dimpled chin and full, sensual lips. By the knot in his brow, he didn't seem to be in a great mood.

Was this the man who had taken her virginity?

Maddy felt suddenly awkward. The spell from last night was broken; the inferno of adrenaline and passion had passed. Now, in the cloudy daylight of a rainy afternoon, she felt much more sensible. When she thought back over their intimate encounter in the woods, she felt like she was watching a porno starring a smutty red-haired actress. They had mated like wild animals. She remembered her wanton cries ringing out in the quiet woods, her little mewls and whimpers, and his deep groan as he emptied himself inside of her.

She was *not* that bold.

"How's your ankle?" he asked. His gravelly baritone gave her a pleasant little shiver.

"Oh, uh, it's fine," she stuttered, "like totally better, no worries."

"Good."

He gently nudged her aside and strode past her to the sink, then turned on the water.

"Um, the power's out," she said.

"Yup, I was setting up the generator for the well pump. Water's on now."

"What's a generator?"

Gareth raised an eyebrow. "You don't have a generator for the trailer?"

"I mean, maybe? Is that like a heater?"

Gareth sighed and turned off the sink. He folded his arms and looked at her.

"It's like a bigass battery. Dean's been letting you live on the mountain all year round with no generator?"

Maddy felt a little defensive, but she didn't know why.

She explained, "We don't lose power every winter. We might have a generator, I just don't know about it."

It was a lie—the whole town lost power at least once a year during the winter storms. It was practically a tradition in the upriver community. Black River was a rural small town buried in the Adirondack mountains. They didn't have the kind of grid system or infrastructure found in larger cities or suburbs. This far in the mountains, any number of things could take out a power line or a converter. She remembered one winter, the power went out for a whole week, and Dean almost set the living room on fire because the woodburning stove wouldn't get hot enough. She didn't think Dean owned a generator. If he did, it was piled in a heap of broken appliances at the back of their property.

Silence stretched between them. Maddy felt cursed by a sudden wave of shyness. After the events of last night, making polite conversation about the weather seemed insane.

If Gareth noticed her tension, he didn't mention it.

"So will the lights work now?" she asked.

"Naw, it's not a big enough generator. It'll run the fridge and the water pump, but not much else. Why? You need to charge your phone?"

Actually, Maddy hadn't thought of her phone yet. With a little gasp, she reached for the pocket of her hoodie, then she remembered she was wearing his clothes.

"Oh, um, where is it?" she asked.

"Behind you, on the counter," Gareth nodded.

She turned and saw a brick of black plastic sitting next to the microwave. She picked up her phone, feeling a sense of relief. The screen was cracked and it wouldn't turn on—the battery was dead. But at least she hadn't lost it. Considering the chaos of last night, it was a miracle. She couldn't afford a replacement.

"I got a battery you can use," Gareth said, reading her face.

"Oh, great, um, thanks."

Nonchalant, he opened a drawer in the kitchen and took out a flat, white square of plastic with a charging port. He handed it over to her. Maddy took it, feeling its weight. It was the biggest phone battery she had ever seen.

"This is, like, industrial sized," she said.

"It's for emergencies. Should last a whole week."

"A *week?*"

"Yup, it's what the Army uses. Here."

He slipped the battery and her phone out of her hand without asking. Maddy felt a little scandalized. He plugged in her phone. Then he leaned past her and set it on the counter behind her. The screen lit up with a white lightning bolt icon. It was charging.

Maddy sucked in a breath as he leaned past her. His delicious scent filled her nose. Her stomach clenched. Despite her misgivings about the werewolf thing, and her general overwhelm about last night, her whole body reacted to his presence.

His seed was inside of her. The thought rose up in her mind, unbidden.

Maddy briefly met his eyes. His face was so close, she could reach up and bite his chin. She considered it. She wondered if he would kiss her. She waited for him to initiate. But he didn't.

Instead, Gareth rested his arms on either side of her, propped up on the counter. His big body hovered a few inches away from her own, his face intimately close. He leaned in, nuzzling her hair. She listened to him breathe deep. The strength of his presence washed over her.

She felt like a lost girl he had found on the mountainside and brought home to his den.

"I like seeing you in my clothes," he said, his voice deep in his chest.

"Sorry, I didn't have anything else . . . ." she mumbled.

"Why are you sorry? I said I like it."

He pressed his lips against her forehead. Maddy closed her eyes. He was still Gareth, despite everything she had learned about him on Friday night. If she was so freaked out, why did she fuck him? She really needed to figure out her boundaries.

"How are you feeling?" he asked in a growl.

She knew what he meant.

"Um, sore," she said.

"A little sore, huh?"

"I mean, it's not bad . . ." her voice faded as a blush grew in her cheeks. She wasn't used to talking this intimately.

Without warning, he grabbed her by the waist and boosted her up onto the counter so she was sitting with her legs astride his hips. She gasped. She was a curvaceous woman; his strength surprised her.

"Um, wow, hi," she said.

"Hi." He gazed into her eyes. "I got something for you."

"What's that?"

He pretended to reach into his back pocket like he was pulling out his wallet. Then he mimicked holding up a card between two fingers.

"Got your V card right here," he grinned.

It broke the tension. Maddy smacked his wide chest. "Oh my god, you're such a nerd! Are you serious?"

"Yup, dead serious. You dropped it in the woods Friday night. For real though, you feeling alright? No regrets? I didn't hurt you, did I?"

"No regrets," she promised. "It was really good, Gareth. I . . . uh . . . ." She really didn't have words for it. She glanced away, feeling her cheeks turning pink again, thinking of his seed still warming her body.

He searched her face, brushing her hair back from her eyes. His gaze grew warm and intimate. In a low voice, he rumbled, "You're cute, little wolf girl. I was worried about you. You slept a long time."

"I was just really tired." Maddy fell quiet, thinking of his words—*wolf girl*. It made her uncomfortable. She tried to change the subject. "So, uh, what about you? Is your back feeling better? It was pretty torn up last night."

"Friday night."

"Yeah, last night."

"It's Sunday, babygirl. You slept through Saturday."

Maddy's eyes widened. "Really?"

"Yup."

So that's what he meant by *"you slept a long time."* Maddy was amazed. She counted back the hours. Had she slept for a full day and night? No wonder her ankle felt so much better.

Now that she thought about it, she had a vague recollection of waking up on Saturday afternoon to use the bathroom and drink some water. She remembered feeling sick with exhaustion. Then she passed out again in his bed. She couldn't remember if he was asleep next to her.

"Did you sleep through Saturday, too?" she asked.

"Naw, I got up in the afternoon. Worked out. Ran some errands. Did laundry."

"Does that mean your back is healed now?" she asked, a little awkward. Talking about his werewolf healing power was a little strange.

Gareth stood up straighter, rolling out his neck and shoulders with a wince. "Honestly, I've been better, but should be good as new in a few days."

"Can I see?"

"Sure, baby."

He lifted up his shirt, revealing his muscular chest and dark tan skin. Maddy felt her mouth go dry. She did not expect him to rip off his shirt quite so quickly. He had a warrior's physique, his torso covered in long, toned muscles, his chest like two little mountains with a deep ravine down the middle. The sight of so much bare skin made her feel flushed and heated. Jeez. She wanted to run her hands up over his chest.

He turned around, pulling his hair to one side so she could see the gouges all over his back. They were caused by werewolf claws, and she was pretty sure she saw bite marks on the back of his left arm. They were mostly scabbed over. Some had healed into thin white lines. It looked a lot better than she remembered, but still painful.

Considering only a day had passed since their altercation with the Grayridge pack, he was healing with miraculous speed. Just like her ankle.

Gareth pulled his shirt back on.

"It looks a lot better, but still a little bloody," Maddy said.

"Yup."

"Does it hurt?"

He popped his neck again. "I'm stiff, but it's fine, babygirl. I've had worse."

"It's amazing how fast you can heal."

"Yeah, well, it's an Alpha thing. Comes with the territory. We call it *vitality*. The same power that allows us to Change also repairs our body fast."

"Oh. I didn't realize."

Maddy paused, remembering the size and ferocity of his wolf form. His gleaming fangs and ravendark coat. He was a lot larger than a regular wolf, almost the size of a horse. His beast form looked majestic and terrifying all at once.

"You sure you don't have regrets?" Gareth asked, trying to read her expression.

"No, not *regrets*," she stuttered. "It's just a lot to think about. Like, Friday night was my first time, and you're not even human." She felt really dumb saying that. She searched his face. She hoped she hadn't hurt his feelings. "What I mean is, you're not just a normal boyfriend, you're a . . ."

"A *monster*, Mads? A big ol' beast?"

He had a humorous glint in his eye, like he was teasing her.

"It's a big deal, Gareth!" she exclaimed.

"I agree it is," he said, leaning closer between her legs. He pressed his crotch intimately against hers. *Oh my.* He was hard. Maddy sucked in a breath. She felt his thickness through his pants. How did he fit all that inside of her? Anatomically, it just didn't make sense.

Gareth grinned, seeing her look of alarm.

"I know *it's a lot to take in*," he murmured, his words laced with implication. "But I've been like this the whole time, babygirl. You just saw a different side of me on Friday night, that's all. Nothing's changed. I'm still that boring dude who owns an auto shop up Highway 20. I just happen to be a werewolf."

"B-boring?" Maddy said, trying to pull her mind out of the gutter. "No way. There's nothing boring about you."

"Yeah, well, you'll find out soon enough, babe. I'm pretty boring."

"Why didn't you tell me sooner about the werewolf thing? Like, you could've told me when we first met."

"I wanted you to get to know me first, babe. And to be fair, I dropped plenty of hints."

Maddy bit her lip. Right. He had told her that first night on his couch that he was a lone wolf without a pack. He had been drawn to her scent: a lost little wolf on the mountain. At the time, she had thought it was a romantic kind of metaphor. She hadn't realized he was telling the truth.

And at Fright Farm, he even told her that drinking turned him into a wolf. She thought he was teasing her with a bad joke. But he was being serious.

"You saved my life," she admitted. "If you hadn't been there at Fright Farm, then those men would've . . . ." Her voice hitched.

Gareth's eyebrows lowered. "Hey," he murmured, "no one's gonna get you long as I'm around. I'll always protect you. You got that?"

She nodded.

"Now give me your pretty mouth."

He leaned forward and pressed his lips to hers, taking her off guard. She felt the brush of his five o'clock shadow against her soft skin. Within seconds, his mouth became her whole world. He kissed her slowly, patiently. Then he deepened the kiss, expertly sliding his tongue between her lips. He took his time tasting her, as though he had never kissed her before. He explored every inch of her mouth.

A swarm of butterflies kicked up in her stomach. Her hands settled on his broad shoulders. A flush of arousal grew in her cheeks. She felt a pleasant tingle in her breasts.

Fuck, she wanted him.

His hand clasped her face. He angled her head sideways. He kissed her like he meant to drown her. Maddy found her hands threading through his long hair, weaving through his silken black locks, so different from her own. She knew sex with him again would probably hurt just like the first time, he was so large. But she was very aroused. They had already crossed that line—was there any reason to stop? They could do it right there in the kitchen.

Then a loud groan from her stomach disrupted the moment. Maddy felt a sudden, gnawing sense of hunger. It had been a full day since her last meal. She was more than just hungry—she was ravenous.

Gareth broke their kiss. He pressed his forehead against hers, breathing heavily. Then he grinned at her. His tongue darted out. He licked the tip of her nose.

"Come on, little wolf girl," he growled. "Let's get you breakfast."

Then he helped her slide down from the counter.

Now, standing outside the Black Bear Diner, the rain pouring down, Gareth pulled her between his legs under the overhang of the building. He settled her against his chest, his big tatted arms looped around her body. She could feel his protectiveness as he held her, his pectoral muscles making a cushion beneath his shirt. He leaned back against the building. The rain fell in little waterfalls from the gutters along the roof. His eyes scanned over the parking lot and the trees behind the diner. Guarding her.

They stayed like that for a little while as she listened to his heartbeat. Then his cell phone buzzed in his pocket. He checked it.

"Table's ready. Come on, let's go," he said, straightening up. He guided her towards the front door of the diner with his big body. Maddy felt like she was being herded along by an overprotective guard dog. As they passed through the crowded lobby, his hand settled on her waist. His body language was clear: *this is mine.*

Continue reading now!

Wolf Girl Running

Available on Amazon:
https://www.amazon.com/gp/product/B0D9R8V9R4?ref_=dbs_m_mng_rwt_c
alw_tkin_1&storeType=ebooks

A STEAMY SUPERNATURAL ROMANCE

BLACK RIVER MOON #2

WOLF GIRL RUNNING

A. MARIPOSA

Heart of the Wolf Podcast

Black River Moon Podcast banner.

Ever wondered what Gareth's voice sounds like? Enjoy the story again in a brand new theatrical, DRAMATIZED format with a full cast of characters, sound effects, music and graphics.

Listen to the audiobook online as a chapter by chapter podcast.

CLICK to Listen FREE on Youtube!!!

About the Author

Meet A. Mariposa!

A. Mariposa's first series, BLACK RIVER MOON, is a gritty Dark Fantasy Romance trilogy, a spicier version of Teen Wolf written for "grown ladies," featuring a strong female lead and swoon-worthy Alpha wolf hero. *Small town life, heavy on the spice.*

Ms. Mariposa grew up traveling between Los Angeles, CA and Washington State, which gave her a love of diversity, Southwest culture, big forests, rainy weather, and a fascination with weird little historic towns. Many of her own life experiences make their way into the fantastical world of Black River. She currently lives in Seattle, WA with her husband and two fur babies.

Check out A. Mariposa's podcast on Youtube: youtube.com/@blackbutterflyproductions